In the Headmaster's Chambers
Part 1

In the Headmaster's Chambers
Part 1
By Kira Takenouchi

PEGASUS
HOUSE

Naples, Florida 34116
Pegasushousebooks.com

ISBN-13: 978-0997902518
ISBN-10: 0997902515

Printed in the USA

www.pegasushousebooks.com

*For Camry
and the Elites*

Chapter 1 - *Disciplining Kyoshi*

"DON'T TELL ME YOU'RE IN TROUBLE already?" Nampo stopped at the door, staring at the glowering youth, who sat slumped in a chair outside the Headmaster's chambers.

Kyoshi shrugged. "I didn't even do anything," he replied, bitterly.

"Hmmm. You're off to a great start. Your first week here and you've already been sent to the Headmaster. That's gotta be some kind of record."

"Fuck off," Kyoshi answered, irritated.

Nampo laughed. "No need to get all pissy about it. I'm just warning you, Headmaster Mitsuwa has a wicked arm. You'd better watch yourself in there, or you'll find out."

Kyoshi tossed his head. "Whatever. I'm not worried." He crossed his arms on his chest, staring back at Nampo as if challenging him to disagree.

"You're braver than me, then," Nampo smiled. "I'd be scared shitless if I were you. My roommate got sent to him last term, and he gave him fifteen strikes with that nasty little whip of his. Kept me up all night with his pathetic moaning."

"Yeah well. I'm not some wimp who doesn't know how to take his punishment. I'll take whatever I've got coming, and that will be that."

Nampo studied the youth for a moment, marveling over his good looks, which had already attracted considerable notice among the other residents of Kensington Hall, where Kyoshi had been assigned. His longish, dark hair looked silky soft, and his eyes, black and glittering, gave him a mysterious, seductive quality. But his rather surly, brooding disposition had put off those who had tried to approach him.

Kyoshi didn't seem to be interested in making friends; in fact, he didn't seem all that interested in being at Valemont, the most prestigious school in the northern provinces. When it was rumored he'd been caught fondling a classmate, Nampo had been sent by his dorm-mates to find out the facts.

"So, what did you do exactly?"

Kyoshi shrugged. "Just screwed around with a cute first year."

Nampo grinned. So, the rumor was true. "Huh. And…who was it?"

"Don't know. Never caught his name."

His name. Encouraged, Nampo leaned forward. "Did you actually fuck or what?"

"No. I hardly got into his pants before we were fucking busted."

"Are you into just guys, or girls, too?"

"Whatever's there."

Nampo stared at the handsome young man, fascinated. He didn't seem the least bit concerned about facing Headmaster Mitsuwa, whose formidable, no-nonsense, corporal approach to discipline instilled pure terror among the residents of Valemont Academy for Distinguished Young Men. No matter what the infraction, Headmaster Mitsuwa answered it with his infamous crop whip; it was merely a matter of determining how many strikes were necessary to complete his answer.

"So, I guess you're used to being punished, then?" he asked, curious.

"Fuck yeah. He'll have to swing pretty bloody hard to get my attention."

Almost as if this comment had been overheard, the door to the Headmaster's chambers opened, and Headmaster Sho Mitsuwa stood, arms across his chest, staring at Kyoshi, a look of uncompromising sternness on his face.

"See ya," Nampo whispered, rushing off.

"Kyoshi Sayuki." The Headmaster's voice was surprisingly soft, almost disconcertingly so; for the way he stared unwaveringly at Kyoshi was decidedly unnerving.

"That's me."

"Please step inside my chambers."

With a sigh, Kyoshi rose, and with deliberate nonchalance, ambled toward the Headmaster.

Their eyes met in a moment of challenge.

Kyoshi was a bit surprised when he saw the Headmaster; he had expected some fat, ancient fellow with an ugly mug. Headmaster Mitsuwa was young, and undeniably attractive. His hair, longer than Kyoshi would have expected, just touched his shoulders, and his eyes met his gaze unwaveringly, an unusual shade of impenetrable grey. The smallest hint of a smile tugged at his otherwise stern face, and as Kyoshi approached him, the Headmaster did not move out of the way.

Stepping past him, Kyoshi was close enough to feel his presence, even catch a whiff of his distinctive, intoxicatingly virile scent, and found that he shivered, his heart beating faster.

Closing the door behind him, the Headmaster then walked back to his chair behind a great wooden desk, and with a disarming air of relaxed ease, sat back, putting his feet up on the desk.

"Sit down," he commanded.

Kyoshi did so, his eyes immediately drawn to the long, thin riding crop that was lying across his desk. So. He was to be disciplined.

He snorted, shaking his head as he sat down.

"You find something amusing?"

"If you're going to discipline me, let's get on with it. Why don't we skip over the pointless lecture and get straight to my punishment."

The Headmaster smiled at this, remaining silent for a moment as he studied the boy, marveling over his physical beauty. He could tell immediately; this one would be trouble. The way he sat slumped in his chair, the way his eyes challenged him, the unveiled disrespect in his voice.

He'd spent the last hour studying Kyoshi's records. The boy was brilliant, scoring highest of all the students currently at the Academy on his entrance exams. He had been expelled from two world-renowned institutions for his behavior, and the Headmaster at the last had written, that he was "amoral, anti-social, with no regard to the sanctity of our institutions, and no respect for rules of any kind." Another had called him "dangerous, and a bad influence on promising young men."

But apparently Kyoshi also had an extraordinarily wealthy guardian, who had donated a ridiculously huge sum of money to the Academy in exchange for Kyoshi's acceptance. And Valemont, like most such institutions, could certainly be bought when it came to admitting students, particularly in this case, when the boy's academic record was sterling, his cognitive capabilities unsurpassed. His disciplinary probations and expulsions were simply overlooked; and Headmaster Mitsuwa found it somewhat annoying that no one from the Board had even alerted him to the young man's presence, given his rather unpromising disciplinary record.

It was inevitable that Kyoshi would eventually end up in his chambers; and the Headmaster found it almost humorous that the unruly youth was already seated before him, not a week into his admittance at the Academy.

He watched the young man's growing impatience with amusement. "When you come into my chambers, Kyoshi, you will do as I say. If I choose to bore you with pointless lectures, I shall do so. And if I choose to discipline you, as is highly likely in this case, I will administer it when I am ready, and not a moment before. Is that understood?"

"Bloody hell," Kyoshi breathed, letting his head fall back against the chair.

Suppressing a smile, Mitsuwa continued. "Now. I've just taken a look at your…record. I must say, your former Headmasters had quite a good deal to say about you."

"I bet they did," Kyoshi laughed. "Those pricks."

"Might I remind you that you are in the presence of your Headmaster now. Such disrespectful commentary about other Headmasters will not be tolerated."

Kyoshi sighed, looking away. "I didn't want to be at those schools, just like I don't want to be here."

"Tell me, Kyoshi. Why have you come to our great Academy, if you have no desire to be here?"

"Because my uncle won't give me my fucking inheritance until I graduate from some bloody Academy or another."

"Ah. And that would be," now the Headmaster peered at his records, "Kiichi Sayuki?"

"Yeah."

"Then I am assuming, you're to inherit quite a fortune?"

The boy shrugged. "A couple million anyway."

"Then, if this is a requirement for your procuring this inheritance, why have you not tried harder to finish your studies? You've been expelled…twice, I see."

Now Kyoshi's eyes glimmered angrily. "The only reason I got kicked out is because everywhere I go, tight-asses control everything. They're always forcing me to abide by ridiculous, pointless rules. I'm just trying to live my life the way I want to live it. Why should I have to follow someone's else's twisted notion of morality? It's fucking absurd."

Mitsuwa listened to the boy's impassioned diatribe, fascinated. He found he rather admired the youth for his courage to challenge authority and all that stood in the way of what he desired. He admired him; but he also knew that, as Headmaster, he would have to punish him.

"Be that as it may, I am afraid that here at Valemont, you will be expected to conform to our expectations and rules regarding your behavior. I highly recommend you consider taking a course or two in philosophy while you're here, where you can discuss these issues in a more appropriate forum. But, Kyoshi, you are going to be coming to my chambers on a regular basis if you persist in the type of behavior we saw from you today."

Kyoshi sighed. "I didn't even do anything."

"Public displays of affection are forbidden on this campus. Yet you were caught fondling a first-year student in the library."

"We were behind a bookcase," he protested. "That's not public."

The Headmaster smiled, finding it interesting that the boy did not try to deny the act. "You do realize, Kyoshi, that sexual congress between two males is frowned on at Valemont?"

"How about three males then," Kyoshi shot back, with a smile.

The Headmaster returned the smile, lowering his gaze as he considered the appropriate response. "Any type of sexual congress among those of the male sex is discouraged at Valemont. The official position of the Academy is that such relationships impede the educational progress of the students, and complicate life in the residence halls."

"The official position of the Academy," Kyoshi whispered. "So, if you don't mind my asking, what is *your* position, Headmaster? Do you think a good fuck complicates life?"

The Headmaster struggled to suppress his smile. "My position is not at issue. The reason you have been sent here is that you blatantly disregarded a stated regulation of the Academy. Therefore, you must be disciplined."

Kyoshi leaned back, smiling. "All right. Now we're getting to it."

The Headmaster picked up his crop, tapping it lightly against his hand as he regarded Kyoshi for a moment. "Ten strikes," he said, finally.

"Fine. Let's do it."

"On your feet."

Kyoshi rose, and the Headmaster did the same.

"Lower your bottoms, and lean over, forearms on the desk."

"My...bottoms?"

"Everything from the waist down."

"But," now Kyoshi looked, for the first time, a bit anxious. "Headmaster," he began.

"Now!" Slamming his crop on the desk with a loud smack, the Headmaster moved around behind him.

Kyoshi hesitated, not sure what to say.

"Did you hear me, Kyoshi? What happened to, *'let's get on with it?'* Very well. You've just graduated to fifteen strikes."

Slowly, Kyoshi unzipped his trousers, humiliated that he was now sporting a massive erection. As he lowered his pants, the Headmaster caught sight of him, suddenly understanding the reason behind his reluctance.

He chose to say nothing, puzzling over Kyoshi's arousal. Had the boy found him sexually exciting? Or did he enjoy being disciplined? Or perhaps...he was merely still aroused from his exploits in the library. Sho stroked the crop between his fingers, fighting his own undeniable attraction to the unruly youth.

With Kyoshi's bare ass presented to him for discipline, Headmaster Mitsuwa found that he was now painfully aroused as well, though thankfully his robes covered this rather embarrassing development. He typically only made the most troublesome students bend over his desk, usually allowing them to remain upright for discipline. And now he found that, if he were truly honest with himself, he had made Kyoshi bend over so he could get a good look at him from behind.

He cursed himself for his impure thoughts, yet found that his eyes devoured the sight of the youth positioned so vulnerably over his desk, his firm ass inviting further exploration. His heart beat a little faster as he filed away the image for use at a more private moment; in truth, he longed to ravish the unruly Kyoshi, to spread him wide apart and penetrate him, plunging into him deeply, violating him completely.

Having never experienced such desire toward a student before, the Headmaster was rather at a loss when faced with it, especially with the intensity of his thoughts. Forcing himself to put such fantasies out of his mind, he concentrated now on the task before him: disciplining Kyoshi.

"So," he whispered. "I'll need to swing pretty hard to get your attention, then? Isn't that what you said?"

"What were you doing, eavesdropping?" Kyoshi demanded.

"You don't deny it, then? I see. Then, let's see if this gets your attention."

With that, the Headmaster whipped his arm back and let the crop whip fly.

Kyoshi's eyes widened when the first strike met with his bare flesh, quite surprised with how hard the Headmaster had struck him. He bore the first few strikes quietly, not even uttering a sound. The discipline at least also quelled his arousal; he lost his erection completely by the second strike. Feeling incredibly exposed, bent so shamefully over the desk, Kyoshi now began to doubt his ability to remain silent under the Headmaster's arm.

Puzzled over Kyoshi's complete silence, the Headmaster now increased the range of his swing to deliver the maximum impact with each strike.

Strike six seemed to slice into his skin; seven burned beyond bearing. When the eighth strike of the Headmaster's whip met Kyoshi's punished flesh, he gasped, his first vocalization since the beginning of his discipline session.

"Ah. Now I've finally got your attention, I think?"

Smiling, Mitsuwa made the last six strikes really count; he used all his strength, finally eliciting a few rather tormented, ragged cries from the stubbornly silent youth, who struggled to hold back his tears.

When at last the punishment ceased, Kyoshi continued to stand, bent over the desk and head down, trying to regain his composure. Much to his mortification, he found that despite his just being disciplined, he was once again developing an erection.

The Headmaster stood silently for a moment. "Pull up your trousers," he said, finally.

Kyoshi did so, wiping a wayward tear from his face. He felt humiliated beyond anything he had ever experienced before. Now the Headmaster was standing next to him, offering him a handkerchief.

"Coming to a new Academy mid-term can be quite an adjustment," he said, soothingly.

"I don't need your bloody pity," Kyoshi shot back, angrily.

The Headmaster studied him for a moment. "I was hardly pitying you. Are you always this cold to everyone, Kyoshi?"

"No. Only people who just whipped my ass raw," he answered grumpily.

The Headmaster laughed. "Fair enough."

Kyoshi, once again in control of himself, looked him in the eyes. "I know you saw me."

The Headmaster swallowed, choosing his words carefully. "You needn't worry. What happens in these chambers…will stay in these chambers."

"Oh really?" Suddenly Kyoshi leaned forward, grabbing the Headmaster by the back of his head to kiss him, his tongue exploring him wildly, his hand moving down to press against his robes, discovering there the Headmaster's own arousal.

Surprised, it took Sho a moment to respond. He pushed Kyoshi away, angrily. "Enough!"

"I knew it!" Kyoshi said triumphantly. "You're a bloody sadist! All turned on from disciplining me. Will *that* stay in these chambers? Or are you going to punish me more now?"

"Get out."

"Let me guess. You're going to have me expelled."

"Out!"

With a smile, Kyoshi turned and left, closing the door behind him as he irreverently blew the Headmaster a parting kiss.

For a long moment, Sho simply continued to stand, completely overwhelmed with what had just happened. Never in his career had he been physically approached by a student; and for Kyoshi to know that he had been aroused, too, was mortifying.

He returned to his chair, wondering what he should do. If he were to follow strict regulations, he should have the boy expelled for his advances. And yet…Sho found that a part of him wanted Kyoshi to remain at Valemont, almost hoped that he would be disobedient again and sent to his chambers for more discipline. And perhaps even…for something else.

Angry at himself for having such thoughts, he was also annoyed that he was now so aroused some sort of release was required. He had never done so before, but that afternoon Headmaster Mitsuwa pleasured himself in his chambers, his thoughts fixed around these new images now burned into his mind — those dark, furious eyes, that hard, angry mouth, that irresistibly sweet bare ass, clenching under the torment of discipline.

The taste and feel of Kyoshi's tongue in his mouth now tormented him, inviting tantalizing thoughts of returning that kiss, of exploring him without restraint. He fantasized taking Kyoshi right there, over his desk, and at the same time felt guilty for having such thoughts, groaning both from agony and pleasure as his semen finally spilled down his eager hand.

For a long time afterwards he simply sat at his desk, wondering, and worrying.

About Kyoshi.

Chapter 2 - *The Invisible Line*

KYOSHI LEFT THE HEADMASTER'S CHAMBERS and made for Kensington Hall, feeling strangely upbeat for having just been disciplined rather thoroughly, and probably having earned yet another expulsion. His ass burned as though it were on fire, and he knew it was only just beginning. It would be a long night.

The look on Headmaster Mitsuwa's face after he'd kissed him was priceless. And though he'd only meant to fluster him, Kyoshi found his thoughts now bent around that kiss, the surprisingly sweet, sensual warmth of the man's mouth that gave him shivers just thinking about. It was an intangible thing, but there was a chemistry there that he had never experienced before, not in all the many kisses Kyoshi had won or stolen.

He was puzzled by it…and intrigued.

But…so much for Valemont. His uncle would be furious; and Kyoshi dreaded having to tell him he'd been expelled yet again.

"So, how many strikes did you get?" Nampo was standing outside Kensington Hall, talking with another young man as Kyoshi walked up, and he gave him a knowing grin when he saw his stiff walk.

"Fifteen."

"Ouch."

"No shit."

"I told you he had a wicked arm." Nampo turned to his companion, putting his hand on his shoulder. "Seiko here knows all about that. How many times have you been to his chambers, Seiko?"

He shrugged, grinning. "Lost count."

"Yeah. We were all starting to think he had a crush on Headmaster Mitsuwa, as often as he went there."

Now Seiko eyed Kyoshi, his eyes sparkling. "Well...I wouldn't kick him out of bed."

Kyoshi laughed. He liked Seiko already. The boy had beautiful, medium-length light blond hair that shimmered gold in the sunlight and a pretty, almost boyish face, with an impish gleam in his bright green eyes. Unlike Kyoshi's fair skin, Seiko's skin was a deep gold that almost seemed to glow from the boy's exceptional health, for he was extremely fit, one of Valemont's finest athletes. He played tennis, soccer, and polo, and was a world-class skier, having just placed sixth in the International Games at Mount Jufi.

His athletic achievements had saved him from certain expulsion for his mischievous behavior, for Valemont—though first and foremost an academic institution—valued excellence above all else, and welcomed the prestige that courted its gates with students like Seiko Shinozaki within.

"You're going to be really feeling that later. If you want, come up to my room and I'll let you borrow my ice packs." Seiko lowered his voice a bit, "and I have some good imported brew and my own special little post-Headmaster cocktail that'll help take the edge off."

Kyoshi nodded, smiling. "Sounds good to me."

Nampo shook his head. "May the gods help us all if the two of you team up on us. Talk about double trouble." He turned to Kyoshi, winking. "By the way, if you get caught with contraband of any kind, you'll really be in for it."

"I'll take my chances. I'm probably going to be expelled, anyway."

"Ah, the eternal optimist," Nampo replied.

"You're welcome to join us, Nampo," Seiko offered.

Nampo shook his head, holding up his hands. "No, no. Unlike the two of you, I can't afford any stains on my record. If I lose my scholarship, I'm screwed. I don't have rich relations to bail me out."

Seiko laughed. "I doubt my father would bail me out if I got tossed out of Valemont. I'd be seriously fucked." He turned to Kyoshi. "What about you, Kyoshi? Would your parents help you?"

"My parents are dead," Kyoshi answered. "As for my uncle, he'd probably take me in, after a mandatory conference with his paddle, that is."

Seiko and Nampo fell silent for a moment.

"Sorry about your parents," Nampo said, finally.

Kyoshi shrugged. "It happened a long time ago."

"Well," Nampo gave them both a salute, "I'm off to the library."

Seiko put his arm around his shoulders. "Nampo here is one of those students at Valemont who actually studies. Quite a rarity, I assure you. He puts the rest of us to shame."

Nampo grinned, shrugging. "I like studying."

"You're a strange fellow," Seiko answered, shaking his head.

"What can I say? I've always liked books."

"I like books," Seiko protested. "Smelling them, anyway."

"Especially the news ones," Kyoshi added, smiling.

"With the two of you around, next thing you know they'll make books illegal," Nampo moaned.

"Then they'd be even *more* fun."

Nampo shook his head. "You're incorrigible, Seiko. Well, anyway I'm off. Though I'm sure I won't be having as much fun in the library as you did," he teased, grinning at Kyoshi.

"What can I say? I've always liked fucking."

"A man after my own heart," Seiko said solemnly.

The three of them laughed and then Nampo gave them a slight bow before departing.

"He's a nice kid," Kyoshi remarked.

"Shit, yeah. Everyone loves Nampo. I seriously doubt he has a single enemy. What's the phrase? A heart of gold? And if you're ever in a jam, Nampo's your man. Though I'll warn you, he does have a penchant for gossip."

"Hmmm."

"I'm on the third floor. You okay? You look a little stressed."

"My ass is bloody killing me," Kyoshi replied. "Fucking Headmaster."

Seiko laughed. "We'll get you fixed up. Although you'll probably be sore for a couple of days."

"Great," Kyoshi sighed, following him inside and up the stairs. As Seiko unlocked his door, curious dorm-mates turned to see who he'd brought with him.

"Hey Shinozaki, who's your new friend?" one called out, while another whistled.

Seiko answered them by flipping them off, rolling his eyes.

"This one's prettier than the last one," another one teased. "Can he come visit me next?"

"I'll come visit you," Kyoshi replied, "though I doubt your virgin ass can handle me."

Everyone laughed at that as Seiko and Kyoshi disappeared inside.

"Sorry about that," Seiko said. "They're assholes."

"Sounds like you have a bit of a reputation."

Seiko shrugged, grinning, and retrieved two icepacks from his freezer, wrapping them in a thin towel. "This will be most effective directly on your skin. Are you shy? Go ahead and lie on my bed if you want, and I'll place them on you."

"I'm not shy," Kyoshi replied, unzipping his pants. "Is this a come on?"

"In your dreams."

Kyoshi laughed. "Asshole." He was, in fact, rather eager to get some ice on his backside, which was now starting to burn rather alarmingly. As he lay down on the bed, his ass now exposed, Seiko examined him.

"Shit. He really did a number on you."

"Feels like it. He broke the skin, didn't he?"

"Yeah. It'll sting like hell next time you shower."

"Maybe I won't shower for a few days then."

"Hmmm. In that case, don't bother coming around for a while," Seiko teased.

"Bastard," Kyoshi replied, laughing.

"Here we go." Seiko placed the towel on his buttocks, eliciting a slight gasp from him. "Give it a few minutes, and it should start numbing you."

"Thanks."

"Now, for my special post-Headmaster cocktail." Seiko went to his desk and retrieved a book from his shelf, opening it to reveal an assortment of bottles and bags in a secret compartment he'd manufactured in the book with a sharp knife.

"That's bloody brilliant," Kyoshi remarked. "I would have never thought of that. What book is that, anyway?"

"Calculus."

Kyoshi laughed. "I take it you're not much of a mathematician?"

"I deplore math. You?"

"Don't mind it. Anyway, it's necessary for all the fun stuff."

"Fun stuff? Like what?"

"You know. Quantum physics, M theory and all that."

"Holy shit," Seiko laughed. "Don't tell me you're some kind of genius."

"Fuck no. Ahh…I think this is helping."

"And this," Seiko grinned, holding up a tiny capsule, "will help you even more."

"What is it?"

"A bit of this and that. I made it myself."

"Hmmm. And…what sort of grades did you get in chemistry?"

"Don't worry, it's safe. I pop 'em all the time." He opened a cold bottle of ale and handed it to him.

"That sounds dangerously like the beginning of an educational anti-drug film. Right before the kid drops dead."

Seiko laughed.

"So, you want me to take this with alcohol, huh? What are you trying to do, kill me?" Kyoshi grinned, taking a drink.

"It won't kill you, but don't go driving anywhere for a while," he answered, moving to stand over him. "Open," he commanded, holding the capsule in front of his mouth.

"I think they call this peer pressure. And I'm in a very compromising position here. My chastity may be at stake."

"No offense, but you're not my type. Though you do have a very nice ass."

"Then, I guess I'll trust you." He opened his mouth and Seiko slipped the capsule on his tongue. Swallowing it with the help of a drink, Kyoshi smiled. "So, I'm not your type? You seriously wouldn't fuck me?"

"I'm not saying you wouldn't be a good fuck. Only that I'd rather be your friend than fuck you. It'd be too much like fucking my brother."

"And...how often do you fuck your brother?"

"Bastard. I just meant I don't want to fuck you."

"Well, I don't want to fuck you either, then."

"Liar," Seiko grinned. "You know you want me."

"Nah. It'd be too much like fucking your brother."

Laughing, Seiko opened an ale for himself, taking a long drink. "You're pretty cool, Kyoshi."

"I know."

"Shit. Quit making me laugh, my stomach is starting to hurt."

"It's probably all that sibling cum you swallowed. That stuff will kill you, you know."

"I can't wait to introduce you to Hisashi. He's gonna love you."

"Who's Hisashi?"

"He's...well, he and I did a lot of pranks together last year; he knows Mitsuwa's arm well, I'll tell you that much. He's great fun. Also he's an awesome yudona fighter."

"No shit? I'm a fighter, too."

"For real?"

Kyoshi grinned. "Fuck yeah."

"What level are you?"

"Master."

"Holy shit. Are you joining the team?"

"I didn't know we had one. But...yeah, I probably will." Then Kyoshi remembered that, most likely, this would be his last day at Valemont. He suddenly found this realization a bit disappointing.

For the first time in a long while, he felt like he'd found someplace he almost...belonged. He actually liked Seiko...a lot. And the yudona team; it would have been fun to fight again. It was too bad he'd blown it already.

"It's a little late in the season—but I know they'd probably still take you, if you're good enough, that is. There's a tournament coming up at the end of the term."

"Do you fight?"

"Me? No...well, yes, but I'm no good at it. I play other sports, though."

"Like what?"

"Soccer, tennis, and polo...but I'm best at skiing."

"Fuck," Kyoshi laughed. "You play ALL those?"

Seiko shrugged. "I like physical things. I'm a terrible student, though."

"I like physical things, too," Kyoshi replied, smiling. "That's probably what will get me kicked out of Valemont. Actually, I'm a bit worried that this might be it for me."

"What do you mean?"

"I mean, I think that the Headmaster is going to expel me tomorrow."

Seiko shook his head. "Not if he already disciplined you. Just watch yourself from here on, I guess." He grinned. "Though I'm not really in a position to give you advice."

"It's just that...in the Headmaster's chambers...." Now Kyoshi fell silent, wondering if he should keep his transgression to himself.

Seiko studied him. "When you were in the Headmaster's chambers...what?" he encouraged.

"After he disciplined me...I...actually...I kissed him."

For a stunned moment, Seiko just stared at him. "You kissed...Headmaster Mitsuwa?"

"Yep."

"You're fucking shitting me!"

"I swear." Kyoshi smiled, remembering. "He was pretty pissed off."

"Hmmm."

"You don't believe me, do you?"

"Honestly? No."

Kyoshi shrugged. "Makes no difference to me if you do or if you don't." He decided then to keep the other critical piece of information to himself, that he had not only kissed the Headmaster, but had also touched him intimately.

"You seriously kissed him."

"Yep."

Seiko cocked his head, dubious. "What did he do?"

"He ordered me out of his chambers."

Studying him for a long moment, Seiko finally decided he believed him. "Shit," he sighed, disappointed. "You probably *are* going to be expelled."

"Yeah. I'm always doing stupid shit like that. Then I end up regretting it."

Seiko crouched down to look him in the eyes. "What was it like?" he whispered.

"Honestly?" Kyoshi returned his gaze, considering. "It was…nice."

"Did he kiss you back?"

"Not really. No…he pushed me away."

"Hmmm."

"So you think I'll be kicked out?"

Seiko sighed again. "Probably. Which fucking sucks. Although…if he didn't expel you there on the spot…maybe you still have a chance. Actually, it's odd that he didn't expel you then. I wonder why he didn't?"

"Probably because of my uncle. He just made a bloody huge donation to Valemont."

Seiko's eyes brightened. "Yeah? Then…maybe you'll be okay. So…it's true what Nampo said, that you're rich?"

"How did he know?"

"He says you drive a Grantley Platinum. You'd have to be pretty fucking loaded to afford that."

"Actually, it's my uncle who's rich. He gave me the wheels, but if I don't graduate somewhere, I'll never see any of it."

"Then why did you do it? Kiss Headmaster Mitsuwa?"

Kyoshi shook his head. "I'm not really sure. I just…did it. I was pretty upset…it's hard to explain."

"Well," Seiko said, smiling, "no question, he *is* pretty attractive."

"Yeah. Although I think I mostly did it just to unnerve him. But…hey, maybe you'd better not tell anyone about this."

"I wouldn't. Although…don't tell Nampo. He can't keep a secret."

"Woah. Shit. This stuff is great. I'm starting to feel it now. So…how did you end up in the Headmaster's chambers?"

"All kinds of dumb shit. The best prank was one Hisashi and I did last term. We set loose a few tarantulas in Professor Zen's boring-ass trigonometry class. It was a riot."

"Shit. I hope you still don't have any of those."

"Don't tell me you're afraid of tarantulas?"

"Fuck yeah. They're creepy as hell."

"They're actually quite gentle and sweet. In fact, one of them seems to like you, he's crawling next to your leg."

"Shit," Kyoshi cried, leaping up.

Seiko laughed hysterically at this. "I was only teasing."

"Wise ass," Kyoshi grumbled, though he couldn't help smiling. "I think I'll be heading back to my room…I feel kinda sleepy."

Seiko nodded. "Yeah, you'll probably sleep a long time. Just make sure you don't oversleep…the professors get really pissy if you're late for class here."

"So you think I should just go to class like nothing happened?"

"Definitely. Although my guess is tomorrow Mitsuwa will call you back to his chambers. And if he's decided not to expel you, you're probably in for more discipline. Which, given your current state, isn't going to be pleasant."

Kyoshi sighed. "Fuck. Does he always use corporal punishment?"

"Pretty much."

"That bastard. Well…hey, do you think I could have another of these capsules then, for tomorrow?"

Seiko grinned. "Sure. And take the ice packs…just give them back whenever you're finished with them."

"Thanks. For all this…it really helps."

"Sure thing. I hope I'll be seeing you around…but if not, have a nice life, and try to stay out of trouble," Seiko answered, with a wink.

"You too."

As Kyoshi left, he couldn't help but feel a bit sad. He didn't make friends easily, mostly because other people typically annoyed him. Though he told himself he preferred being alone, in fact, he sometimes felt quite lonely. He and Seiko had hit it off from the very start, and he rather wished now he was staying at Valemont.

Perhaps…when the Headmaster called him to his chambers, he could apologize, and ask for a second chance. He sighed, unenthusiastic about having to suck up his pride and grovel before Headmaster Mitsuwa, and even less enthusiastic about facing whatever punishment was in store.

He smiled. At least, no matter what, he would always have the memory of that kiss.

HEADMASTER MITSUWA REMAINED LOCKED in his chambers well past sundown, trying to decide what to do about Kyoshi. Finally, he placed a call to Dean Gerard, hoping for some guidance in the matter.

"Sho. Good to hear from you. I trust the term is going well?"

"Typical, at any rate," Sho replied, smiling. "At least up until today."

"Oh? And I suppose that's why you're calling me at this hour."

"Did I interrupt your dinner? I'm terribly sorry—"

"No, no. I only meant…you only call me at home when something's on your mind."

Sho laughed. "I'm sorry. It often takes me a few hours to sort out my thoughts. Especially in this case."

"Then let's have it."

"Does the name Kyoshi Sayuki mean anything to you?"

A short pause. "Don't tell me he's come to see you already?"

"I'm afraid so."

The Dean sighed. "I was afraid of that. I went round and round with the Board about it. I guess you've read his record?"

"Yes."

"Yes, well. It all came down to the simple fact that Valemont needs a new stadium, and the uncle—Mr. Sayuki—offered us such a huge sum that we really couldn't turn it down."

"I should think that the Academy might benefit from an expanded library before another stadium is built."

The Dean chuckled. "I suppose you're right, but it's not so much what the University needs, as it is what the community demands. At any rate, whether it's a new stadium or more books, the Board voted to accept the donation and the young man's application."

"You know my views on buying admission. It is hardly fair to less affluent students—"

"Sho. Forgive me but…it's been a long day."

"Very well. Let me get to the point of my call. As I said, Kyoshi was sent to my chambers today."

"I can't say I'm too surprised, I suppose. Then, you disciplined him?"

"Yes." Now Sho hesitated, feeling a bit awkward.

"And?"

"The boy…the truth is, he made a sexual advance."

"With another student?"

"No…well, yes, in fact. That's why he was sent to me initially. But I mean he also made a sexual advance toward me."

A long silence followed this statement, and then a sigh.

"And you want to expel him," the Dean finished.

"No—not necessarily. That's why I'm calling you. I'm really at a loss, Gabe. That is, I'm certainly willing to give him a second chance, but I thought you should know the situation."

"Then...I'll leave it to your discretion. I'll certainly understand if you feel he must be expelled. I'll deal with the Board and Mr. Sayuki."

"You misunderstand me. I'm calling to see if the action *compels* expulsion. If you're saying I can use my discretion, then I'm inclined to resolve it in another way."

"But you see...this puts me in an awkward position. In fact, I don't think I can advise you, simply because of...shall we say...a conflict of interest. I'll only say that you're not compelled to any action. As Headmaster, the decision is entirely up to you. Just let me know what you decide."

"Understood. Then...I'll think on this a bit more and then contact you tomorrow."

"Very good. Good night, Sho."

Headmaster Mitsuwa hung up the phone, already certain what he would do. He would allow Kyoshi to stay. This would make the Dean happy as well as the Board of Trustees, and it would prevent the dissemination of a potentially embarrassing incident.

He would, of course, have to punish Kyoshi, and he felt a bit guilty that this thought excited him. He'd never really taken pleasure in disciplining students; it was simply what he was required to do as Headmaster. But Kyoshi was altogether a different story.

Eyes closed, he remembered the taste of the boy's mouth in his, allowing his thoughts to accelerate the moment to completion, once again ravishing Kyoshi there on his desk through the unfettered wanderings of his mind.

"Stop," he whispered, biting his lip.

As delicious as the fantasy was, Headmaster Mitsuwa knew that continuing to imagine such a scenario was unwise. He had already climaxed once that afternoon, right there in his chair, thinking of Kyoshi.

It simply wasn't appropriate to consider a student sexually, and he knew he needed to stop. Yet even as he tried to repress his urges, images of Kyoshi bent over his desk tormented him, and he found his hand fumbling again beneath his robes, his twitching organ demanding release. It was almost as if, the more he tried not think about young Sayuki, the more aroused he became.

Finally giving in completely to his desires, he threw his head back, pumping himself with masterful strokes until the sweet release was achieved. He was so transported by his orgasm that he had difficulty staying quiet, gasping and clutching onto the arm of his chair.

Twice. And in the same afternoon. Both times, because of Kyoshi.

Letting his head fall back against his chair, he groaned. Perhaps he should expel the unruly youth. For his own sanity. But...that was hardly fair to Kyoshi. Why should he be penalized because of his Headmaster's untoward desires?

He laughed at himself, realizing that he was once again thinking up excuses for Kyoshi to stay.

His thoughts once again returned to Kyoshi's punishment, only now the Headmaster was able to focus on what was fair without the distraction of becoming sexually aroused. Once he came to a decision, he put the summons on his secretary's desk, and finally went home for the night.

"FUCK," KYOSHI GROANED, READING the summons to the Headmaster's chambers. He'd just finished his classes for the day and was almost starting to think he wouldn't be called. But the summons had arrived at the residence hall, not at one of his classes as he'd expected.

He made his way to the Administration building, wondering what the Headmaster had decided and if there was still time to change his mind.

This time he didn't wait long. Almost as soon as he arrived, Headmaster Mitsuwa opened his door, beckoning him inside with the same, soft, rather unnerving command.

"Please step inside my chambers."

This time, though, Mitsuwa returned to his desk immediately, sitting down in a less relaxed fashion than the previous day, and looking rather stern.

When Kyoshi saw the crop whip lying on his desk, he felt hopeful. Deciding to advance his ass-kissing strategy, he stopped before the Headmaster's desk, bowing. "Please, Headmaster, accept my apology for my inappropriate behavior yesterday. I would like to ask you to consider letting me stay at Valemont."

Headmaster Mitsuwa was rather surprised at this, and stared at him for a moment, silent. "Very well. I will accept your apology, Kyoshi. Please sit down."

Kyoshi did so, and Sho noticed immediately that he sat more upright, his deportment completely altered from the previous day, now humble and respectful.

Suspicious, he leaned back in his chair, studying him. "Is this the same unruly lad that was in my chambers yesterday? How came this magnificent change? Let me guess. You are afraid to tell your uncle that you were expelled once again."

"That's not it," Kyoshi protested, now dropping his façade and speaking honestly. "I mean, well, that's true. He'll be pissed as hell. But it's just that I've decided I might want to stay here after all."

"Is that so? And…what brought about this sudden change of heart, Mr. Sayuki?"

"It's because...well, I meant this really cool guy. And I found out we have a yudona team."

"I see. You're a yudona fighter then?" Sho asked, feeling an unexpected stab of jealousy when Kyoshi mentioned meeting someone. Of course, he'd been in his office the previous day for sexual misconduct, so it was hardly surprising. Yet something about the way his face lit up when he mentioned the "really cool guy" bothered Headmaster Mitsuwa. He was so distracted by it that he realized he hadn't heard Kyoshi's answer, and it wasn't until he heard the name "Seiko" that he snapped to attention.

"Seiko Shinozaki?"

"Yeah. That's it."

"Don't tell me the two of you," now the Headmaster fell silent, realizing his question was heading in an inappropriate direction.

"I know what you're thinking," Kyoshi laughed. "You don't have to worry. I know Seiko's been to your office plenty but...we won't cause trouble, I promise. Not all that much any way."

"I'll hold you to that," he replied. "Now, as for my decision, I must tell you that I did consider expulsion. However, I've decided to allow to stay at Valemont. You will, however, need to be disciplined."

"Thank you, Headmaster," Kyoshi murmured, watching him anxiously.

Sho was silent for a moment, then picked up his whip, looking the boy directly in the eye.

"Twenty strikes."

"What!" Kyoshi cried, his eyes flashing. "That's bloody fucked and you know it!"

The Headmaster smiled at the return of the Kyoshi he remembered.

"I think it's quite appropriate, given the offense. There is a...an invisible line between you and I that should never be crossed. You crossed it."

"Well, what about you?" Kyoshi demanded. "You bloody crossed it too! I felt you — you were hard as tank!"

"I must ask you to lower your voice," Sho replied, sharply.

"See! You're trying to hide it, because you know you're to blame, too! Don't you think I should get a break on account of the fact that you enjoyed it?"

"Having certain thoughts are one thing," the Headmaster replied, carefully, "but acting on them is quite another."

Kyoshi shook his head at this, sinking down in his chair and then wincing.

"I take it you're still a bit sore from yesterday."

"Yes, if you must know. I'm fucked up." The thought of twenty additional strikes was simply too much; Kyoshi felt sure he couldn't take it.

"I'll give you a second option. Eight strikes. With that paddle." The Headmaster nodded to a paddle that hung from the wall.

Sighing, Kyoshi closed his eyes, trying to decide between two equally unpalatable options. He knew full well how much a paddle hurt, and eight strikes was almost ridiculous. Still...it would be over quicker than the crop whip, and it was a different kind of pain.

Headmaster Mitsuwa watched him, curious as to what he would choose. He had made the punishment severe so that Kyoshi might entertain a third option—simply dropping out. As much as he didn't want to see the boy go, he knew that it might be better for everyone concerned—at least, Sho thought, for himself. He had a feeling that if Kyoshi stayed, he would be in his chambers rather frequently, and already he felt he was starting to lose his head when it came to the rebellious youth.

Opening his eyes, Kyoshi gazed at the Headmaster for a moment. "I'll take the paddle."

"Have you ever been paddled before, Kyoshi?" he asked, curious as to his choice.

"Yes." Kyoshi's dark eyes glared back at him defiantly.

"Very well," Mitsuwa answered, rising. "On your feet. Drop your bottoms and lean over the desk."

The Headmaster was careful to keep his eyes away from Kyoshi as he retrieved the paddle from the wall. He rarely used the paddle and was actually a little surprised that he had chosen it, especially if he knew what he was getting into. It would be far more painful, though it would be over quicker.

Positioning himself behind the boy, he almost felt pity for him when he saw his punished flesh; he was bruised and torn, every strike of the crop whip still imprinted on his skin. But, this was good. The paddling would be excruciating and Kyoshi would no doubt come to hate him, if he didn't already. He would not need to worry about future advances from young Sayuki, advances that the Headmaster was not altogether sure he could continue to resist. Best end the matter now.

Holding the paddle with both hands, he took aim, and then, with a mighty swing, let it fly. The loud smack it produced was matched by an equally loud vocalization from Kyoshi, who had been simply unprepared for how much it would hurt. Whether it was his previous day's punishment or Headmaster Mitsuwa's strength, the pain was beyond his wildest dreams.

A second strike proved equally barbaric; the third unbearable.

"Please, Headmaster," he pleaded.

"Negotiations are over." A fourth strike illustrated this point, eliciting a strangled cry from the boy.

"I'm begging you. I can't...I can't take it."

Whack!

"You'll take it, Mr. Sayuki. You have three more strikes."

"No."

Suddenly Kyoshi spun around, putting out his hand to stop the paddle.

"Turn around, Kyoshi!"

"It's too much. Please."

"You'll finish your punishment, or you'll take your expulsion."

"Please." Desperate, Kyoshi tried to think of anything that would get him out of the paddling. He looked at the Headmaster, who was careful to keep his eyes locked on his face, and he thought he saw there something he detected the previous day...desire.

"Let me...do something else," he whispered.

"Kyoshi! Turn around and bend over, NOW!"

"I'll suck you...would you like that? Or...you can fuck me if you want. I know you want it."

Stunned, for a moment the Headmaster was speechless.

"Come on. It will be just between us. No one will ever know."

Kyoshi looked at him with unveiled desire, spreading his legs a bit and reaching down to fondle himself.

The beautiful boy's offer sent a surge of carnal excitation to Sho's loins, and a part of him very much wanted to accept. He tried to keep his gaze on Kyoshi's face, but finally he could not resist glancing down. There he beheld Kyoshi in all his male glory, stroking himself to full arousal.

"That's it. Let's cross that invisible line."

"This...is precisely why you're being disciplined today, Kyoshi," the Headmaster said, finally, looking up. "And I should add to your punishment for your inappropriate solicitation. But I won't. I'm simply going to insist that you complete your punishment. You have three more strikes. If you fail to obey me on this, you may leave my chambers and I will draft up your letter of expulsion this very afternoon. Turn around, Kyoshi."

Disappointed, the boy finally did so, presenting his already reddened backside for the rest of his discipline. These three strikes were the worst thing Kyoshi could ever remember experiencing in his life, and at the end of it, he wept openly.

"Pull up your trousers, Mr. Sayuki."

The youth did so with some difficulty. This time when Headmaster Mitsuwa offered him a tissue, he took it, mortified that the man had actually made him cry.

Sho put the paddle back on the wall, and sat back down, allowing Kyoshi to regain his composure.

"I think we understand one another now, Kyoshi. I sincerely hope I will not need to repeat this lesson again. You may go."

Gifting him with a look of hate, Kyoshi turned and left, slamming the door behind him.

For a long time afterwards Headmaster Mitsuwa sat in his chambers, replaying the youth's offer in his mind, the seductive way he had looked at him as he stroked himself with graceful fingers. He was angry with himself for being tempted by it, even for a moment. He sighed, staring down at his crop whip, wondering when he would see Kyoshi again and if he would once again make another such offer.

And he wondered if he would be able to resist him again, if he did.

Chapter 3 - *The Sixteenth Strike*

"You're not allowed to smoke in here."

Kyoshi, who had darted into the library to get out of a sudden downpour, was standing next to an open window, trying to finish his cigarette. When confronted by Masami Rin, the resident informer and student security assistant, he shrugged. "Fuck off."

Masami, hands on hips, was not so easily put off. "That's against the rules. And secondhand smoke kills people, you know."

"I'm blowing the smoke out the window," Kyoshi protested.

"The air's still contaminated."

"I told you to fuck off!"

"You'd better do what I say or I'll report you to the librarian."

"Oh no. What will happen if you report me to the librarian," Kyoshi answered, in mock distress. "What if she holds me down...and...and...*reads* to me?"

"You'll be in trouble, that's what. I know who you are. You're Kyoshi Sayuki. Everyone knows you're a troublemaker."

"Listen here, asshole. I'm telling you for the last time. Fuck off or I'll be forced to mess up that pretty little face of yours."

"You can't talk to me like that! Fine! I'll report you then. And I'm going to tell her that you threatened me!"

Kyoshi, now rather irritated with Masami's annoying banter, stood up, threw his cigarette out the window and, with one good swing, punched the boy in the face, knocking him out. Several students, upon witnessing this, cheered him, as Masami was hardly a favorite at Valemont.

Then the librarian came rushing over and Kyoshi was immediately sent, once again, to the Headmaster's chambers.

Kyoshi was almost glad to be sent to the Headmaster—if only to see the man. In the three weeks since he'd last visited him, he'd thought about him nearly every day, wondering if he was just imagining it, or if Mitsuwa had really had been attracted to him. But Kyoshi felt sure he was not imagining the desire in his eyes—the way the Headmaster had looked at him when he offered himself.

As he waited outside his chambers, he wondered what waited for him inside. He supposed it was too much to hope it wouldn't be corporal punishment. He desperately hoped it wasn't the paddle—he had regretted choosing the paddle last time and felt certain he would never opt for it again, if given a choice. It had been an entire week before he was completely free of soreness after his punishment. The Headmaster must have struck him with all his strength; Kyoshi was certain he'd never experienced anything so painful. Not even his uncle, who had paddled him many times, came close to delivering blows like the Headmaster.

So while Kyoshi wanted to see the Headmaster again, he was much less enthusiastic about bending over his desk for more punishment, which, as the moment drew closer, he began to dread.

Finally, the door to the chambers opened and Headmaster Mitsuwa beckoned him. "Mr. Sayuki. Please step into my chambers."

Mitsuwa managed to suppress a smile that threatened to compromise his stern demeanor as he watched the unruly youth rise to his feet in a deliberately unhurried fashion, ambling toward him with his hands in his pockets.

Kyoshi looked him dead in the eyes, smiling in an arrogant, smug way.

"You find something amusing?" Sho demanded, as Kyoshi passed him.

Kyoshi did not reply, shaking his head when he saw the crop whip laid out on the desk. "Bastard," he muttered softly, not quite loud enough for the Headmaster to make out.

"What's that? If you have something to say, Mr. Sayuki, then say it." The Headmaster closed the door firmly behind them and returned to his chair behind the desk, leaning back comfortably as he waiting for Kyoshi's response. "I'm waiting," he said, finally.

"I don't have anything to say."

"I see. And...have you anything to say about the fact that you're once again sitting before me on a disciplinary issue, not three weeks after the last time you were here?"

Although the Headmaster feigned being disappointed in Kyoshi's behavior, he had, in fact been secretly thrilled when he learned of the boy's disobedience. He had fantasized about Kyoshi every day since his last visit to his chambers and had now developed something of a private infatuation for him, though he would never let him know. And now, to see him again, his heart was most definitely pounding a cadence faster than normal.

The boy looked...beautiful. His hair, wild and unkempt, nevertheless looked silky soft, though slightly wet, and Sho longed to bury his hands and face in it. Though it was cold and rainy, he wore a thin, short sleeve shirt—very tight, so that his well-cut arm and chest muscles were emphasized.

Kyoshi shrugged, gazing back at him defiantly, sitting comfortably in the chair with manner of deliberate nonchalance, his legs stretched out in front of him.

"It seems my discipline failed to curb your unruly ways. Or wasn't that paddling hard enough for you?"

"It was hard enough," Kyoshi replied softly, his eyes narrowing.

"I think not. Perhaps I'll have to take things up a notch this time."

"You'd like that, wouldn't you, you pervert," Kyoshi retorted, angrily.

Headmaster Mitsuwa simply stared back at him for a moment, a little stunned with the boy's audacity, but also privately conceding that there was some truth to his remark. Kyoshi seemed to wither a bit under his gaze, sinking down a little further in his seat and looking away.

"Whether I like it or not is of no consequence," Sho answered, finally. "But you will not speak to me in such a manner again, Mr. Sayuki, or I will expel you from Valemont on the spot. Is that understood?"

Kyoshi sighed, closing his eyes and letting his head fall back against the chair.

"I said, IS THAT UNDERSTOOD?"

"Yes," Kyoshi shot back, annoyed. "It's bloody well understood. And expel me for all I care."

The Headmaster opened Kyoshi's file, looking at his record again. "Now, Kyoshi, I find it hard to believe you want to be expelled. It seems you've become quite the...star on the yudona team. You've won every fight since you joined. You're telling me you want to just...throw all that away?"

Kyoshi sighed again. He really didn't want to be expelled. The yudona team was great fun, and he and Seiko and some of the others had been having a blast together. But he was still angry at the Headmaster for paddling him so brutally and for turning down his offer, especially after the Headmaster had LOOKED at him so unabashedly.

"Mr. Sayuki, you—"

"Headmaster, there's a call from Ukita Kajiyama from the Jufi Philharmonic," his secretary said over intercom.

Cursing silently, Sho thought for a moment. "Tell him I'll be there tonight at 7:00 as we discussed."

"He insists on speaking with you."

Sighing, the Headmaster took the call. "I apologize," he said to Kyoshi, who shrugged, looking away.

"Sho Mitsuwa."

"You've been avoiding my calls," Ukita accused.

"Not so. I have not been avoiding them, but I've been very busy," Sho replied, lowering his voice.

Kyoshi raised an eyebrow at this, immediately guessing the intimacy between the Headmaster and whoever it was on the other line, this Philharmonic person.

"Then, if you're not avoiding me, come to my hotel tonight, after rehearsal."

"I can't. I have...things to attend to."

"Right. Why am I not surprised? I demand to know where I stand with you, Sho. You can't keep putting this conversation off forever."

Sho sighed. "I have a student in my office. This isn't the...appropriate time."

"Send him out!"

"Ukita...all right. We'll talk later tonight, after rehearsal. But not at your hotel."

Ukita fell silent for a moment. "You...you're killing me, Sho. I already know what you're going to say."

"Then why must I say it?" Sho whispered, angrily, then saw that Kyoshi was watching him.

"That's it. I get it. It's because of...what happened."

"No, Ukita—that happens to everyone occasionally. It's nothing to be...ashamed of."

Kyoshi laughed at this, eliciting a glare from the Headmaster.

"Ukita, I must go. We'll discuss this later."

With an exaggerated sigh, Ukita finally relented. "All right. See you tonight."

Sho hung up the phone and for a moment said nothing, trying to remember where he and Kyoshi had left off.

"Are you breaking up with your boyfriend or something?" Kyoshi asked.

"I'm quite certain that is none of your business."

"What, do you play an instrument? With that Philharmonic?"

"As a matter of fact, I do. I'm a pianist. Though...I only play occasionally."

"No shit?" Perhaps that was why the Headmaster had such beautiful, graceful hands; Kyoshi had noticed his hands before, admiring them and the way he held them. He was also intrigued with the thought of the Headmaster having a lover. So. There was no question that he was sexually active. Once again, Kyoshi found his thoughts bending around what it would be like to be intimate with the man.

"Don't tell me you have some appreciation for music?"

"Fuck no," Kyoshi lied. "Not that kind of music anyway." Secretly, Kyoshi did enjoy the classics, but he had always kept this a secret. It simply didn't fit his image of being the tough rebel to admit listening to a cantata or concerto, or having an appreciation for fine arts.

His uncle had exposed him to world music at a very young age, and Kyoshi also had a good eye for art, though he possessed no talent himself. He had helped his uncle purchase several works that had later turned out to be excellent investments.

Now he tried to imagine Headmaster Mitsuwa at the piano, and he found his heart seemed to skip a beat. He wondered when the concert would be, and where, and if he could somehow go to secretly watch the Headmaster play.

"I see." The Headmaster smiled, puzzling over Kyoshi's vacillations. And was he mistaken, or was the boy giving him that look again? "Is there something on your mind, Kyoshi?"

"Just tell me one thing," Kyoshi replied, softly. "Why...did you *look*?"

Immediately guessing what he referred to, Headmaster Mitsuwa remained silent for a moment, closing his eyes with a small sigh. "That was...quite wrong of me. Quite inappropriate. I...apologize."

"Why? Why was it inappropriate? You were feeling me, I could tell. Just like you're feeling me now."

His heart now beating very fast, the Headmaster picked up the crop whip and began twirling it between his fingers. "I believe I made it very clear to you last time, Kyoshi, that you and I have very distinct...roles. I am the Headmaster. You are the student. And so, whatever...feelings may or may not exist between us are irrelevant. They can't be acted on."

"You choose to accept these...roles. But why does it have to be that way? So what if I'm a student? I know you want to be my lover. I can see it in your eyes. I could tell by the way you looked at me. And I'll admit it...I want to be your lover. I want to fuck you and let you fuck me, hard, and —"

"Enough. This conversation has gone far enough, Kyoshi."

"I say it hasn't."

"Kyoshi!"

"What? Can't you fucking be honest with me about this?"

"Mr. Sayuki. You are here today for assaulting a classmate, and that is the only thing we will be discussing. You're lucky he wasn't seriously hurt; fortunately, I've spoken to his parents and they are not going to press charges."

"Masami's a total dickhead."

"Be that as it may...that is," Sho quickly caught himself , "what I meant to say is, regardless of your feelings toward that student, violence will not be tolerated at Valemont."

"Unless it comes from your whip, I take it," Kyoshi shot back.

Now the Headmaster, a little annoyed with the boy's insolence, tapped the whip against his hand, deciding to increase his punishment from what he had initially planned.

"Twenty strikes, Kyoshi."

"What! I didn't even hurt him!"

"You knocked him unconscious."

"I can't help it if he can't take a punch!"

"Twenty strikes. On your feet."

Sighing, Kyoshi stood up, glaring at the Headmaster. Sho had intended to allow him to stand upright, with his pants up, but Kyoshi had already lowered them and was bending over the desk before he could say anything.

Trying to keep from trembling, the Headmaster positioned himself behind Kyoshi, biting his lip to keep from uttering a sound. The sight of the boy once again so vulnerably positioned was almost too much. He felt a surge of blood rush to his groin; this was precisely why he had been planning to allow Kyoshi to keep his pants up.

He longed to toss the whip aside and spread him, sinking his now rigid cock into his depths, plundering him without restraint.

As absurd as it was for a Headmaster to wish for a student's disobedience, he'd almost been disappointed that Kyoshi hadn't come to see him earlier. He had craved another good look at his enticingly tight little ass bent over his desk and had fantasized numerous times about disciplining him again...followed by other salacious, frightfully lascivious deeds.

He'd played Kyoshi's offer over and over in his mind, his heart beating faster each time he contemplated the boy's proffered "wicked blow job" or his seductively tendered, "you can fuck me as hard as you want." These thoughts inevitably lead to the same conclusion, and while Sho felt extraordinarily guilty each time he masturbated over Kyoshi, he could not seem to stop.

And now, to have him once again presenting himself for discipline, after his shameless solicitations, was wildly erotic to the sex-starved Headmaster, who had not had a good fuck in some time.

His trysts with Ukita had been disastrous; on the one hand, Ukita had been unable to last more than a few seconds, and on the other, Sho was disappointed with every aspect of their intimacy—he didn't like the way Ukita kissed; the chemistry just wasn't right, and the conductor seemed sadly at a loss when it came to orchestration in the bedroom.

Kyoshi wondered why the Headmaster took so long to begin, and just as he was about to complain, he felt the first strike. It stung, no question, and the second hurt even more than the first. He closed his eyes, trying to remain completely silent. He hated giving the Headmaster the satisfaction of hearing him cry out. By the ninth strike, Kyoshi knew he would no longer be able to remain silent, and his choked cries and gasps were enjoyed by the Headmaster, who was now so aroused that he was having difficulty resisting touching himself.

Each strike aroused him more than the last. Sho felt guilty for deriving so much pleasure from disciplining a student, but he simply could not help it. He longed to do other things to Kyoshi, to whip him a bit more and then fuck him...and fuck him hard, or make him kneel and suck him, swallowing every last drop.

Finally, the temptation was too much, and Sho reached down to adjust himself after the sixteenth strike. As it happened, Kyoshi turned to look back at precisely that moment, planning to beg—however futilely—for a cessation to his punishment, and catching Sho in the act of fondling himself, immediately stood up.

"I knew it," he cried, grabbing the Headmaster's wrist before he could strike him again.

"How dare you! Take your hands off me!" Sho demanded, furious.

"I saw you! You bloody pervert!"

"You have four more strikes, Kyoshi! No, TEN more!"

As Kyoshi tightened his grip on his wrist, Sho suddenly realized he was no match for the boy's strength. Kyoshi was strong, and the warmth of his hand around his wrist was disconcertingly arousing.

"No. We're finished with the discipline, Headmaster. I think perhaps I should discipline *you*." Kyoshi smiled, once again giving him a seductive look.

"Stop...stop it," Sho whispered.

"You don't want me to stop. You know it, and I know it."

With that, Kyoshi pulled Sho close and began kissing him.

Sho meant to push him away. He meant to...but suddenly, when Kyoshi's hot tongue began exploring him so exquisitely, he found that he could not. Or rather...that he did not *want* to stop the kiss.

Before he realized what he was doing, he was kissing Kyoshi back, passionately, wildly, descending down an intoxicating spiral, the path of his tongue taking him deeper and deeper into that kiss, until all he wanted was to pull Kyoshi deep inside him and imprison him there. It was the most erotic moment of his entire life, and even though he knew how very wrong it was, he could not seem to resist the moment.

Or rather...he did not *want* to resist.

He had dropped his crop whip, which went rolling across the floor, and now put his hands in Kyoshi's soft hair, pulling him even closer. When he felt the boy's hand fumbling under his robe, touching him, trying to unzip him, he nearly ejaculated from his mere touch; he felt Kyoshi's hand encircle his shaft and then, realizing how quickly things had spun out of control, he finally broke off the kiss, pushing Kyoshi firmly away.

"Stop."

"Why?" Kyoshi demanded, now stroking himself openly. He was quite ready to take things to the next step, and felt angry with the Headmaster for pushing him away. He took a step toward him but Sho put out his hand to stop him, shaking his head.

"No, Kyoshi. Please forgive me. That was...what I did was...unforgivable. I'm quite...mortified. Please...leave my chambers. Your punishment is finished."

"I don't want to leave. I want to finish what we started."

"We can't," Sho whispered, fiercely. "Go, Kyoshi."

"I'm not leaving until I come. If I have to stand here and masturbate, then I guess that's what I'll do."

"Kyoshi," Sho begged, but could not help following the movement of the boy's arm down to the place of origin, where he now began pumping his immense cock with his beautiful, strong fingers. Spreading his legs apart a bit more and leaning back against the desk, he closed his eyes. He quickly brought himself to orgasm, gasping, his head thrown back, as his semen erupted, dripping down his hand and onto the floor of the Headmaster's chambers.

Transfixed, Sho felt as though his heart had stopped. He was now desperate for Kyoshi to leave simply so he could relieve himself. He handed him a tissue which the boy accepted with a smile, wiping off his hand and then pulling up and zipping his pants.

"Are you sure you don't want me to...suck you off before I go?" he asked, eyes gleaming dark.

Sho most definitely *did* want Kyoshi to do so, but he managed to resist the offer.

"Just go, Kyoshi."

Kyoshi, quite pleased with himself for having nearly seduced the Headmaster as well as getting out of the rest of his punishment, left without further argument. His ass was burning from the crop whip, but he didn't even mind that much. The Headmaster had kissed him back. All his suspicions were confirmed; Sho Mitsuwa was attracted to him.

The Headmaster mumbled his apologies again and then practically pushed him out the door. He shut the door and stood, leaning against it, trying to fumble with his zipper to release himself before he stained his pants. His cock swollen and aching, it only took a few quick strokes to ejaculate. He groaned as he watched his semen arc to the floor, remembering how enticing Kyoshi had looked as he masturbated, leaning against the desk — the same desk over which Sho had punished him but moments before.

For a long time he continued to stand, sorting through what had just happened in his chambers, his shame now eating away at him. He could not believe what he had done; he had kissed Kyoshi — a student — and had almost allowed things to go even further. What would happen next time Kyoshi came to his chambers?

And...what should he do now?

Chapter 4 - *Over the Line*

SHO LEFT HIS OFFICE EARLY FOR THE FIRST TIME since he had become Headmaster at Valemont. But after what had happened that afternoon, he felt he had to leave the campus. He had to...get away from Valemont.

From Kyoshi.

He needed to talk to someone. To his brother, Nishi. He wasn't sure what he would say to him; he doubted he could actually confess what he'd just done. But Nishi had a way of calming him down, no matter what the circumstance.

Nishi was surprised to hear from him and could tell right away that something was wrong. But, as was his usual way, he did not question him or act any differently.

"Sure. Come on over, brother," he answered, in response to Sho's call. "What's that noise?"

"I'm in the car," Sho replied. "Are you sure I won't be...interrupting things?"

"If you mean sex, then no. Takashi and I had a fight earlier this week. I told him to clear out."

"I'm...sorry to hear that."

"Liar," Nishi laughed. "I know perfectly well you didn't approve of Takashi."

"It's not that I didn't approve," Sho argued. "It's just that...I guess...I didn't trust him."

"Well, your instincts are good, anyway. He cheated on me, the little bitch. Although King didn't like him either. I guess from now on I should either trust my dog or my brother when it comes to partners."

Smiling, Sho already felt better just hearing Nishi's voice. "Thanks Nish. I appreciate this."

"No problem. See you in a few minutes then."

Nishi lived close to the Academy, so it wasn't long before Sho pulled into his drive. He was watched lazily by King, Nishi's Siberian Husky, who looked completely uninterested in his arrival.

"You don't care much for me either, do you, King?" Sho asked. King put his head on his paws, looking bored.

Nishi opened the door, grinning. "Come in, come in," he announced, bowing formally. "Although you'll have to excuse the mess. I don't keep a tidy house the way you do. And I'm right in the middle of a....new painting."

"I *am* interrupting you," Sho replied, worried.

"Hell no. I need a break. Anyway it sucks; I think I'm scrapping it."

"Can I see it?"

"No."

"You know, I've yet to see any of your art, Nishi. I'm starting to doubt you're actually an artist at all."

"So am I," Nishi answered, with a grin. "Anyway....what can I get you — coffee, tea, beer, soda?"

"If you don't mind, coffee would be quite nice, thank you. But only," Sho began, then stopped.

"If it's fresh," Nishi finished. "I remember. You're very anal when it comes to your coffee. It has to be just freshly brewed, a medium roast, with a dash of real cream."

"If it's too much trouble...."

"Hush. I'm just thrilled to see you. We never get together any more, these days."

"You're right. We should....do this more often."

"Are you going up to see mom this weekend?"

"I can't — I have that concert with Jufi Philharmonic."

"Oh right. Well...she was asking about you."

Sho nodded. "I know. I'm a bad son. I'll be sure to go up next weekend."

Nishi laughed. "You're the bad son? I think not. You're her pride and joy."

Sho did not answer, suddenly wondering what his mother would think if she knew that he had gotten involved with a student.

His brother studied him, noticing his sudden change of mood. "I'll...go make that coffee. Come into the kitchen with me, if you like."

Sho followed him into the kitchen and then startled when he saw a mouse running along the wall and then scurrying behind the stove, fast as lightning.

Nishi laughed. "That's Alfred. I've been trying to catch him for the last five months. He's too smart."

"Don't you think you should...do something about it?"

"I thought about trying to poison him. But then...I just couldn't do it. I don't know. I'm kinda used to him now. He's really pretty cute."

Sho smiled. Nishi hadn't changed at all since when he was a boy and, as an aspiring naturalist, had decided to collect butterflies. But when it came right down to it, Nishi couldn't bring himself to kill the butterflies, so instead, he set them all free.

"But...what if he's a *she*? Then you might have a bit of a problem."

"Now that's where you and I are different. You worry."

"Do I?"

Nishi, having started the coffee brewing, sat down at the table with him, nodding. "Yes. You do."

"I suppose...that's true," Sho conceded.

"So...maybe you'd like to tell me what's on your mind?"

Sho sighed. "It's...awful."

"Now, Sho. I doubt it's as bad as you think it is."

"But it is." Sho shook his head. "I'm so...ashamed."

Nishi raised an eyebrow at this, curious, wondering what could possibly make his brother so upset. "You don't have to tell me...unless you want to."

"Maybe...it would help to tell someone. I mean, you. I can't imagine telling anyone else."

"I'm listening."

"It's...there's a new student. Kyoshi Sayuki." Sho stopped for a moment. Just saying Kyoshi's name made his heart beat a little faster. "He's...been to my office three times already." Now Sho fell silent, looking a bit nervous.

Nishi studied him, puzzled. "So...he's been to your office three times," he prompted.

Sho nodded. "Yes. And...one time...he kissed me."

Nishi could not resist a smile at this. It was just like his brother to be flustered over something like that. "So what did you do? Expel him?"

Sho shook his head. "No. I didn't. Not only that...but," now Sho broke off, looking rather tormented.

"But what, Sho?"

Sho raised his eyes to look at his brother. "I...today, that is...I kissed him back."

A bit surprised, Nishi remained silent for a moment. "Wow," he said, finally.

Sho put his face in his hands, groaning.

"Then, all you did is kiss?"

Sho looked up, sighing. "No...there was all sorts of...touching and grasping going on....Nishi, what am I going to do?"

"All sorts of touching," Nishi repeated, slowly. "Who was touching who?"

"He...was touching me...but I let him. I let him, Nish. And I wanted to touch him. I wanted to do more than that. I wanted to take things to the next level. And I...watched him masturbate."

Nishi was undeniably a bit shocked. It was completely out of Sho's character to have done something like that. Nishi probably wouldn't have hesitated, but Sho? Sho was a different story altogether.

"Well," Nishi replied, after a moment, "I confess I'm a little surprised. But he must have really made an impact on you for you to...respond, Sho." The gurgling from the coffeemaker alerted him that the coffee was finished. "Hold on. Let me get your coffee."

As he poured Sho a cup of hot brew, he pondered what his brother had just told him.

"What do you think I should do?" Sho asked.

"I can't really answer that for you. I think you know...you're taking a risk. With your position and all." He fell silent for a moment. "I take it he's a looker, then?"

"He's perfect."

Nishi lowered his voice, intrigued. "What was it like? Kissing him, I mean."

"It was...idyllic."

Nishi smiled at his brother's word choice. "You mean it was good, I guess?"

"Oh yes." Sho sighed. "It was the most...erotic moment of my life. I...can't stop thinking about him."

"Hmmm. Well, like I said, I can't really advise you. But if it were *me*, of course, I'd give him a good hard fucking."

Sho laughed. "You're incorrigible, Nish."

"Oh, come on. That's what you want to do, isn't it? You didn't really expect me to tell you to turn your back on, what was it? The most erotic moment of your life?"

Smiling, Sho shook his head.

"Life is short, brother," Nishi whispered.

"What are you saying?"

"You know what I'm saying. Go with your gut."

Sho felt silent, considering. "If I did that, I could lose my position...my entire career at Valemont would be jeopardized."

"Only if you're caught," Nishi answered, eyes twinkling.

"And there are...certain ethics involved. I'm in a position of authority."

"I guess that means you'll be on top."

Sho laughed. "I don't know. I think he's stronger than me."

"Hmmm....maybe he'll be on top, then. Or maybe you'll have to take turns."

Sho punched his brother in the arm. "Stop it, Nish. You're very bad."

Nishi grinned. "What, you're just now realizing that? So...what are you going to do?"

"I don't know."

"Promise me one thing. If you decided to fuck him, I get to hear *all* the juicy details."

Sho shook his head, sighing, though he couldn't help smiling.

"So what happened with that conductor...what was his name?"

"Ukita." Sho groaned. "I'm trying to break it off. I'm supposed to talk with him about it tonight after rehearsal and I'm dreading it."

Nishi studied him. "That bad, huh?"

"It just wasn't...that is, he wasn't my type."

"Hmmm. He was rather attractive though, if I remember correctly?"

"Yes. But...when we kissed...it was so—I don't know. Almost like kissing a dead person. He just stuck out his tongue and let it sit there."

Nishi laughed. "Poor Ukita. I hope you didn't tell him he kissed like a corpse."

"God, no. In fact, I haven't officially broken things off. I've been...avoiding him."

"I take it the sex wasn't much better?"

Sho shook his head. "The absolute worst. First, he came on my leg. Then," Sho sighed, "I can't possibly describe it. He just...doesn't know what he's doing. I tried to fuck him but he kept tightening up. Then I asked him to suck me, and he actually bit me, just a bit."

"Ohh," Nishi winced.

"But it wasn't really any of that. The truth of the matter is, there's no chemistry. I can't explain why."

Nishi shrugged. "No one can. It's just one of those things. But I take it this...Kyoshi? Has it."

Sho nodded, feeling the blood rush to his face. Whatever that mysterious, intangible *it* factor was, Kyoshi most certainly had it. If it had been Kyoshi rather than Ukita fumbling around and ejaculating on his leg, Sho probably would have climaxed right afterwards, just from pure excitement. No, it wasn't Ukita's awkwardness that had been the deciding factor. It was simply that...he wasn't Kyoshi.

"EVERYONE'S TALKING ABOUT IT," SEIKO SAID, grinning. "You really knocked him out with one punch?"

"Yeah." Kyoshi winced as Seiko placed the ice pack on his ass.

"Headmaster Mitsuwa sure doesn't hold back with you," Seiko commented. "He broke the skin again."

"Where's that cocktail thing," Kyoshi demanded. "I'm dying here."

"Coming right up. So...tell me, did you kiss him again?"

"No," Kyoshi lied. He didn't feel like sharing what had happened in the Headmaster's chambers with anyone, not even Seiko. Because now he had a definite agenda when it came to Headmaster Mitsuwa.

Kyoshi was going to seduce him.

"Hey, did you know he plays piano with some orchestra? Jufi Philharmonic?"

"Yeah. He's supposedly really good. I don't know, I'm not really into that stuff."

"Me either," Kyoshi replied quickly.

"I think he was some child protégé or something. But now he only plays occasionally."

"Yeah, because he's too busy disciplining students in his chambers. Hey, it would be fun to go to his concert and throw spitballs at him."

"You'd get tossed out on your ass if you did that," Seiko laughed. "Besides, you'd never get a ticket. Those things are sold out months in advance. My sister's always complaining about it, how she can never get a ticket because the patrons buy out season seats."

Disappointed, Kyoshi fell silent. Then he realized all he needed to do was call his uncle. His uncle could get him a ticket; he was sure of it.

"What are you smiling about?" Seiko demanded. "You must be pretty sore by now."

"I don't feel so bad. Must be those endorphins kicking in."

"Whatever the fuck *that* is, you nut. Hey, isn't your tournament this weekend?"

"No. Next weekend. In Jufi." He smiled. "You going?"

"Of course. Afterwards Hisashi's having a get together over at his parent's old lake cottage. So I thought we could all go together."

"Sure. Sounds fun."

"Then, here's your prescription," Seiko replied, handing him two little pills, "and now I must ask you to get the fuck out. I've got company coming, and if he comes over and sees you with your pants down like that I might have some explaining to do."

Kyoshi grinned at this, standing up and preparing to leave. He winced as he zipped up his pants, even the mere touch of the fabric against his ass too much to bear. "Who's your new friend? And how do you know he wouldn't like to see me with my pants down?"

"Don't even think about it. He's mine," Seiko grinned. "And it's Kimura Jiro."

"Shit. You mean that musician from Abort Mission?"

"The same. Hot, huh?"

"Fuck yeah. How'd you ever manage that?" Kyoshi teased.

"Asshole," Seiko replied, pushing him toward the door. "Out."

"Anyway, thanks again. I owe you."

"Yes, you do."

Flipping him off, Kyoshi then left and retired to his own room to contemplate his designs on Headmaster Mitsuwa. Unlike most of the other students at Valemont, he had a private room, which suited him just fine. He fantasized about the Headmaster for about an hour, masturbated, and then, once he was flying high from Seiki's post-Headmaster cocktail, finally called his uncle — who sounded surprised to hear from him.

"Are you in trouble?" he demanded.

"Nothing like that. I wanted to ask you...for a favor."

"Uh huh. I'm not sending you more money, Kyo."

"That's not why I'm calling. Not exactly, anyway. I want to go to a concert. At the Jufi Philharmonic this weekend. Only...the tickets are sold out."

"You want to see the Jufi Philharmonic?" Surprised, his uncle thought about this for a moment. "They're not sold out. Give me a few moments and I'll call you back. How many tickets do you need?"

"Just one."

"Ah. I'll only be a moment."

Kyoshi hung up the phone, smiling. His uncle had almost sounded...friendly.

He called back, as expected, less than ten minutes later.

"I have your ticket. Front row, Saturday night."

"Wow. Thanks, uncle. I really appreciate it."

"Just give your name at the ticket booth. And...attire is formal. I've reserved credit for you at Paxton's Formalwear there in Hiracho. You'll need to get fitted tomorrow. And you have a room at the Swan Hotel in Jufi so you can spend the night rather than drive back afterward. I don't want you driving after dark at this time of year—the weather is too unpredictable. I've also left a little spending money for you with the concierge. You might consider visiting the Jufi Art Museum while you're there."

Kyoshi could not help smiling over his uncle's sudden, rather atypical, generosity. "Thank you, uncle."

"I'm very pleased that you're developing a taste for the arts, Kyo. I want to do everything I can to encourage you in that regard." He paused for a moment. "How is school? Are you doing well in your studies?"

"Yes, uncle."

"Have you had any...disciplinary problems?"

"No," Kyoshi lied. He knew better than to tell his uncle the truth; he'd found out the hard way, his uncle paddled him each time he got into trouble, so his punishment was essentially doubled. Of course, if his uncle ever thought to call the Headmaster to verify his behavior, he'd be screwed.

"That's good to hear. Because as you know, Kyoshi, if you pull the same stunts at Valemont as you did at Edgewood and Gremley, I'm going to very hard on you. I'll get out the paddle *and* the bench."

"Yes, uncle," Kyoshi murmured, instinctively shuddering a bit. He hated the "bench" — a restraining device that had apparently been in the family for over 300 years — handed down from one generation to the next for one purpose only — discipline. Restrained on the bench, there was no escape from whatever punishment was then doled out. Kyoshi had only been disciplined over it a few times, but was in no hurry to be punished in such a manner again.

"Very good. Ah, Kyoshi, I should tell you — I'll be abroad over the Holidays. You can still come back to the house, if you like. Rosa should be here."

"I'll stay here." Though Kyoshi told himself he did not really care that he had nowhere to go for the Holidays, in truth, he felt a bit hurt that once again his uncle was abandoning him. Although he had no great love for his uncle, he was, nevertheless, the only family he had. Rosa — the housekeeper — had always been good to him, but Kyoshi could not bear the emptiness of the mansion and the memories of his unhappy childhood there. It would be better to stay at Valemont, or maybe go to Jufi and explore the city, than to go back to an empty house.

But....he had his ticket to the concert, and a hotel room, too. Kyoshi spent the next few days fantasizing about how he could lure Headmaster Mitsuwa back to his hotel after the concert...and what he would do to him afterward.

The night of the concert finally arrived. Kyoshi managed to slip out of Valemont without anyone noticing him; he wore a long overcoat over his formal attire. He didn't want anyone to know where he was going, though he wasn't even exactly sure why.

He arrived at Jufi early enough to get settled in his room, which turned out to be a posh penthouse suite far more extravagant than was necessary. Kyoshi couldn't help but smile; although his uncle had never been overly affectionate toward him, there were times, like this, when it almost seemed as if he were attempting to express some sort of caring for him.

Kyoshi was prepared for the night ahead. He had lubricant, ropes, a flogger, and toys—just in case. All he had to do was lure the Headmaster back to his room; once he got him inside, he suspected Mitsuwa would not be able to resist. The look in his eyes when they last parted left no mistaking its meaning—Sho Mitsuwa lusted for him. And of course, had he been able to conceal his look, his body had quite betrayed him. Kyoshi longed to get his hand around that shaft again, and his lips—he ached to taste the man's sex.

By the time he was ready to leave for the concert, he was so aroused he contemplated relieving himself before he left, but then opted against it, preferring to be deliciously tormented for a few hours.

The Jufi Concert Hall was packed. As Kyoshi pulled up to the entrance, he was immediately greeting by a gloved valet. Heads turned to admire his sleek grey Grantley Platinum, then to regard its occupant; for Kyoshi, dressed head to toe in the finest formalwear money could buy, was hard not to notice. Although his hair was a bit longer than others attending the opening night of the Jufi Philharmonic, it suited him well. There was no question that young Sayuki was exceedingly handsome, and undeniably affluent.

He made his way inside to the ticket counter, where he retrieved his front row ticket — perhaps the best seat in the house.

The proprietor of the Concert Hall was waiting for him to arrive; he immediately greeted him, insisting on escorting him personally to his seat.

"Please give your uncle my kindest regards," he smiled. "And thank him once again for his most generous contribution."

"I will," Kyoshi promised, trying to suppress a smile. It was nothing new; wherever he went, people asked him to thank his uncle for one thing or another, and he was, in truth, a bit proud of the man's generosity. It would be horrid to be the nephew of a stingy old miser, no matter how wealthy. And although he demanded Kyoshi graduate before he received his inheritance, privately he had to acknowledge that his uncle was asking very little from him.

Lost in his thoughts, it seemed to him only a few moments had passed when the lights began to dim. Then, the curtain rose, and the orchestra stood, bowing as the audience applauded. The conductor was surprisingly attractive, and Kyoshi flipped through his program to be sure: Ukita Kajiyama. Yes. That was the name, wasn't it? He looked him over again, trying evaluate what sort of an obstacle he would present to his agenda of seduction.

As he stared at him, it seemed that Ukita suddenly looked right at him, giving him a little smile and a nod as if he knew him. Before he could puzzle over this overly much, he was distracted by the standing ovation when Headmaster Mitsuwa came out onto the stage. Kyoshi managed to get to his feet, staring at him in disbelief.

Mitsuwa looked stunning in his tuxedo, and he smiled a dazzling smile that Kyoshi had never seen before. As he sat down at the grand piano, a hushed silence then fell upon the hall.

Then, Sho began to play.

From Kyoshi's seat, he could see everything — the side of his face, his hands flying across the keyboard, and he found that he was mesmerized by Mitsuwa's performance. His heart began to beat faster and his erection ached. The Headmaster was absolutely amazing, and now Kyoshi wanted him more than ever.

He *had* to have him.

Much as he enjoyed watching the Headmaster play, Kyoshi soon became anxious for the concert to end so he could pursue his evening's agenda. He now deeply regretted not masturbating before he arrived, as he wriggled uncomfortably in his chair.

When the concert finally ended, it was all he could to keep from whipping out his cock and ejaculating right there on the stage. Fortunately able to restrain this more unrefined impulse, he waited until the people began to file out of the hall. Then, he quickly ascended to the stage and slipped behind the curtain.

No one even noticed him; backstage was nearly as noisy as the hall itself, as the musicians mingled about in post-concert mania, congratulating one another on their performances.

He surveyed the crowd until finally he saw Mitsuwa, off in a corner with the conductor. As he approached them, it became clear they were having some sort of argument, though it appeared they were trying to keep it hushed. Ukita's face was red, and his mouth moved quickly. Sho was looking away, shaking his head.

Slowly, with devilish nonchalance, Kyoshi sauntered toward them, hands in his pockets.

Mitsuwa was the first to see him. The look on his face was nothing less than pure shock.

"Kyoshi," he breathed.

Ukita turned, surprised. The conductor appraised him and, once again, seemed to nod as though he recognized him.

"Mr. Sayuki, I believe?" he said, with a polite smile.

"At your service."

Sho felt as though his heart had stopped. The sight of Kyoshi, ambling toward him so sharply attired, his hair bouncing a bit against his shoulders, eyes glimmering, lips in a half-smile—had rendered him, for a moment, completely speechless. His knees felt weak beneath him.

"What...are you doing here?"

"I came to see *you*, of course," Kyoshi replied, smiling. "And I wasn't disappointed. I don't mind telling you, it was bloody awesome."

Ukita turned back to Mitsuwa, watching his reaction with interest.

"You...had tickets?"

"My uncle got one for me."

Sho nodded. "Of course." Had Kyoshi specifically gotten a ticket just to come and watch him perform?

"Do you two know each other?" Ukita finally asked, perplexed.

"Kyoshi is...a student. From Valemont." Although Sho tried to be casual about it, Ukita immediately picked up on his signals.

"I see." Now Ukita looked at Kyoshi again, this time through jealous eyes. "You've come to see your Headmaster play, then?"

"Yes." Kyoshi met his gaze levelly, making his intentions known through a challenging look that spoke far more than words.

Although Ukita now decided disliked Kyoshi, he could not very well be rude to him, given that his uncle had just made an enormous contribution to the Philharmonic as well as the Jufi Concert Hall.

"Then, I will excuse myself," Ukita answered, giving Sho a final look of anger.

Ukita then moved away, much to Sho's relief.

"I'm...in your debt," he whispered, with a small smile.

"So it seems. You were getting grilled, I think?"

Mitsuwa nodded. "A bit. I'm...pleased to see you. At a cultural event, I mean."

"You mean you're not pleased to see *me*?" Kyoshi prodded.

Unable to reply to this, Sho simply smiled, feeling a little uncomfortable.

"Actually I came...because I wanted to talk to you. Can we go somewhere private around here?"

Sho looked around nervously. "I suppose we could go behind the curtains — I'll show you."

Kyoshi followed him, aware that they were being closely observed by Ukita. He turned and gave the conductor a little nod just for spite.

Fuming, Ukita turned away. Now he was starting to get the distinct impression there was more to Sho's breakup than he was letting on. This student...Kyoshi Sayuki no less...was definitely *more* than a student. And there was no mistaking what the boy had on his mind.

Sho led Kyoshi back behind the curtains to a little secluded corner under a scaffolding.

"How's this?" he asked.

"Perfect."

"So...I suppose...you want to talk about what happened."

"No. I don't want to talk." Kyoshi suddenly pushed the Headmaster back against the wall, pinning his arms as he began to kiss him.

At first, Sho made some attempt to struggle against him. But almost immediately, he surrendered to the kiss, spiraling down again in its intoxicating warmth and groaning as Kyoshi's tongue explored him deeper. His cock went rigid within seconds.

Kyoshi pressed his body up against him so that there was no mistaking he was equally aroused. The kiss was so perfect, so exquisite, so erotically sensual and sweet, that suddenly Sho no longer cared how inappropriate it was.

Something inside him broke, releasing his inhibitions. He returned his kiss wildly, thrilled with the way the boy had him pinned up against the wall.

Kyoshi broke away and whispered in his ear. "I'm going to suck you now. I know that's what you want."

And Headmaster Mitsuwa, biting his lip and closing his eyes, did not object as Kyoshi had expected.

Smiling, the boy released his hold on the Headmaster's wrists, then slid his hands down his body as he knelt, unzipping him. Sho leaned back against the wall, looking down with shining eyes.

He knew he should have Kyoshi stop. It was...wrong. And...ill-advised, given the entire Philharmonic orchestra was only a few feet away. It was inappropriate. Unconscionable. Forbidden.

And deliciously erotic.

Giving into the moment, he put his hands on the youth's head, letting his fingers run through his hair. He spread his legs a little wider, moaning softly as Kyoshi released him, his warm fingers firmly encircling his shaft.

Looking up at him seductively, Kyoshi then flicked his tongue along the top of his head, licking up his wetness. Sho began to pant as Kyoshi continued to pleasure him — and tease him.

"Naughty boy," Sho whispered, urgently. "Take me in your mouth now."

Obeying this mandate, and thrilled that the Headmaster had given it, the youth did so.

"Mercy." Mitsuwa let his head fall back against the wall, overcome with pleasure. Kyoshi hadn't been boasting when he'd claimed he gave a "wicked good blow job." Headmaster Mitsuwa could now attest to the veracity of this assertion.

He looked down again, wincing as he watched his entire shaft slide into Kyoshi's mouth. "God yes," he moaned. "It's imminent now, Kyoshi."

As if to punctuate this announcement, his climax followed on its heels, sending him into a realm of pleasure he had not experienced in a long time—perhaps ever. Floating on the wake of his release, Headmaster Mitsuwa then realized that nothing between them could ever be the same again.

They'd stepped over the line and there was no going back.

Chapter 5 - *A Night at the Swan*

EVERYTHING ABOUT THE MOMENT WAS perfect—Kyoshi's soft hair between his fingers, the boy's wickedly skilled tongue vibrating against his cock as his mouth explored him intimately, the thrill of being caught in the act of fellatio, the forbidden pleasure of being sucked off by a student.

Once he had made up his mind to submit to the temptation, Headmaster Sho decided to savor their naughty encounter completely; he leaned back against the wall, spreading his legs and thrusting a bit into Kyoshi's mouth.

It was all he could do to keep from groaning; he clenched his teeth and sucked in his breath, desperate to cry out his pleasure. As he approached his ascent, he looked down and saw that Kyoshi was gazing up at him, seductively, his eyes gleaming dark and triumphantly, and the mere sight of his cock disappearing into the boy's mouth was the deciding stimulus that pushed him over the brink.

Kyoshi was thrilled beyond words—not that he was in a position to utter any. He loved performing fellatio generally, but he'd never experienced anything as erotic as this—sucking off the Headmaster. He was actually rather surprised that Mitsuwa had given in, and the fact that he had done so confirmed his suspicions that the Headmaster wanted him.

"God yes," Sho moaned. "It's imminent now, Kyoshi."

Excited, Kyoshi watched anxiously as the Headmaster's face began to twitch, his fingers desperately tangled in his hair, his eyes starting to roll back, his breathing erratic and dangerously audible. Kyoshi almost hoped they'd be caught, but at the same time, he knew there would be repercussions that would bring their delightful affair to an end, and he hoped the Headmaster was conscious of the noise he was making.

"God. Oh god," Sho whispered. "Oh dear god."

The look on the Headmaster's face as he climaxed was exquisite, and Kyoshi nearly lost his seed just watching him come. His cock aching with need, he rose to his feet and unzipped his pants, nuzzling Sho on the neck and then whispering in this ear, "you liked that, I think?"

"Oh yes," Sho admitted, trying to catch his breath. "I won't deny it."

"Good. Then," now Kyoshi took hold of his hand and directed him to his own erection, "you won't mind returning the favor, I hope?"

For a moment the Headmaster hesitated, trying to determine in his mind if it was more profoundly unethical to pleasure a student or to be pleasured by one.

"Don't tell me...you're a taker but not a giver? I find that hard to believe." With a firm hand, Kyoshi forced the Headmaster to confront his ready cock.

Sho stroked him for a few seconds. "I want to pleasure you, Kyoshi," he whispered. "But not here. I'm a bit worried that Ukita will come back here any moment."

Kyoshi smiled. It was just as he'd hoped. "Then...come with me to my room. I'm at the Swan."

"The Swan?" For a moment Sho was surprised until he recalled that Kyoshi—or at least his uncle—was fabulously wealthy. The Swan was a hotel that only the richest patrons could afford. Even Ukita could not afford a room at the Swan.

"Yes. It's quite nice, I assure you. I'm not taking you to an old motel, if that's what you're worried about."

"I have my own car," Sho began, uncertainly.

Kyoshi gingerly removed Sho's hand from his organ, which was so hard he could barely stand the stimulation of the Headmaster's touch. Zipping up his pants with an awkward grin, he pointed to himself. "Think anyone will notice?"

Sho could not help but laugh with he saw the boy's enormous bulge. "They might."

"Let's wait a minute then. I'll try to think of something revolting. Let's see...I've got it. The thought of you and Ukita having sex."

The Headmaster laughed again. "You're incorrigible."

"But you don't deny it was revolting."

"My car?" Sho hedged, smiling evasively.

"Leave it here. Ride with me and I'll bring you back tomorrow."

Sho nodded, wondering what Ukita would think if he saw them getting into the same vehicle.

"I want to put my hand on your back as we walk out," Kyoshi said. "Can I?"

"You know very well you cannot," the Headmaster replied, sharply. "Perhaps this isn't such a good idea."

"Chill out, I'm just fooling around," Kyoshi grinned. "It doesn't take much to get you all flustered though."

The Headmaster gave Kyoshi a warning look, though couldn't help but smile at the boy's impish expression. "Stop looking so naughty," he whispered.

"I can't help it. We just did something very naughty. I still have all that naughtiness in my system."

"I'm serious, Kyoshi."

"Oh very well. And what are you going to do this time, Headmaster? How many strikes do I get for sucking you off?"

"Hush," Sho hissed, as they stepped back into the crowd.

"How many?" Kyoshi whispered in his ear.

"You'll find out soon enough," the Headmaster shot back. "Only you're in trouble for deliberately disobeying me and teasing me inappropriately."

"Punish me tonight then."

"Kyoshi," the Headmaster pleaded, though he had some difficulty maintaining a serious expression.

Ukita, who had been waiting for them to return from their suspiciously long dalliance behind the curtain, changed his trajectory to avoid the concert master and immediately headed straight for Sho.

"I need to talk to you," he whispered, urgently.

Kyoshi smiled slightly at this, which Ukita found exceedingly irritating.

"Alone," he added, shooting Kyoshi a dark look.

"I'm afraid that's not possible," Sho replied. "I have plans at the moment. Besides, we really have nothing more to discuss, Ukita."

"Please, Sho."

"He just told you to fuck off," Kyoshi advised. "How about you do so, and pronto? We're late."

Although Sho did not exactly approve of the way Kyoshi handled the matter, he was nevertheless grateful to avoid yet another confrontation with Ukita, who had been hounding him for days.

Ukita was so stunned at Kyoshi's bluntness that he simply stood there as they slipped past him.

Kyoshi struggled to keep from laughing. Sho punched him in the arm. "Hush," he scolded, though he was having difficulty keeping a straight face himself.

As soon as they stepped outside, they saw that the valet was already waiting with Kyoshi's vehicle. The Headmaster raised an eyebrow as he admired the sleek, shiny vehicle. "My my. So this is what you drive?"

Smiling, Kyoshi took the keys from the valet and got in the vehicle. The valet opened the door for the Headmaster, who slid onto the plush seats with a grin. "I could get used to this."

"Good," Kyoshi replied. "I want you to."

Mitsuwa suddenly realized the absurdity of their situation. He shook his head. "No. We can't get used to this. What happened tonight...it can't happen again."

Incredulous, Kyoshi took off, his tires squealing in a manner rather out of place at the Concert Hall.

Sho shook his head. "Did you hear me, Kyoshi?"

"I heard you. But I don't agree with you. You're saying we can only have one night together? All right, then tell me. Why?"

"You know perfectly well why. What we're doing...is inappropriate. More than that—it's...it's...unconscionable."

"Then why is it all right to be all deliciously unconscionable tonight but not tomorrow night?"

Sho sighed. "It's not."

"Then?"

"I see your point. There's no excuse for tonight. But...if we continue, that would only compound the infraction."

Kyoshi laughed. "That's absurd."

"I beg to differ."

"Ooo, you can beg. But I'm tying you up first."

"Kyoshi!"

"Tell you what. Let's not talk about anything else other than tonight. Deal?"

Sho nodded. "Agreed."

"So when we get to my hotel, Headmaster, you're in for a fucking."

Mitsuwa smiled. "Is that so?"

"Yes. That's most definitely so. I have an agenda planned."

"I see. But, if I'm not mistaken, you're in for some punishment tonight, Mr. Sayuki."

"Okay, you win. I must be punished. Just a little. But then I'm punishing *you*."

Sho laughed. "I don't think so."

"No? We'll see about that."

The Headmaster stared over at Kyoshi, his heart starting to pound. What was it about this young man that was so exciting to him? Now that they'd stepped over the line, Sho was anxious to explore Kyoshi more thoroughly; he couldn't wait to get him alone in his room, to see him undressed and then push him down on the bed, spread him wide and penetrate him, fuck him without restraint....

"You're turned on again," Kyoshi noted, smiling. The Headmaster was practically leering at him, which he found rather flattering.

"Yes," Sho admitted.

"I wish I could see into that mind of yours. You should see the look on your face."

Mitsuwa looked away, embarrassed.

"Now," Kyoshi chided, resting his hand on the Headmaster's thigh. "Don't get all uptight on me. Just let go tonight. Make it count."

Sho closed his eyes, expelling a long breath. He could feel another erection developing again, just from the boy's warm hand so close to his groin.

Kyoshi brought the car to a stop, then leaned over and began to kiss him.

Sho felt intoxicated by the boy's tongue, the slow, confident paths he traced inside his mouth, Kyoshi's distinctive, masculine scent.

"So. Is that a deal? You'll open up to me tonight, completely?"

"Deal," Sho replied.

"Let's go."

They got out of the vehicle, once again being greeted by a valet, and entered the hotel. As they passed the lobby, they were stopped by the concierge.

"Master Sayuki, your uncle has left some more funds for you."

Kyoshi nodded, accepting the proffered envelope with a grin. He would have to remember this little trick. His uncle could be unusually generous if he thought Kyoshi was engaged in anything to do with the arts. Perhaps he'd have to develop a new interest or two....

"All the way at the top, then," Sho said nervously, when he saw Kyoshi select the 39th floor.

Kyoshi laughed. "It's the penthouse."

"I see."

"What's wrong? Don't tell me you're....afraid of heights?"

The Headmaster made a face, ashamed to admit his fear.

"You are. You're afraid!"

"It's not so much the heights...as it is I'm afraid they'll be a fire and I won't be able to get out."

At this, Kyoshi grew grave, nodding. "Fair enough."

Puzzled, Sho studied him for a moment. "Did I...say something wrong?"

"No."

"But...you seem--"

Kyoshi silenced him with another kiss, this time running his hands up and down the Headmaster's body. He was now quite anxious for release. He groaned, breaking away.

"I want you," he whispered.

Now equally aroused, Sho returned his kiss, allowing his hands to explore his body, sliding down to grab his buttocks and squeeze them suggestively.

"Oh," Kyoshi groaned. "You're driving me wild."

They reached their floor and it was all Kyoshi could do to keep from ejaculating right there in the elevator. He suddenly realized his big plans for Sho would have to wait—he wasn't going to last more than a few seconds. Not the first time.

He managed to key in his code; the door slid open, revealing a luxurious suite the likes of which Sho Mitsuwa had never before seen.

"Heavens," he muttered, eyeing the spacious, posh rooms in disbelief. "This is where you're staying?"

"Get on your knees and suck me," came Kyoshi's blunt reply. "I'm dying here."

Mitsuwa smiled at this, but obeyed the boy's command. Kyoshi sucked in his breath as he unzipped his pants and pressed his cock up against the Headmaster's lips.

"Oh fuck yeah," he groaned, as Sho's warm fingers encircled him and his hot tongue began snaking a teasing path along his head. "Open," he ordered, slapping Sho's face gently to make the urgency of his request clear.

The Headmaster did so, admitting young Kyoshi into his mouth.

Overcome with lust, pleasure, and mounting need, Kyoshi grabbed the Headmaster's hair and thrust a few times into his mouth. "Fuck. I'm coming. Oh yeah." Biting his lip, Kyoshi released, savoring every spasm. "Drink me," he pleaded, and Sho obliged him, enjoying the taste of his sex.

"That was fucking awesome," Kyoshi breathed. "Sorry...I couldn't wait. I was too turned on."

"As was I...earlier," Sho replied, standing. "But perhaps I should go, Kyoshi."

"Why?"

"Because," now Sho's eyes drifted to the bed, where he saw Kyoshi's sex toys, ropes, flogger, and tubes of lubrication laid out. "Oh dear."

Kyoshi smiled, guessing what the Headmaster had just perceived. "Because?"

"Because...the truth of the matter is, Kyoshi, I most definitely want to stay, but if I *do* stay, you can no longer trust me to behave in a way fitting of a Headmaster."

"I think you've already established that," Kyoshi teased.

"But I mean," now Mitsuwa took a deep breath, looking directly at him. "I mean to violate you, Kyoshi. Without restraint."

"You're turning me on already."

"I'm not teasing."

"Neither am I. And I intend to violate *you*. Completely."

Sho smiled. "Then I suppose the question is...who will be first?"

"Now you've got me at a disadvantage, since I just came."

"Then I guess we've settled that. Get undressed."

"Now? Don't you want a drink or something first?"

"Now, Kyoshi."

Sho walked over to the bed and picked up the flogger, smiling. "What's this?"

"I told you. I'm punishing you later."

"Ah yes. And I'm punishing you *now*."

Kyoshi now stood before him, completely naked. Sho felt his heart nearly stop. "You're incredible," he whispered.

Grinning, Kyoshi flexed his muscles playfully and then stood, hands on his hips. "So what now, Headmaster?"

"Come over here. Hands down on the bed. You need some discipline."

The boy obeyed, and when he bent over, Sho could see the marks from his last discipline session. "Are you still sore?"

Kyoshi shrugged. "A little. Tell me something."

"What?" Sho walked back and forth behind him, enjoying the view.

"When you disciplined me in your office, did you fantasize about fucking me?"

Sho smiled. "That's my secret." With that, he whipped his arm back and gave Kyoshi a punishing strike — not too hard, but hard enough to get his attention.

"Ow! Take it easy with that!"

"I'm the one who'll be issuing the commands, Mr. Sayuki."

Strike!

"Remember, I'm going to have my turn with that later, so you'd better be a little nicer."

"I don't think so."

Strike!

"Ouch, dammit! That's too hard."

"Naughty boy!"

Strike!

"What? You're as naughty as I am!"

Strike!

Kyoshi stood up and grabbed the Headmaster's wrist to prevent him from striking him again. "Enough."

"Very well. Then...get on the bed, on your hands and knees, right here on the edge."

"Are you going to fuck me?"

"Yes." Mitsuwa picked up a tube of lubrication and prepared himself, then put some additional lube on his fingers. "Yes, Kyoshi, I'm going to fuck you."

"Use plenty," Kyoshi advised. "And you'd better go gentle. Remember I'm fucking you later."

"Don't tell me what to do," Sho shot back, sternly.

"Oh, I get it. You're the master?"

"Hush!"

Kyoshi giggled. "You're fun."

Sho answered that with a sharp spank to his buttocks. "No giggling allowed." With that, he inserted one of his fingers in the boy's ass and began slowly thrusting and wiggling it.

"That feels nice," Kyoshi remarked.

"What about this?" Sho inserted a second finger, thrusting a little harder.

"Yeah. Oh yeah. Fuck me, Headmaster."

"Oh, Kyoshi." Excited by the boy's addressing him as *Headmaster*, Sho now pressed himself up to his portal, anxious for entrance. He pushed against his sphincter, eliciting a small yelp.

"Hold up. I have to...relax."

Sho used the moment to run his hands up and down Kyoshi's bare legs, enjoying the smooth tautness of his skin. He felt extraordinarily aroused by the marks of his discipline still on his flesh, reminding him of how recently Kyoshi was bent over his desk in his chambers.

"Okay."

Sho proceeded, and suddenly his cock slipped all the way inside, far faster and deeper than he had intended. "I'm sorry," he apologized.

"No. You're good."

Realizing then that Kyoshi was apparently quite accustomed to being penetrated, Mitsuwa found himself suddenly a bit jealous.

"I'm completely inside you," he remarked. "And apparently I'm not the first."

Kyoshi laughed. "Of course you're not."

Sho thrust harder. "So? Who is he?"

"There's more than one, Headmaster. Don't tell me you're jealous?"

Grabbing hold of his hips, Sho now shifted his position and began fucking Kyoshi, hard. "Perhaps. Are you still seeing them?"

"What do you care? I thought this was just one night?"

"Suppose it *is* more than one night. Would you stop seeing them?"

"Is this a proposal?"

"Kyoshi!"

"I can't help it. You're so fun to tease!"

Sho pulled back on his hips and began thrusting so hard that the boy began to object.

"That's a bit rough, Headmaster."

"You'll take it however I give it."

Grinning, Kyoshi submitted to his wishes, enjoying Sho's enthusiasm. "You said before...suppose it were more than one night? Are you saying you want this to continue?"

"Oh, Kyoshi," Sho groaned, now quickly approaching his ascent.

"Answer me."

"Yes. God yes."

"Does that mean yes you want it to continue, or yes—"

Sho cut him off with his sex cry, this time not holding back. He groaned so loud that Kyoshi was almost worried someone in the hotel might complain. But the sound of the Headmaster's pleasure seemed to reverberate inside his very soul, pouring into a void that he had long waited for something, or someone, to fill.

Though he told himself it was only sex, Kyoshi found that, for some reason, intimacy with Headmaster Mitsuwa was much more than just carnal gratification. He felt almost as if...they belonged together. As if he had been waiting for Sho, all these years.

Mitsuwa withdrew, and Kyoshi excused himself to go clean up, pondering the Headmaster's apparent jealousy over his other partners. Sho's jealousy gave him a kind of pleasure; he felt flattered that the man cared who he'd been with.

As he returned to the bedroom, he found Sho lying in bed, one arm behind his head, eyes closed. Though he was still fully dressed, just the sight of him in the bed was enough to arouse him.

"So...I take it you liked that?"

Sho opened his eyes, sighing. "It was...exquisite."

"Don't fall asleep yet. I'm not finished with you."

"Ah. Yes. You have an agenda worked out for me, isn't that right?"

"Yes," Kyoshi answered, picking up the rope and pulling it taut in front of him. "Now it's your turn." He grinned. "And...I like to *play*."

Chapter 6 - *Coitus and Caprice*

"IF YOU THINK I'D BE FOOLISH ENOUGH to let you tie me up, you're sadly mistaken," the Headmaster said, smiling, as Sayuki stood before him, rope in hand.

"Oh, come on," Kyoshi pleaded. "I let you fuck me. Don't tell me you're not going to reciprocate?"

"I didn't tie you up," Sho pointed out.

"So? It'll be fun."

The Headmaster laughed. "For you, perhaps. If I let you tie me up, I'd have no way to escape should I find the situation unpleasant."

"I'd let you go, if you asked me," Kyoshi promised.

"You expect me to trust you? I think not. And, while we're on the subject, I certainly hope you'd never let a partner tie *you* up— one you hardly knew, that is."

Kyoshi shrugged. "I'd let you tie me up."

"Oh?" The Headmaster raised an eyebrow, considering the possibilities.

"Sure. If you let me tie you up *first*."

"Ah. But we've already established I'm not going to do that."

"Dammit," Kyoshi cursed, tossing the rope onto the bed. "Get undressed, then."

Sho obeyed, though rather unhurriedly, standing up and slowly doffing his long concert cape, and then his tuxedo shirt, and finally his shoes, socks and pants. Kyoshi watched, growing excited. "You're sexy as hell," he announced, once the Headmaster stood before him, completely naked.

Rewarding him with a slight smile, Sho leaned back against the wall by the bed, arms across his chest. "What now?"

"Lie on the bed," Kyoshi whispered. "Facedown."

"As you wish." The Headmaster situated himself on the bed, and was about to comment on how comfortable the mattress was when he suddenly felt Kyoshi straddle him, pulling his wrists behind him.

"Kyoshi!" he scolded, as the boy began binding his wrists. "I told you no!"

"Hush," Kyoshi replied, as he quickly restrained the Headmaster. Though Sho made some attempt to resist him, he was simply no match for the young yudona fighter.

"Let me go this instant!"

Kyoshi answered that by gagging him with a handkerchief, tying it behind the Headmaster's head in a secure knot.

Sho, now starting to panic, began to buck. Kyoshi immediately lay on top of him, trying to calm him.

"Relax," Kyoshi whispered. "I'm not going to hurt you. Not *too* much, that is. Anyway not any more than you've hurt me, Headmaster."

Unable to reply, Sho now grew still, finding the pressure of the boy's naked body on his back undeniably interesting, despite having just climaxed. And as much as he didn't want to admit it, he rather enjoyed Kyoshi's boldness in tying him up and, in the space of a few minutes, managing to render him completely vulnerable to whatever the deviant youth had in mind. His heart was pounding, and as Kyoshi began to kiss his neck and upper back, he shivered with pleasure and apprehensiveness.

"That's it. Just try to enjoy this. I know I will." With that, Kyoshi blindfolded the Headmaster.

Sho was both terrified and intrigued. He told himself that surely Kyoshi wouldn't do anything too horrendous...after all, he was still in a position of authority. Although, at the moment, Sho most definitely did not feel in charge of the situation. He was naked, blindfolded, and gagged, with his hands bound firmly behind his back. Now he began to wonder exactly what agenda of punishment Kyoshi had planned for him.

Kyoshi teased him by raking his fingers down his back. "You're trembling, Headmaster," he remarked. "Are you really so afraid of me?"

Wanting to reply but unable to, Sho simply lay, waiting. When Kyoshi abruptly withdrew, he instinctively stiffened…he couldn't see what the boy was up to, though he could feel some movement on the bed.

Then he felt what seemed to be pillows being pushed under his body…several pillows, beneath his stomach, so that his ass was now elevated above the bed. Sho felt extremely vulnerable and exposed but at the same time, strangely aroused.

"All right, Headmaster. It's time for your punishment. Now, I guess I should warn you, you probably won't like this part too much. But it won't be any worse than what *you* did to *me*. And I've decided to use my belt, since you're a naughty little boy who needs to be punished."

With that, he proceeded to give the Headmaster a thorough strapping, much to Sho's dismay. Unable to do much except squirm and make sounds of protest, he was forced to endure discipline he hadn't experienced since his childhood, when his father had punished him for various juvenile grievances.

Kyoshi was enjoying the Headmaster's muffled vocalizations and the way he struggled against the ropes that bound his wrists. He knew he was probably taking things a bit too far, but it was hard to resist—the sight of the Headmaster bent so submissively over the pillows, his ass growing redder by the minute, was exquisitely erotic.

Finally, he brought the punishment to an end, mostly because he was nearly ready to burst. He could tell from the way the Headmaster's muscles flexed that he was angry.

"Don't be too hard on me, Headmaster," he whispered. "But I must confess…I *did* enjoy that."

In fact, Sho was furious; he couldn't wait to be released so that he could administer some retaliatory discipline. He had half a mind to turn Kyoshi over his knee and spank him like a child.

But it soon became apparent he wasn't being released anytime soon. Sho waited, feeling rather anxious when he couldn't tell what Kyoshi was doing. Then, he felt the boy's warm breath near his ass. He gasped—as much as he could gasp while being gagged—when Kyoshi spread him apart and began licking him, his hot tongue slithering up inside him.

It was tremendously stimulating, and Sho, though fairly experienced when it came to sex, had, oddly, never really been treated to analingus, and the fact that he now experienced it while bound and gagged made him feel deliciously violated. He groaned, unable to help himself, biting down on the handkerchief in his mouth.

Kyoshi withdrew, smiling. "Feels good, huh?" Next he picked up a plug vibrator with ascending widths, coated it with lubrication, and then inserted the first nodule into the Headmaster's ass.

Sho found he rather liked this. He waited, intrigued, ready for a little more stimulation. He was not disappointed; Kyoshi pushed the plug in a bit further, and the Headmaster could immediately feel the change in width. When the youth sunk the plug in deeper still, the Headmaster began to experience some anxiety over just how long and wide the device was. He was so focused on this concern that he was startled when Kyoshi flipped on the vibrator.

Laughing at the Headmaster's obvious surprise—Sho's buttocks clenched in alarm—Kyoshi began to slowly thrust the plug in and out. "You're doing good," he encouraged. "We're almost ready."

In fact, Sho was grateful for the preparation, as it had been quite some time since he'd engaged in such activities, and was accustomed to being on the giving—rather than the receiving— end. The vibrating plug was pleasant, now that he had relaxed a bit, and he was actually starting to enjoy it, especially when Kyoshi moved it around.

Kyoshi was so excited, he could no longer wait. He removed the plug and tossed it aside. "Stay just like that. Don't tense up," he commanded, as he positioned himself, on his knees, behind the Headmaster.

Sho nervously waited, hoping the boy would go easy on him, as there wasn't much he could do, should Kyoshi decided to opt for a violent acquisition.

"I'll be gentle," Kyoshi promised, as if hearing his thoughts. And he was true to his word; he penetrated slowly and carefully, giving him plenty of time to adjust to his considerable size.

The Headmaster was stunned at how big the boy was. Although Kyoshi progressed slowly, Sho winced with every movement, unused to being stretched so wide. Eventually, however, he began to relax, and he had to credit Kyoshi for his patience, his complete mastery over his own desires as he waited for Sho to open.

In truth, it was all Kyoshi could do to keep from plunging in and fucking the living daylights out of the Headmaster. When he finally felt confident that Sho was ready, he switched gears into full-fucking mode, alternating between spreading him and pulling back on his hips as he enjoyed the Headmaster's exceedingly tight depths.

It was abundantly clear that the Headmaster was unaccustomed to being fucked. Perhaps he was even a virgin? Although Kyoshi doubted this, he relished Sho's tight grip, the slight, almost inaudible sounds he made with every thrust, and most of all, the sight of his engorged cock sinking into the Headmaster's punished flesh.

"You feel so good," Kyoshi groaned, increasing the cadence of his fuck. "You should see how sexy you look, all punished and at my mercy. You don't get fucked often, do you, Headmaster?"

Although now the boy was taking him with appreciably more enthusiasm and force, Sho was starting to enjoy the experience, having finally acclimated to Kyoshi's considerable size. He found himself instinctively wiggling a bit to redirect the boy's trajectory, his breathing erratic.

"You're taking me in deep," Kyoshi exclaimed. "Oh fuck. You're gonna make me come. I don't want to come yet. I want—"

Kyoshi's desire would forever remain unarticulated, as he was then overcome with the throes of his release, ejaculating with such intensity that he was, for a brief moment, rendered completely silent. Then he groaned, loudly, as his pleasure erupted from deep within, spreading throughout his body.

"Holy shit," he gasped. Then, after he had fully recovered, he finally withdrew, and for a moment simply contemplated the Headmaster. "You're not going to punish me when I untie you, are you?" he asked, rather stupidly, as Sho was hardly in a position to answer.

Sho waited, once again feeling his anger return, now that his release was imminent. As soon as Kyoshi removed the ropes around his wrists, and then released him from his gag and blindfold, he leapt to his feet, furious.

"How dare you, Kyoshi! I made it perfectly clear to you I did *not* want to be tied up."

"Oh, come on," Kyoshi countered, still basking in his post-coital bliss. "You enjoyed it."

"I most certainly did *not*."

"Liar."

"Kyoshi!"

"What?"

Sho sat down on the bed, grabbing Kyoshi's wrist. "You're going to be punished." He pulled the boy over his knees, a bit roughly.

Laughing, Kyoshi did not try to resist. "What, I'm getting a spanking?"

"Yes. You're very naughty."

"You'd better be careful. You might turn me on, and then I'd have to fuck you all over again," Kyoshi teased.

"Let's see how funny you think this is in about five minutes." With that, the Headmaster secured Kyoshi's wrists behind his back and then proceeded to give him a good, hard spanking, eliciting, at least initially, laughs of protest from the unruly youth.

"Ow! Fuck," Kyoshi laughed. "Okay, I get your point. That's enough."

"I think not."

"Seriously, Sho! Damn, that hurts!"

"You'll call me Headmaster," Sho replied, smiling, spanking him a little harder.

"Fuck! Cut it out already!"

"I'll stop when I feel you've been sufficient punished for your transgression, and not a moment before. Naughty Kyoshi!"

Kyoshi, though perhaps physically stronger than the Headmaster, was in a position from which it was difficult to wriggle free. Not only were his wrists secured awkwardly behind his back, the Headmaster had placed one leg over his, pinning him down. Suddenly realizing his peril, Kyoshi quickly changed tactics.

"The people in the next room are going hear," he protested. "They'll call the front desk!"

"Let them call," the Headmaster calmly replied. "I don't plan on staying at the Swan again any time soon."

"Dammit, Sho! Ouch! Stop it!"

"I told you," Sho whispered, giving him an especially hard series of spanks, "call me Headmaster."

"This is…undignified!" Kyoshi tried, feeling desperate.

"And how do you suppose I felt, tied up and exposed for your pleasure?"

"Ow! Please!"

"Hush."

"Please, Headmaster!"

"No, Kyoshi. You're being punished."

After pleading a bit more to no avail, Kyoshi finally submitted to the spanking. He was rather dismayed over how hard the Headmaster struck him, feeling his transgression hardly justified it. He realized then he had greatly underestimated how angry Sho would be.

His ass burned excruciatingly, and he wiggled miserably on the Headmaster's knee, as much as he was able to, desperate for a cessation to the discipline.

"Please," he finally whispered again, his voice choking back tears.

At this, Sho brought the punishment to an end, releasing Kyoshi and helping him to his feet. "I think we understand one another now, Kyoshi?"

"Whatever," the boy muttered, rubbing his ass. "I'm going out for a smoke."

With that, Kyoshi went out onto the balcony, completely naked, though it was the dead of winter. Seeing this, Sho was about to insist the boy get dressed, when his cell phone rang.

He found it where it had fallen from his pants pocket, onto the floor, and flipped it open. "Sho Mitsuwa."

"Sho. It's Nishi."

"Nish." Sho smiled. "Guess where I am. Guess who—"

"Sho. I have some bad news."

From the sound of Nishi's voice, it was immediately apparent that his brother was extremely upset. A horrible, sick feeling pressed into Sho's stomach.

"Bad...news?"

"It's mom. She's...gone."

"What?" Sho felt as though his heart had stopped.

"I just got a call from the home. They said she had...buzzed the nurse asking for some aspirin. But when the nurse got to her room, she was...dead."

Unable to digest this news, Sho simply sat there, silent, trying to keep the phone up to his ear. "No," he finally said, weakly. "Oh, god...."

"Can you...come over?" Nishi asked, trying to hold back his tears.

"Of course. I'm in Jufi now. It will be...about an hour before I can get there."

"All right."

There was a short pause. "I feel like I should say something. But I don't know what to say," Sho confessed.

"I know. Me too."

"I don't understand. She was doing so well."

"It's just one of those things. Life is capricious. I guess…you never know what might happen."

"I was going to go and see her…next week," Sho whispered. "I should have gone sooner."

"Don't start thinking like that. It won't do any good."

Sho nodded, although his brother could not see this. He felt devastated by the news, but at the same time was struck with how unreal it all seemed, as though he were speaking to Nishi in a dream.

"So, you're coming now, right?"

"Yes. I'll be there soon. That is, in an hour or so."

"Don't speed or anything. Drive…you know…safely."

"I will."

Kyoshi, who had initially enjoyed the cold air on his hot punished flesh, now was uncomfortably cold. He saw that Sho was on the phone and he watched him for a moment, curious. It was obvious the Headmaster was having a serious conversation. When Sho finally put the phone down, burying his face in his hands, Kyoshi realized something was dreadfully wrong.

Tossing his cigarette over the balcony edge, he went back inside, slowly approaching Sho.

The Headmaster did not look up.

"All you…all right?" he asked, softly.

When Sho did not answer, Kyoshi sat down beside him on the bed, putting a hand on his knee. "Sho?"

"My mother died," Sho answered, his voice thick with emotion.

"Oh, Sho. I'm…so sorry." Kyoshi truly meant this, knowing all too well what it felt like to lose someone he loved. He could feel the Headmaster trembling. "It's okay to cry. I won't think less of you for it."

And Sho did cry, unable to stop the tears once they began. Kyoshi held him, rocking him as the Headmaster sobbed his grief, his tears warming the boy's cold, bare skin.

"I should have…visited her more. I should have told her I loved her."

"I'm sure she knew," Kyoshi comforted. "It doesn't do any good to think like that."

"That's what Nishi said," Sho replied.

"Nishi?"

"My brother. He wants me to go over there. So...I should go."

"You're driving back now?"

"Yes."

"But...let me drive you. I don't think you should be driving when you're...upset."

"But my car?"

"I'll take care of it. Anyway, it's still at the concert hall. I'll go up tomorrow with Seiko and have him drive my car back. Then I'll drive your car back."

"That's not necessary," Sho began, then was overcome with another flood of tears.

"Yes. It is. Really...you can't drive safely now. I insist."

Sho nodded. "All right. Thank you, Kyoshi."

Kyoshi grinned, standing up and rubbing his ass. "I really shouldn't be so nice after that spanking."

"You deserved it," the Headmaster replied, though he didn't feel much like engaging in banter with the boy, at the moment.

Sensing Sho's mood, Kyoshi nodded. "Perhaps I did deserve it, just a little bit. Then...let's get dressed, and we'll get going."

Chapter 7 - *Blood and Tears*

IT WAS A QUIET DRIVE BACK TO Hiracho. Sho, still numb from the shock of learning his mother had died, now felt uncomfortable on several counts; not only had he engaged in inappropriate sexual contact with a student, but he'd actually wept in his presence. The typically impassive Headmaster found this last point particularly embarrassing, and now he was plagued with remorse over his licentious behavior with Kyoshi, feeling almost as though he was being punished.

But more than this, he felt bewildered and devastated over his mother's death. It didn't seem real. Yet he knew it was real, and he felt as though his heart was being gripped by a cold hand, an evil hand that squeezed him mercilessly. Though he managed now to hold back his tears, Sho felt that part of him was no longer the same. There was a hollow place inside that he knew could never be filled.

He felt alone. At least he had Nish. And he wished, rather passionately, that he could have Kyoshi. But he knew that, after tonight, he could never be with him again.

Kyoshi was silent, but for other reasons; he was mulling over the night's events, his thoughts racing. Though it seemed impossible that he'd managed to seduce the Headmaster as he'd hoped, he now worried that Sho would enforce his earlier promise, that they could share but one night—and one night only—together.

Finally, he could bear it no more. "This isn't really going to be it, is it?" he asked, his voice betraying his anxiety on that point.

Sho sighed, closing his eyes. "Kyoshi. I told you. We just…can't."

After a moment's pause, Kyoshi replied, "but we didn't actually have an entire night together."

At this, Sho almost smiled. "That's a technicality. You know perfectly well we can't continue."

"But...I'm not just saying this...tonight, I felt something. Something special. And...I know you did, too."

Sho stared out the window as they passed Lake Willow, gazing at the dark waters illuminated only by the pale glow of the moon. He knew exactly what he meant; in his heart, he wanted nothing more than to continue to see Kyoshi, but he knew that it would only lead to disaster, for both of them. He'd had his taste of what was forbidden—that had to be enough.

"I won't deny I enjoyed it," he answered, finally. "But I should never have allowed it to happen."

"Why not?" Kyoshi demanded.

"Kyoshi. Please."

Kyoshi fell silent again, wanting to press Sho on the point but feeling restrained, because of the Headmaster's loss. He decided it wasn't the time to push the issue. He knew what it felt like...to lose someone.

They were back in Hiracho. Sho directed him to his brother's house, and as they approached, Kyoshi drove more slowly, reluctant for the night to come to an end.

Sho did not seem to notice, staring down at his hands.

"Do you mind if I smoke?" Kyoshi asked.

"Yes."

"Bloody hell," Kyoshi sighed. "Don't tell me you're one of *those* people."

"You mean, one of those people who prefers to breathe clean air?"

"I fucking need a smoke."

"Please, I'd rather you didn't. Anyway, it's a nasty habit, Kyoshi. You really ought to stop."

"You sound like my uncle," Kyoshi grumbled.

"Then your uncle is a very smart man."

"Ha," Kyoshi snorted. "He's a total dickhead who takes pleasure in paddling my ass raw, for no reason."

"Hmm. I like him already."

Kyoshi smiled. "At least you still have your sense of humor."

"I don't think I'd survive without it," Sho replied.

Kyoshi nodded. "I hear you. So…you're really not going to let me smoke? In my own car?"

"Obviously I can't stop you from smoking. But I'm asking you not to smoke."

"All right then. I won't smoke, on one condition."

"What's that?" Sho asked, suspiciously.

"You let me kiss you, one last time."

Just hearing Kyoshi say the words made his heart beat a cadence faster in response; Headmaster Mitsuwa swallowed, trying to steady his voice before replying. "Very well. One last kiss. This is it…up here on the left. The house with the…dog there, yes…that one."

"What a beautiful dog," Kyoshi remarked.

"That's…King. He doesn't really…like people."

Kyoshi laughed at this. "That's fucking brilliant. Sitting out in front of the house. I bet I'd like your brother."

"You can meet him if you like. I'll introduce you." In fact, Sho was quite anxious to show off Kyoshi to Nish, who he knew would appreciate the boy's physical beauty.

Pulling into the driveway, Kyoshi brought the car to a stop, turned off the engine, then leaned toward the Headmaster.

"Now. It's time for that kiss."

Nodding almost imperceptibly, Sho tried to remain detached when Kyoshi pressed his mouth open with his tongue, but found that he was unable to resist the boy's intoxicating kiss.

He moaned into Kyoshi's mouth when he felt him fumbling with his zipper, then his warm hand stroking his hardened cock; already he was erect, despite everything that had happened and all the sex they had already enjoyed.

There was just something about Kyoshi that excited him beyond bearing. He didn't understand it, couldn't control it, and didn't want to stop it. Once again he was spiraling down into Kyoshi's kiss, falling to a deep place where he felt he could not return. Nor did he wish to return. He felt comforted there, safe, far from his troubles and the torment of his mind.

Kyoshi broke off the kiss and began assaulting Sho's exposed throat.

"Kyoshi," Sho gasped. "We...shouldn't. It's just not...the right time."

The Headmaster opened his eyes, and saw that Nish had opened the front door and was standing there, staring at the car.

"Don't worry," Kyoshi said, following his gaze. "The windows are darkened from the outside."

"I should go inside," Sho replied, gently removing Kyoshi's hand. "Nish is waiting."

"Oh...all right." Kyoshi hadn't seriously expected the Headmaster to engage in more sexual exploits, especially considering his mother's death, but he'd figured it was worth trying.

Sho zipped up his pants. "Come up to the door with me. I'll introduce you."

Kyoshi reached out and stayed Sho before he could open the door. "Hold up. Please. Tell me this isn't really going to be it."

"I'm sorry, Kyoshi. As I said, I freely admit I enjoyed everything that happened between us tonight. But...we just can't continue. And it wouldn't be appropriate for me to ask you not to tell anyone, but I should say that if word of this ever got out, I would most likely lose my position at Valemont. So I suppose you could say I'm hoping for your...discretion. Don't misunderstand me. I would love nothing more than to continue what we've started. But it was wrong of me to let it happen. You're a student, Kyoshi. And as Headmaster I've behaved abominably. I should have shown restraint. But I didn't. There's nothing I can do to change that now, but I feel I have a duty to ensure that nothing like that ever happens again."

"You say that now. But wait until you get horny again," Kyoshi replied, with a devious smile.

"Kyoshi," Sho scolded, but couldn't help smiling at the boy's teasing.

"Oh, all right. Whatever. I guess you're back in full Headmaster mode now."

"Yes. And that reminds me. Don't think you're going to receive special treatment if you continue to disobey University policy, Kyoshi. I *am* Headmaster, and if you get sent to me, for whatever reason, I should make it clear — I won't spare my arm."

"That's because you're a pure sadist at heart," Kyoshi replied, grinning.

Sho smiled. "Be that as it may, I'll have you bent over my desk, pleading for mercy."

"Is this before or after you fuck me?"

"Smart ass."

Kyoshi laughed at this. "Well. For what it's worth, I thought tonight was awesome. I think we could be great together. I don't know why you're so hung up on this whole Headmaster/student thing. But whatever. You're old school, I guess."

"Old school? And I suppose the new school condones Headmaster-student congress?"

"New school condones fucking on general principle."

"Get out of the car, Kyoshi," Sho replied, sighing.

Kyoshi laughed, but obeyed him.

King, Nishi's Siberian Husky, immediately stood up and walked over to him, wagging his tail.

"I don't believe it," Sho remarked, smiling.

"What?" Kyoshi bent down to pet the dog, who seemed anxious for Kyoshi's attention. "Hey, I thought you said he didn't like people?"

"He usually...doesn't."

Now Nishi came outside, and the brothers hugged for a long moment. Kyoshi remained silent, continuing to pet King, who now was sitting down at his feet, looking up at him expectantly.

"You okay?" Nish whispered.

"Yes. You?"

Nish shook his head. "It...still hasn't sunk in."

"I know."

Nish turned his attention to Kyoshi, an eyebrow arching as he took in the boy's youthful, lean, decidedly male form. "Kyoshi?" he mouthed, eyes wide.

Sho nodded, returning the smile.

Nish slapped Sho on the back. "Well done, brother," he whispered.

Sho jabbed him in the side with his elbow.

"Ow!" Nish protested, laughing.

"Kyoshi...this is my brother, Nishi. Nish, this is...Kyoshi Sayuki."

"Sayuki," Nish repeated, his brow furrowing, feeling somehow that the name was familiar. "You've made quite an impression on King. He isn't usually so friendly."

Kyoshi shrugged, smiling. "I like animals."

"Hmm." Nish gave his brother another smile, conveying his approval of the animal-loving, incredibly sexy Kyoshi. "Would you like to come for some coffee, Kyoshi?"

Kyoshi shook his head. "No. You two...have a lot to discuss." He looked at Sho uncertainly. "Are you...going to give me your keys? So I can bring you your car?"

"That won't be necessary, Kyoshi,' the Headmaster replied. "We'll take care of it."

"Oh." A little disappointed at the loss of a good excuse to see Sho again, Kyoshi hesitated. "Then..."

"Thank you for...everything, Kyoshi. Driving me back...and all."

Kyoshi's eyes narrowed a bit at this. And all? It seemed to him a good deal of fucking and other delightfully devious activities had been collapsed into the miserable space of these two paltry words, and for a moment he felt a bit hurt. But, unwilling to reveal this to the Headmaster and his brother, he shrugged again, putting his hands in his trouser pockets. "No problem. See ya around."

With that, he turned and left, his face burning. As he approached his car he lit up a cigarette, turning to look back at the Headmaster and a little surprised to find that he and his brother were still watching him. King followed him to the car and then waited, as if he expected Kyoshi to let him get into the car.

"What is it you want there, pup?" Kyoshi asked, taking a deep drag.

King whined, putting his head down on his paws.

"He's beautiful," Nish whispered in his brother's ear. "Please tell me you violated him."

Sho smiled, saying nothing.

"Oh yes," Nish breathed. "I want to hear ALL the details. Look at him. He's sexy as hell. And King likes him. That's saying a LOT."

"I'll tell you all about it. But…it's not going to happen again."

"Uh huh." Nish grinned, smacking Sho on the bottom.

"Ow! Dammit, Nish!"

Nishi laughed. "I barely touched you."

"Well, I'm…sore."

"Sore? Oh god. Don't tell me…all right. Get your ass inside right now and tell me everything."

Sho nodded, glad for an excuse to talk about something other than what was weighing on both their minds.

Kyoshi watched them go inside, then gave King a final pat. "I've gotta go, pal. I'll see you around…I hope. You watch the Headmaster for me, all right?"

King answered that by licking his hand, and as Kyoshi got into the car and pulled away, the dog remained where he was, looking after him.

"WHERE THE FUCK HAVE YOU BEEN? AND WHY are you all dressed up?" Seiko demanded, as Kyoshi ambled into Kensington hall.

"I went to receive the Best Fuck of the Millennium Award in Jufi," he replied.

"Yeah right. Like they'd give that to *you*."

"What would you know about it? You refuse to sleep with me."

"I told you, you're not my type."

"You mean I'm not a virgin."

Seiko shrugged, grinning. "Can I help it if I like 'em green?"

"Yeah well. You can have them. Babies are too much work. When you've broken them in, send them over to me."

"Hey, why don't you change into something else and let's go out somewhere."

"Where?"

"Anywhere. Maybe the strip. Let's just check out the scene."

"On one condition."

"What's that?"

"We both get completely plastered."

Seiko smiled. "Deal. But let's take your car."

"Like I'd really be dumb enough to drive wasted. If I wrecked my car, Uncle would tie me to the bench forever."

"What the heck is *the bench*?" Seiko laughed.

"His torture device. You don't want to know."

"Well, I hope you don't expect ME to drive."

"No. Let's just walk."

"Walk? It's like…at least a mile to the strip!"

Kyoshi smiled. "So? Aren't you the big athlete? You're saying you can't do a mile? Or you're just upset you can't wear high heels?"

"Asshole. Go change then, I'll wait for you here."

Kyoshi came back to the lobby dressed in tight black jeans, with a sexy, skintight tank and a black jeans jacket, a chain necklace and a belt with a silver buckle that read "Fuck Me".

Seiko laughed hysterically. "Don't tell me you're a gigolo now."

"What?" Kyoshi replied innocently, trying to hold back his smile.

"If we go out together, everyone will think I'm your pimp."

"So? I'll let you take 3%."

"Three percent! You're out of your mind. I'll take 60%."

"As long as I get to fuck you."

"I already told you—"

"Yeah I know," Kyoshi replied, grinning. "I'm not your type."

Several hours later, both of them were so drunk they were kicked out of the Corkscrew, the club where they'd been hanging out, and they staggered together down the street, giggling hysterically for no reason.

"Which way is home?" Kyoshi asked, confused.

"Let's just walk and we'll find it," Seiko suggested.

"Good idea."

"They keep moving the sidewalk," Kyoshi remarked.

"We should complain."

"Ahh! You stepped on my foot again."

"No, that was you. You stepped on MY foot."

"Like I don't know which foot is my own? Shit." Kyoshi looked down. "Okay I guess that *is* your foot."

"You shouldn't drink."

"Neither should you...."

Now Seiko looked around, mystified. "Fuck. We accidentally walked into that one dream."

"It's not a dream. I know because my foot still hurts from where you stepped on it."

"You stepped on *my* foot."

"Does it hurt?"

"No."

"Maybe it *is* a dream," Kyoshi replied, contemplating this for a moment. "I wonder if they have bathrooms here."

"Yeah, where are they? I need to piss."

"Oh shit. I think we're going the wrong way."

"No, look!" Seiko yelled. "That's the clock tower, see?"

"What time is it?"

"I don't know. They keep moving it."

"Fuck. I think I drank too much."

"You're fucking brilliant. I think you might be…a genie."

"You mean genius, moron."

"Shit. Do I still get three wishes?"

"Seiko. Can't you walk normal…you're making me dizzy."

"I *am* walking normal."

"No, you keep zigzagging. You're…hogging up the whole sidewalk."

"You keep getting in my way!"

"Here. Let me…put my arm around you," Kyoshi replied, flinging his arm around Seiko's shoulders.

"I told you…you're not fucking me."

"If you think this is fucking…you're really missing out, Seiko."

"You're an asshole."

"You love me. Admit it."

"No."

"Say I'm your best friend in the whole…world."

"That's true. You're my best friend in the whole world."

"And you love me so much, you're going to let me fuck you."

"Ha ha. You think I'm an idiot, I guess."

"Yeah. But I'll still fuck you. I don't discriminate just because you're mentally handicapped."

"Quit leaning on me. You're going to push me into the street."

"I can't help it. These beers are heavy."

"I told you we didn't need to buy any take-homes. I've got beer already in my room."

"Yeah but yours suck," Kyoshi protested. "I only drink…the finest brew."

"Oh yeah. You're a real connoisseur."

"Damn right."

"I thought you liked my beer."

"I just said that so you'd sleep with me."

"Ha! It didn't work, did it?"

"But I'm not finished yet. I'm still in the…process of seducing you."

"Is this how you seduce people? Stagger around completely nailed and drool all over their shirt?"

"That depends. Is it working?"

"No," Seiko answered. "And if you step on my foot one more time I'm going to fucking kill you."

"Don't kill me. I've got...so much to live for."

Seiko laughed hysterically at this, confusing Kyoshi, so that they began walking in a circle.

"No! We just came from there," Seiko protested, giggling.

"You're the one moving! I'm just standing here."

"Look at your feet. They're moving."

"How did that happen?" Kyoshi exclaimed, bewildered. "Because I thought I was standing."

"Stop! I'm getting dizzy!"

"But which way do we go?"

"There's the clock tower."

"Right. The...clock. Hey! We're close."

"Yeah, we're on the main lawn. There's the main sign and the...statue."

"Shit. I really have to piss. Who is that a statue of anyway?"

"Like I fucking know? Probably Lord Valemont or something."

"Valemont was a Lord?"

"I think so. He was...rich as hell."

"Sounds like my uncle. I'll piss on him, then."

With that, Kyoshi whipped out his cock and relieved himself on Lord Valemont's shoe, staring up at the dark statue as he did so.

"I'm pissing too," Seiko replied, joining him.

"Shit! He's looking at me."

"He looks mad," Seiko agreed.

"Fuck him. I'm writing my name on his...crotch." With that, Kyoshi attempted, rather unsuccessfully, to leave a memento of his visit on the statue, but succeeded only in flinging his spray everywhere.

"Watch it! You almost got me!" Seiko complained.

"It works better in the snow."

"Ah! I feel so much...better."

"Me, too," Kyoshi agreed. "But now I'm tired. Let's...sit down on this bench."

"Okay."

They sat down and Kyoshi put his arm around Seiko again. "If you really really really really *really* REALLY loved me...you'd let me fuck you."

"If I let you fuck me, will you shut the hell up?"

"Okay."

"Then I guess you can."

"Well, let go of your dick, then. Let me have it."

"It won't do anything. I can't feel it."

"Yes, it will. I'm a sex god."

"Ha. You can try, I guess. But I think...I'm too drunk."

"Let me see." Kyoshi pushed Seiko's hand away and began to try and arouse him, without success. "You're not trying," he accused.

Seiko giggled. "A sex god, huh?"

"Hey. You two. What do you think you're doing?"

Seiko and Kyoshi looked up in surprise to find a security guard staring down at them.

"We were just...resting," Kyoshi replied, still, in his inebriated state, stupidly trying to pump Seiko.

"Just resting. How about you stop fondling this gentleman here."

"Oh he's not a gentleman," Kyoshi retorted. "He's a total slut."

"Hey!" Seiko protested.

"Get your hand off him, NOW."

Kyoshi looked down and, seeing what he was doing, let go of Seiko, giggling. "Oh. Sorry."

"You *will* be sorry, when I tell the Headmaster about this," the guard replied, sternly. "I assume you're both students here?"

"Yeah," Kyoshi admitted.

The guard picked up the six-pack of beers, frowning. "You realize alcohol is prohibited at Valemont?"

"Those aren't ours," Seiko tried. "They were just sitting there."

"Yeah," Kyoshi continued. "We don't need beers, because Seiko already has some in his room."

"Is that so?"

"Kyoshi," Seiko wailed, alarmed. "You just told him about my beers!"

Now the guard looked at the statue, shaking his head. "I thought that's what I saw you doing. I can't believe you'd actually deface this statue in this manner."

Kyoshi blinked up at the statue, confused. "What? He still has a face."

"All right. On your feet, both of you. You'll dry out at Security and then you can go back to your rooms. But I'll be reporting this to the Headmaster, so I imagine you'll hear from him on Monday."

"Shit," Seiko moaned. "Not the Headmaster."

Kyoshi began laughing, unable to control himself.

"Let's see how funny you find this when you're in the Headmaster's chambers," the guard remarked.

HEADMASTER MITSUWA LEANED BACK IN HIS CHAIR, studying the report for a long moment without speaking. Finally, he looked up, frowning.

"Public intoxication. Urinating on the Valemont statue. Possession of contraband. And... engaging in sexual contact in a public place. I assume both of you realize these are serious transgressions." Although Sho had avoided looking directly at Kyoshi, he did so now. "And that you will both be punished."

Kyoshi did not respond, simply staring back at him. He found the Headmaster's manner exciting, and was actually looking forward to being punished.

"You find something amusing, Kyoshi?" the Headmaster snapped.

"Huh? No," he replied.

"Then I suggest you wipe that grin off your face."

Kyoshi tried his best to comply, but had difficulty doing so. He kept imagining the Headmaster tied up, bent over his pillow and at his mercy.

Sho was, in fact, furious. It wasn't so much that Kyoshi had gotten drunk; he didn't care about that. But the guard's report that Kyoshi had been found fondling Seiko angered him. He was jealous, so jealous that he could hardly see straight. Although he knew he had no right to feel so, he could not help it.

Seiko jabbed Kyoshi with his elbow, worried when his friend continued to defy the Headmaster. "Kyoshi," he whispered.

"What?"

"Silence," the Headmaster hissed, picking up his crop. "You'll each take 30 strikes."

"Thirty!" Kyoshi cried, dismayed. "That's bloody sadistic!"

"You'll take forty, Kyoshi," the Headmaster replied, looking levelly at him. "One more word out of your mouth and I'll bump it up to fifty."

Kyoshi no longer found the situation amusing. He slumped down in his seat, letting his head fall back against the wall with a long sigh.

"Kyoshi, please leave room. I'll call you when Seiko and I have finished."

Slowly, Kyoshi got to his feet, daring a backward glance at Seiko, who looked a bit pale.

"NOW, Kyoshi."

Reluctantly, Kyoshi left his chambers, closing the door behind him quietly.

"On your feet, Mr. Shinozaki."

"Yes, Headmaster," Seiko replied, meekly.

"You know the routine. Lower your trousers. Forearms on the desk."

Seiko obeyed, his fingers trembling as he fumbled with his zipper. He'd been to the Headmaster's chambers many times, but the most he'd ever endured from Mitsuwa's infamous crop was twenty strikes. He was about to take thirty, and he was not looking forward to it. Especially because, for some reason, the Headmaster seemed unusually angry.

Sho waited behind him, tapping the crop against his hand, eager to punish the boy. His jealousy was pumping him up, making him anxious to release some of his pent-up anger. He wondered how far Kyoshi had gone with Seiko. Were they lovers?

He suspected they were. And he found he was quite angry with Kyoshi for all his talk, but a few nights before, of their having shared "something special." Now he realized the boy had played him.

Seiko waited, bent over the desk, feeling extraordinarily anxious when he could hear the Headmaster pace behind him for a few moments. Then, Mitsuwa unleashed the first strike, and Seiko realized he was in for pure torture. He cried out his anguish, much to Sho's satisfaction.

"Did you feel that, Seiko?" he asked, smiling, then struck him again.

Once again Seiko cried out. "Please, Headmaster."

"Pleading already, are we?"

"Yes!"

Strike.

"That's three, Seiko. You only have 27 to go."

"Oh god!"

It was all Sho could do to keep from laughing. He loved hearing Seiko beg for mercy, and he found the boy's punishment exceedingly gratifying. It was not long before Seiko began weeping, continuing to beg shamelessly for an end to the punishment, an end that was not granted until every one of the thirty strikes had been delivered.

"You may go now, Seiko," he said, softly, offering the boy a handkerchief.

Seiko wiped his face and pulled up his trousers, mortified that he had begged throughout the entire discipline session. He desperately hoped Kyoshi had not heard him.

He shuffled out of the Headmaster's chambers, finding it a bit difficult to walk. Sho followed him, standing at the door with his crop whip.

"Please step into my chambers, Kyoshi," he said, with a slight smile.

Kyoshi looked at Seiko with concern, having heard his friend's cries quite distinctly. "Go on back," he whispered. "Take care of yourself. I'll come by in a bit."

Seiko nodded, his face burning red.

Headmaster Mitsuwa, hearing this, once again felt his jealousy spinning darkly within. "I haven't all day, Kyoshi," he snapped.

Kyoshi narrowed his eyes, daring to give Sho a little glare as he passed him.

Sho closed the door behind them, then reached back and locked it quietly.

"Lower your trousers. Forearms on the desk," the Headmaster ordered.

Kyoshi hesitated for a moment, staring back at him. "You're acting as though...nothing happened between us."

"Kyoshi, I made it perfectly clear to you, that if you were sent to my chambers for *any* reason, that I would not go easy on you."

"What is it? Why are you so pissed off?"

"Your punishment is *not* open for negotiation, Kyoshi. Did you hear me? Drop your pants."

"Forty strikes...seems like a lot."

"Shall we make it fifty?"

"No, thank you." Kyoshi unzipped his pants angrily, letting them fall to his ankles, and then bent over the desk, feeling a bit confused. He could tell Sho was upset, but he wasn't sure why.

"You've been a very naughty boy, Kyoshi," the Headmaster whispered.

A bit surprised at this remark, which seemed rather *un-Headmaster-ish*, Kyoshi looked back to find Sho tapping the crop whip against his thigh, gazing at Kyoshi's nakedness with unveiled lust.

"I haven't really been that naughty," he protested.

"Turn around."

Kyoshi obeyed, his heart beating a little faster.

Then Sho let the first strike fly, hitting his still sore backside with such force that Kyoshi could not help but wince. He closed his eyes, shuddering. How would he endure 40 strikes? It seemed an interminable length.

The Headmaster continued his punishment, slowly, methodically, pausing between each strike. As he disciplined Kyoshi he fondled himself, for he had almost immediately become aroused at the sight of the boy bent over his desk. Kyoshi's cries only stimulated him further, and Sho adored that he remained in position, submitting to every strike.

Somewhere around the twentieth strike, Kyoshi began to beg, feeding the Headmaster's lust. His cock was so hard he felt he might ejaculate on the spot; he longed to sink into the boy, to spread him wide and take him without mercy.

Kyoshi's tears excited him to no end; when at last he reached the 40th strike, the boy was sobbing. Sho unzipped his pants and released himself, then came up behind Kyoshi and, without any preparation, penetrated him, holding his hand over Kyoshi's mouth to muffle his cry.

"Here's a little extra punishment for you," he whispered, angrily. "For taking Seiko."

Kyoshi, although in undeniable pain from the Headmaster's unannounced entrance, quieted at this. He was surprised—but thrilled—that Sho was taking him by force. And suddenly, he understood the source of the Headmaster's fury.

He was jealous.

Sho, having completely lost his rational mind in his fury, took Kyoshi violently, pinning his wrists behind his back with one hand and spreading his legs wide with his knees, as he continued to hold one hand over his mouth. Only when he finally climaxed did his senses begin to return to him. He withdrew, shaking.

"What have I done?" he whispered, staring at the blood on his organ. "Oh, Kyoshi…."

Chapter 8 - *Sho's Remorse*

"Does this mean the punishment's over?" Kyoshi teased, pulling up his trousers and turning around. Although he was trying to make light of it, for the Headmaster's sake—and to preserve his own sense of dignity—he knew he had a long night ahead of him. Mitsuwa hadn't gone easy on him, and he would be feeling the effects for hours.

Sho's look of utter horror almost made up for it all. The man was truly mortified at what he'd done, and Kyoshi—though fully intending to milk the situation for all he could—at the same time didn't want the Headmaster to take the matter too seriously.

"Hey. I was just teasing," he whispered, smiling. "It's all right, Sho."

Headmaster Mitsuwa shook his head. "No. It's not all right. You should...we should call the police."

Kyoshi laughed. "Why? Wanna borrow their handcuffs?"

"This is serious, Kyoshi! I...have used my authority in the most egregious way. I should be punished."

"Oh, don't worry. I'll punish you. But how about we save it for another time—my ass is killing me." Kyoshi gave Sho a little wink, hoping to lessen the Headmaster's obvious angst. He found a tissue and handed it to him, and Sho wiped the blood from his hands as though in a daze.

"Then...you forgive me?" he whispered, finally.

"Yeah, I forgive you. But I was serious, you know. I *will* punish you, Sho. You were very *very* bad."

Mitsuwa stared at the strikingly handsome youth before him in disbelief. The boy seemed hardly affected by what had just happened. "But...how can you forgive me? When I just took you...by force?"

Kyoshi shrugged, grinning. "I like it rough."

"Kyoshi." Sho shook his head, feeling overcome with remorse. He leaned back against the desk, burying his face in his hands. How could he have done such a thing? To a student? "I must give up my post," he whispered, weakly.

"What? Don't be bloody absurd. Look." Kyoshi put a reassuring hand on his shoulder. "I deserved the punishment—most of it anyway, since forty was a bit much, in my view—but I know pissing on statues is against school policy and whatnot, so, I guess you were justified in tearing up my ass with your little crop whip here."

The Headmaster made no reply.

Kyoshi sighed. "As for what happened afterwards, if you want to know the truth, it's actually something of a turn-on that you'd lose control like that and rape me. I'll probably jerk off about a thousand times thinking about it—maybe not tonight since I'll be groaning most of the time, and by groaning I mean as in pain groaning, not as in shooting my wad groaning, but once I'm healed I guarantee I'll have a special place in my fantasy collection for this little incident. And you know why? Because I know why you did it. You were jealous."

Sho let his hands fall away from his face, nodding. "Yes. I admit it. I was."

Kyoshi laughed. "The funny part is, you had nothing to be jealous about. Seiko's my friend—and we were both really drunk. It would have never happened under normal circumstances, and actually—for the record—nothing *did* happen, because Seiko couldn't even get an erection."

Sho frowned at this, not wanting to hear the details of the episode, though he felt somewhat pacified by Kyoshi's reassurances.

"Besides...you told me there couldn't be anything between us. So I wouldn't have been in the wrong if I *had* fucked someone."

"I know." The Headmaster sighed, feeling defeated. "I hardly understand myself these days."

Kyoshi reached out and brushed the hair back from Sho's eyes. "That's to be expected, you know. You've been through a lot." He swallowed, remembering a time in his own life when he'd nearly gone mad with grief over a similar loss. But he wouldn't allow himself to dwell on such memories; not now...not ever.

He leaned closer, his voice dropping to a whisper. "I bet you'd be less tied up in knots if you'd just admit that we were made for each other so we could get on with the fucking. That's my advice for you — fuck therapy."

Sho could not help but smile at this. "I see. Is that your view?"

"Yes. That's my view."

The Headmaster sighed again, closing his eyes. "As much as I'd like to...take you up on your offer, Kyoshi...I think you and I both know this simply must stop. Right here and now. I've abused my authority in the most unforgivable fashion. You may think you want this, now, but you'll probably feel differently in a few years. I may have done irreparable damage by taking advantage of you in such a manner. I couldn't live with myself if I were to continue hurting you."

"You're not taking advantage of me," Kyoshi protested, with a mischievous smile. "I want to be violated. By you, anyway. As long as I get to violate you every now and then."

But the Headmaster had made up his mind. He shook his head, taking the boy's hand from his shoulder and pushing him firmly away. "No. This goes no further. I hope you'll accept my most sincere apology, Kyoshi. And I advise you to report this...incident to the Dean."

"Sho—"

"You'll address me as Headmaster," Sho interrupted, his voice suddenly stern. He knew it was far too late in the game to insist on formalities, but he had to discourage the boy from addressing him in such a familiar fashion, at least from this point on.

"I'm not going to report anything."

"That's your choice. But, in that case, I'll contact the Dean myself."

"Don't do that. You really want to give up your whole career?"

Sho made no reply, his heart a turmoil of emotions. No, he most definitely did *not* want to give up all that he'd worked for. But did he even have a choice? He had to confess his transgression. That was the proper thing to do. He'd take whatever the Dean decided was fitting punishment. He would most likely be asked to resign; but he deserved it.

Kyoshi was quiet for a moment, studying him. He could see from Sho's features that he was still upset, but trying to hide it. "Look. Why don't you talk to your brother — Nishi — before you do anything rash. All right? He seems like a reasonable guy. Why don't you see what he has to say about all this?"

The Headmaster thought about this for a moment, staring at the floor. Perhaps it *would* be good to talk to Nishi, if only to clear his conscience. But now, he had to do all he could to discourage Kyoshi — even if it meant angering him. He took a deep breath, then met the boy's gaze with a steely look of resolve. "That will be all, Kyoshi. Return to your quarters."

Kyoshi gave a slight laugh, though he was a little hurt by Sho's coldness. "Yeah, I get it. Headmaster."

"NOW, Kyoshi."

"Don't you want to talk about this some more?"

"I've said all that needs to be said. And…just so we're clear on this, I have no feelings for you, Kyoshi. I simply took advantage of you to satisfy my sexual needs." This was a lie, and Sho was unused to being anything but brutally honest, but he had decided that he would have to take drastic action to dissuade Kyoshi's further interest.

A little taken aback by Sho's harsh tone, as well as his words, the boy hid his hurt with a shrug. "Whatever." He felt the back of his neck grow hot as anger started to heat his blood. "And just for the record, I don't give a fuck about you, either. Maybe I *will* report this."

"I highly recommend that course of action."

Kyoshi stared at him for a long moment, as though expecting him to change his tone. "Maybe I will," he repeated, somewhat lamely.

"Then, I believe we're quite finished here."

"Yes. We're finished. We're bloody well fucking finished."

Hurt, and angry, Kyoshi turned and left the Headmaster's chambers, slamming the door behind him.

For a long moment Sho stared at the door; then, he moved to his chair behind the desk and sat down, staring at the phone.

He should call the Dean. Just get it over with, rather than let Kyoshi be the one to broach the subject. Besides, the Dean probably wouldn't even believe Kyoshi, at least not at first, and he didn't want the boy to be badly treated.

He continued to stare at the phone, picked up the receiver, and then set it down again on the cradle, indecisively. He stood up, and then sat down again.

His hands were trembling as he instinctively reached into his pocket to worry a small, smooth stone he kept there.

Perhaps he should talk to Nishi first.

Nishi opened the door, surprised to see Sho on his doorstep.

"Sho! Why didn't you call? My place is a mess, but—"

"I've done something terrible," Sho blurted out. "Something…of the most amoral, licentious sort."

"Hmmm. I hope you took pictures, then." Nishi smiled reassuringly, trying to comfort his brother, who he could see was clearly distressed.

"This is no joking matter. I must tell you what I've done."

"And I'm all ears but, wouldn't you like to come inside—or were you intending to announce your indiscretion to the whole neighborhood?"

Sho nodded, blushing. "Of course. Thank you."

Nishi cleared a path from the door; the house was littered with art supplies and aborted paintings, the canvases torn where he had angrily thrown them against the wall. "I'm having some...issues," he explained.

His brother only nodded, too upset to comment.

"You look like you could use a fresh cup of coffee. I'll start some." Nishi fumbled around in the kitchen, dropping things and muttering his apologies.

Despite himself, Sho had to smile. His brother was just too precious. "You ought to hire a maid."

"I've thought about that," Nishi replied. "Only, I can't stand for strangers to touch my stuff."

"I'm sorry to...barge in on you like this."

"No trouble, Sho. That's what brothers are for. You just sit back and relax, and we'll work this out, whatever it is. It's going to be fine, you'll see."

Sighing, the Headmaster relaxed in his chair, feeling strangely comforted by his brother's clumsiness and the familiarity of the old kitchen. At that moment, an old Higishi cuckoo clock announced the hour, the tiny red bird peeping his head out from behind his blue door, while a set of colorful miniature dancers waltzed around the base of the clock to the tune of an ancient melody. It was a clock they'd had since childhood, and suddenly hearing its chime made Sho think of his mother.

He began to cry.

"Oh, fuck. Here." Nishi handed him some tissues, surprised to see his brother in such a state. "Surely...it can't be as bad as all that."

"I was only thinking of mom, just now," Sho replied, sniffing. "I'm sorry...the clock...."

Nishi looked at the clock. "Want me to break it?"

Laughing, Sho dried his tears with a tissue. "No. I'm being...ridiculous. I was just thinking how ashamed she'd be of me now, if she knew what I'd done."

Sitting down at the table, Nishi waited for him to continue. When Sho remained silent, he reached for an old tin sitting on the table. "Want some cookies? They're really good. With icing and everything."

Sho smiled. "You know I can't resist a good biscuit."

Grinning, Nishi opened the tin, holding it out to him. "I made them myself."

The Headmaster peered into the tin, and then broke out into a laugh. "Nish! They're all...phallic-shaped!"

"Aren't they lovely? I made them for HP Day."

"HP Day?"

"Happy Penis Day. I invented a new Holiday, and I think we should celebrate it every year."

Smiling, Sho reached out and selected an especially big cookie, shaking his head. "You're something else." He took a bite, closing his eyes. "Mmmm. Delicious, Nish. So, when is this new Holiday you're proclaiming?"

"I'm thinking...next weekend? It's a Holiday weekend anyway."

Sho laughed. "And what are you going to do to celebrate, now that Takashi's out of the picture?"

Nishi shrugged. "Dunno. Got any suggestions? If you're finished with Kyoshi, perhaps I could try him out."

At this, the Headmaster immediately grew grave, the light fading from his eyes.

"That was a stupid thing to say," Nishi announced, wincing. "I'm sorry. I'm such an idiot."

"No. You were only teasing. But...oh, Nish."

"All right. Let's have it."

"I...I...raped him."

Nishi waited for more details, and when they were not forthcoming, he nibbled his cookie, thinking. "Hmmm. And...does *he* think you raped him?"

"He should."

"Ah." Nishi smiled. "But he doesn't?"

"I don't know. Maybe he does now. It's...complicated."

"What happened?"

Sho sighed, closing his eyes. "He came to my chambers. I had to punish him. He was intoxicated last night and apparently...defaced the Valemont statue with his bodily fluids, and then—"

"Wait," Nishi interrupted, eyes gleaming. "What do you mean, defaced the Valemont statue with his bodily fluids?"

"He urinated on it."

Nishi laughed aloud at this.

"Nish! It's hardly a laughing matter!"

"I'm sorry." Nishi tried to suppress his laugh, but couldn't wipe the smile from his face. "Okay...and then what?"

"And then...well, apparently he was caught fondling another student. So...I had to punish him."

"Hmmm."

"The thing is...I was...jealous. It's hard to admit, but I was furious with him. And so I made his punishment a bit more severe than was probably justified."

"How many strikes?"

"Forty."

Nishi raised an eyebrow. "That *is* a bit extreme."

Sho shook his head. "But that's not even the worst of it. There he was, bent over my desk, in tears after begging me to stop, and I...I took him. By force."

"How so? Be more explicit."

"I came up behind him and kept him pinned down on the desk and then penetrated him while I put my hand over his mouth to muffle his cries."

Nishi studied his brother for a moment. He was surprised; such an action was so unlike Sho that he hardly knew what to say.

"You're shocked."

"Well...maybe a little."

Sho hung his head. "I should resign."

"I don't know about *that*. Tell me, what happened, right afterwards? What did he say?"

"He tried to brush it off like it was no big deal. He told me he *wanted* to be violated."

Sounds like my kind of boy, Nishi thought, though he decided to keep this to himself.

"Then, he wasn't upset?"

"No...well, yes. After I told him to get out, and that I didn't have any feelings for him. Then he was upset."

"What did you tell him that for?" Nishi demanded.

"Because! This...can't continue. I told him to report the incident to the Dean."

Nishi sat back in his chair, thinking. "Do you think he will?"

"I don't know."

"Well, what if he doesn't?"

"Then...then, I should just resign."

"Well...who was the other boy? The one he fondled?"

"Seiko Shinozaki."

"Seiko! You mean the athlete?"

"The same."

"Fuck! He's bloody hot," Nishi exclaimed, then tried to rein in his enthusiasm when Sho gave him a disapproving look. "I mean, from a purely artistic, aesthetic point of view."

"Who am I kidding? You're right. That's why I was so jealous."

Nishi paused for a moment. "You told Kyoshi you have no feelings for him. But that's not true, is it?"

Sho stared at the table. "No."

"How bad is it?"

"I can't say—that is, I've never felt this way before. For anyone."

Nishi smiled. "Are you in love with him?"

"I don't know! I barely know him, Nishi!"

"So? Sometimes love is just that way, from the very start."

"It doesn't matter how I feel about him. He's a student, and I'm the Headmaster. This can't go on."

"Are you trying to convince me or yourself?"

Sho sighed, closing his eyes. "Oh, Nish. What am I going to do?"

The coffee pot began to gurgle, and Nishi moved to retrieve some of the fresh-smelling brew. He poured his brother a cup and then one for himself, and then brought both mugs to the table.

"Cream, right?"

"Yes."

Nishi added a splash of white, rich liquid to his brother's coffee, then sat down again.

"I you want my opinion, I don't think you should do anything. Just wait and see what he does. If he feels violated, he'll report the incident. Sounds like you gave him plenty of incentive to do that. And if he doesn't, then you'll know either he doesn't feel like he was taken completely by force, or he cares about you too much to say anything."

"But...don't you think I have a moral obligation to confess my transgressions?"

"I wouldn't know about that," Nishi answered, sipping his coffee. "I'm hardly the poster boy for morality." He paused for a moment. "I know you hate it, Sho, but would you mind terribly much if I smoked?"

Sho shook his head. "No, of course not. This is your home."

"Thanks." Nishi lit up a cigarette, inhaling deeply, and then exhaling, taking care to blow his smoke away from Sho's face. "You know, I think you worry too much about what's 'right' and 'wrong'. I mean, in your dying moment, what are you going to care more about, whether you did the 'right' thing according to society or whether you had a life you enjoyed? Aren't you entitled to happiness?"

"Even if I am, I'm not entitled to hurt Kyoshi."

"But what do you think is going to hurt him more, fucking him or blowing him off after you've fucked him?"

"I don't know," Sho admitted. "He *was* pretty upset when he left."

"I bet. And my guess is, he was mostly upset because you told him you didn't care about him."

Sho nodded, considering. "You can see why I did that though, right?"

"Yeah, I get it. But do you really think shutting everything off now is going to make things right? And what if...Kyoshi and you are meant for each other? He's only going to be a student for a few years, you know. Then you could do whatever you wanted."

"Technically maybe," Sho conceded. "Although it would definitely raise a few eyebrows, if we were together in a few years."

"So? Maybe you could transfer to another school or something."

"That's actually not a bad idea. I should probably get as far away from him as possible."

"That's not what I meant."

"I know, but surely you're not saying we have a chance at a real relationship, Nish. We're off to a very bad start."

"I don't know about that. Sounds like you're off to a pretty *kinky* start, though." Nishi smiled, studying his brother. "So, he wasn't all like, '*You raped me!*' or anything, afterwards?"

"No…he told me he forgave me. I said we should probably call the police."

"And what did he say?"

"He said…he said something about borrowing their handcuffs."

At this, Nishi threw back his head and laughed. "Oh fuck! If you don't want him, Sho, I've got dibs. He sounds like my sort of boy."

Sho stiffened at this. "Go near him and I'll be forced to beat the life out of you."

"I'd like to see you try! Anyway, no need for conflict. How about a threesome?"

"Nish!" Sho punched his brother in the arm, though couldn't resist smiling. "You're impossible."

"Hmmm. Is that a definite *no*?"

The Headmaster shook his head, laughing softly. "I hope you're not going to start that up again."

"What? I bet I'm not the only male in the world who wanted a little sibling sugar."

Sho laughed, remembering. "I practically had to fight you off, that last year at home."

"Well? Who can blame me? You kept walking around naked."

"It was my room, too, you know. I had to get dressed, didn't I?"

"It's your fault for having such a sexy body."

"Nish," Sho scolded, though his voice was gentle. He shook his head. "You were always the naughty one."

"Tell me about it. My ass was paddled so raw sometimes I thought I'd pass out. Whereas you, of course, were always the perfect darling of the family."

Sho's smile faded at this. "Not anymore."

"Oh, come on. Everyone's entitled to some mistakes. That's what you need—a good paddling, then you'll feel like you've been properly punished."

Sho laughed. "I probably do deserve it."

"Of course you do. That's it! How about I give you a few hard whacks? Would that make you feel better?"

The Headmaster took another bite of his cookie, shaking his head.

"Hey, I'm serious. Wait right here."

Nish put out his cigarette, jumped up and dashed out of the kitchen, then came back with a long wooden paddle—one that had been used many times on both boys, and particularly Nishi, when they were young.

"Remember this?" Nishi held the paddle up in the air, grinning.

"Nish—"

"No arguments! On your feet, brother. You've been very naughty, and now I'm going to punish you. Come on, get up. You can take it. You deserve it, and you know it."

"What are you going to do?" Sho laughed, continuing to sit.

"Just what I said. Work you over so you can stop obsessing about this. You'll feel better, knowing you've been punished. On your feet!" Nishi reached out and grabbed his brother, dragging him out of his chair.

"Ow! My arm—take it easy, Nish!"

"Are you going to submit to your punishment or not?"

"Oh, all right," Sho laughed. "Give me a few good whacks."

"A wise decision. Now, put your hands on the table and lean over."

The Headmaster obeyed this mandate, smiling at his brother's serious expression. "You're quite the disciplinarian."

"That's right. Now, you'll feel this, I think."

With that, Nish gave Sho a good smack with the paddle, eliciting an involuntary cry from him. "Ow! That bloody hurt, Nish!"

"Quiet. You're being punished, remember? Here's another one."

WHACK!

"All right, that's enough," Sho replied, frowning.

"You think you're getting off with such a slim punishment as that? Two whacks for raping a student? Be a man and take it, Sho."

Nishi delivered yet another punishing strike, and then a fourth.

"This really hurts, Nishi," Sho complained.

"Silence!"

WHACK!

"Ow! Okay, that's it." Sho attempted to turn around, but his brother grabbed hold of him, managing to deliver three more brutally hard whacks before Sho was able to wrench the paddle away from him.

"Dammit, Nish," he whispered, his voice choked from tears and anger. "That wasn't funny."

"It wasn't supposed to be. You had to be punished. Do you feel punished?"

His brother answered that with his silence as he struggled to regain his composure.

"Good. I think I hear you. Now, stop worrying about what happened today. I've punished you, so let this whole thing go. Got it?"

Sho nodded, offering Nishi a small smile. "Yes."

He did already feel a little better. Nishi knew him well, understanding that he would feel a bit less guilty once he'd been "punished."

"All right then. Want another penis cookie?"

"SOMEBODY FUCKING KILL ME," SEIKO groaned.

"I can't. I'm too busy suffering miserably," Kyoshi replied, bitterly. "When are those pills gonna kick in?"

The two young boys were face down on Seiko's bed, with icepacks on their punished flesh.

"Not soon enough. Fucking Mitsuwa! He was more of a prick than usual," Seiko grumbled.

"I'll say." Kyoshi almost smiled over the double meaning, though he wasn't in much of a mood for jokes.

"He sure kept you in there a long time. Did he really give you all forty?"

"Every last fucking one. That's not all he did, either."

"What do you mean?"

"I mean...I don't know if I should tell you."

Seiko turned his head to look at him, resting his cheek on his arms. "What?"

"You wouldn't believe me if I told you."

"Probably not, 'cuz you're a fucking liar," Seiko agreed. "But tell me anyway."

"It's complicated."

"So? I'm not going anywhere."

"I think he was especially angry with us—and you—because he was jealous."

"What do you mean?" Seiko laughed.

"I mean, he was jealous of *you*. Of my fondling you, or whatever."

Seiko snorted. "In your dreams, Kyo. He punished us because we were fornicating and pissing on the Valemont statue."

"Technically but…there's a lot you don't know."

"I know. You told me you kissed him. I don't know if believe you but…."

"Not only that. We've done a lot more than that. We — this weekend, in Jufi, I went to see him play at the Philharmonic. And…we were together."

"What do you mean, you were together?"

"I mean, we fucked. First I blew him off at the Philharmonic, and then we spent part of the night together at the Swan."

Seiko stared at him for a moment, expressionless. Then a smile tugged at his lips. "Fucking liar."

"I'm not lying. I wouldn't…not about something like that."

"Headmaster Mitsuwa would never do something like that. He's…I don't know…got *principles*. He teaches Ethics, you know."

Kyoshi shrugged. "Guess I'm just irresistible."

"Yeah, right."

"Fine. Don't believe me. But you have to believe that, to believe what he did in his chambers just now."

Seiko sighed. "I really don't care for these sorts of games, Kyoshi. I hope you don't think you're going to impress me with stories like this."

"It's not a game."

"You're fucking with me."

"I'm not."

The blond-haired, green-eyed youth studied him for a long moment. "Shit. You're for real?"

"Yes."

"Then…what happened today?"

"He held me down over the desk and fucked me raw."

Seiko opened his mouth to challenge this assertion but could see from Kyoshi's expression that he was clearly upset.

"Holy shit. He really did that?"

Kyoshi nodded. "And then he told me to get out."

"That fucker! What are you going to do?"

"I don't know. He said I should report what happened to the Dean."

"Are you going to?"

Sighing, Kyoshi closed his eyes. "I don't think so."

"Why the hell not?"

"Because," he whispered, "I...have feelings for him. It's my fault, you know. I deliberately seduced him."

"Still...." Seiko was silent for a moment, letting all this new information sink in.

"You can't tell anyone about this. All right?" Kyoshi cautioned.

"Yeah, sure. But...I mean, don't you think you should tell someone what he did?"

"I didn't mind it. I was glad. It proved he...cared."

As Kyoshi said this, he suddenly realized that it didn't matter what the Headmaster had told him afterwards. It couldn't be true that he didn't have feelings for him—otherwise he would never have done such a drastic thing, something that could jeopardize his position at Valemont.

He smiled.

"What are you smiling about?" Seiko demanded.

"I just realized...the Headmaster is in love with me."

Seiko shook his head. "I don't even want to know the logic behind that. You say he rapes you, tells you to get out, and now you say he loves you. That's twisted."

"Yeah," Kyoshi whispered, dreamily.

"I think that cocktail's kicking in now," Seiko sighed, closing his eyes. "So, what are you going to do?"

"Nothing. I'll let him come to me."

"Mmmm."

"He will, you know."

"Will...what?" Seiko struggled to open his eyes, the double-dose of the pharmaceutical analgesic cocktail making him suddenly drowsy.

"Come to me."

"Do you really want him to, after that?"

"Yes."

"Kyoshi," Seiko announced, after a long pause, "you're one sick little fucker."

"I know." Kyoshi smiled, slipping off into his dreams.

Chapter 9 - *The Ethics of Fucking*

THE NEXT FEW DAYS WERE PURE TORTURE for Headmaster Mitsuwa, who flinched every time the phone rang, anticipating a summons from Dean Gerard and a shameful end to his career at Valemont. It was bad enough that he had to attend his mother's funeral. But that wasn't even what was on his mind.

It was all about Kyoshi. He wavered back and forth on whether or not he should confess his transgressions to the Dean rather than wait for Kyoshi to turn him in.

On the one hand, it seemed the honorable thing to do, and on the other, Sho couldn't help but wish for at least a few more trysts with the boy, if he was planning to turn himself in, just to make his disgraceful retirement a little sweeter. Yet no matter how guilty he felt about what he'd done, he couldn't quite bring himself to make the call.

Nor could he stop fantasizing about Kyoshi or resist squeezing in some special alone time each day in his office. Thus he vacillated wildly between wanting to do the right thing and wanting to call Kyoshi to his chambers for a thorough fucking.

Nishi, anticipating his distress, had sent him a tin of cookies—phallic-shaped, no less—and Sho had eaten nearly the whole batch by midweek. He had downed an extraordinary volume of coffee as well, neither of which had done much to calm the anxious man, who tossed and turned at night with a belly full of cookies, his blood wired with caffeine.

After a few days, exhaustion took over. Sho finally surrendered to his dreams, sleeping entirely through his first alarm the next morning and aroused only by the second, an emergency alarm that he always kept by his bedside but had never before actually had to use. He awoke refreshed and in better spirits, and the rest of his day seemed to go well — at least better than the few days previous.

He was at home that evening, sitting at his kitchen table, a fresh cup of coffee just off the pot as he nibbled on one of the last remaining iced biscuits. His thoughts were starting to wander away from the worries that had gripped him since he'd last seen Kyoshi. In fact, he was almost starting to relax. Evidently Kyoshi wasn't going to say anything after all; he had spent a good part of the week fretting for naught, and now it was time he put his attention to other matters at hand.

Just as he came to the conclusion that the situation was resolved, the phone rang. A deep feeling of dread overcame the Headmaster, a sensation only exacerbated when he discovered the identity of the caller: Dean Gerard.

"I'm sorry to bother you at home, Sho. I assure you, I wouldn't if this weren't something of…well, an emergency. I'm afraid I have rather disturbing news for you."

"Oh?" Sho struggled to keep the fear out of his voice but was so nervous he dropped his cookie into his coffee. The penis bobbed up and down in the hot sea of java as frosting slid down perilously into the brew.

This was it; he was finished. He was trying to amass up a sense of dignity so he could face what was coming with some semblance of honor, but his heart was heavy with shame.

"Yes, I'm afraid so. Though I would have thought you might have heard?"

"Yes," Sho exhaled quickly, then caught himself. "That is, no. I'm not sure? What is it?"

"I'm referring to Shin Yumi? You've heard, then?"

Sho's relief was so great that for a moment he could not speak.

"Forgive me, no. I thought you were speaking of something else."

"Then, if this is news to you, this may come as something of a shock. He died late this afternoon."

"Surely not," Sho breathed, not having to feign his disbelief.

"Yes, it was quite horrific, apparently. He was up on his rooftop putting up decorations for the Holidays when he fell and was…my understanding is…impaled on his fence post."

"Heavens! That's…terrible!"

"Yes. Especially seeing as he didn't die right away. Horrible way to go, I must say."

"That's positively frightful," Sho agreed, feeling secretly relieved that the "disturbing news" the Dean had called to share with him was Shin Yumi's death rather than his own dismissal. He immediately felt guilty for this, trying to refocus upon the tragedy of Shin's death rather than his own good fortune. "Is there anything I can do?"

"Yes, in fact, there is. We'll have to replace him, of course, but that's going to take some time. Until then, I was wondering if you would consider taking on one of his classes? He's only teaching three this term, all upperclassmen, and I've managed to convince Yori and Susumu to each take one, so if you could possibly take on the third?"

"Of course. Which one?"

"Civilization, Past and Present?"

"Well, certainly I'll do my best, but I don't have much background in history."

"I realize that; I was hoping you could do a segment on Comparative Ethics? That would finish up the term nicely, I believe, and that's your area, is it not?"

"Yes," the Headmaster conceded, glad that the Dean could not see him blush. Although he had taught Ethics in the past, to teach it *now* seemed…well, hypocritical.

"Then it's arranged?"

"Yes, of course."

"Excellent. I knew I could count on you. You should already have a copy of the roster. Or do I need to send another copy?"

"Not necessary. I have all the rosters at my office."

"Very good." The Dean paused for a moment. "What was the other bad news you heard today that you thought I was going to tell you?"

"Oh...just that, we had lost the...yudona tournament."

The Dean laughed at this. "Where have you been getting your information? The tournament isn't until this weekend, and moreover, it seems we have a good chance of winning with Kyoshi Sayuki on the team."

"Ah! That's...good news, then."

"Speaking of which, how is he doing this term? Any more trouble from the boy?"

"Some," Mitsuwa replied, feeling the heat rise to his cheeks, "but all in all...he's a good kid. Just a little...misguided."

"I'm glad to hear that. So are you going to the tournament, then?"

"Oh. I'm not sure."

"I hope you do. You've never seemed to take much interest in our first-rate athletic program, Sho. You may not think anyone notices that you never go to any of the events, but they do. *I* do."

"Well, I may go," Sho lied, feeling rather put on the spot.

"Good! I hope to see you there, then. Thank you for your willingness to help out, Sho, with our little crisis. Your willingness will not go unrewarded come Review time. I realize this must be an especially hard time for you — I'm sorry to hear about your mother."

"Thank you," the Headmaster murmured. "Have a good evening, Dean."

"And you."

Sho hung up the phone, feeling overcome with a variety of emotions — relief, shock over Shin's death, anxiety over having to pick up a class mid-semester, and excitement over the thought of seeing Kyoshi perform at the yudona tournament. His thoughts turned to the class; he would have to come up with a curriculum that very night, or at least a starting point, and have some readings prepared. It would need to be some combination of ancient ethics and modern, and he wondered which civilizations Shin had focused on.

As he was contemplating this, a thought suddenly occurred to him: who exactly was *in* the class?

What if….

Seized with panic, he grabbed his coat and headed over to the University, unable to wait until morning to find out. His office seemed disconcertingly eerie late at night, and he almost expected to see Shin sitting in his office, waiting for him, the gatepost still impaled in his chest. Shaking his head at his own foolish fears, he rushed inside — turning on all the lights to relieve his anxiety — and then made for his desk.

He didn't need to sort through his files to find Kyoshi's file; he kept it in his drawer and knew exactly where it was. Although he felt a bit ashamed about it, there were a few pictures of the boy that he enjoyed looking at while pleasuring himself; he had tried to stop this rather inappropriate behavior but found that he could not, especially now that they had been intimate.

Fumbling through his records, hands trembling, he finally came to the document he was looking for: Kyoshi's schedule. He glanced over the listing, gasping aloud when he found what he had dreaded — or perhaps secretly hoped for:

3:00 Rm 25 Prof. Shin Yumi Civ., Past and Pres - *Sayuki Kyoshi*, **registered**

He collapsed into his chair, bringing a hand to his mouth.

So. Kyoshi would be one of his students. It almost seemed like some practical joke fate had gifted him. That he would be teaching Ethics to Kyoshi seemed completely absurd. He had no doubt the boy would find the situation amusing.

But there was nothing he could do about it, and Sho found that, despite how awkward the situation would be, he was secretly excited by the thought of seeing Kyoshi every afternoon. He was so excited, in fact, that he found himself fumbling with his zipper, and within a few minutes had relieved his sexual tension, his warm semen dripping down his fingers as he gazed longingly at Kyoshi's photograph.

"HEY! DID YOU HEAR THE NEWS?" NAMPO RUSHED up to Kyoshi and Seiko, who had just left the mess hall after breakfast.

Seiko shrugged. "Can you be more specific?"

"I mean about Professor Yumi!"

Seiko shook his head. "No."

"He's dead."

"No shit?" Seiko's eyes widened.

Nampo nodded. "And it was a really gruesome, horrible death, too."

Kyoshi frowned. "What happened?"

By now some of their other classmates had gathered round, having overheard the conversation.

"Apparently he fell off his rooftop and was impaled on his iron gate."

Exclamations of horror and disbelief followed this announcement.

Masami Rin, however, laughed. "You're lying."

"I'm not," Nampo retorted. "You'll find out soon enough."

"Does that mean class is cancelled?" Seiko asked hopefully.

"No. They've already found someone to replace him."

"Who?"

Nampo shook his head. "I don't know. Only that all his classes are covered."

Amidst groans of disappointment, Kyoshi asked, quietly, "Will there be a Memorial?"

The others hushed at this, feeling a little ashamed to have been only concerned about their schedules. Professor Yumi, though not exactly a great favorite at Valemont, had been respected, and the boys suddenly seemed to realize how inappropriate their reaction had been.

"Yeah. This evening after dusk in the Old Cathedral," Nampo replied.

After a moment of silence, Seiko spoke. "Should we bring tribute flowers or something? I mean for his family."

"That seems only right," Nampo answered. "I'll go purchase them, if everyone wants to chip in. Only…I don't have a vehicle."

"I'll get them," Kyoshi volunteered.

The boys then fumbled through their pockets, handing bills and coins to Kyoshi, who took their donations without comment.

"Want me to go with you?" Nampo asked.

"No; I'll place the order and then pick them up later this afternoon. I might miss part of class."

"I'm sure whoever's covering the class will understand," Nampo remarked.

"Speaking of missing class, we're going to be late for first period," Masami announced, staring at his watch.

The group broke up then as the boys all hurried to class.

Seiko fell into step with Kyoshi, noting his gloomy mood. "Are you still sore today?"

"What? Oh. No. Well, a little." Distracted, Kyoshi ran a hand through his hair.

"I am," Seiko laughed. "I think I'll try to avoid Mitsuwa's chambers for a while."

"Mmmm."

After a moment of silence, Seiko leaned toward him to ask in a low voice, "Has he called you?"

Kyoshi shook his head, frowning.

"Have you decided what you're going to do?"

Blinking, Kyoshi looked toward him, seeming confused. "About what?"

"About," now Seiko lowered his voice to a whisper, "what he did to you."

"Oh. I'm not going to do anything."

"Maybe you should."

Kyoshi stopped, turning to him. "You're not going to say anything, are you?"

"No, I'm just saying—"

"You'd better not. I'll fucking kill you."

Seiko frowned at this, looking a bit annoyed. "Ha! In your dreams. I'll take you on any day."

"You'd lose."

"Oh yeah? I bet I'd—"

Before he could finish, Kyoshi had pinned him face up against the building wall, his arm painfully wrenched behind him.

"Ow! Dammit, Kyoshi!"

"Just trying to make a point," Kyoshi whispered in his ear. "I'll fuck you up good, make no mistake. You promised you wouldn't say anything and I'm going to hold you to it."

"All right! Fine! Bloody...hell," Seiko gasped, wincing when Kyoshi tightened his grip on his arm. "I won't tell. Let me go already!"

"I don't know," Kyoshi teased, thrusting up against him from behind. "I've got you perfectly positioned for a nice fucking."

"Kyoshi!"

Some of their classmates laughed as they passed by upon apprehending the pair so intimately engaged.

"Do it, Kyoshi!" Takumi, another third-year, called out.

"Woo!" Nampo jeered, joining in. "Seiko's getting it up the ass!"

"Mr. Sayuki," came a familiar voice.

Kyoshi turned to see Headmaster Mitsuwa, standing behind them with his arms across his chest, looking decidedly displeased. The other boys, spying the Headmaster, scurried off, hoping to evade his notice.

"Yeah?" he grinned, lamely.

"This is hardly appropriate behavior. It seems your last visit to my chambers hardly made an impression on you."

"I don't know about that," Kyoshi replied, his lips curled into a suggestive smile.

Ignoring the sudden pounding of his heart, Sho now felt annoyed. "Release him, Kyoshi, this instant!"

Kyoshi did so, and Seiko rubbed his arm, wincing. "That hurt," he complained, giving Kyoshi an irritated glare.

"Mr. Sayuki, you will report to my chambers today immediately following your afternoon classes. Expect to be disciplined."

"All right," Kyoshi answered, his eyes shining. "And...what implement of discipline will you use *this* time, Headmaster?"

Mitsuwa stared back at him, his gaze unwavering. Kyoshi was deliberately taunting him. "You shall find out," he replied. "Now, get to class, both of you."

"Yes, Headmaster," Seiko murmured.

Kyoshi only shot him a deliberately provocative look, winking.

Sho turned and made for his chambers, glad his robe was hiding his quickly developing erection.

Naughty boy, he thought, trying to suppress an instinctive smile. He was looking forward to Kyoshi coming to his chambers. He would give him a good whipping...and then...and then....

No. He was not going to touch the boy this time. He would be disciplined, and that would be the end of it.

Nothing more.

He found his pace increasing as he hurried to his chambers, anxious to have a private moment to contemplate Kyoshi's punishment and release his own mounting lust.

Kyoshi spent the rest of the morning fantasizing about what he would do in the Headmaster's chambers. He wasn't about to submit to more discipline—at least nothing more than a few strikes—and he was desperate for Sho's kiss, anxious to explore the Headmaster fully, right there behind closed doors. Although he knew Sho had tried to hide it, he was well aware that he had been aroused, and he couldn't wait to be alone with him.

In the afternoon he skipped his classes, driving into town and finding the most expensive-looking flower shop he could, a posh establishment called Blooms of Paradise, and there he ordered a beautiful arrangement for Professor Yumi's Memorial, charging it on the credit card his uncle had given him. Then, using nearly all the cash he had on hand, he purchased a second arrangement of exotic rose orchids, signing the card and sealing it before handing it over to the clerk, who promised that the arrangement would be sent that very afternoon.

Then he returned to Valemont, feeling quite smug.

Headmaster Mitsuwa spent the entire day in his chambers, preparing for his afternoon class and fantasizing about Kyoshi. It was late in the afternoon, only minutes before his class, when he received an arrangement of flowers.

Assuming it was from Ukita, he sighed. It had been awhile since he'd heard from him and he was starting to hope Ukita had given up. Still, he had to acknowledge that the flowers were quite beautiful and elegant—a definite departure from his usual fare. He opened the card, feeling a bit distracted, and caught his breath when he read the following:

I need a good fucking. -K

Smiling, the Headmaster tucked the card away in Kyoshi's file, then headed to class.

SEIKO, NAMPO, AND HISASHI WERE SITTING on their desks, whispering together.

"Are you sure?" Seiko asked.

Nampo nodded. "He'll be teaching the class for the rest of the semester."

"Shit!" Hisashi scowled. "I'll bet he brings that bloody crop whip of his."

"Yeah," Seiko agreed. "And personally, I've seen enough of it this term."

"You and Kyoshi really got it, I heard."

"It was fucked up. And sooo over the top. Like, we didn't even do anything, not really."

"I heard you were caught fondling in public," Nampo piped up.

"I don't know, maybe. We were both too drunk to know what the hell was going on."

"What I heard," Hisashi whispered, "is that you pissed on the Valemont statue."

Nampo giggled at this, bringing a hand to his mouth.

"You laugh like a girl," Seiko teased.

"I know," Nampo acknowledged good-naturedly. "But did you really?"

Seiko shrugged. "It's possible. I really don't remember. Poor Kyoshi though...he's already been called to Mitsuwa's chambers for discipline later today."

"Speaking of Kyoshi, he's not back yet," Nampo remarked, worried. "I'm not so sure the Headmaster will understand after all."

"I'll tell him where he's at."

"But what if he—"

The noisy classroom suddenly hushed as Headmaster Mitsuwa walked into the room, carrying his leather attaché case in one hand and his crop whip in the other, his long dark robe swirling behind him as he strode across the floor to the front of the class. Placing both firmly on his desk, he turned around to face the class, leaning back against his desk, his gaze immediately moving to Seiko, Nampo, and Hisashi.

"Off the desks, gentlemen," he scolded. "Class, please take your seats."

The boys immediately sat down as Sho scanned the room, frowning. "Where is Mr. Sayuki?" he demanded.

Nampo raised his hand. "He…he went—"

"I'm right here," Kyoshi announced, sidling into the classroom with both hands in his pocket, grinning. He was surprised to see the Headmaster, but thrilled. "Hey, are you teaching?"

"Kyoshi, class begins on the hour. You're late. You will address me properly as Headmaster, and you will not speak until I have called on you. Is that quite clear?"

Grinning, Kyoshi shrugged, slipping into his chair in the front row and watching Sho's reaction with obvious pleasure.

"I hardly see what you find so amusing, Kyoshi. You're already slated for a visit to my chambers this afternoon. And now you arrive late. I suppose you think you can saunter in here whenever you please with no consequences?"

"I was busy romancing a new love, Headmaster," he replied, his eyes gleaming.

Sho felt his throat constrict at this as he struggled to maintain his composure. "Mr. Sayuki, if you have personal affairs to attend to, you will do so during your own time…not during the school day."

"Yes, Headmaster," Kyoshi purred, gazing up at him with a disconcertingly seductive look.

Ignoring him, Sho now directed his remarks to the entire class. "As you probably all know, Professor Yumi is no longer with us. He passed away yesterday, and there will be a Memorial this evening in the Old Cathedral that I encourage you all to attend. I will be taking this class for the remainder of the term."

Nampo raised his hand.

"Yes, Mr. Toyama?"

"Is it true Professor Yumi was impaled?"

Sho paused for a moment. "It is, regrettably, true. He fell from his roof onto his iron gate post."

The boys vocalized their horror at this, the imagery almost too gruesome to contemplate.

Sho raised his hand to silence them. "That's enough. Yes, it is a horrible tragedy, though it seems inappropriate to focus on the gory details. Now. As far as this class is concerned, let me clarify a few ground rules. First of all, class starts precisely on the hour, and you will all be on time. Anyone who is late will automatically be given seven strikes, no negotiations." Sho's gaze now drifted to Kyoshi, who was watching him with a half-smile.

"Secondly," he continued, keeping his eyes locked on Kyoshi, who continued to smirk, "I expect order in this classroom. I'll tolerate nothing less, and will punish any infractions on the spot. You'll bare your white ass before the entire class, should discipline be necessary."

Some of the boys snickered at this, especially at the Headmaster's uttering the phrase "white ass."

"Silence! Shall I be forced to make an example of one of you?"

"Headmaster," Kyoshi said, without bothering to raise his hand, "I was late. Aren't you going to punish me?"

The boys all held their breaths at this, watching the Headmaster's reaction with interest.

Seiko flicked Kyoshi in the back of the head. "Idiot!" he whispered.

Sho was silent for a moment. "Kyoshi, do you enjoy being punished?" he asked, finally.

"Depends who's doing the punishing," came the boy's surly reply, which brought titters from his classmates.

"Very well, Mr. Sayuki, since you seem anxious to be disciplined today, I shall oblige you. On your feet."

Kyoshi stood up slowly, gifting the Headmaster with a drop-dead sexy gaze.

Sho straightened, picking up his crop whip and pointing it toward the desk. "Lower your trousers and bend over, forearms on the desk."

Kyoshi obeyed, seeming completely unaffected about exposing himself in front of the class. When his bare ass was revealed, however, the marks of his recent discipline still clearly imprinted on his flesh, the watching boys reacted with small gasps of surprise and laughter. Nampo's giggle could be heard above all of them, and it was infectious, causing others to laugh harder.

"Silence!"

Mitsuwa slammed his crop whip down on the desk and the room went dead silent. The sight of Kyoshi's punished buttocks and thighs had quite a different effect on the Headmaster, who was suddenly overcome with a desire to ravish the boy. He wanted to push him down onto the desk, spreading his ass and sliding his cock deep inside. Kyoshi wanted a good fucking...and Sho found he wanted to oblige him. He couldn't wait to get him back to his chambers.

He began walking back and forth behind him, swinging his crop whip in the air a few times to warm up his arm. *What was Kyoshi doing?* he wondered. It was as though he deliberately *wanted* to be punished. And so soon after...what had happened.

It made no sense.

But he couldn't have Kyoshi making a spectacle each day. He'd let him know right here and now how he'd answer his insolence.

"Mr. Sayuki, you will be on time for class from this day forward," he announced, sternly, and then, whipping his arm back with all the force he could muster, let the crop whip fly.

The crack of the whip announced the first strike on Kyoshi's backside; this was followed by six more equally vigorous strikes. The Headmaster struck so hard that the *whish* of his whip as it moved through the air could be heard, and the smart snap of the crop against Kyoshi's behind left no doubt that the boy felt his arm.

Kyoshi closed his eyes, taking the punishment without uttering a single sound. He found the situation excruciatingly erotic, and relished his punishment as though the Headmaster was loving him through his whip. Somehow he had come to associate punishment with pleasure and — at least when only a *few* strikes had to be endured — he enjoyed the intimacy of being punished by the Headmaster. Moreover, the mere knowledge of their previous coital engagement made his blood run hot. The fact that Headmaster was going to be teaching his class was almost too much to hope for. He could toy with him each and every day; he had already decided he would most definitely be late every single day.

As Sho finished he moved in front of his desk, mostly to satisfy his curiosity, and then — spying the boy's erection, struggled to keep his own arousal under control. Kyoshi opened his eyes and looked up at him suggestively.

Sho knew that only he could see Kyoshi's look and his aroused state, and it was almost more than he could take.

Naughty boy, he thought, marveling at Kyoshi's audacity in playing such a dangerous game publicly.

He set his crop whip down on the desk, allowing his gaze to drift momentarily to the boy's twitching organ, longing to press his lips up to the swollen cock and explore him, slowly, with his tongue. "You may take your seat, Kyoshi," he instructed, trying to maintain his composure. "But you are still to report to my chambers after classes today. I'm not finished with you."

"Yes, Headmaster." Kyoshi raised his trousers, fastened them, and sat down, a smile teasing his lips.

Seiko leaned forward. "Are you out of your mind?" he whispered.

"Mr. Shinozaki," the Headmaster barked. "Are you hoping for some discipline as well?"

"No, Headmaster," Seizo murmured, bowing his head.

"Good. Now, on to the curriculum. We'll be doing a series of readings spanning several major civilizations. Mr. Rin, please hand out the revised syllabus."

Masami leapt to his feet, eager to please the Headmaster. "Yes, Sir," he answered, taking the stack of papers from him gingerly as though he had been asked to distribute sacred documents.

Mitsuwa paced slowly in front of the class as he spoke.

"I expect you all to come to class prepared to discuss the readings. Anyone *not* prepared will be dealt with accordingly; I think you all know my threat to use my whip is not an idle one. And you'll each be writing a term paper on comparative ethics, so I suggest you start thinking about your topic."

A collective groan from the class was halted by the Headmaster's icy glare. "Hush, gentlemen. Haven't I made myself clear on my expectations? There will be order in the class. No exceptions!"

Kyoshi raised his hand, struggling to keep from smiling.

Sho frowned. "Yes, Mr. Sayuki?"

"Can we write on any topic?"

"Any topic that deals with an issue of ethics."

"What about sex between professors and students?"

Amidst gasps and laughter, the Headmaster moved directly in front of Kyoshi's desk. The boy looked up at him, his eyes twinkling mischievously.

"Mr. Sayuki, you are trying my patience. I think you want a good whipping and I assure you, you are going to get one. I suggest, if you have any desire to sit down in the near future, that you rethink your strategy for behavior in this classroom."

"I've thought it over," Kyoshi replied, "and I still want to do the paper about fucking."

Aghast, the other students looked from Kyoshi to the Headmaster, curious to see how he would handle the boy's completely inappropriate response.

Now the Headmaster was forced to take action. "Mr. Sayuki. It seems you're bent on punishment today; I suppose my crop whip wasn't enough for you. You want the paddle. Very well. I shall oblige you. On your feet. You'll accompany me to my chambers this very instant; class is dismissed."

The other students began whispering excitedly as Kyoshi stood up and was led away by the Headmaster.

"What is wrong with him?" Nampo exclaimed, voicing what many others were thinking. "Mitsuwa's gonna take his skin off."

Seiko shook his head, keeping his thoughts to himself.

"Can you believe he actually said, '*fucking*'?" Hisashi whispered. "I about pissed my pants."

"At least we got out of class," Seiko answered, shrugging.

The Headmaster kept his grip tight on Kyoshi's elbow, striding so quickly that Kyoshi almost had to jog to keep up.

"Ow! You don't have to squeeze me so tightly," he complained.

"Hush, Kyoshi," Sho replied.

"Oh, come on. You can stop with the Headmaster act. I know perfectly well you about shot your wad in there."

"If you think you won't be punished, Kyoshi, you're sadly mistaken," the Headmaster whispered.

"Did you get my flowers?"

Sho was silent for a moment, his lips twitching as he tried to suppress a smile. "And your note," he said, finally.

"Ah! You're going to take me up on it, I hope."

"The first thing on our agenda is your punishment."

"What! Come on, Sho. You already gave me seven wicked hard strikes with that thing."

"And you deserved it. You were very naughty, Kyoshi."

They had reached the Headmaster's chambers and Sho opened the door and pushed the boy inside, closing and locking the door behind him.

"You were turned on. Admit it," Kyoshi replied.

Sho contemplated him for a moment, then moved past him, pointing to the chair before his desk.

"Have a seat, Mr. Sayuki."

"Is this a game?"

"I assure you, it is not." Sho went to the wall, removing the paddle that hung there, and then moved around behind his desk and sat down, setting the paddle across his knees. "Sit."

Kyoshi continued to stand, crossing his arms in defiance.

"Very well," the Headmaster sighed, standing. "We'll forgo the lecture. Bend over." He pointed to the desk with the paddle.

Laughing, Kyoshi ignored this order, waiting to see what Sho would do. When the boy refused to obey, the Headmaster moved around to the front of the desk.

"*Now*, Kyoshi."

"I'll paddle *you* before you use that thing on me," Kyoshi replied.

Irritated, Sho lunged forward, pulling Kyoshi toward the desk. Caught off balance, the boy fell forward into the desk as the Headmaster wrenched one arm behind his back. He took a mighty swing and gave Kyoshi a hard whack with the paddle.

"Fuck! Dammit, Sho!"

"You will address me as Headmaster!"

Whack!

But by now Kyoshi had managed to wriggle free from Sho's grip, turning around and struggling with him for control of the paddle.

"Turn around!" the Headmaster commanded, once again disconcerted by the boy's amazing strength.

After a few minutes, Kyoshi won the paddle. "Now it's time for *your* punishment," he whispered, holding the paddle up threateningly.

"Kyoshi! Release me this instant, or I shall call for assistance!"

"Oh, come on, Sho!" Kyoshi was now behind the Headmaster, having secured both his arms against his back. He tossed the paddle onto a chair and then pressed his body close, whispering in his ear. "I saw you lock the door. Let's fuck."

Still keeping a firm hold on the Headmaster, he forced him back around behind the desk and into his chair.

"No, Kyoshi!"

"You know you want this," Kyoshi replied. He took hold of the Headmaster's arms, pinning them to the chair, and leaned down to kiss him.

Sho resisted…for perhaps half a second. Almost immediately he gave into the kiss, returning it eagerly, hungrily. Kyoshi moved onto the chair, straddling him, then released his hold on Sho's arms.

The Headmaster immediately pulled the boy closer, running his hands down his back to squeeze his ass. All his plans to show restraint were now abandoned. "Take off your clothes," he whispered.

"Are you going to punish me some more?" Kyoshi replied, smiling.

"Yes. I am going to punish you…I am going to fuck you harder than you've ever been fucked in your life."

"You're fucking sexy as hell, Sho." Kyoshi kissed him again, unzipping the Headmaster's robes.

"Obey me," Sho replied, his voice thick with lust.

"I will," Kyoshi promised, sliding a hand down inside the Headmaster's pants. "Ah, you're huge. And you're already wet."

Sho closed his eyes, trembling from the boy's touch. "Undress," he repeated again, this time urgently.

Smiling, Kyoshi slid off the chair and began removing his uniform. "Aren't you getting undressed?"

"No. I'll take you like this." Sho unzipped his pants, releasing his swollen cock with a breathy moan.

"That's kinky," Kyoshi replied. "You, still in your Headmaster's robes and all." Now completely naked, he stood before Sho, waiting for instruction.

"Straddle me," Sho ordered, holding out his hands.

"I thought you were going to fuck me hard," Kyoshi countered, as he positioned himself over the Headmaster's legs. Sho slid a finger up his ass to ready him, then slid his hands around to the boy's hips, pushing him down on his cock.

He closed his eyes and then opened them, a long breathy sigh escaping his lips. "Ohhh Kyoshi. You feel so good." He lifted Kyoshi's hips and then forced him down on his cock again, this time harder. "I'll fuck you hard. Don't worry."

"Then will you suck me off?"

"Yes," Sho promised, a little breathlessly. "Oh. This is good. But I want something else now."

"What should I do?"

"Get down on the floor on your hands and knees. Kiss me first."

Kyoshi complied, gifting him with an exceptionally long, sensual kiss.

As he broke away, Sho looked up at him through half-closed eyes. "I love the way you taste," he whispered.

"What do I taste like?"

"Mmmm. Like a naughty boy fooling around with the Headmaster."

"Between the two of us, you're the one who's the naughtiest. I don't know any better, I'm just a student."

"Perhaps," Sho conceded. "But in any case, I still must punish you."

"So by punishment you mean a good fucking?"

"Yes. On your knees."

"All right." Kyoshi slid off him then, repositioning himself on the floor on his hands and knees. He looked back at Sho, who had slid off the chair and now was kneeling behind him. "Like this?"

"Spread your legs more. As wide as you can. And put your head down on the floor."

"Ooo, kinky."

As Kyoshi offered himself, Sho entered him again, spreading his ass apart with his hands and penetrating with a bit more force, grabbing his hips and pulling back on them roughly with each thrust.

"Yeah," Kyoshi encouraged. "I like it hard like that."

"It's not hard enough, then," Sho replied, through gritted teeth. "This should be punishment."

Kyoshi laughed. "You're fun."

"No laughing during sex," Sho scolded.

"Oh! That hurt, actually."

"Good."

"Ow! That's too hard!" Kyoshi made a half-hearted attempt to move away, but the Headmaster kept his hips firmly in position.

"I told you this was punishment. You'll take it."

"Sho," Kyoshi whispered, wincing and closing his eyes as he tried to submit to what the Headmaster wanted.

"Good boy," Sho hissed, when Kyoshi stopped struggling. "Ahh, yes." Eyes rolling back, he gave the boy a few more violent thrusts before succumbing to his need, biting his lip as he ejaculated.

"I can feel that," Kyoshi whispered, after a moment. "Your hot semen inside me."

Slowly Sho withdrew, still shuddering from his orgasm. "Kyoshi," he whispered. "That was so very good."

"You fucked me way too hard," Kyoshi complained. "I'm not a girl, you know. Now," the boy turned around and lay down on the floor, stroking his erection, "I'm ready for that blow job."

"We can't make a habit of this," Sho warned, as he slid between the boy's legs.

"Why not?" Kyoshi demanded.

"You know perfectly well why not."

"Whatever. Just suck me."

The Headmaster obliged him, holding his cock with one hand as he offered his lingual arts. He slid his other hand between his legs, stroking the boy's perineum.

"That's good," Kyoshi encouraged, reaching down to rest his hands on Sho's head. "Oh, this is nice. I'm getting blown by the Headmaster!" Pleased with this observation, he continued to watch Sho, grinning. "I like it when you...vibrate your tongue like that."

Although the Headmaster was hardly in a position to reply, he answered by increasing the vibration Kyoshi had praised.

"Oh! That's," Kyoshi gasped, realizing suddenly he was going to come far more quickly than he wanted, "that's perfect."

In the next instant the boy came, his semen pumping onto the Headmaster's tongue. Sho tasted him, relishing him, then drank him dry.

"Shit. That was beautiful," Kyoshi groaned.

Sho moved up next to him, propped up on one arm. He looked down at Kyoshi, frowning.

The boy opened his eyes. "What?"

"We can't keep doing this."

"I know."

"You do?" Sho was almost disappointed.

"Yeah. You're back in Headmaster mode. We won't do anything for a few days until you can't stand it and need a good fuck again."

At this, Sho threw back his head and laughed. It had been a long time since he had laughed so loudly and openly, and in that moment he felt exceptionally happy. He gazed down at Kyoshi, love shining in his eyes.

Kyoshi returned his gaze, smiling.

Chapter 10 - *Lover's Spat*

SHO PULLED HIS COAT AROUND HIM, CHILLED by the sudden gust of cold air. The weather had turned decidedly cooler, though the stars shone brightly in the night sky. As he approached the Old Cathedral, his gaze drifted to a group of students standing in a group just outside the main entrance; Kyoshi was among them, and appeared to have said something the others found especially entertaining.

Headmaster Mitsuwa had spent the evening reflecting on his afternoon tryst with the boy, feeling simultaneously aroused and ashamed of what they had done. While he had vowed that he would not let such an incident happen again, just seeing Kyoshi immediately made him doubt his resolve.

Kyoshi Sayuki had to be the most attractive young man the Headmaster had ever encountered. It was more than just his devilishly good looks—his longish dark hair and gleaming, intense eyes, his extraordinarily fit physique—it was the manner in which he carried himself, his confidence, his very presence—that Sho found so difficult to resist.

As he approached the group, the boys quieted.

"Headmaster," Seiko murmured, nodding toward him.

Mitsuwa nodded back, his gaze then locking with Kyoshi's.

Kyoshi smiled slightly, shivering suddenly, either from the cold or the Headmaster's intense look. "Evening, Headmaster," he said, with atypical, almost exaggerated courtesy.

"Good evening, Kyoshi. Gentlemen. I believe the Memorial will start soon; I suggest you make your way inside."

Kyoshi nodded almost imperceptibly, awed by Sho's ability to resume his stern Headmaster demeanor so easily, as though nothing had ever taken place between them. If anything Sho had given him a warning look. But Kyoshi found, rather than be offended by Mitsuwa's aloofness, the knowledge that they had been intimate together only made his impassivity even more intriguing, even sexy.

It was almost like a game. His most recent visit to the Headmaster's chambers that afternoon had left him breathless. Sho was beginning to surprise him, and he could not help but wonder what would happen next between them.

The Headmaster's coat had fallen open, and Kyoshi could see he that had donned his more formal robes for the sad occasion, with gold trim around the collar and a long gold and silver sash that hung down the front of his robe. His hair, though no doubt carefully combed when he had left his home, was now tussled from the wind, giving him a decidedly sexy look.

The boys shuffled inside, their former revelry now extinguished by the solemnity of the Old Cathedral. An impressive, exquisite arrangement of flowers decorated a long table in front of the dais, and the hall was hushed. Near the front of the Cathedral the family of Shin Yumi sat on a pew—his widow trying to calm a fractious toddler, and next to her sat a small boy of about eight, staring down at his lap.

Once everyone had settled into their seats, the Memorial began; Sho hardly heard what Dean Gerard said, for his attention was focused entirely on Kyoshi.

Kyoshi had opted to sit next to the grieving family, and the Headmaster watched, hardly believing his eyes, as he proceeded to direct his energies toward folding a piece of paper in an intricate fashion, as though completely ignoring the service and the pain of the boy next to him, who had now begun to cry.

Sho was incensed, and his anger only increased when Kyoshi continued with his paper-folding project. He wanted to get up and yank him out of the Cathedral; he was both appalled and enraged over Kyoshi's insensitivity and rudeness. More than this, he was genuinely surprised, for he had never believed the boy could be so tactless.

Kyoshi was in for some serious discipline, and this time there would be no getting out of it. He would make an example of him and paddle him in front of the entire student assembly. He would....

Just as he was about to stand up and take action, Kyoshi turned to the boy and handed him something. The boy took it and looked up at him, tears still wet on his face, and Sho thought he saw something of a smile press into his trembling lips.

He strained to see what Kyoshi had given him and then realized, his heart melting, that the boy was holding a small paper creature that Kyoshi had folded for him. Kyoshi leaned down and whispered something in the boy's ear, which brought a second almost-smile to the wee one's face, who now examined the paper animal again, turning it over in his hands.

Sho closed his eyes, breathing hard. In that moment he knew with complete certainty he had fallen in love with Kyoshi. He felt a strange heat rise within him, a searing open of his heart by the boy's subtle kindness. With that single act, all his plans to end their forbidden relationship were swept away. He still wanted to yank Kyoshi out of the Cathedral, but now for other reasons; tonight he wanted to take him home, and make love to him in his own bed.

Once the service was finished, Sho rose to speak with him but was distracted by Dean Gerard, who came to ask him how his class had gone and whether he needed any assistance. Out of the corner of his eye, the Headmaster saw Kyoshi slip behind the curtain near the dais leading to the passageways that connected the even older parts of the Cathedral with the newer sanctuary. Kyoshi looked back at him, as if wanting him to follow.

As soon as Sho could break away, he made his way stealthily toward the curtain and then pulled it aside, peering into the darkness within. The passageways were only lit by a few candles, flickering in the sconces on the old stone walls, for the Cathedral was considered a sacred place and no form of electricity or modern lighting were allowed.

He walked a few steps into the dimly lit passageway. "Kyoshi?" he whispered.

Kyoshi moved from the shadows, seizing him from behind.

Sho nearly jumped out of his skin, but Kyoshi had put a hand over his mouth to muffle his cry.

"Kyoshi!" he scolded angrily, once he'd caught his breath and managed to break free.

The boy only grinned. "You sure are nervous back here. Don't tell me you believe all those stories about ghosts in the old passageways." He pushed Sho up against the wall, pressing his body up against him and pinning his wrists to the cold stones.

"Release me," Sho demanded, though not very convincingly, for Kyoshi could feel the Headmaster's erection developing under his thin robe.

"I want a kiss first," he whispered, and proceeded to take one, coaxing Sho's mouth open with his own and slowly tasting him with his tongue.

Sho, far from resisting, allowed the boy to keep him pinned to the wall, responding to his kiss with equal ardor.

"I've been thinking about you all evening," Kyoshi confessed, breaking away. "I was hoping I'd see you here tonight."

"Hmmm." Sho feigned indifference, but his heart was pounding. He was enjoying being held up against the wall, feeling deliciously vulnerable. Even in this small act he could feel Kyoshi's incredible strength, something which he found extraordinarily arousing.

Kyoshi laughed. "Is that all you have to say? I rather thought you enjoyed our time together, but perhaps I was mistaken."

Sho smiled. "I enjoyed it. I confess to it; but you are very naughty luring me back here. This is dangerous."

"Then why did you follow me?" he countered, arching up against him in a disconcertingly erotic way.

"Stop...doing that," Sho whispered, closing his eyes.

"Why? You seem to be enjoying it. Unless I'm quite mistaken." With this, Kyoshi released his grip on one wrist and slid a hand under the Headmaster's robe, then deftly slipped it down his pants to apprehend the man's raw lust.

Sho grit his teeth to contain his arousal, seizing Kyoshi's arm. "Stop."

Ignoring him, Kyoshi moved his thumb over the Headmaster's head, spreading the new wetness over his warm skin. "You're so ready for me, already," he whispered, smiling. "And we just fucked a few hours ago."

"Hush," Sho scolded, now using a bit more force to remove Kyoshi's hand from his pants.

"Why are you resisting?"

"Not here, Kyoshi," the Headmaster replied, urgently.

Encouraged, Kyoshi leaned forward and began kissing the man's exposed throat, which Sho allowed, letting his head rest back against the wall.

"In your chambers?" he suggested, between kisses and bites.

"No. Too dangerous. Kyoshi...."

The boy pulled back, looking up at him with a naughty smile. "Yes?"

Sho took a deep breath. "Come to my bed tonight," he whispered, finally.

Just hearing the Headmaster say the words set Kyoshi's heart pounding. "Seriously?"

"Yes. I want to...make love to you."

Thrilled, Kyoshi simply returned his gaze for a few moments; then they were kissing again, now more passionately. "I want that, too."

"We should stop now," Sho suggested, gently pushing him away. "I want to explore you...slowly. In my bed."

His head spinning with the Headmaster's provocative words, Kyoshi could barely manage a reply. Although he was curious as to why Sho was suddenly ready to move forward, he didn't want to ask about it, afraid the Headmaster would think better of it and change his mind.

"Then, we're going to your place?"

"Yes. Drive over later…in about an hour. I'll leave the garage door open for you. Don't get out of the car until I close the garage door—that's important, Kyoshi. Are you listening to me?"

Kyoshi nodded, stunned with Sho's devious plan. The Headmaster wanted him in his bed. That meant fucking, and lots of it—a whole night of it, if Kyoshi had any say in the matter.

"I'm on the corner of Siam and Cherry Blossom, a two-story house with an old tower. 960 Siam. Can you find it?"

Nodding, Kyoshi adjusted himself, wincing.

Sho noted this with a smile of amusement. "I'm going back into the sanctuary now. You wait a few minutes before you leave. Understood?"

"Yes," Kyoshi murmured, swallowing. He was so aroused he felt ready to burst; he was even calculating whether he should relieve himself beforehand to be a little less eager for the night ahead, but decided against it. It would make the night even more erotic to arrive ready to spill his seed; their first time together would be passionate, and after that they could slow down.

"You might consider preparations," Sho remarked, giving him a pointed look.

For a moment Kyoshi was confused, not quite sure if he understood the Headmaster's meaning.

Sho leaned forward. "I intend to explore every part of you," he whispered.

"Oh fuck," Kyoshi groaned. "You're bloody torturing me now."

Smiling, the Headmaster turned and left, moving quietly down the dimly let passageway and then drawing the curtain aside to move back into the sanctuary.

Kyoshi was trembling with excitement; he was so aroused that he once again contemplated tending to his needs, but again forced himself to wait. The Headmaster's artful seduction had left him weak at the knees. He leaned back against the wall, Sho's words echoing in his mind.

Come to my bed tonight.

I want to make love to you.

I want to explore you slowly…in my bed.

I intend to explore every part of you.

He shook his head, unable to believe what had just transpired. He forced himself to wait several minutes, like Sho had instructed, though he was anxious to proceed with the evening's preparations. It would be hard to wait an entire hour before going over to the Headmaster's home, even harder to keep quiet about it.

Sho was in a similar state of excitement, though maintained a calm, almost impassive demeanor as he made his way out of the Cathedral and back home. He'd done the unthinkable. He'd made the first move, luring a student to his bed for a night of unrestrained sex. Though he knew he should feel guilty about it, he was so excited about the evening that he didn't care.

Now that he'd decided to proceed, it was as though a tremendous passion in him had been released, and all he could focus on was what he would do with Kyoshi.

There would be lovemaking, yes. But there would also be fucking. Hot, violent sex…raw and abandoned, messy and wet and thoroughly wicked. Perhaps he would even tie the boy up. Perhaps Kyoshi would even resist, just a bit, which would make his violation of him even more gratifying. And he would be gentle, too--at least part of the time, for he fully intended to pleasure Kyoshi completely, and make him cry out and beg for more.

THE HEADMASTER WAITED BY THE WINDOW, PEEKING out behind the curtain. He'd changed into more casual clothes—a dark pair of pants and an ivory turtleneck—after showering thoroughly and preparing himself for the night ahead. He sipped a fine cognac, twirling the honey-amber liquid in his glass, as he tried to calm himself.

Finally, the blue-white soft glow of Kyoshi's headlights moved up his driveway and Sho went to the garage, immediately shutting the door once the car had rolled inside. Kyoshi got out of the car, dressed in a skintight T-shirt that showed off his incredible arms and chest, and a pair of old blue jeans.

Kyoshi smiled, nodding at the cognac. "Can I have one of those?"

Sho hesitated for a moment.

"What, you can fuck me, but you can't serve me alcohol?" Kyoshi teased.

"It's not that. I don't want you dulled."

"What do you mean, dulled? So *you* can drink, but I can't? And for the record, there's not much chance of my being dulled, I'm so horny I can barely think straight."

"You may have a sip," Sho offered, as Kyoshi approached him.

"You take a drink," Kyoshi whispered, sliding his hands to Sho's waist. "And then let me kiss you."

Smiling, Sho did so, and Kyoshi lapped up the cognac from his mouth.

"Mmmm. That's nice. You smell good."

"As do you," the Headmaster replied, nuzzling his neck. "You showered."

"Not just that."

"Ah," Sho breathed, making his way up to the boy's ear. "You're ready for me, then?" he whispered.

"Hell yes. I'm more than ready."

"Come inside." Sho pulled him into the house.

"I'll come all right," Kyoshi muttered. "I'll come so hard my semen will bloody hit the wall."

Sho answered this by putting his cognac down and kissing him, his hands slowly moving down his back to rest on his ass.

Kyoshi moaned. "I'm so turned on, Sho. I can't wait much longer."

"Get undressed."

Needing no second invitation, the boy immediately stripped, and the Headmaster did as well, noting Kyoshi's twitching erection with delight. "No, you won't last long, this first time," he observed.

"I can't help it! Quit torturing me!" Kyoshi held his swollen cock by the base, grimacing. "Come on. Get on your knees and suck me."

"Very well." Sho moved to his knees, and Kyoshi grabbed him by the back of the head, hands in his hair, pressing his organ up to his lips, and sighing when the Headmaster admitted him.

"Yes. Oh, yes. That feels...so good." Kyoshi closed his eyes, groaning. "I'm warning you...this won't last long. Oh! Oh god!"

Unable to hold back any longer, and completely undone by the Headmaster's wickedly perfect tongue, Kyoshi climaxed, crying out like a newly matured boy in rapture for the very first time.

Sho broke away, rising to his feet with a smile. "Feeling better now?"

"I'm sorry," he murmured. "I should have taken care of that before. Then I'd be ready for more now."

"I hope you don't think we're finished." The Headmaster took him by the hand and led him to his bedroom. "Since you've just released, I'll give you a good working over. And then we can start over again in a bit. Lie face down on the bed."

"I suppose you think you can order me around," Kyoshi teased.

"Yes." Sho gave him a smack on his bare ass. "I most certainly can. I'm the Headmaster."

Kyoshi dove onto the bed playfully, rolling onto his side. "Is this where you bring all your students?"

"Only the especially naughty ones." Sho crawled onto the bed, pushing him back onto his stomach. "Now, be a good boy and spread your legs."

"I'm still sore from this afternoon, you know," Kyoshi complained. "So take it easy, okay?"

The Headmaster answered this by wetting his finger and inserting into the boy's rectum, wiggling it. "You don't know the meaning of sore," he warned, pushing Kyoshi's legs further apart with his knees.

Kyoshi laughed at this, which the Headmaster punished by giving his ass another smack—this time a bit harder.

"No laughing during sex."

"Ow! Watch it! I'm still—I'm going to shove that crop whip up your ass one of these days, by the way."

"Perhaps if you arrived to class on time you'd be less sore now."

"It's not just *that*. You already rammed me pretty hard. Anyway I thought you were going to make love to me. What happened to that?"

"First I'm fucking you," Sho replied, removing his finger and retrieving a vial of oil he'd left by the bed. He poured the warm oil onto his hand and lubricated his cock thoroughly, and then, wiping the excess on Kyoshi's buttocks, repositioned himself for entry, and then eased in, penetrating slowly until the boy accommodated his full length.

He lay on Kyoshi's back, sliding his arms under his chest and nuzzling his neck, his eyes rolling back. "I'm completely inside you," he whispered.

"I know that," Kyoshi shot back. "Like I can't feel your huge dick up my ass?"

"Don't you like it?"

"I like it. I'll like it more in about an hour."

"I can't wait an hour." With that, Sho gave a decisive thrust, eliciting a small grunt from Kyoshi. He pulled back and then sunk into him again, reveling in the boy's exquisite tightness. He wiggled a bit inside him, spreading Kyoshi's thighs even wider with his knees, and then proceeded with the full agenda of his fuck, increasing the force and velocity with each thrust, until at last he was grunting and gasping, unable to contain his seed any longer.

He ejaculated, groaning his pleasure in such an erotic manner that Kyoshi shivered, now starting to feel aroused again. Although Sho had been a bit rough, Kyoshi found that he rather liked it; there was something inexplicably exciting about being so intimately violated by the Headmaster.

For some moments Sho continued to lay on top of him, breathing hard. Then, withdrawing slowly, he rolled onto his back.

Kyoshi snuggled up to him, pleased to see Sho looking so content. "You're sexy when you climax," he remarked.

"Mmmm." Sho kept his eyes closed for a moment, then, after feeling something warm twitching against his leg, opened one eye, peering down at him. "Are you getting another erection?"

"Yes," Kyoshi admitted.

Sho laughed. "We need to work on our timing."

Kyoshi answered this by biting his shoulder. "No laughing during sex," he scolded.

"We're not having sex."

"Yes we are."

"Give me...just a few moments, then. Just lie here with me."

"All right."

Kyoshi lay his head on the Headmaster's chest and Sho pulled him close, one hand toying with the boy's soft hair.

"I can't believe you asked me here," Kyoshi whispered, finally.

"Nor can I, to be honest," Sho admitted.

"But you couldn't resist me."

The Headmaster smiled. "I guess you could put it like that."

"It's just that...earlier today, you said we had to stop."

"I know. We probably *should* stop."

"I don't want to stop."

"Neither do I."

For a few moments they lay quietly.

"This feels good," Kyoshi announced, finally. "Your body feels good. You're so warm."

"Kyoshi...."

"What?"

"What was it you gave Shin Yumi's boy? In the Cathedral?"

"Oh. That was...just a paper bird. Poor kid."

"That was extraordinarily kind of you."

"Not really. The kid was crying. I just thought it might help distract him."

"It was kind," Sho insisted, turning to look down into his eyes. "You...surprise me, at times."

"Hmmm. Is that a compliment or an insult?"

"A compliment. Ah." Sho laughed. "I see your point."

"Anyway, I kinda knew how he felt. That's about how old I was, when..." Kyoshi stopped, falling silent.

"When you lost your parents?" Sho prompted, quietly.

"Yeah. I don't like to talk about it."

"We don't have to."

"This is great insider information for my Ethics paper," Kyoshi reflected. "Lying here in the Headmaster's arms."

"I hope you're being facetious. You don't seriously intend to proceed with your proposed topic?"

"Why not?"

"You know perfectly well why not. It's inappropriate. Pick another topic."

"What, it's okay for you to fuck me but not okay to write a paper on teacher/student relationships?"

"Precisely."

"Hypocrite!"

"Please remember that I am still Headmaster. I'll have you bent over my desk."

"I know you will, that's exactly my point."

"I meant I can still punish you. I *will* punish you, Kyoshi. Which reminds me, if you're late again for my class I'm going to double your strikes."

"You can't do that! You said seven strikes!"

"Seven for the first time. Each time I'll add seven more. I'll clarify that tomorrow."

"Hmmm." Kyoshi fell silent, reevaluating his plan to be deliberately late to Sho's class.

"You do realize, Kyoshi, that we need to take extreme precautions now in public. You must be on your best behavior. And we can't be intimate in my chambers. If you come to my chambers, it will be for punishment only. Nothing more."

Kyoshi smiled at this. "We'll see."

"Kyoshi!" The Headmaster give his ass another smack.

"Ow! Dammit, Sho!"

"Stop being naughty and I'll stop spanking you."

"I'm not being naughty. I'm just being my normal self."

"Your normal self *is* naughty."

"Um...I need to...clean up. Where can I...?"

"Ah. Down the hall, to your left. Come right back."

"I intend to." Kyoshi got up from the bed, giving him a meaningful look as he stroked his now matured erection. "I'm ready for more."

Sho eyed him, smiling. "You're a very handsome young man, Kyoshi."

"So are you. You've got a hot bod. Even better than what I imagined. You must work out?"

"I take good care of myself. I go for long walks, eat right, get plenty of sleep."

"It shows."

"Thank you. But I must say, between the two of us, you're the one with the extraordinary physique."

Kyoshi responded to this by posing, flexing his muscles. "I know. I'm a god."

Sho threw a pillow at him and Kyoshi caught it, laughing.

"It must be the yudona training?"

Kyoshi nodded. "It's pretty rigorous. It's a rough sport. Speaking of which, why haven't you come to any of my tournaments?"

"To be honest, it's a bit barbaric for my taste."

"Hmmm." A little disappointed, since he had hoped to show off a bit at the tournament, Kyoshi shrugged it off, making for the Headmaster's water closet.

Sho watched him go, enjoying the view. He was feeling surprisingly calm with his decision to take Kyoshi to his bed, though he wondered if this might be due, in part, to the boy's presence; perhaps he would feel differently in the morning.

At the moment, however, he was looking forward to a long night of lovemaking. Feeling mischievous, he got out of the bed and hid behind the door. When Kyoshi returned, looking at the empty bed in confusion, he slipped out and seized him from behind.

"Fuck! Bloody hell, you scared the living crap out of me!" Kyoshi yelled.

Sho laughed. "It's only payback."

"Yeah, well. I just lost my erection."

"That can be amended."

Kyoshi leaned back against Sho's naked body, smiling. "Although, you *do* feel good behind me like this."

The Headmaster answered this by allowing his hands to move up and down Kyoshi's body, gently biting and kissing his neck.

"Okay. Now I'm turned on again. Oooo. That feels good."

Sho slid his hand around the boy's hips and across his abdomen, finding his erection and working it with gentle fingers.

"Yeah. That's good, Sho."

"Get on the bed," Sho whispered. "On your hands and knees."

Trembling, Kyoshi obeyed, thrilled when the Headmaster moved behind him, pressing his buttocks apart with his hands. He could feel a warmth and then...a hot wetness, as Sho's tongue moved across his portal, gently penetrating.

"Holy fuck," he breathed, his eyes rolling back, overcome with pleasure. When the Headmaster began stroking him again, it was almost too much. He wiggled back, wanting more of Sho's tongue, completely unaware that he was gasping and moaning rather wildly.

The Headmaster was enjoying Kyoshi's obvious excitement, deliberately prolonging the experience by releasing his hold on the boy's cock every few minutes, much to Kyoshi's dismay.

"Keep touching me, Sho!" he begged, finally. "Don't stop! Why do you keep stopping?"

Sho struggled to keep from laughing, continuing to torment him for a while, and then he suddenly withdrew altogether.

Kyoshi wailed his despair. "Keep going!"

"I thought you might want something different now?"

"Such as?"

"Take me, if you like."

It took Kyoshi a moment to fully comprehend the Headmaster's offer. "Where's the oil?" he asked, breathlessly.

Sho tossed him the vial, and the boy immediately poured a ridiculous amount on his member, groaning as he massaged the warm wetness onto his engorged shaft.

"I don't know if you put enough on," Sho teased. "Where do you want me?"

"On your knees. No! On your back. No, wait! I'll get on my back. You straddle me."

Amused with Kyoshi's excitement and indecision, he waited for him to move into position and then straddled him, positioning himself over the boy's throbbing cock.

"Wait a minute," Kyoshi whispered, probing him with the tip of his organ as he tried to locate Sho's entrance.

The Headmaster reached down, guiding him confidently, then slowly easing down onto him.

"Fuck yes," Kyoshi moaned, grinning. He let his hands slide to Sho's hips, encouraging his descent. "You're so sexy, Sho. And you're fucking tight as hell."

"That's because I'm not a whore like you."

"What's that supposed to mean? Are you saying I'm not tight?"

Sho smiled. "You're tight. But you accommodate me very easily."

"Well, you didn't think I was a virgin, did you?"

"It wouldn't have been out of the question to presume as much," the Headmaster replied. "You're younger."

"So? You're not that much older than me. How old *are* you?"

"That's my own business."

"Oh, come on. We can be intimate like this and you can't even tell me your age?"

"A gentleman never reveals his true age."

Kyoshi closed his eyes. "Sho. What you're doing there, the way you're...undulating...moving your body...that's so good. You're so sexy."

The Headmaster, who had been working hard to provide Kyoshi with just the right stimulation, was now distracted by his own mounting needs.

The boy opened his eyes and, spying his developing erection, smiled. "Are you always this easily aroused?"

"No," the Headmaster confessed. "Are you?"

"Not really. I mean, not this quickly. You just really turn me on."

"It's the same, for me." Sho was moving against the boy slowly, deliberately, rising and lowering onto his shaft. He reached out and took hold of Kyoshi's hand, guiding him to his anxious member.

Kyoshi's hand was still coated with oil, and the Headmaster gave a little moan as he began stroking him. He adjusted his position to maximize his own pleasure, gasping when he achieved the stimulation he was looking for.

"Ah. Right there?"

"Yes," Sho whispered. "Yes. Right there."

For a few moments they fell silent, but for their mutual gasping and moans, and heavy breathing.

"I'm coming," Kyoshi announced. "I'm about to come."

Sho answered this by placing his hand around Kyoshi's, increasing the intensity of his strokes. "Kyoshi," he whispered. "Ah...Kyoshi."

The boy gasped and then, sucking in his breath, released a sex cry that pushed the Headmaster over the edge; he followed him almost immediately, his semen pumping up and down both their hands.

After a few moments, his heart still pounding, Sho withdrew, moving next to Kyoshi on the bed and pulling him close.

"That was bloody amazing," Kyoshi proclaimed.

"Yes," Sho agreed, closing his eyes.

They lay together quietly, enjoying the moment, both of them so relaxed that they almost dosed off.

"Mmm." Sho stretched, giving Kyoshi a tap. "Let's not fall asleep yet. I'm getting a drink. Would you like something?"

"Sure. What do you have?"

"Lemonade, cream soda, water...I'm not sure what else. Nishi keeps sneaking in and raiding my fridge."

"Nishi?"

"My brother?"

Kyoshi nodded. "Oh, right. I'll take a cream soda. Though I never would have thought you'd be drinking it."

"And why not?"

"It's so...like something a kid would drink."

Sho smiled. "To be honest, I buy it mostly for Nishi. He really is like a kid, sometimes."

"Sounds like it, if he actually raids your fridge? Does he have a key to your house?"

"He knows where I keep it."

"So, you know he's sneaking in and you stock the fridge especially for him? That's so sweet."

"Yes, well. He makes me cookies and always offers them when I visit him."

"Does he know that *you know* he sneaks in?"

"No, that would ruin it for him."

Kyoshi laughed. "I like him already."

"Yes, the two of you...well to be honest, you remind me a bit of him, how he was when he was younger."

"In what way?"

Sho smiled, getting up from the bed. "Your...general naughtiness."

"I like him even more. Hey! Make sure you put lots of ice in it."

The Headmaster nodded, and Kyoshi whistled as he watched him leave. "Nice ass!"

Ignoring him, Sho retrieved the drinks, after cleaning up a bit first and brushing his teeth, for the Headmaster was always very meticulous about cleanliness, especially when it came to sex.

Kyoshi was waiting for him on the bed, fondling himself.

"How can you possibly be aroused already?" Sho demanded.

The boy shrugged. "I'm young."

"Your soda." Sho handed him his drink and then moved onto the bed next to him, eyeing Kyoshi's exceptional physique, his ripped abdomen and muscular chest and arms, and narrow waist and hips. "My, you really are a pretty boy."

"Pretty?" Kyoshi wrinkled his nose. "And I'm not a boy."

"Hmmm."

"Do I look like a boy?"

"No," Sho conceded, smiling.

"Then why did you call me one?"

"I meant nothing by it. It's...of course you're not a boy. You're a young man."

"Thank you. I'll have you remember that."

"However, you *are* a student."

"So?"

"So, I'm always going to think of you...well, as a student, not as a lover."

Kyoshi sulked at this for a few moments. "That sucks, Sho. You're saying...you can fuck me, but you don't consider me your equal."

"I didn't mean it like that."

"How did you mean it, then? Explain."

Sho sighed. "Never mind."

"I consider *you* a lover."

"Do you?" The Headmaster smiled at this.

"Yes. And, if I'm not mistaken, you promised to make love to me tonight. Which means we *are* lovers."

"Point taken." Sho took a drink and then set his glass down on the table next to the bed. Then, slowly, he slid his hand across Kyoshi's abdomen, admiring the tiny hollows and his perfectly sculpted muscles, which twitched and flexed reflexively under his touch.

Kyoshi's response was immediate; his erection swelled, and he spread his legs, breathing harder, as he watched the Headmaster slowly explore him.

"I'm...gonna spill this. Here. Take it." Kyoshi held out his glass, which Sho took and set down on the table next to his own.

Then he continued to run a hand down Kyoshi's body, enjoying the way he stiffened and gasped every now and then.

Suddenly impatient, Kyoshi seized his hand and guided him to his swollen member.

Sho began gently stroking him, smiling when the boy began thrusting into his hand. "Is this...how you like it?"

"Perfect. Kiss me."

The Headmaster obliged him, teasing his mouth open with his own while continuing to stroke him. They kissed; but what they shared was more than a mere kiss, it was a merging between them, forging new paths of intimacy. Before long their initial gentleness had transformed into wild abandon, and they began rolling around on the bed, each feeling as though he could not get enough of the other.

"Ah, Kyoshi," Sho whispered, his voice thick with lust. "Let me make love to you now."

"You're already doing that," Kyoshi replied. "But if you mean you want to go to the next level, I'm ready."

"I want to prepare you again, like before."

His heart beating faster, Kyoshi swallowed. "I won't refuse that."

"Let's try it a different way. Hold your legs up for me."

Kyoshi grabbed hold of his thighs behind the knees and brought his legs toward his shoulders. "Like this?"

Nodding, Sho repositioned himself to gain access to the boy's exposed portal, flicking his tongue sensually along his salty skin before tasting him more intimately.

"Ohhh," Kyoshi moaned, beside himself with pleasure. He began crying out, without even meaning to, completely undone by the Headmaster's skilled lingual arts. Desperate to fondle himself but prevented from doing so by the task of holding his legs open, he began panting. "Sho...Sho!"

Sho stopped. "Yes?"

"I...can you please?" Unable to articulate his desire, Kyoshi lowered his legs and took hold of his shaft, wincing.

Smiling, the Headmaster moved up and continued to pleasure him, taking his cock into his mouth and loving him with his tongue.

"You're so good!" Kyoshi exclaimed. "So...fucking good, Sho! I'm going to come soon."

Hearing this, Sho stopped and took a moment to pour more oil on his now almost painfully rigid erection. He repositioned himself again, hooking Kyoshi's legs with his arms to spread him as he began small tentative thrusts, searching for his entrance.

"Oh!" Kyoshi cried, as the Headmaster finally penetrated. "Fuck yeah! Right there, Sho!"

Careful to keep the boy in exactly the position that seemed to bring him such pleasure, Sho eased into him with a few gentle thrusts before advancing to a more deliberate, slow fuck, his breathing coming hard and fast.

"Sexy boy," he whispered, almost hissed, as he watched Kyoshi's rapture approach.

"Don't stop!"

"I wasn't planning on it," Sho retorted, fucking him a little harder.

"Right there! Holy...oh god!" Shuddering, his eyes rolling back, Kyoshi made a strange, almost choked sound and then let out a wail that could only be described as otherworldly.

"Yes," Sho encouraged, feeling his own ascent rising. "Oh, Kyoshi...."

Then, in a bright white dream, the Headmaster surrendered to his need, riding the waves of his rapture seemingly forever, deep into the inner reaches of his being.

Sho awoke, feeling strangely disoriented. He turned and saw Kyoshi sprawled on the bed, snoring loudly.

Alarmed, he looked at the clock, gasping when he realized they had both overslept.

"Kyoshi!" he shook the boy awake.

"Huh?" Kyoshi opened one eye, looking extraordinarily confused.

"Get up! We...we've overslept."

Kyoshi turned and, apprehending the time, sat up. "Shit."

"I'm such an idiot," Sho hissed. "Now we're *both* late."

"Which sucks for me," the boy agreed, his voice raspy with sleep. "Professor Zucyu doesn't tolerate tardiness. And *he* keeps a paddle on the wall."

"I'll write a note for you," the Headmaster replied, almost dismissively. "But get dressed, we need to get going."

"I can't wait to see that note," Kyoshi grinned. "Dear Professor Zucyu. Please excuse Kyoshi's late arrival. I fucked him so hard we both inadvertently fell asleep; I apologize. - Headmaster Mitsuwa."

"Get up, Kyoshi! We need to get moving."

"What, no breakfast? You expect me to sit through my classes on an empty stomach?"

Sho sighed. "I suppose you're right. We're already this late; get dressed, and I'll meet you in the kitchen."

"Are you going to cook for me?"

"Depends what you want."

"Hotcakes?"

"Try again."

"Eggs and bacon? And toast?"

"Very well. How do you want your eggs?"

"Sunny side up, please," Kyoshi grinned. "This is great. Being waited on by the Headmaster!"

"I'm not waiting on you, I'm simply providing nourishment for you. Don't get used to it."

"Awww. Why not? I love a man who can cook."

"I never said I could cook. I said I would make you breakfast."

"I know you can cook. You live by yourself. I bet you're a great cook."

"Hmmm."

"Well...do I have time for a shower?"

Sho nodded. "Just hurry." He slipped on his robe and rushed to the kitchen, starting a fresh pot of coffee and slamming two skillets onto the range.

Kyoshi was right about Sho's cooking; he was quite experienced at it, and had a good breakfast whipped up in no time. By the time Kyoshi wandered into the kitchen, a towel flung around his shoulders, food was on the table, and fresh, steaming hot coffee gurgled into the carafe.

"Mmmm. I want some coffee, too," Kyoshi said, putting a cigarette in his mouth and preparing to light up.

"You can't smoke in here. And you can't have coffee. You'll have orange juice."

"But I need a smoke! And why can't I have coffee?"

"Both are very bad habits. I'll not encourage either."

"Bloody hell," Kyoshi sighed, returning his smoke to his pack and tossing it on the table. "But *you're* drinking coffee."

"That's because I'm already addicted to it. I don't want to get you hooked on it."

"Oh come on, Sho. Let me have a cup. It smells really good."

"No." The Headmaster sat down at the table, nodding to the other chair. "Now, sit down and eat. We haven't all morning."

Sighing with exasperation, Kyoshi sat down. "You're a bloody tyrant," he mumbled.

"Hush, and eat your food. Or shall I give you a spanking instead?"

Kyoshi sulked at this, stabbing at his eggs with his fork. He took a bite, and then began munching on a piece of bacon. "Hey. This is really good."

Sho smiled, nodding. "I'm glad you approve."

Kyoshi took another bite. "I still don't see why I can't have *one* bloody cup of coffee."

"Don't talk with your mouth full," Sho scolded. "And I told you, *no*, Kyoshi."

Frowning, Kyoshi swallowed. "What makes you think you can start bossing me around? I don't have to answer to you!"

"When you're in my house you'll do as I say. For that matter, when you're at Valemont, you'll do as I say."

"You mean even after you've fucked me, I presume," Kyoshi shot back. "So doesn't that put us on the same level? Why should I have to do what you say?"

The Headmaster studied him for a moment before replying, slowly chewing his food. He took a sip of his coffee, then set the mug back down on the table. "You'll do as I say," he replied calmly. "Otherwise we'll call this whole thing off."

Frowning, Kyoshi finished his meal in silence. "Maybe we should call it off, then," he answered, finally.

"Is that what you want?"

Although this was most definitely *not* what Kyoshi wanted, he suddenly felt too proud to admit it. He shrugged. "Yeah, fine. I don't take orders from my lovers."

Sho gazed at him, trying to judge how serious he was. "Very well," he replied calmly, deciding to call his bluff.

"Good. Because I had a date this weekend anyway."

The Headmaster, though suspecting Kyoshi only said this to provoke him, could not help but feel jealous at this remark. "With who?" he demanded.

"That's my own business."

"Are you finished?" Sho said, abruptly. "Let's get going."

"Fine." Kyoshi stood up, already wishing he could take back his words when he saw Sho's angry look. This was a horrible way to end what had been an incredible night together, and he wasn't even sure how it had happened. He grabbed his smokes, lighting one up deliberately.

"I told you not to smoke in the house!" Sho yelled.

"Fuck you."

Furious, Sho stood up, lunging for him and managing to seize the cigarette from him, putting it out on Kyoshi's half-finished plate of food.

"Dickhead!"

The Headmaster, fed up with Kyoshi's insults, struck him hard across the face.

Kyoshi answered this by giving him a firm shove, knocking him into the table and sending a few dishes crashing to the floor.

They both glared at one another for a few moments. Then, without another word, Kyoshi turned and left.

Chapter 11 - *The Tournament*

SHO PACED THROUGH THE KITCHEN, brooding. He was angry at himself, already, for allowing his night with Kyoshi to be ruined by such a ridiculous squabble. And then he had struck the boy—which was completely uncalled for. After all, he was in a position of authority—he ought to be modeling maturity and restraint, and instead he had lashed out with a violence that actually surprised him, now that he had time to reflect on it.

He had been jealous—ridiculously so—when Kyoshi had taunted him about his date. But he was hardly in a position to demand anything of Kyoshi. The boy was no doubt going out with a peer—completely appropriate. And then he, the Headmaster of Valemont Academy, had lured him back to his house to violate him sexually—completely *inappropriate*.

After anguishing over his behavior for a few moments, he decided to call in with an excuse—something he had never done before—and rather than go directly to the Academy, go visit his brother, Nishi.

He fretted all the way to his brother's house. When he finally arrived, Nishi opened the door with a surprised look on his face.

"I should be publicly whipped," Sho wailed.

Nishi blinked. "Is there nudity involved? Because I might be for it, actually."

"Nish! I'm…a sexual deviant! I'm a perverted old fool!"

"You've come to the right place," Nishi replied, grinning. "Come right on in!"

"This is serious!"

"I can see that. But once again you are attracting the interest of the neighbors with your proclamations." Nishi waved at Old Lady Hammond, who was peering out her window at them, frowning. "Hi Mrs. Hammond!" he shouted. "Don't worry, it's just a penis thing. You wouldn't understand!"

At this, Sho seemed to suddenly snap to life, looking toward the old woman's house in horror. "Nish! You can't say *'penis'* to an old lady!"

Nish giggled, as Sho pushed him inside. "Why not? I bet she gets her freak on, same as anybody." And to taunt his brother a bit more, he stuck his head back outside. "Penis!' he yelled.

Mortified, Sho yanked him inside. "You're impossible!"

"What? You're the one who was screaming about being a sexual deviant on my front porch! Which turned me on, by the way."

Sho sighed. "I *am* a sexual deviant. God, Nish. I can't believe what I did."

"Ooo this sounds good. Hey! Let's get some cookies and coffee and then you can tell me everything. Details! I want details, Sho! And maybe a physical demonstration as well. You can use my penis as a prop, if you need it."

Despite himself, Sho had to smile at his brother's teasing. "You're incorrigible," he laughed.

"Thank you very much! That's just the effect I'm trying to achieve," Nishi shot back. "Do you think it makes me seem all, you know, corrupt and sexy?"

"No," Sho shot back. "It makes you seem like a wiseass."

"Now, let's get back to the important thing. Your sexual deviance." Nishi pointed to a kitchen chair. "Sit your deviant ass down and tell me everything. And, for the record, you're probably not as deviant as you think. Although, personally, I hope so, I already have an erection just contemplating it. So! Fresh coffee coming right up!"

Sho shook his head, sitting down with a sigh. "I should really be at work."

"Ah yes! I noticed that! The Headmaster is skipping work! My, my, you are a bad boy. Perhaps I'll have to give you another paddling."

"Paddling! Oh no!" Sho stood up, suddenly remembering what Kyoshi had told him about Professor Zucyu and the paddle he kept on the wall.

"Relax, Sho. I was just teasing—although if you're that frightened about it, it only makes me want to do it even more."

"I didn't give Kyoshi a note. He was late, too. We...overslept."

"Now we're getting to it. Overslept? This implies sleeping, which suggests that you were in bed together. Am I right?"

Sho nodded, sitting down again with a sigh. "I had him stay the night."

"Oh brother, if you only knew what hardening hath commenced down south at those words—that gave me a boner, and I haven't even heard everything yet. So, you seduced the poor boy into spending the night with you?"

"Yes. I'm ashamed to say it, I did."

"Lots of fucking, then?"

"It was...glorious, actually. But very wrong of me. And then, we quarreled. Everything was spoiled, for no good reason whatsoever."

Nishi poured his brother some coffee, and then set a carton of fresh cream on the table. "I bought that just for you. Now, I'm sure you want to talk about this 'quarrel' or whatever, but how about we start with the glorious night of fucking, first. Like, what positions?"

Sho sighed again. "Where are those cookies you promised?"

"Hmmm? Oh! Here they are!" Nishi opened a tin, showing him what appeared to be heart-shaped cookies with white frosting.

"What? No perverted shapes this time?"

"They're perverted. See?" Nishi held one up. "They were hearts but I cut off the tip. So now they're cute little asses. Here—I made this whole tin for you. You can take them with you."

Sho laughed at this, shaking his head. "What would I do without you? I love your cookies."

"I know you do. That's why I make them. I'm going to seduce you with my baking skills. And, speaking of seduction, you still haven't told me anything. Might I suggest filming it next time? I can set up the camera for you, if you want."

"Can you be serious for five seconds? I'm in a jam, here, Nish. I don't know what to do."

Nish looked at his watch. "Are you timing this or am I?"

"Nish!

Nishi laughed. "I'm sorry. All right. I'll be serious." He put on a stern expression. "But it's really difficult, because you're so cute when you're stressed out like this. I've never seen you this way before. And I have to say, I absolutely love that you seduced a student. I adore that you did that! So maybe I'm not the best person to talk to, because I don't really see anything wrong with it. It's deliciously naughty and a huge turn-on. But besides that, I think you're being too hard on yourself. You're entitled to a little fun. And it's not like you're seducing boys left and right. I think you're in love."

"Perhaps," Sho conceded. "Perhaps I am. Though I know I shouldn't be."

Nishi smiled. "You can't help who you fall in love with."

"I know. But I can help what I do about it. It's not appropriate for me to pursue this relationship."

"But it's a little late for that, don't you think? You're already *in* the relationship."

Sho shook his head. "Maybe not any more. We…had a fight."

"So? A lover's spat. That doesn't mean the relationship is over. So what exactly did you argue about?"

"He wanted to smoke in my house."

Nishi, who had been just about to light up a cigarette, paused. "Um…? Do you mind if I do?"

"No, this is your home. You're entitled to smoke in your own home, go ahead. But I'm equally entitled to insist no one smokes in mine."

Nishi nodded, lighting up and taking a drag. "Yep. I agree with that. So what did he do?"

"He lit up anyway."

At this, Nishi smiled, privately applauding Kyoshi for daring to defy his brother. "Naughty boy. So, you didn't care for that?"

"No...and we quarreled, about, I don't know exactly what. I think I said that since I was older, I'd make the rules. I wouldn't let him have any coffee."

"No coffee? How barbaric." Nish broke off a piece of a cookie and put it on the floor. Immediately, a mouse came scurrying out from under the stove and made himself at home, nibbling on it.

"Nish! You still haven't got rid of that mouse yet? And now you're feeding him?"

"So? He's pretty cute, right?"

"You can't have a rodent running around in your house! It's...unsanitary! Nish, the mouse has to go."

"But I love him," Nishi protested.

"Oh, for heaven's sake! You can't love a mouse!"

"Why not? I'm lonely. He's...my friend. Right Alfred?"

The mouse continued to nibble the cookie, seeming completely relaxed.

"I have an idea. Get a cat! Then you'll have a companion, and take care of the mouse problem at the same time."

"What! Alfred, don't listen to him. He doesn't mean it."

Sho sighed. "Fine. Don't take my advice. But cats make marvelous companions."

"I'm not sure King would agree with you," Nishi remarked. "I don't think he'd be too happy if he saw me bringing a cat inside."

"And how exactly would you tell? You mean he might actually lift his head, or something?"

"Are you insulting my dog?"

"No. I'm sure he's...a fine dog. It's just that he's not the most enthusiastic creature I've ever encountered."

"He's a deep thinker," Nishi replied defensively, "and I don't know why you've never liked him."

"What makes you think I don't like him? I actually have no opinion about him. He doesn't have enough attributes from which to form an opinion."

"You *are* insulting my dog! Or maybe you're jealous, because he seemed to like Kyoshi."

At the mention of Kyoshi's name, Sho grew serious again. "Oh, Nish. Whatever shall I do about Kyoshi?"

"Whatever shall you do?" Nishi teased. "You sound like a princess in a tower, looking off into the sunset."

"Nish!"

"All right. You want to know what I think, honestly?"

"Yes."

"You want it both ways. You want to have authority over him, but at the same time you want to be able to fuck him. If you're in bed together, you're on equal footing. Period. You can't be his lover one moment, and then try to boss him around the next. And that's going to be a problem, since you're the Headmaster at the Academy he's attending."

Sho sighed. "You're right. I know you're right. I do want it both ways. But what should I do?"

"If you want to continue the relationship, I'd do everything you can do avoid him when you're wearing that Headmaster's robe."

"But...I'm teaching his class!"

"What? Since when?"

"Oh! I didn't tell you...one of the teachers, Shin Yumi, passed away. So I'm taking over the class."

"Hmmm. Can you get out of it?"

"I don't think so."

"Well, that's a problem. And I hate to say it, brother, but I don't know what to tell you."

Sho nodded. "I know. I don't know what to do. But...maybe it's resolved itself. Kyoshi was pretty angry after he left. After...I struck him."

"You struck him? Why?"

"Because he deliberately lit up in my house, just to annoy me! He said he wanted to break things off, that he had a date this weekend. And he...called me a name."

Nishi tried to keep from laughing. "A name? What did he call you?"

"Dickhead, I think."

"Brother," Nishi smiled, "isn't that overreacting a bit?"

Sho buried his face in his hands. "Yes. I don't know. Oh, Nishi. What am I going to do? He brings out...the very worst in me."

"And the very best, too, I think," Nishi replied softly. "Well at the very least, I think you should apologize for striking him."

"Yes. I agree. I'll...do that."

"And perhaps the two of you need to talk things out. Tell him everything you've just told me. There's got to be a solution. Perhaps you can transfer over to Kemberly? Maybe the Headmaster there would consider doing a switch?"

"The girl's Academy?" Sho blinked, considering. "I'd never thought of that. Although it still doesn't change the ethics of engaging with a student."

"No, but at least it wouldn't be a student in your Academy. And it would be less awkward for both of you."

"Perhaps so. Although, I don't think I could switch until the term is finished."

"Well, by then you'll have a better idea about how serious this relationship is. Can you survive a few more months?"

Sho nodded. "I think so. I don't really have a choice."

"Good. Then, the next thing I'd do is apologize to Kyoshi. Perhaps you could, I don't know, send a gift of some kind?"

"Yes. All right. I can do that. But...I don't know what to give him!"

"I'm sure you'll think of something. And by the way, I seriously doubt he had a date, after he'd just spent the night with you. I think he told you that to make you jealous."

"You think so?" Sho gazed up at his brother hopefully.

Nishi smiled. "You look so sweet, Sho. But yes, that's what I think. And speaking of this weekend, isn't Kyoshi in the big yudona tournament? That's tomorrow night, you know. Are you going?"

"I told Dean Gerard I would. He gave me tickets. Although, I really don't want to. It's such a violent sport."

"But Kyoshi's the big champion, right? Don't you want to see him fight?"

"I don't know. I don't think so."

"What? You know, they look sexy as hell in those outfits. It's worth going, just to see him in that! Come on, Sho, you're not even the slightest bit curious?"

"Maybe, just a bit," Sho confessed. "But...will you go with me?"

"Of course. I'd love to! Let's call it a date." Nishi grinned, giving him a wink. "Now, you'd better get to work, don't you think? Or were you planning on taking the entire day off? Not that I care one way or another, but if you decide to go on Holiday, I don't want to hear you moaning and groaning later about how you're such a bad person for shirking your responsibilities."

"You're right. I'll go in now," Sho murmured, rising. "Thanks so much, Nish. You're such a big help. I don't know how I'll ever repay you for all the support you've given me lately. If there's anything I can do...."

"Well, you can suck my dick, if you like," Nishi teased, pretending to unfasten his jeans.

"Nish!"

Sho gave him a little shove, which Nish reacted to with a girlish giggle. "Ow! Okay, fine! Be that way! And here I made you ass cookies and everything."

KYOSHI WAS SO ANGRY, HE DIDN'T EVEN CARE that he was late for Professor Zucyu's class. He walked in halfway through the class, and attempted to make for his seat.

"MISTER Sayuki," Professor Zucyu bellowed. "You have missed nearly half the class. What makes you think you can saunter in here without an explanation?"

"I was fucking the Headmaster," Kyoshi replied hotly. "And he forgot to give me a note."

Amidst shocked gasps and titters, Professor Zucyu stood for a moment, hands on hips, a look of utter disbelief on his face. "Kyoshi Sayuki! How DARE you! What insolence! Insulting Headmaster Mitsuwa—I shall save him the trouble of punishing you, for I shall do it myself. Come here, Kyoshi. And I need two volunteers."

With the exception of Seiko, Nampo, and Hisashi, hands shot up eagerly.

Seiko and Nampo exchanged worried looks.

"He's in for it," Hisashi whispered.

"Mr. Konomi and Mr. Rin, please come to the front of the room. You will hold Mr. Sayuki down."

Masami Rin and Eiru Konomi both leapt to their feet, grinning as Professor Reginald Zucyu took his paddle from the wall.

"Mr. Sayuki! I told you to come here! NOW!" With that, the professor slammed the paddle down onto the desk, which made such a deafening sound that nearly everyone in the class jumped.

Slowly, Kyoshi walked toward him, now fully regretting his remark, but seeing no way out of the situation. Masami, in particular, looked utterly thrilled with Kyoshi's fate, gloating at him as he approached.

"Bend over the desk, forearms on the desk. I am going to teach you, Mr. Sayuki, to show a little respect. By the time I'm finished I imagine you'll have a new attitude."

The professor spun the paddle in his hand, waiting as Kyoshi moved into position. It was an immense paddle, nearly a foot long and three quarters of an inch thick, with holes drilled into it for sadistic speed. The man was quite fit, and though it was hard to tell beneath his robes, he was rather muscular, for he lifted weights three times a week, without fail. His hair, nearly as long and dark as Kyoshi's was only barely streaked with gray, and this was only because he had grayed prematurely. He was, in fact, the last person in the world one would want to take the paddle from, for he was also the Coach for the Gentlemen's Racquetball Team, and played tennis, polo and squash regularly.

"Gentlemen, hold him down, and don't let him move," Professor Zucyu ordered.

Masami and Eiru grabbed hold of Kyoshi's arms, pinning him to the desk. Almost immediately, a loud *WHACK!* announced the first strike. It was dreadfully hard, striking the boy on his ass and thighs. Kyoshi winced, closing his eyes. *WHACK!* A second strike. *WHACK!* Strike number three. *WHACK!* Now Kyoshi gasped, instinctively trying to move off the desk. The professor was paddling him so hard he could hardly believe it was possible.

"Hold him down, gentlemen," Professor Zucyu repeated, and then swung again.

WHACK!

Kyoshi whimpered, despite himself, his ass now feeling as though it were about to erupt in flames.

The professor paused for a moment. "You may think, that because your uncle has so generously endowed this institution, that you are permitted to behave like a barbarian, with no recourse. But you'll find no favoritism from me. You'll show the proper respect that's due Headmaster Mitsuwa, and all the professors at Valemont, Mr. Sayuki. I take it, you're feeling this now? Starting to regret your words, perhaps?"

"Yes, professor," Kyoshi murmured.

"Good. However, your punishment is not over yet. These next seven strikes are going to be difficult for you, but I find them necessary, to fully discipline you for your outrageous conduct."

Seven more strikes? Stunned, Kyoshi could only close his eyes, attempting to brace himself for what was coming.

WHACK!

This time he could not help it; he cried out and from that point on, with each strike, his cries became increasingly desperate. The professor gave him twelve strikes with the paddle, which was the most anyone could ever remember having been given at Valemont Academy. The classroom was dead silent, as everyone watched the brutal paddling in horror.

Kyoshi, in tears, could barely stand. Even Masami seemed to feel a bit sorry for him, his eyes wide as Kyoshi slowly stood up.

Professor Zucyu, confident that his point had been driven home, put the paddle back on the wall. "You are dismissed from the rest of class today, Kyoshi," he announced.

Nodding, Kyoshi left the room, his face burning nearly as red as his ass.

SHO SPENT THE REST OF THE DAY FRETTING over how he would apologize to Kyoshi and what he could give him as a gift. The gift had him stumped; what could he, a humble Headmaster, offer a wealthy young man like Kyoshi, who was to inherit a fortune?

After hours of thought, he finally came up with an idea. It was ridiculous, he knew, but he hoped it would at least convey his regard for Kyoshi, and how he viewed him as an equal.

He had decided that he would ask him to his chambers after their class that afternoon; the day seemed to last an eternity, and when it was finally time for class, he rushed to the room, arriving before the students.

The boys filed in, slowly, talking and laughing loudly. Sho tried not to make obvious that he was watching them, but he was keenly aware of each and every person who entered the room. He waited anxiously for class to begin, frowning when Kyoshi's seat remained empty. The bell rang, and the boys immediately fell silent.

"Where is Mr. Sayuki?" he demanded, studying the boys. He could tell by the looks on their faces that they knew something, but no one volunteered any information. "Seiko. Do you know where Kyoshi is?"

Seiko frowned, looking down at his desk. "He's probably in his room, Headmaster. He was paddled today, awfully hard, in Professor Zucyu's class."

"I see," Sho murmured, his heart sinking. It was his fault, he knew, and now it would be even more difficult to patch things up with Kyoshi. He desperately wanted to find out more details, but decided that it would seem odd if he were to inquire too much into the matter. He proceeded with his lecture, finding he was nearly as impatient as his students for the class to end.

Afterwards, just as he was about to leave the room, he ran into Reginald Zucyu.

"Ah! Sho, might I have a moment?"

"Yes?" Sho waited, feigning complete ignorance as to what the professor might want to speak to him about.

"It's about one of your students, Kyoshi Sayuki. You know him, I think?"

Sho nodded. "Ah. Yes. I heard he took a few strikes from you today."

"That he did," Reginald replied, smiling slightly. "Twelve, to be exact."

"Goodness."

"I felt it was well deserved. Do you know, when he arrived late for class, the excuse he gave me?"

Sho swallowed. "I shudder to think."

"He told me—forgive me, I'm sure this is an embarrassment for you—that he was engaged in sexual relations with you—although, of course, I'm paraphrasing—he put it in a much more vulgar manner—and that you had forgotten to give him a note."

Headmaster Mitsuwa blanched at this, unable to even find the words to reply.

Reginald nodded. "Yes. You're quite shocked, I can see. As was I, I assure you. These boys today," he sighed, "are far more bold and disrespectful than they were in my day. I would never dream of making such a proclamation, heavens! But, like you, I believe such unruly behavior deserves swift and uncompromising punishment. I paddled him, on the spot. And I assure you, I put my arm into it. He'll be feeling it for several days. Of course, you may want to give him a few strikes yourself, and at any rate I wanted you to know what he had said."

"Thank you, Reginald," Sho answered, relieved once he realized that the professor hadn't even entertained the possibility that Kyoshi's remark might be true.

After that he made his way back to his chambers, feeling a bit depressed. He wanted to talk to Kyoshi but wasn't sure how to arrange it. He couldn't very well go marching over to the dormitory—unless of course, he wanted to feign being angry over Kyoshi's remarks—but the last thing he wanted to do was to add to the subterfuge, or be seen with Kyoshi any more than was absolutely necessary.

No, he would simply have to wait for the opportunity to talk to him, or allow Kyoshi to come to him. Perhaps, at the yudona tournament, he would be able to corner him, under the pretense of congratulating him for his efforts there, and beg for a few minutes alone.

So, with a heavy heart, he returned home that day without seeing or talking to the boy, wishing that he had not been so foolish as to allow the day to get off to such a bad start. He could only hope that he would be able to amend matters the following day, at the tournament.

"Oh, Kyoshi," Seiko whispered, aghast when he saw the dark bruises on the boy's buttocks and thighs. "That's completely brutal. It must hurt something awful."

"It hurts a bit," Kyoshi conceded, sighing. "So how about you give me three of those pills?"

"I'll give you two," Seiko offered, "but three is too much. Your heart could stop, or something."

Kyoshi groaned as Seiko placed the icepack on his exposed rear. He was lying on his bed, face down, his pants pulled down to his knees. "Even the ice hurts," he complained.

"I'm sorry. It should numb it, though, pretty soon. The Headmaster asked about you in class today."

"I bet he did," Kyoshi replied, scowling. "That fuck!"

"Um...Kyoshi? Was it true what you said? I noticed you weren't here last night."

"Yes. It's true. But that was stupid of me to say so. I was so pissed off, I wasn't thinking straight."

"I don't understand. You spent the night with him? Then why are you angry?"

"We had a fight. And the prick struck me! Bloody asshole."

"Oh. What did you fight about?"

"Just...stupid shit. I don't know. He wants to control everything I do. So I told him, the whole thing was off."

Seiko paused for a moment. "Well, maybe that's a good thing. It doesn't seem right, the Headmaster being involved with you."

"Yeah, maybe. I don't know. How the hell am I going to fight tomorrow, when I can hardly move?"

"I'm sorry, Kyoshi. I wish I could do something to help."

"How about giving me those pills!"

"I've got them," Seiko answered. "And here's some water. Open your mouth."

Seiko helped him take the pills and a drink of water. "Is there anything else I can do?"

Kyoshi paused for a moment. "Yeah. There is. Bring me my phone, and my address book—it's that silver book there, on the desk."

"This?" Seiko held up the small, shiny silver book.

"Yeah. Or, actually, just look up a name for me. Rieko...no, wait. How about...Jiji." Kyoshi smiled slightly. "Give me the number."

Seiko flipped through the book. "Geez. These are all girls."

"So, is that a crime? Girls can be interesting you know."

Hmmm. Maybe for *you*. Personally I never cared much for them."

"Sometimes they're amusing."

"What, are you planning on going on a date or something?"

"Yep. I want to bring someone with me to the tournament tomorrow." Now that Kyoshi had told Sho he had a date that weekend, he intended to make good his boast. Besides, he needed a good fuck. Jiji was just the thing—beautiful, buxomly, with a shapely ass, and silky smooth thighs—and eager for him. He'd had her a few times before and she was easy to grease—she came even faster than he did, with a cute little squeaky cry that gave him an erection just thinking about it.

Seiko read him the number, and Kyoshi keyed it in, waiting for the relay signal.

"Hello?"

"Hi doll. Remember me?"

"Kyoshi? Kyoshi Sayuki?" The girl sounded ecstatic.

"Guilty. You doing okay?"

"Sure! But we miss you...where are you? They said you'd transferred somewhere else."

"I'm at Valemont now. I just now got all moved in and I found your number. I'm glad I didn't lose it, 'cuz I wanted to ask you out this weekend. I'm in the yudona tournament tomorrow night, wanna come?"

"Oh! Yes, I'd love to! I have another date but...I'll break it, for you."

"Great. I'll pick you up at six. And baby, can you wear those cute over-the-knee socks you know I like? You look so cute in those. Underwear is optional."

Jiji giggled. "You're so bad, Kyoshi."

"You like me that way. I'm serious about the socks, though. Six then?"

"Okay!"

"Bye, doll."

Kyoshi hung up, smiling smugly.

Seiko shook his head. "You snake."

"You're just jealous, because I'm getting some ass tomorrow night, and you're not."

"What makes you think I'm not?" Seiko demanded. "I'll have you know I have a date. With Kimura Jiro."

"Again? Then you two are really hitting it off, I guess?"

"Yep. And remember that party I told you about after the tournament, at Hisashi's cottage? Well, the entire band's coming. They're going to put on a concert for us."

"No shit? Abort Mission?"

"Yep."

"Good, then we can double. That'll be a blast. Though I doubt I can wait until we get to the cottage to have my way with Jiji. I intend to find a dark corner somewhere at Kingsley Hall. I always need a good hard fucking after a match."

Seiko nodded. "I'm the same way, with my sports. But what makes you think she'll agree to your agenda?"

"She'll be begging for it. How could she not?"

Seiko tossed the book at him, which hit Kyoshi on the head. "Ow! Asshole!"

"You're an arrogant fellow."

Kyoshi laughed, rubbing his head. "What? Can I help it if I'm a sex god?"

"Yeah right. In your dreams."

"I told you, Seiko, anytime you want a little demonstration, all you have to do is ask."

"And I told you, you're not my type. Anyway, I don't think friends should fuck. It always spoils everything."

Kyoshi snorted at this. "Yeah, well, what makes you think I'm your friend?"

"Dickhead! And I just gave you two of my pills!"

"Calm down," Kyoshi laughed. "You know I'm just teasing."

Seiko leaned against the desk, nodding. "Yeah. I know. Shit. I can't believe you actually said that in Zucyu's class. I thought he was going to implode or something. You've got a lot of balls, you know that?"

"Yeah, well. It was a pretty stupid thing to say. This is...probably the worst I've ever felt."

Seiko nodded. "He was pretty brutal. You're going to be black and blue for days."

"I know it. Although...I'm starting to feel those pills, now. Ahhh...finally!"

There was a moment's pause. Then, Seiko, who had been aimlessly flipping through one of Kyoshi's books, suddenly grew serious. "Kyoshi. I feel like I should tell you this...as a friend. What you're doing with...Headmaster Mitsuwa. I don't think it's right. I mean, I'm really surprised that he'd do something like that...with you. He's the Headmaster. Shit, he's always whipping our asses raw for misconduct, but then he gets to fuck one of his students? It's...it bothers me. It makes him seem...well, I wouldn't have admitted this before, but I always sort of respected him. He seemed like, you know, the sort of person you could trust. But now, with you...I just find it very peculiar. If you want my honest opinion, I think you should report him to Dean Gerard. Or maybe I should."

At this, Kyoshi's head shot up. "No! Please, Seiko! Don't."

Seiko frowned. "But...I thought you were angry with him. Don't you think he should face the consequences for what he's done?"

Kyoshi shook his head. "I don't want him to lose his position or anything. Yeah, I was pissed. I still am. But...Seiko...I, to be honest, I think I'm falling in love with him."

Seiko was silent for a few moments. "I don't know, Kyoshi. I'm starting to feel really uncomfortable about this."

"You promised you wouldn't say anything! Please, Seiko! I'm begging you, as a friend. Please don't say anything. Besides," Kyoshi continued, quickly, "I'd get expelled from Valemont, for sure."

"That's true," Seiko nodded, frowning. "I didn't think of that. They might expel you, you're right."

"And then Uncle would have my balls in a vise! So promise me again you won't say anything!"

"All right," Seiko sighed. "But I just want it to go on record that I'm not comfortable with it."

"Duly noted," Kyoshi replied, relieved.

In truth, he didn't care whether or not he was expelled from Valemont. But when he thought of Sho facing some sort of disciplinary committee, or even losing his position—he couldn't bear the thought.

He had been stupid to say such a thing in Professor Zucyu's class, he knew—but at the same time he had been perfectly aware that no one would take his words seriously. And now that he had spent the afternoon thinking about what had happened, he felt a little sorry for how he'd left things with Sho that morning. The night had been extraordinary, and even though he was still upset, he didn't seriously want any harm to come to Sho. It was true, what he'd told Seiko.

He was falling in love with Headmaster Mitsuwa.

"IS THAT WHAT YOU'RE WEARING?" NISHI DEMANDED, as he got into Sho's car.

"What? It's a formal school function. Why shouldn't I wear my robes?"

"Sho! No one goes to games dressed like that! What, were you planning to bring your crop whip, too?"

Sho smiled at his brother's teasing. "No, I left that in my chambers."

"Hmmm. On the other hand, that might have been kinky, if you'd brought it. Hey! Want to punish me sometime?"

"You really think I shouldn't wear my robes?"

"Hell no! Take them off—what are you wearing under them?"

"Just, I don't know," Sho murmured, unzipping his robe and tossing it into the back seat.

He was wearing a pair of neatly pressed dark trousers and a skintight, black turtleneck.

"Ah! Much better. You look sexy in that shirt," Nishi grinned. "I can see your chest and arm muscles. Very nice."

Sho raised an eyebrow at this, though couldn't help smiling at his compliment.

"Are you wearing cologne?"

"Maybe."

"Oooo. It's sexy as hell. Damn, brother! This really *is* a date, huh?"

"What makes you think I'm wearing it for *you*?" he countered.

"Admit it. You're finally caving to my advances. You know, we could pull over somewhere right now, if you want. There's still time for a little penis play before the tournament."

Sho laughed at this, despite himself. "Penis play?"

Nishi grinned. "Come on, brother." He slid a hand teasingly between Sho's legs.

"Ahh!" Sho startled, swerving on the road. "Nish! I'm trying to drive, here!"

Nishi giggled, pulling away. "Oh, all right. Big baby. Hey! Do you suppose Kyoshi's friend will be there tonight, you know, Seiko?"

Sho shrugged. "How should I know?"

"Because he's a dream. A wet dream, anyway. Damn. I'd love to get the boy on his knees."

"Don't even think about it."

"What? Are you trying to suggest you're the only one who gets to frolic with the natives?"

Sho only smiled, refusing to answer.

"Hypocrite. Rogue!"

"Rogue?" Sho laughed, turning to give Nishi a smile. "Brother. I love you, you know that?"

"Oh, Sho. Pull over now, I think I just stained my pants."

The Headmaster only shook his head at this, rolling his eyes. "You know what I mean."

"Yeah. I know," Nishi smiled. "And I love you, too. So, did you and Kyoshi patch things up?"

Now Sho frowned. "No. I didn't get a chance to see him."

"So, you're going to approach him tonight, then?"

"If I can...garner the courage."

"Garner the courage?" Nishi laughed for several moments. "You're so funny, Sho. Garner the courage. Ha!"

"What? What's funny about that?"

Nishi was now coughing, he had been laughing so hard. "Shit! I can't breathe!"

"Oh, for heaven's sake. Must you make a mockery of everything?"

"Yes," Nishi gasped, between giggles, "I must. I must make a mockery of everything, dearest brother. Providing I can garner the courage, first."

Sho answered that by punching Nishi in the arm.

"Ow!" Nishi complained holding his arm. "Help! I'm being abused!"

"Ha! That's nothing," Sho teased, grinning. "I'll pull over this car and show you what abuse really is."

"Will you, please?" Nishi begged. "Please abuse me, brother! Oh! I really did practically stain myself that time. Shit! I have the biggest erection, Sho. I'm serious, actually."

Sho turned to regard his brother, his eyes lowering to the bulge his pants. "You're disgusting," he sighed.

"What, you're blaming me? You're such a tease!" Nishi adjusted himself grumpily. "Would you mind, awfully, if I just relieved myself here? You don't have to look."

"Nish! Don't you dare!"

"I won't get it on the car seat! I promise, I...I'll use a tissue."

"Oh, for heaven's sake! You can't be serious!"

"Well, pull over then, so I can run down to that little wood down there. Please? Seriously, I'm about to burst, here."

Sho shook his head, pulling the car over to the side of the road. "You're really something else. Hurry up—and not in the car."

Nishi reached out and grabbed his wrist. "Sho. How about just this once? Just touch me."

"Nish!" Sho cried, yanking his hand away! "Cut it out!"

"Please?" Nishi unzipped his pants, revealing himself. "I'm begging you."

"Ahh!" Sho covered his eyes with his hand. "Put it away! Nish!"

Then, Nishi had moved close, and was trying to kiss him. Sho pushed him away, and for several moments they wrestled, as Nishi tried to force his brother to touch his erection.

"What is WRONG with you?" Sho bellowed. "Have you gone completely insane?!"

"Oh, Sho." Nishi managed to straddle his brother, his ass touching the horn of the vehicle, which blared so loudly it startled them both. "Just touch me! Just...oh god! Oh GOD!" Nishi then ejaculated, his semen spraying onto Sho's shirt and pants.

"You disgusting little freak!" Sho shoved his brother away violently, horrified to see the semen on his clothes. "You...you...came on me! I'm going to be sick!"

"I'm sorry," Nishi mumbled, seeming actually a bit embarrassed. "I'm sorry, Sho. Really, I...I'm not sure how that happened."

"What do you mean you're not sure how it happened! You just attacked me, exposed yourself to me and then ejaculated on me!"

"I didn't hurt you, did I?"

"No," Sho grumbled, wiping the semen from his clothes with a handkerchief. "Just psychologically. God! Now I'm going to be in therapy for ten years."

"I'm awfully sorry, Sho," Nishi whispered, his eyes filling with tears. "I didn't mean for it to go that far. Honestly. But then...well, suddenly...it was like I couldn't control myself."

Sho sighed. "All right. Forget it."

Nishi bowed his head. "I am a freak. I'm...a bad person."

"No, Nish. You're not. I said that in anger."

"I was just playing around...but then it...I just," Nishi's voice cracked as a tear slid down his cheek.

"Oh, Nish. Don't cry. You know I can't bear to see you cry."

"Do you forgive me? Do you still love me, Sho?"

"Of course I love you."

"I don't know what's wrong with me," Nishi wailed.

"Hush. Come here." Sho held his brother, who cried for a few moments in his arms.

"I miss Mom," Nishi whispered.

"Me too," Sho replied, finding his own eyes filling with tears.

"I'm so lonely, Sho."

"Oh, baby. It's okay. I didn't mean to yell at you." Sho put his hand in Nishi's hair, stroking him in a comforting way. "I love you, Nish. I'll always love you."

"Good," Nish replied, his voice muffled by Sho's shirt, "because I'm getting another erection."

"Nish!" Sho pushed him away, disgusted.

"I'm teasing! I'm teasing!" Nishi laughed. He wiped the tears from his face, then turned to Sho, his expression serious. "You won't tell anyone about this, will you, Sho?"

"Of course not, love. Let's just forget about it."

Nishi nodded, swallowing hard. The rest of the drive to the tournament was mostly in silence, the brothers each deep in thought.

THE YUDONA TOURNAMENT WAS HELD AT KINGSLEY HALL, in Jufi. As soon as the brothers arrived, they realized it was going to be difficult to even find a parking place.

"Shit," Nishi exclaimed. "I wasn't expecting THIS much of a crowd. Hey! What seats do we have? Are they any good?"

"I...don't really know. Dean Gerard gave them to me. Here," Sho said, tossing Nishi his wallet, "they're in there."

"Hey, thanks, brother! Mind if I take a bill, too?" Nishi teased.

"I don't care," Sho replied honestly. "Do you need money, Nish?"

"I was just joking around," Nishi replied. "Holy shit! You're loaded! Do you always carry this much cash around with you?"

"Hmmm? Oh. I don't know. I guess I just like to be prepared for anything. Go ahead, Nish, if you need something—take as much as you want."

"Really? You're really cool, Sho. You're like, the best brother ever!"

"Yeah, I know."

"Wow! These seats...holy shit! You've got seats in the FRONT ROW! You're on the floor, Sho!"

"Really? Huh. I didn't realize that." Now Sho frowned, suddenly realizing it would be hard to hide the fact that he had come to see Kyoshi if they had front row floor seats.

"And look—did you even bother to look at these tickets, Sho? You have reserved VIP parking!" Nishi held up the red stubs, grinning. "No walking for us!"

"But where's the reserved parking?"

"Over there, where those red flags are, see? VIP Parking? Right by the entrance!"

"Well, that was very kind of Gabe," Sho murmured. "He didn't even mention how good the seats were, when he gave them to me."

"So I can really take a couple bills? You don't mind?"

"Sure, no problem." Sho smiled at his brother, who rewarded him with a beautiful, heart-melting grin.

"This is going to be awesome, tonight," Nishi exclaimed. "I've never seen a yudona match up this close before. Hell, we might even get splattered with blood!"

Sho flinched at this. "Heaven forbid."

Nishi laughed. "You don't look too excited, brother. You really don't like yudona, do you?"

"I told you, I find it completely barbaric. Although I suppose it has some redeeming elements, in terms of the discipline involved to attain it."

"Not just that. It's an ancient art form, really. When you see it in motion you'll understand. It's really beautiful. Plus the fighters are almost always hot."

Sho smiled slightly, wondering what it would be like to see Kyoshi pumped up for the match, his upper body shining with oil, wearing nothing but the loose, but very thin silk-like pants that were the hallmark of the yudonii.

"Do you know his best?" Nishi asked.

"What?"

"His best—which of the Three Rounds is his best?"

"Nish. I really don't know anything about yudona."

"Well, surely you've watched a match before, somewhere?"

"No. I've seen...scenes, like in films and whatnot."

"Wow. Okay, there are Three Rounds. The First is with the toika—you know what that is, right?"

"You mean that...long stick?"

Nishi nodded. "Right. And the Second Round is bare hands, just basic fighting, from the set of legal moves. If either yudonii wins both Rounds, the match is over. But if they're tied, they move to the Third Round. That's the most exciting Round, and the roughest. There are no rules, no illegal moves. Just whatever it takes to bring the other fighter down without any weapons, other than the toika."

Sho shivered, worried. He hoped the match would be over in two Rounds, because he couldn't bear the thought of Kyoshi being hurt.

"Don't worry, Sho," Nishi whispered. "He'll be okay. He must be pretty good, to have made it to the finals."

"We're here," Sho replied, pulling into one of the reserved spots. An attendant rushed over to secure their VIP stubs.

"We've never been here before," Sho remarked. "Which way is the arena?"

"Just follow the red arrows. You go in this entrance, here, which takes you straight to the floor."

"Woo hoo! No standing in line," Nishi cheered, gleefully. "And it's getting ready to rain, too!"

The attendant smiled. "Yes, you're the lucky ones, to be sure. Have a nice evening."

"This is great, Sho," Nishi avowed, as they got out of the car and proceeded inside. "VIP parking and our own private entrance! What did you do, give the Dean a blow job?"

Sho shook his head. "I guess the Dean gets a certain number of reserved seats, or something. I really had no idea."

"Well this is definitely the way to do it, no fighting the crowds, no searching for parking, no walking, no standing in line! Hell, I bet they'll even bring us a cup to piss in! If you don't enjoy this match, tonight, I'm giving up on you."

But Sho knew he wasn't going to enjoy the match. He was dreading it, now that Nishi had described what was in store, and frightfully worried for Kyoshi. As they moved into the arena, he realized, with a bit of awe, what a big deal the tournament was. The arena was packed—and loud. They were escorted to their seats, which were, in fact, directly on the floor, just a few feet away from the fighting mats.

The moment they sat down, Sho saw Kyoshi. He was standing with his back to him, the muscles in his arms bulging and flexing, his long hair pulled back and fastened behind his head with a knotted cord, the tail hanging down between his shoulder blades. He wore only the low riding silk pants, his upper body bare and glistening from the oils that had been rubbed into his skin.

"Hey! There he is—whoa! He is gorgeous, Sho! Look at him!"

Sho nodded, swallowing hard. Then his eyes narrowed as he studied Kyoshi. "Who's he talking to?"

At that moment, Kyoshi took a step back, and Sho could then see a young girl sitting on the front row, grinning up at him. She was dressed in the merest pretense of a skirt, her legs crossed in a manner that exposed a good expanse of her thighs, and her upper body garbed only in a tiny top that was laced up the front, tightly, over her rather generous breasts. Kyoshi bent down and whispered something in her ear, allowing a hand to rest on her thigh.

"He *did* bring a date! And it's...a girl!"

Nishi smiled at his brother's unveiled jealousy. "Now now, brother. I hate to break it to you, but young men do sometimes like to date girls. Not any that I know personally, but I've heard it's the case."

"She's...look how she's dressed! The little harlot!"

Nishi laughed. "Sho! You're being a bit severe on the poor girl, don't you think? She just wearing the latest fashions, I'll wager."

"He's got his hand on her thigh! Such audacity! Perhaps he should just throw her down on the mat and take her right here, in front of everyone!"

"Hmmm. That might be interesting," Nishi teased. "Now, calm down. He *is* a young man, after all. And as far as he knows, you and he are fighting. I seriously doubt she means anything to him. He probably just asked her because he had told you he had a date. I'll bet he asked her after you had that fight."

Sho opened his mouth to speak, but was silenced when Kyoshi suddenly turned around. He was breathtaking, the low-riding silken pants revealing every hollow in this lower torso, the muscles in his upper body sharply cut and defined, his manner confident and suddenly serious and brooding.

"Oh my," Nishi remarked.

Sho couldn't speak; Kyoshi had stopped, staring directly at him.

"He sees me," Sho breathed.

Kyoshi and Sho stared at each other for a long moment. Then, with a slight smile, Kyoshi bowed to him, then turned away.

"See that?" Nishi exclaimed. "He bowed to you!"

"I saw," Sho whispered, unable to keep from smiling.

"I'll bet you anything he ditches his date. He's thrilled you came, that much is clear."

Sho swallowed, looking over again at the young girl who Kyoshi had been talking to. She was pretty, no question, but Headmaster Mitsuwa found it absurd that he was competing with a young girl.

What could Kyoshi possibly want with her? Someone so inexperienced...surely, when it came to matters in the bedroom, Sho was the clear choice. Or had he only imagined that their sex had been that good? Perhaps Kyoshi had only been pretending.

He thought for a moment, then smiled. No. Kyoshi's cries had been genuine. He was sure of it. That was one thing Sho had to his advantage—experience and skill in the pleasuring arts.

"He keeps looking over at you, Sho," Nishi whispered. "See that?"

Sho looked back at Kyoshi, just in time to see him quickly turn away.

"Oh look! Seiko did come. He's sitting next to that girl," Nishi announced, then frowned. "Fuck. Looks like he has a date, though."

Sho's attention was suddenly diverted by the other young yudona fighter on the mat. He gasped. It was hard to believe the boy could be a student—he looked like a full-grown man, his muscles immense. "Oh no," he breathed.

"What? Oh," Nishi fell silent upon seeing Kyoshi's competition. "Wow. This is going to be a tough fight. He's rather good-looking though, don't you think?"

Sho could only gape at the young man, whose fierce dark eyes hinted at the intensity he was capable of. Now the two yudonii, who had previously ignored each other, had locked gazes, each sizing up the other. For some moments they both stood, silently, neither one wanting to be the first to break the gaze.

"Look at that," Nishi whispered. "Oh, brother. This is going to be an awesome match!"

The Headmaster's feelings on the match couldn't have been more different than Nishi's. His heart was now pounding; he felt dreadfully worried for Kyoshi.

"This can't be right," he whispered. "He ought to be disqualified! He...he can't possibly be a student!"

Nishi put a reassuring hand on his knee. "It will be all right, Sho. Kyoshi wouldn't be here if he couldn't hold his own."

"I hate this sport!" Sho exclaimed.

"Give it a chance! It hasn't even started yet."

"I don't think I can watch."

Nishi only smiled, knowing full well Sho would be as riveted as everyone else. There was nothing boring about yudona. It was a tense, violent sport that was utterly captivating to watch. A true test of physical strength, agility, and cunning.

The arena was now completely full, and the loudspeakers came on to announce the beginning of the match. "Welcome to the National Young Gentlemen's Yudona Championship!"

The crowd went wild, screaming and applauding, and stomping their feet.

"Goodness," Sho remarked, holding his hands to his ears.

"The yudona fighters you see before you have proven themselves to be the best in the entire nation! From Grandview Park Academy, we have Yon Yoshimatzu! And from the Valemont Academy for Distinguished Young Men, Kyoshi Sayuki! Gentlemen! Round One begins now!"

The crowd, which had been positively deafening, now suddenly fell almost completely silent, but for a very low murmur.

The two young men picked up their toikas, slowly circling each other on the mat. The toikas were long, wooden rods about an inch in thickness, nearly six feet in length. Yon swung first, aiming for Kyoshi's calves, but Kyoshi jumped, easily evading the swing, and then answered him with a jab toward his chest. But Yon managed to jump back, then blocked him with his own rod. Kyoshi spun around and knelt down, managing to strike Yon on the thigh.

"Good one!" Nishi whispered.

Yon barely flinched, although it was clear the impact of the toika had to be painful. He had already launched a counterstrike with a hard hit to Kyoshi's upper arm.

Sho immediately stood up, concerned when Kyoshi winced. Nishi pulled him back down. "He's all right, brother."

"This is absurd!" Sho whispered. "He'll be killed!"

The two fighters had picked up the pace and now fought wildly, each successfully blocking the offensive of the other. Both Kyoshi and Yon were sweating, but neither let up.

Then suddenly, Yon's troika went flying, rolling off the mat. The crowd gasped and Kyoshi, smiling, now began chasing Yon around the mat, as the yudonii desperately tried to evade his blows.

"What's going on?" Sho whispered. "Why doesn't he pick up his stick?"

"He can't. Now all Kyoshi has to do is strike him once, and he's won the Round."

Encouraged by this, Sho smiled. It was clear Kyoshi knew he would win the Round, from his body language. He was toying with Yon, making him dash around the mat, trying to tire him out.

"Why doesn't the other one just give up?" Sho whispered.

"It's not allowed, brother. He has to take his blow. This is Kyoshi's chance to injure him as much as possible."

"This...this is completely barbaric," Sho announced.

"But, fortunately, Kyoshi's won this Round. You should be proud."

Kyoshi, finally seeming bored with his game, finally leapt forward and swung with all his might, hitting Yon on his thighs. The fighter cried out, doubling over.

"Round won by Sayuki!"

At this, about half the people in the arena, including Sho and Nishi, leapt to their feet, cheering. The other half—who had come to cheer Yon, watched him with concern. The young fighter had five minutes to recover from the First Round before the Second Round began, and he appeared to be in severe pain.

Sho, though relieved that Kyoshi had won, now sat down, scowling. "I hate this," he announced. "That poor boy—look at him."

"Show a little patriotism, brother. It's our national sport."

"It's sick. I deplore it. I wish I hadn't come."

"Kyoshi fought well. And he gave the boy a good hit—which will make the next Round more difficult for Yoshimatzu."

"I can't believe how popular this is! I'm living among savages!"

Kyoshi, who had been wiping the sweat from his face and taking a long drink of water, now turned toward the Headmaster, curious as to his reaction. He had been stunned to see Sho there — especially since Sho had so openly proclaimed to hate the sport. He could only assume he had come specially to see him. And he found this thought excited him. He was anxious to patch things up with Sho, and more than that, dying to spend another night with him.

He almost wished he hadn't brought a date, though there wasn't much he could do about that now. Besides, the girl was a knockout, and Kyoshi knew he would need some immediate sexual relief. As soon as the match was over he was going to drag her off to one of the classrooms and have his way with her. She had already shown her interest, by wearing the cute over-the-knee socks he'd asked her to wear. And when he had leaned down to ask her whether she'd opted for underwear or not, she had replied, coyly, "You'll have to find out."

He found his gaze moving toward her, pleased to see that she was staring back at him with a look of utter adoration. She waved at him, smiling. He nodded slightly, then drained the rest of his water, turning his attention back to his opponent, who seemed to show a miraculous recovery, now standing up and cracking his knuckles. He was glaring at Kyoshi, looking decidedly displeased.

Despite himself, Kyoshi shivered slightly, secretly dreading the next Round. Yoshimatzu would have the advantage, because they were limited to a small set of moves.

With his tremendous physical strength, Yoshimatzu would be difficult to defeat. In fact, Kyoshi rather suspected he could not do it. But he was confident in his ability to win Round Three, as long as he could survive Round Two. But he knew it was entirely possible that Yoshimatzu would disable him completely, perhaps even knock him out. The boy looked furious, and Kyoshi knew he had been a bit cruel with his blow, but he had felt it was the only way he would even have a chance at winning Round Two. Besides, it showed his opponent he wasn't afraid to be ruthless, if he had to. Yudona was a game as much about psychology as physical strength.

"Gentlemen, begin Round Two now!"

The crowds quieted as Kyoshi and Yon once again circled each other on the mat. Kyoshi already knew his strategy—he would strike him as often as he could, as hard as he could, on his thigh, in the very area where he had struck him with the toika, which now boasted a long welt-mark. Yon was clenching and unclenching his fists, gritting his teeth.

Though Kyoshi was careful to stare him down without showing fear, his heart was pounding. He knew the championship could be over in a matter of just a few minutes. If Yoshimatzu managed to strike him hard enough, in the right place, Kyoshi would go down, perhaps even be seriously injured.

Just as he was thinking this, he saw Yoshimatzu rush toward him, and then, in the next instant, he felt a tremendous pain in his face, and he saw a bright white, spinning light, and then, he was falling, endlessly, into a dark abyss.

Chapter 12 - *Sho's Jealousy*

"KYOSHI!" SHO LEAPT OUT ONTO THE ARENA FLOOR before Nishi could even stop him.

"Sho! You can't do that! He'll be disqualified!" Nishi tried in vain to stop his brother, but the crowd was so loud that Sho didn't even hear him.

But even if he had heard Nishi, Sho wouldn't have stopped. He dashed across the floor toward his fallen lover, scowling when one of the referees put a hand out to stop him.

"Off the floor! Off the floor!" the referee screamed.

"I'm Headmaster Mitsuwa of Valemont Academy, and you will step aside and allow me to examine my student or I'll pull Valemont out of this and every other tournament!"

Sho stood with his hands on his hips, shouting, and looking about ready to punch the referee in the face. The referee frowned and turned back to the others, unsure of what to do. Never before in the history of the tournament had anyone dared step out onto the floor.

"We seem to have a... situation," the announcer remarked. "Who? Just a moment...yes, we have confirmation...that is Sho Mitsuwa, Headmaster of Valemont Academy demanding to examine Kyoshi Sayuki. This may mean a disqualification."

The crowd began to boo to show their displeasure at the match ending in such a fashion. Sho pushed past the referee and rushed to Kyoshi's side, brushing his hair back from his face. There was a dark red area on his cheek where he'd been hit, but more worrisome than this was that Kyoshi was completely unconscious.

"Kyoshi," Sho whispered, shaking him. "Kyoshi! Wake up!" He turned to look around, furious. "Where's the medic?"

"Right here," the medic replied, rushing over with an icepack, his face reddening. He'd been flirting with one of the students from Grandview and hadn't reacted as quickly as he should have to Kyoshi's knock-out.

"Nice of you to join us!" Sho was so furious he grabbed the icepack from the medic and put it on Kyoshi's face himself.

"I'm sorry," the medic murmured.

Kyoshi stirred and then groaned.

"Kyoshi! Come on now, open your eyes!" Sho bent close to him, almost forgetting himself. All he cared about was Kyoshi. He was already kicking himself for not forbidding him to attend the tournament. What if he were seriously hurt?

Kyoshi's eyes fluttered open and he looked at Sho with confusion.

"Sho?" he whispered.

The referees exchanged glances, a little surprised at the intimacy obviously shared between Kyoshi and the Headmaster.

Sho was overjoyed but managed to catch himself before he began planting kisses all over Kyoshi's face, which he longed to do. "I beg your pardon?" he answered. "It's Headmaster Mitsuwa to you."

Kyoshi blinked, frowning, suddenly seeming to realize where he was. "What are you doing here? Get off the floor! You'll have me disqualified!"

"You're not disqualified," one of the referees informed him. "However, you need to be up in three minutes or you'll forfeit the Round."

Sho stood up, a little hurt by Kyoshi's anger. He wanted to say something but realized it wasn't the time, so he simply turned and left, returning to his seat.

"We've just had word...there is no disqualification, Sayuki may proceed to Round Three."

Yon Yoshimatzu had watched the situation with growing concern. Though of course he wanted to be named the champion, he didn't want to be responsible for seriously injuring another player.

He'd already come to respect Kyoshi Sayuki and secretly hoped his opponent would make it to the Round. When Kyoshi finally found his feet he nodded, walking away to prepare himself for Round Three.

"You lunatic," Nishi laughed, when Sho returned to his seat. "What made you run out there like that?"

"He could have been killed! I ought to pull Valemont out of the tournament!"

"Come now, you know perfectly well you can't do that. It's a very popular sport, you know."

"Why? What on earth is the appeal? I'm mystified."

"You're lucky Kyoshi wasn't disqualified. He would have been pretty angry with you, I'll wager."

"I wish he had been," Sho muttered, scowling. "I can't stand watching this."

"There's only more Round and then it will all be over."

"I'm not watching," Sho announced, sitting down and staring stubbornly at his lap, his arms crossed on his chest.

"Brother, I haven't seen you this upset since, well...since I don't know when."

"I never should have come!"

Nishi sat down next to Sho, throwing an arm over his shoulder. "Oh come on, now. He's fine. It was worth it just to see him in those sexy yudona pants, right?"

"I can't sit through any more of this."

"Sure you can. It will be over in just a few minutes."

Sho shook his head. "No, I—"

"Gentlemen, begin Round Three now!" the announcer proclaimed.

The Headmaster immediately looked up, the blood rushing from his face. "They've got those sticks again."

Nishi nodded. "That's right. They'll use those as long as they can. Kyoshi's got the advantage, there."

Kyoshi and Yon circled one another, each holding their troika before them. Kyoshi grinned, which seemed to fluster his opponent. In the next instant Yon's troika went flying, and then Kyoshi swung with all this strength.

But Yoshimatzu surprised him by suddenly reaching out and seizing the troika, yanking it from Kyoshi's hands.

"Can he do that?" Sho cried.

"Unfortunately, yes."

Kyoshi reacted to the loss of his troika by spinning around in the air and landing a flying kick on Yoshimatzu's forearm; Yon immediately dropped the troika, holding his arm with a look of horror.

The crowd howled their approval as Yon backed away from Kyoshi.

"What just happened?" Sho demanded.

"I'm not sure, but I think Kyoshi may have broken Yoshimatzu's arm," Nishi answered.

"Shouldn't they stop the Round?"

"There are no time outs allowed," Nishi answered.

Kyoshi leaned toward Yon and seemed to be saying something; the crowds watched excitedly as the two rivals suddenly appeared to be in deep conversation.

"He's going to forfeit," Nishi whispered, tugging on Sho's shirt sleeve.

"Who's going to forfeit?" Sho cried.

Yoshimatzu, now obviously in severe pain, bowed to Kyoshi, and then removed his headband, tossing it to the floor.

"Yoshimatzu has forfeited the Round, Sayuki has won Round Three! Ladies and gentlemen, the winner of the National Young Gentlemen's Yudona Championship, from Valemont Academy for Distinguished Young Men, Kyoshi Sayuki!"

"He won! He won!" Nishi exclaimed, as the crowd erupted with wild cheering and hooting, chanting Kyoshi's name.

Sho, suddenly feeling as though his legs had turned to jelly, sat back down, his head in his hands. He was trembling; he was so upset, in fact, that for a long moment he could say nothing.

"Aren't you happy for him, brother? Kyoshi won!"

Down on the floor, Kyoshi seemed to ignore the announcement of his victory, his attention entirely on Yoshimatzu, who was in agony as the medic attempted to examine his arm.

"Is it broken?" Kyoshi asked anxiously.

"I think so," the medic answered. "He needs to go to a hospital."

"I'm sorry," Kyoshi whispered, frowning.

Yoshimatzu shook his head, wincing. "It was a legal move. You deserved to win."

"You played well. I'd like to play against you again sometime."

"I think I'll pass," Yon replied, with a wry smile.

"No hard feelings?" Kyoshi held out a fist, and Yon punched it softly with his own fist.

"No hard feelings. It was a good fight."

Kyoshi watched as Yoshimatzu was led away, his brow furrowed with concern. He felt bad about breaking the fighter's arm — that hadn't been his intent. He had only hoped to get Yon to drop the troika.

He didn't have long to dwell on the matter, however, as soon he found himself lifted up on the shoulders of the other members of Valemont's yudona team, all of whom were beside themselves with excitement over Kyoshi's victory. The trophy awarded Kyoshi and Valemont Academy was so huge it took several fighters to hold it up.

Kyoshi grinned, looking around him at the cheering crowds, and enjoying the chanting of his name. He scanned the faces of those near him, searching for Sho, but the Headmaster seemed to have disappeared.

Jiji, however, had managed to push her way through the crowds, and now stood just beneath him, tugging on his silken yudona pants. "Come on, Kyoshi," she yelled, giggling when Kyoshi shook his head, pointing to his ears.

"What?" he laughed.

"I said, come on! I have a special prize for you!"

Kyoshi managed to jump down to the floor, picking up Jiji and attempted to swing her around. But there were too many people around him and so he just held her against his body, his cock going rigid.

"I need to fuck you," he whispered in her ear.

"What?" she yelled.

"I said, I need to fuck you!" Kyoshi called out, his voice managing to rise above the noise of the crowds. His teammates began to laugh and cheer even louder at this, slapping him on the back.

"Go, Kyoshi!" Seiko teased, laughing. "You man-stud, you!"

Jiji seemed delighted with the situation, thrusting her chest out provocatively against Kyoshi's body.

"Gods! I'll fuck you right here if you don't watch yourself!" Kyoshi warned.

Sho watched the scene from a distance, his face darkening when Kyoshi lifted the girl up against his body.

"Let's go," Nishi suggested, tugging at his shirt.

Sho, too jealous and upset to answer, only nodded, following Nishi as they fought their way through the crowds to the VIP exit. Once they were outside, Sho reached out and grabbed one of the red VIP banners, angrily yanking it from the wall.

"Hey!" one of the guards protested. "That's public property!"

"He's feeling ill, he didn't mean anything," Nishi said, stepping between the guard and Sho. "Hey, is that a 4509 unit?" Nishi pointed to the walkie-talkie the guard was proudly wearing at his belt, feigning interest.

"Yes, it is," the guard replied, softening a bit.

"Wow! I've heard those are amazing! Where did you get it?"

"We had them imported from Yihara. And yes, they are amazing. They have built in cameras that can transport any picture as a holographic projection to the receiver. In fact—"

"That's incredible," Nishi interrupted, pushing Sho toward the car. "You must be pretty important to have one of those."

"Well yes, I suppose that's true," the guard replied, puffing up a bit and looking rather pleased with himself. "I was promoted last fall. Before that—"

"Okay, see ya!" Nishi jumped into the car and slammed the door. "Peel out, brother, peel out!"

Sho was still so angry that he actually did so, putting the car in reverse and then taking off with a rather high-pitched squeal of his tires.

"Woohoo! Take the VIP ramp!"

Unlike the rest of the parking lot, which was bumper-to-bumper traffic, the VIP ramp allowed unobstructed access out of the area to the main road. Sho drove faster than usual, his hands clenching the steering wheel.

"Okay, slow down now, Sho. I see some cops up ahead."

"Did you see him? He was practically plastered on her!"

"Sho...pull over here until you calm down," Nishi suggested, pointing to a space just off the VIP drag.

Headmaster Mitsuwa did so, slamming on the brakes and coming to a skidding halt. The glove compartment opened, sending its contents into Nishi's lap.

"Holy shit," Nishi gasped, grabbing his arm rest. "Maybe I should drive."

"I can't go on like this," Sho exclaimed, shaking his head. "He's making me crazy."

"Well, at least he won."

"He could have been killed! Or hurt far worse, like that other poor boy!" Sho alternated between feeling worried to death for Kyoshi and feeling jealous and angry of the girl he'd brought to the tournament, unable to focus his thoughts.

"Arghh!" Nishi suddenly screamed.

"What?! Good heavens, Nishi, you startled me!"

Nishi was holding a kaleidoscope that had fallen out of Sho's glove compartment. "Is this what I think it is?"

"Nish," Sho sighed, bringing a hand to his head.

"It is! It's a kaleidoscope!" Nishi let the object drop as though on fire, pulling his leg up when the object threatened to roll against his shoe.

"Nish, act your age," Sho scolded.

"You know I'm terrified of those! Why would you intentionally have one in your glove compartment, just waiting to fall on me?!"

"Who ever heard of anyone being frightened of a kaleidoscope? It's absurd."

"But you know I hate those things!"

Sho, momentarily distracted from his personal angst by the absurdity of his brother's phobia, reached down and snatched the kaleidoscope off the floor of the car.

"Don't let it touch me!"

"Nish, it's time you got over this ridiculous fear. This is...it's a toy! It's a delightful toy! What in the world could you possibly fear about it?"

"I don't know! There's...like, too many triangles! And they keep changing!"

"You're being extraordinarily silly. Nish. Look inside the hole." Sho attempted to put the kaleidoscope in front of his brother's face, but Nishi only backed away into the corner of the car, alarmed.

"I don't want to look!"

"Nish! It's...quite interesting, I promise."

"Too many triangles," Nishi whispered, shaking his head emphatically.

"Who on earth is afraid of triangles?" Sho demanded, exasperated.

"They're not just regular triangles. They're scary ones. They keep going into each other and...no! Quit waving it at me!"

"This is a ridiculous fear and I refuse to hear any more about it! It was one thing when you were scared of kaleidoscopes when you were four," Sho scolded. "Now, just look inside the hole."

"You can't make me look! Nothing you can do would make me look! I'm not looking!"

Sho sighed, letting his head fall back against the seat of the car. "What am I going to do with you?"

"I'll look if you give me a kiss," Nishi answered, after a long pause.

"What sort of kiss?"

"On the lips. With a bit of tongue."

"I don't think that's a good idea to keep encouraging your unnatural obsession," Sho replied.

"It's not unnatural," Nishi protested. "Come on. In other cultures brothers love each other."

"We're not in those other cultures."

"Please? I'll look, I promise. And I won't...you know...." Nishi pointed down at his pants.

"I can't believe I'm even entertaining this," Sho groaned, rubbing his eyes.

"Come on, Sho. Kiss me."

"All right. One kiss. And no...funny business. But you'll look first." Sho held out the kaleidoscope.

"One kiss, with tongue, right?"

"Yes, all right."

"Okay then." Nishi swallowed, leaning forward to peer inside the kaleidoscope. "Hey! This is pretty cool, actually."

"Hold it and turn the end around."

"Ooo! How psychedelic."

Sho could only shake his head, rolling his eyes. "I trust I'm not going to hear any more complaints about kaleidoscopes?"

Nishi tossed the kaleidoscope aside, grinning. "So you were right. My big brother comes to the rescue again. Pucker up, brother. I'm ready for that kiss now."

Sho leaned back in his seat, his arms behind his head. "Hmmm. And what makes you think I'd actually do something perverted like that?"

"Sho!" Nishi punched his brother in the side, scowling. "You promised!"

"Ow," Sho laughed, rubbing his side. "So it's payback, or have you already forgotten that you ejaculated on me on the ride here?"

"I can't believe you'd actually lie to me!"

"And I can't believe you would actually come on me," Sho countered.

"Now I'll never be able to trust you," Nishi lamented.

At that moment a car went whizzing by them. Sho sat up straighter. "That was Kyoshi!"

"What are you going to do?" Nishi demanded, when Sho immediately pulled the car back onto the VIP exit.

"I'm going to follow them. They're up to mischief, I'll wager."

"You can't be serious. Come on, let's go back home. Can I stay at your place tonight?"

Headmaster Mitsuwa made no answer, his jaw set as he shifted gears.

"What, you're really going to follow them? What are you going to do, crash their party?"

"That's exactly what I'm going to do," Sho answered.

Nishi shook his head. "You just want to keep him from nailing that girl. Admit it."

"I admit it," Sho replied, speeding up to keep pace with Kyoshi's vehicle.

"You're just going to piss him off. He's off to his victory party, and you're out to ruin it for him."

"Maybe so," Sho sighed. "But I won't get any sleep tonight if I don't do something."

Nishi argued with his brother for a good half hour, but to no avail; Sho was set on his mission, and nothing Nishi said dissuaded him.

"Where the hell are we?" Nishi wondered, looking out the windows. "I hope you've been paying attention to where we're going."

"That's it, up ahead," Sho answered, allowing the car to roll to stop. They were out in the country near the lakefront, and had stopped in front of a large cabin that was obviously Kyoshi's destination. Young people could be seen dancing inside, the music from the party blasting out into the cool winter night. Cars were parked haphazardly in front of the cabin, and Kyoshi's was among them.

"What are you going to do?" Nishi asked, as Sho turned off the engine.

"I'm going inside. Come if you like; either way, we'll be leaving in just a few minutes."

"Oh, I'm coming," Nishi answered, scrambling out of the car. "I wouldn't miss this."

They walked toward the cabin, the snow crunching under their shoes. But for the music coming from the cabin, the night seemed quiet; they were far from the noisy city of Jufi, and the trees that surrounded the cabin seemed to make the place seem even more isolated.

"Fuck! It's bloody cold!" Nishi muttered, zipping up his coat.

Sho made no answer, opening the front door to the cabin without even bothering to knock.

As it turned out, their entrance made little impact on the party going on inside. No one even seemed to notice them, except for one young man who tossed Nishi a beer.

"Hey, thanks!" Nishi caught the beer, grinning.

"One for your friend?" The boy held out another beer, preparing to toss it to Sho.

But the Headmaster was already scoping the place, making his way through the crowds in his search for Kyoshi. Most of the young people he didn't recognize, but when he moved into the kitchen the members of the Valemont Yudona Team all startled at his entrance.

"Headmaster!" Hisashi gasped, clumsily trying to hide his beer behind his back.

"Where's Kyoshi?" Sho demanded.

Hisashi was so surprised he couldn't even reply.

"Mr. Shinozaki," Headmaster Mitsuwa said, turning toward Seiko. "Perhaps you can answer my query. Where is Mr. Sayuki?"

"Um...I don't know...upstairs, I think," Seiko answered, his face reddening as he realized he had just ratted Kyoshi out.

"Gentlemen, I'll see all of you in my office in the morning immediately after the Holiday break," the Headmaster announced, giving the young men a meaningful look before turning and heading for the stairs.

"Fuck," Seiko groaned, his sentiments echoed by the others there.

"At least he's not breaking up the party," Hisashi pointed out.

"Yes, but he's summoned us. You know that only means one thing."

"What's going on?" Kimura asked, walking up and putting his arms around Seiko from behind. "Who was that guy?"

"Headmaster Mitsuwa," Seiko sighed.

"No shit? He's pretty good looking. For a Headmaster, I mean."

Seiko scowled at this, pushing Kimura away.

Kimura only laughed. "Jealous?'

"Hell no. But I can't think of Mitsuwa like that...not any more, anyway. He's probably going to whip us raw, the prick."

"Poor Kyoshi," Hisashi sighed. "He's about to get busted."

"How on earth did he find us here?" Seiko wondered aloud.

Upstairs, Kyoshi had just barely gotten Jiji into one of the spare bedrooms, pushing her down on the bed.

"Let's see," he said holding her legs apart with a grin. "Ah, no panties. Naughty girl."

Jiji giggled, gasping when Kyoshi slid a finger inside her.

"Oooo. You're already wet." He moved his finger to fondle her clit, rolling the swelling knob under his finger. "Is this my prize?"

The girl moaned and wiggled against him, her eyes dilating.

"I can't wait," Kyoshi announced. He reached out and ripped open her blouse, sending buttons flying.

"Oh! You just ruined that!"

Kyoshi answered her with a groan, groping her bare breasts. "And no bra. You're begging to be fucked." He leaned down and sucked a nipple, then bit it gently.

Jiji cried out, arching up against him. Kyoshi tugged on his yudona pants, pushing them to his knees and freeing his rigid erection.

"I'll take care of you in a minute," he whispered, eagerly spreading her legs apart with his body and sliding inside her. "I want a good long taste of you. But right now I have to fuck you."

"Oh, Kyoshi," she cried, wrapping her legs around his back.

"You're so sexy," he growled, biting her neck as he rubbed a nipple between his thumb and finger. He began thrusting inside her, hard.

"Oh! That's too rough, Kyoshi!"

"Shhhh," he whispered, fucking her even harder.

"It's too hard!"

"You like it hard," he countered, pinning her wrists to the bed. "Don't you? Don't you, naughty girl?"

"It—oh god! Oh god! I'm going to come!"

"Oh yeah," he panted. "Come for me, baby."

Jiji began to squeal and writhe, contracting against him. "Kyoshi! Right there, right there!"

"Good girl," he whispered, his eyes rolling back. "I'm right behind you, doll. I'm coming, too."

He slid his hands under her hips, wiggling to penetrate a bit deeper, and then groaned as he climaxed. For a moment he simply lay on her, panting. Then he got up on his arms, looking down at her.

"Sorry I didn't last too long. But that's just round one. I've got at least two more rounds in me tonight."

"Are you going to love me with your mouth like you promised?" she asked, batting her eyes.

"Oh yes. And you're going to do the same for me, aren't you, love?"

The door to the room creaked open and Jiji suddenly gasped. "Who's that?"

"What the fuck?" Kyoshi turned, scowling toward the open door. "Hey! Get the hell out!"

"Get up Kyoshi. We're going."

Headmaster Mitsuwa stood in the doorway, his arms crossed on his chest.

"Sho!" Kyoshi scrambled to his feet, tugging up his pants. "Shit! What are you doing here?"

Jiji screamed, covering her body with a sheet.

"Don't bother," the Headmaster said dryly, "you already showed all your assets at the tournament, young lady."

"Leave her alone," Kyoshi said, lowering his voice. "She hasn't done anything wrong."

"Oh? I must say, it doesn't look like that to me. In fact, I'd say this is sexual congress, which as you know is prohibited among students at Valemont and Kemberly. I'd say both of you are in for a bit of punishment."

"Oh, please," Jiji said, her voice wavering as tears filled her eyes. "Please don't report me. I'll get the paddle for sure."

"Save your tears, they won't work on me," Headmaster Mitsuwa answered. "You deserve a good paddling, young lady, and I intend to be sure you get one."

"Come on," Kyoshi whispered. "Don't take it out on her."

Jiji had begun to cry. "Please don't report me," she begged.

"Mr. Sayuki. Please accompany me immediately," Sho hissed, grabbing Kyoshi by the elbow. "As for you, young lady, I'd advise you to cover up that pretty little ass of yours. You'll be baring it soon enough for the Headmaster at Kemberly."

Kyoshi turned to give Jiji a parting shrug of apology as Sho led him from the room, gripping him painfully on the arm just above the elbow.

"Give me a break," Kyoshi pleaded. "We were just celebrating."

"Hush," Sho snapped, so angry he could hardly see straight. The crowds parted for them as they made their way toward the front door.

"Hey, where ya going, Sayuki?" one boy demanded. "This party's for you!"

"Mr. Sayuki is going home for the night, and I suggest you all do the same," the Headmaster replied.

Nishi, who was starting to enjoy himself, looked disappointed when he saw it was already time to go.

"Come on, Sho," he sighed. "Chill out for once, how about?"

"Kyoshi's leaving?" Seiko rushed into the great hall, frowning. "But...he's my ride! I can't drive a stick!"

"Come with us, we'll give you a ride home," Nishi suggested.

Seiko regarded Nishi with a look of confusion. "Who are you?"

"I'm Sho's brother," Nishi replied, rolling his eyes as though embarrassed. "Sorry about all this."

Seiko smiled. "Oh. I'm Seiko Shinozaki. Kyoshi's friend."

"I know who you are," Nishi answered, winking. "You've had a great year, by the way. I've followed you since you came to Valemont."

"Thanks," Seiko answered.

For a moment the two of them locked gazes, the chemistry flowing between them like fireworks. Nishi smiled and Seiko returned the smile, intrigued.

"We're off, then," Nishi announced, following Sho as the Headmaster stormed out of the cabin. He turned to regard Seiko, his eyes shining. "You coming?"

"Yeah," Seiko answered, his heart already starting to beat faster.

"Hey," Kimura complained, as he watched his date leave. "What about me?"

Chapter 13 - *Pinned*

"OW! WOULD YOU EASE UP, SHO? YOU'RE CUTTING off my circulation!" Kyoshi had to jog to keep up with the angry Headmaster, who practically dragged him all the way to the car. "Come on! She doesn't mean anything to me. I just needed a good fuck!"

"Hush," Sho hissed, pushing him toward the car. "Get in."

"Why are you so upset? I thought we were, you know, broken up."

"Keep your voice down," Sho warned, opening the door for Kyoshi and giving him another push.

"What, NOW you're worried about appearances? Don't you think everyone found it a bit odd when you barged into the party—which was for ME, by the way—and made me leave? Only me?"

"Perhaps I should go back inside and cart off the rest of the team," Sho threatened, slamming the door closed.

He walked around to his side of the car, the snow crunching beneath his shoes, the sound of his breath loud in the quiet of the night.

"Sho, wait!" Nishi called out. "We don't have keys to Kyoshi's car!"

The Headmaster turned to see his brother and Seiko approach him.

"Hold on," he sighed.

He opened the door to the car, leaning inside. "Give me your keys, Kyoshi."

"Why? Hey! That's right, I drove here! You've got to be crazy if you think I'm letting anyone drive my car!" Kyoshi fumbled with the door, exiting the car and slamming the door closed. "You can't MAKE me go with you, you know!"

"All right. You can drive. But I'm riding with *you*," Sho announced, tossing Nishi his keys.

"Okay so, I guess we'll follow you, then?" Nish said, cheerfully.

"Um, who should I ride with?" Seiko wondered, looking toward Kyoshi.

"Ride with me," Nishi whispered. "Believe me, you don't want to be in the same car with either of them right now."

Seiko nodded. "Yeah, okay."

Kyoshi and Sho glared at one another.

"Thanks for ruining my night," Kyoshi muttered finally, turning and trudging off toward his car. "In case you didn't notice, I WON the whole fucking tournament!"

"I noticed you fucking," Sho shot back.

"You've got a lot of nerve! She's hot! She's young! Young people are supposed to fuck! YOU'RE the one who's twisted! You have no right—"

"Kyoshi, keep it down," Sho urged, looking around him.

"Don't worry, no one cares! You know why? They're all inside having a blast! Which is where I should be!" Kyoshi unlocked his doors with an angry flip of his remote, pushing so hard the doors locked again. "Fuck!"

"Calm down," Sho scolded.

"You're telling ME to calm down? You're the one who drove all the way out here—by the way, what were you doing, following me? You storm in uninvited and you know good and well it's not because you care there's a party going on. You only wanted to ruin it for me. Because you're jealous of me fucking Jiji!"

"Kyoshi, please," Sho begged, his voice lowered to a quivering whisper. "Wait until we get into the car."

"Fine!"

Kyoshi slid into the front seat, slamming the door shut. Sho got in on the other side, starting to feel a little less sure of himself. He knew that what Kyoshi was saying was true. He'd come to the party because he was jealous.

"You've got a lot of nerve," Kyoshi repeated, as soon as Sho was in the car.

The Headmaster was silent for a moment. Then he closed his eyes with a sigh, bringing a hand to his head. "You're right," he admitted. "I am jealous."

This helped calm Kyoshi down, though he still simply sat in the car, staring at the steering wheel. "We were just celebrating."

"I shouldn't have come here after you," Sho continued after a moment, shaking his head. "I don't know what's wrong with me."

"Yeah, well. I probably would have done the same thing," Kyoshi conceded, softening.

"You can go back inside, if you want. You should go. I have no right spoiling things for you."

Kyoshi turned to look at the Headmaster, his eyes shining with love. "There's nothing in there I really want."

Sho met his gaze, sighing. "Oh, Kyoshi." He reached out and touched the bruise on his cheek, anger and worry filling his eyes. "I about lost my mind watching you today."

"Yeah, I noticed. You almost got me disqualified."

"I'm sorry about that. But when I saw you go down, I couldn't just stay in the stands."

"Yeah? You were that worried, huh?"

"Of course I was worried! I thought you were going to be killed out there! That…that barbaric, savage—I hate yudona," Sho finished abruptly, crossing his arms on his chest.

"Hmmm. I hope you don't expect me to give it up."

"I couldn't stand watching you get hurt."

"I got that much. But don't you think it might have looked a bit strange when you went running out on the floor? Aren't you worried about that?"

"Yes," Sho sighed, shaking his head. "I know I shouldn't have done that."

"And then afterwards you followed me to the party. I'm not trying to lecture you, Sho, but people are going to start talking."

Sho brought his hands to his face, closing his eyes. "I know, I know."

"I'm crazy about you, Sho."

The Headmaster looked up at him, surprised.

Kyoshi nodded. "I only went out with Jiji to make you jealous. I mean—I'll admit she's a good fuck—but that's it. I was mad at you. I wanted to show you that you didn't mean anything to me. But that's a lie. I'm totally into you—seriously—and I want to know if you feel the same."

"Yes," Sho whispered. "I can't stop thinking about you. Night or day, you're all I think about now."

For a long moment they gazed at one another, the anger and jealousy melting away. Then they were kissing, at first gently, and then with increasing ardor.

"Kyoshi," Sho murmured, burying his hands in the young man's hair. "I want you back in my bed."

"I GUESS THEY'RE TALKING," NISHI REMARKED. He and Seiko were sitting in Sho's car, waiting for the couple to leave. He squinted at the darkened glass, wondering what was going on inside. "Maybe I'll just shut off the engine for a bit."

"So you're the Headmaster's brother?" Seiko asked.

"Unfortunately, yes."

Seiko laughed.

"Actually, Sho's a great guy. He's in a mood tonight, though."

"I noticed." Seiko picked up the kaleidoscope that was sitting on the seat, smiling. "Hey, a kaleidoscope! I haven't seen one of these in years." He looked inside it, turning it with his hands to watch the effects. "You know, I never really understood the appeal of these things. I mean, they're interesting for about ten seconds. Anyway, why does the Headmaster have a totally random kaleidoscope sitting in his car?"

"That's what I'd like to know. Some people are scared of those, you know."

Seiko tossed the kaleidoscope back onto the seat, and Nishi instinctively jumped, shifting his position to be as far as possible from it.

"Hmmm. *Some* people, huh?" Seiko laughed. "Would YOU happen to be one of those people?"

"Why would I be scared of a kaleidoscope?" Nishi demanded, looking offended.

Seiko picked up the toy, grinning. "Oh, I see. You're not scared of this, then?" He shook the kaleidoscope near Nishi, who instinctively put his hands up in defense.

"Aahhh!" he yelped.

Seiko laughed so hard he started coughing, his face turning red. He continued to wave the kaleidoscope at Nishi, enjoying his reaction. "Oh fuck!" he gasped. "This is fucking hilarious."

"Give me that," Nishi muttered, grabbing the thing and tossing it into the back seat.

"I'm sorry." Seiko wiped his eyes, trying to stop laughing. "I shouldn't make fun of you. I mean, we just met and everything. But that's about the funniest thing I've ever heard of. Scared of a kaleidoscope!"

"Humph." Nishi pouted, crossing his arms on his chest. "Well, I'm sure there's something equally funny about you. You're probably scared of…I don't know…snakes or something."

"Nope."

"Spiders?"

Seiko shook his head.

"Heights? Clowns?"

"No. Anyway, how would that be funny? Lots of folks are scared of those things."

"You must be scared of something."

"Well, okay. You win. I *am* a little scared of Mitsuwa's whip."

Nishi smiled. "That's understandable. Are you well acquainted with it?"

"More so than I want to be," Seiko admitted. "A few weeks ago he gave me 30 strikes with it. Damn, that hurt."

"Thirty? I had no idea Sho was so sadistic."

"He was really pissed, for some reason. Kyoshi and I were drunk and got caught, but I don't think I deserved 30 strikes just for that."

"Hmmm. Are you sure that's all you did?" Nishi gave him a knowing smile.

"What's that supposed to mean?"

"I'm just saying, I thought there was something a bit more involved."

"You mean Mitsuwa TOLD YOU about it?"

Nishi raised his hands as if in defense. "No, no. Forget I said anything."

"He *did* tell you!"

Nishi laughed, shrugging. "Okay, so maybe he did. I really shouldn't tell you that."

"What did he say?" Seiko demanded.

"He claims Kyoshi was caught fondling you."

"Oh that. Right. I almost forgot about that. That was nothing, honestly. I was just too drunk to push him away."

"Ah, I see. So is that the secret to getting in your pants? Just get you drunk?"

"It was hardly a big thrill for either of us. I wasn't even aroused. So that's why Mitsuwa was so mad? That explains it, I guess."

"Yeah, he can get a bit jealous." Nishi looked toward Kyoshi's car. "I wonder if they're still fighting or what. Hopefully they made up."

Seiko was quiet for a moment. "So, I guess you know about them, then."

"That I do," Nishi replied, nodding.

"Um…what do you think about it?"

"I think Sho's in love."

Seiko looked genuinely surprised at this. "Really? You think so?"

"I'm sure of it," Nishi confirmed. "I've never seen him this way with anyone."

"Yeah, Kyoshi seems pretty soft on him too. It's a bit awkward, though, don't you think? I mean the whole Headmaster-student thing."

"That just makes it even more kinky," Nishi replied, winking.

"I suppose so. Aren't you worried about what could happen? Suppose people start to talk…well, I don't know. Seems like the Headmaster might get into serious trouble."

Nishi looked toward the car again, nodding. "He's worried sick about it. That's how I know he really cares about Kyoshi. He wouldn't risk losing everything—his position, his reputation—if he wasn't serious about him."

"Do you think it will come to that? Will he lose his position as Headmaster?"

Nishi shrugged. "I don't know. I hope not, for his sake. He loves it at Valemont."

"Well, I won't say anything."

Nishi turned to regard him, puzzled. "Of course you won't. You're Kyoshi's friend, right?"

"Yeah." Seiko frowned, looking away.

Nishi studied him for a moment, piecing things together. "I get it. You're worried for Kyoshi."

"Yes," Seiko admitted, turning to look back at him. "I'm not a prude or anything like that. But it doesn't seem right. The Headmaster is…well, he's in a position of authority. He shouldn't be messing around with students. And if Kyoshi gets expelled again, his uncle is going to disinherit him. At least that's what Kyoshi claims."

"Sho would agree with you. He's been saying the same exact thing to me since this whole thing began. But like I said, this is serious business for him. I think he wants to stop, but he can't." He shook his head. "Like tonight—you saw the way he ran out onto the floor. And then following Kyoshi here—he was out of his mind with jealousy over the girl Kyoshi brought. He's acting with his heart, not his brain. Believe me, he'll be kicking himself for tonight, by tomorrow. I'll be hearing about it all week. As for Kyoshi, do you really think he'll be disinherited?"

"That's what he told me. He says his uncle is fed up."

"Well, hopefully it won't come to that. I hear his uncle is filthy rich."

Seiko nodded. "That's what I've heard, too. Kyoshi always seems to have plenty of cash anyway. And his car alone must be worth a fortune."

"What's his uncle's name? Sho never mentioned it."

"Kiichi Sayuki, I believe."

"What! Are you sure?" Nishi exclaimed, his eyes widening. "THE Kiichi Sayuki?"

"Yes. Why? You've heard of him?"

"Fuck yes I've heard of him! He's a HUGE patron of the arts! I've heard if you can get him to sponsor you, your career is made!" Nishi's dark eyes lit up, his features suddenly animated.

"What, are you some kind of artist or something?"

"Hmmm?" As if lost in thought, Nishi slowly focused on Seiko. He ran a hand absently through his straight shoulder-length, brown hair as though to move the hair from his face—a pointless task, for his locks immediately settled back again in the same place. "Oh, yeah. I guess. I'm a painter."

"Really? What do you paint?"

"I paint…well, nudes, mostly."

"I wish I could paint. I have no artistic talent whatsoever."

"Well, you have plenty of talent when it comes to sports. Tennis, soccer, polo, skiing—shit, is there anything you can't do?"

"I can't fight," Seiko laughed. "I mean I'm no good at yudona."

"Yes, well, you're the best athlete Valemont has seen in years. I've had my eye on you since I first saw you four years ago at the Jufi Slam. What a serve! I've never seen anything like it!"

"Thanks," Seiko replied, grinning. He enjoyed the flattery, his green eyes sparkling. "You've really been watching me for four years?"

"Hell yes. I've been admiring your body that long, too. I'd love to paint you. I'd give anything to see you naked."

"Oh yeah? Anything?"

"Anything in my power," Nishi replied. "Why, are you interested?"

Seiko shrugged. "Maybe. I've always wanted to be painted. Are you any good?"

"I'm the best artist on the planet," Nishi replied confidently.

"Then can I see something you've done?"

"Oh, no. I'm not showing anything yet."

Seiko laughed. "Well, how am I supposed to judge your talent if I can't see anything?"

"Tell you what. Come over to my place and maybe I'll let you take a peek at my latest painting. If you like it, will you let me paint you?"

Seiko thought about this for a moment, enjoying Nishi's flirting. The man was positively oozing with sex. He loved the way his hair moved, how it brushed against his shoulders, and the teasing look in his handsome brown eyes. "You mean paint me naked?"

Nishi leaned forward, widening his eyes mischievously. "Yes. Naked."

"Are you sure you want to paint me? What if you change your mind when you see my body?"

Nishi laughed. "There's no chance of that. You're gorgeous." He reached out, tugging on the hem of his shirt. "Let me take a peek at your abs. Please?"

"Oh, all right." Seiko took no persuading whatsoever, as he loved being admired. He lifted his shirt, revealing his rock-hard, perfectly chiseled muscles, the hollows of his V-curve visible at the top of his jeans.

"Holy shit," Nishi breathed. "Now you've GOT to let me paint you. Even if you don't like my work. I'll pay you...whatever you want, I'll pay you."

"You don't have to pay me. You really want to see me naked, huh?"

"Oh, yes. And if you want to know the truth, not just for artistic purposes." Nishi gave him a meaningful look, brushing a finger across Seiko's abdomen.

"Can I ask you something personal?" Seiko asked.

"Sure."

"Are you a bottom or a top?"

"A top. Absolutely."

"Oh." Seiko looked disappointed, letting his shirt drop.

"You're a top, too?"

"Yeah."

"Bet I can turn you into a willing bottom," Nishi whispered. He leaned closer, reaching out to put a hand in Seiko's hair. "You have gorgeous hair. It sparkles like gold."

"I don't think I can be a bottom," Seiko replied, though he didn't pull away.

"I love your eyes," Nishi continued. "Green. I've never seen eyes like yours. They're so bright and beautiful against your skin. Are you tanned all over, by the way?"

"I'm not telling."

Nishi stroked his cheek with his thumb. "Trust me, you'll love being a bottom. I'm a good lover. I'm gentle."

"I'm used to being the one in charge."

"I want to kiss you. May I?"

"All right. But, like I said —"

Seiko's protest was left forever unuttered when Nishi began to kiss him. It was one of those moments that seemed to stand on its own, away from time and space. Seiko met Nishi's kiss with enthusiasm, and for a long moment they were engaged thus, each of them delighting in the taste of the other.

Finally, Nishi broke away. "Nice."

"You're a good kisser."

"So are you." Nishi kissed him again, this time sliding his hand under Seiko's shirt, letting his fingers trail over the boy's taut muscles and then moving up to a nipple, which he rolled gently between his finger and thumb.

Seiko immediately went rigid as a pole, reaching down to unfasten his pants. "I'm horny as hell," he whispered huskily, breaking away.

"Me too." Nishi began kissing his neck, pulling his shirt up to have better access to his nipple, which he then began to suckle. He slid a hand down his body, helping Seiko release himself from his pants. "I don't want to rush this," he warned. "Maybe we should wait until we get to my place."

"I don't know if I can wait now," Seiko replied. "I'm younger than you. I'm about to spill."

"All right. I have an idea."

Nishi moved down, tugging on Seiko's pants to give himself full access. Then he took Seiko into his mouth.

"Fuck yes," Seiko breathed, closing his eyes and letting his head rest back against the seat of the car. He buried his hands in Nishi's hair, moaning. "You're amazing. Oh, that's good. That's really good!"

Nishi gave him the best blow job he could in the short amount of time that Seiko lasted. Within moments the boy climaxed, groaning his pleasure. "Yes! Swallow me! Gods yes!"

Nishi pulled away, smiling and wiping his mouth. "Sounded like you enjoyed that."

"Yes, it was awesome. Sorry I didn't last long." He shook his head. "I can't believe the Headmaster's brother just blew me!"

"Will you still come over to my place?"

"Sure. I can't promise I'll give you exactly what you want, though."

"Just come over," Nishi pressed, knowing full well that once he had the beautiful young boy in his bed, he would convert him to an enthusiastic bottom. "You won't regret it. I promise."

"You're still going to paint me, right?"

"If you'll let me. I thought you wanted to see my work first."

"Nah, you can paint me. Shit. I can't believe I just came in your mouth. And we met, like…half an hour ago?"

"Oh shit," Nishi exclaimed, when he saw Kyoshi's car suddenly take off. "They're finally leaving." He turned on the engine and pulled out after them, turning to give Seiko a grin. "I've got to tell you, you have the sweetest tasting seed of anyone I've ever blown."

"I find that hard to believe. Sweet?" Seiko laughed.

"You know what I mean. I love the way you taste."

"That's a fucking turn-on."

"It is for me, too." Nishi pointed to his erection, arching a brow.

"Want me to take care of you while you drive?"

"No, I want to wait until we get to my place." He eyed Seiko as the boy fastened his jeans, marveling over his sexy young body. "I can't wait to see you completely naked."

"Well, you've already seen the critical parts," Seiko pointed out.

"I want to see every inch of you. I want to love you all night long."

"I don't know about that," Seiko protested. "I told you, I'm not a bottom."

"We'll see."

"I'm serious. If I tell you no, I mean no."

Nishi raised a hand in defense. "Understood. But you'll be saying yes before the night is through."

"I'll give this to you: you sure are confident about your abilities."

Nishi only smiled, saying nothing. He knew perfectly well that his skills as an artist weren't restricted to his paintings alone…he was a master in the bedroom.

Seiko would find out…soon.

"KYOSHI, KYOSHI," SHO BREATHED, PLANTING A SERIES of kisses up his neck and then nibbling his earlobe before kissing him again. "I missed you."

"I know. It's only been since yesterday that we argued, but it seems like forever."

"Let's go to my place. I want you in my bed tonight."

"So, does this mean we're together again?"

"Actually I have something for you," Sho admitted, reaching into his pocket and pulling out his University pin. He showed it to Kyoshi. "It's from my University, Jufi. I know it's foolish. But I want to pin you. I meant to do this yesterday, after our stupid argument. And I'm sorry about Reginald—Professor Zucyu. I heard he really gave it to you yesterday."

"Yes, he did." Kyoshi took the pin, surprised. "You want to pin me?"

"Yes. But of course...you can't tell anyone it's mine."

"Obviously. Then you want to be exclusive?"

Sho frowned. "Don't you?"

"Yes," Kyoshi answered, laughing. "Of course I do. I have to tell you that you're a little old-fashioned. Kids don't pin each other these days. But I like the idea...I'll wear it. I don't have a Valemont pin—although I do have the tournament pin I won today. You can have that." He unfastened the golden trophy pin from his shirt, handing it to Sho.

The Headmaster took it, smiling. "I'll wear it under my robes. Yes, I suppose my age is showing. When I was at University, we pinned each other to show we were exclusive."

"That can't have been so long ago."

"It's been ten years."

"Nowadays kids don't do anything special to show they're together. So I like this idea."

"To do it properly, I'll pin you. Then you can pin me."

"Cool."

Kyoshi handed him back the pin, and Sho carefully fastened it to his shirt, being careful not to stick him. Then he held out the yudona tournament pin.

"Now you pin me."

Kyoshi took the pin, fumbling with it a bit before it was properly fastened to Sho's shirt. "The gold looks good against your black shirt," he remarked. "You look sexy as hell in this, by the way. It's skin tight and I can see every muscle." He slid a finger down Sho's turtleneck, pausing to twist his nipple. "So that's it? We're officially pinned, then?"

"We're official," Sho agreed. He suddenly remembered Nishi, turning to look at his car. "Goodness, I forgot Nishi is waiting for us. Let's head back to my place."

"Sho?"

"Yes?"

"Do you love me?"

The Headmaster paused for a moment, and then reached out to touch the pin on Kyoshi's shirt. "I just pinned you. That should tell you how I feel."

"You can't just say you love me?"

"I care deeply for you, Kyoshi."

The dark-haired youth frowned at this. "You mean you don't love me?"

"I didn't say that." The Headmaster looked down at his hands for a moment, thinking. "Honestly, I've never told anyone I loved them."

"I've never told anyone that either," Kyoshi admitted, starting the engine. He wanted to tell Sho that he loved him, but now he felt like he couldn't, if Sho was being so evasive about it. He felt a little hurt that Sho wouldn't come right out and say he loved him. He knew he loved Sho, even if the Headmaster wasn't sure if his own feelings.

"I don't know where all this is going," Sho added, after a long moment. "With us, I mean. I know we shouldn't even be seeing each other."

"It's a little late for that. We've already fucked."

"Yes, I know," Sho sighed.

Kyoshi fell silent as he pulled away from the cottage, squinting at the dark road. "I can't see shit out here. So, you have no problem fucking me, but you're not sure if you love me?"

"Let's not get into another argument," Sho pleaded.

"I wasn't arguing."

"Kyoshi," Sho sighed.

"What? I'm just trying to get some clarification here."

"Why are you asking me if I love you when it's obvious you don't love me?"

"What makes you say that? How do you know I don't love you?"

"Because you wouldn't have come here with that tramp if you did," Sho replied, his eyes flashing angrily.

"I told you, I just went out with her to make you jealous."

"You accomplished that much just by hanging all over her at the tournament. You didn't have to actually sleep with her."

Kyoshi shook his head, rolling his eyes. "Come on. You've seen her. She's hot as hell. And she puts out. I get really wound up after a good yudona fight. I need release."

"You could have waited for me," Sho protested.

"I looked for you after the tournament but didn't see you."

"Oh really? You were all over that girl when I saw you there."

"Sho, don't be jealous," Kyoshi pleaded. "And you're getting all worked up again."

"Why wouldn't I be worked up? I caught you in bed with her!"

"You know, she probably would have been game for a threesome. Wouldn't that have been kinky?"

"In your dreams," Sho muttered, sulking.

Kyoshi laughed. "Oh, come on. You wouldn't do a threesome?"

"Not with her."

Kyoshi raised a brow, intrigued. "With someone else, then?"

"You'd do that? Wouldn't *you* be jealous to see me with someone else?"

"It would be fucking hot as hell."

"I know I wouldn't like to see you with anyone else. It would drive me crazy."

"All right. Calm down. I'm just teasing you." Kyoshi put his hand on Sho's thigh, rubbing him reassuringly.

"That's the whole point of the pin!" Sho exclaimed. "It means we're EXCLUSIVE. Only two people in the bed. No other partners involved."

"You're so sexy when you're angry," Kyoshi whispered. "I bet you're going to be a wild man tonight."

"Oh, you're getting a good fucking, if that's what you mean," the Headmaster confirmed. "And maybe a spanking, too."

"I'll have to pass on the spanking. My ass is still black and blue."

"I'll save it for another time, then," Sho replied. "But don't think you're getting away with what you did without some recourse."

"Hey, we're going back to your place, I know, but I just had an idea. My uncle is gone for the Holidays. How about we go to my estate? We'd have the whole place to ourselves."

Sho was intrigued with this idea, though he felt a little anxious about it. "You're sure your uncle won't be there?"

"Positive. He's not even in the country. And I already dismissed the servants for the Holidays."

"The servants?" Sho laughed. "Goodness. It must be quite a place."

"Oh, it's very nice. I'll admit to that. Come on, it would be fun."

"I suppose that might be all right."

"Great! We'll just—oh shit! I just remembered, I already invited Seiko over for the Holidays. But that's okay...I mean, he knows about us and everything."

"What exactly does he know?" Sho demanded, narrowing his eyes.

"Erm...well, pretty much everything."

"Kyoshi!"

"It's okay, you can trust him. He's cool about it."

"I don't think it would be such a good idea, then. You two have fun."

"What's that supposed to mean? You know we're just friends."

"Hmmm." Sho looked suspicious.

"Seriously. We are. That one time on campus...we were just drunk. Although, would you consider doing a three-way with him?"

"Kyoshi!"

The dark-haired boy laughed. "I'm just teasing you! Chill out!" He fumbled with his mini-disc player, flipping the unit on and turning up the volume. "Hey, listen to this. It's you at the Jufi Phil. I just bought the recording."

Sho listened, smiling. "You bought it?"

"Of course. You're fucking unbelievable on the piano, you know that?"

"It sounds strange, hearing it when I'm not playing," Sho murmured.

"Don't tell me you've never sat back and listened to your own stuff?"

"Not really."

"If it were me, I'd be doing that all day! I mean, listen to it! It's perfect!"

Sho beamed at Kyoshi's praise. Although he knew he was gifted, it meant something to hear Kyoshi's adulations.

"Do you have any original stuff? Or do you just play other people's work?"

"I write my own music," Sho admitted. "Though I've never performed it."

"Seriously? Will you play it for me tonight?"

"If you like."

"I think you should have a concert with just your original works."

"I don't know if the Jufi Philharmonic would go for that. They're afraid original works won't pack the house."

"Don't worry about that. I'll have my uncle set it up. He'll pay for the whole thing."

Sho shook his head, alarmed. "Oh, I couldn't possibly accept his help."

"Are you kidding? Don't you know what my uncle does? This is just his sort of thing. He's always launching the careers of artists and musicians. Anyway, I'll tell you a secret. He's buying the Jufi Philharmonic."

"He's *buying* it? But...that would cost billions!"

"I don't know about billions," Kyoshi laughed. "But yes, I'm sure it's got a pretty price tag. But he already invested a ton into their new auditorium. He told me he's pretty sure he's going through with it. That means you could have a concert there anytime you want! My uncle would love to support you, I'm sure of it."

Sho sat back, trying to digest this information. "Are you sure he'd feel the same if he knew about us?"

Kyoshi frowned, considering this. "Oh. Well, perhaps not. But he doesn't have to know about us."

"I'm not sure we can hide this forever."

"I know that. But I'll be graduating in a few months. Then it won't matter, right? I won't be a student, so we can be together."

"True, though if we go public with our relationship, folks will naturally wonder if we were intimate while you were at Valemont."

"So? Let them wonder. They won't be able to prove anything."

"What about your uncle? Don't you think he'll have something to say about it?"

"Probably," Kyoshi admitted, wincing as he thought of his uncle's reaction. "Still, I just have to hang on until I graduate. Then I get my inheritance, and after that it doesn't matter what my uncle thinks. I'll buy some other orchestra if I have to. I really want you to perform your original music, Sho."

"You haven't even heard it," the Headmaster protested, laughing.

"So? I know I'll love it."

They were at Sho's house. Kyoshi parked in front, while Nishi pulled into the driveway.

"Hey. Check it out," Kyoshi remarked, when Nishi and Seiko got out of the car. Nishi's arm was around Seiko. "Looks like they made a connection."

"Nish," Sho muttered, shaking his head.

"What? He's not allowed to have a bit of fun and you are?"

"So, is the drama over?" Nishi asked, as Sho and Kyoshi approached them.

"For now," Kyoshi answered, grinning. "Looks like you two met and everything."

"Yeah. We met," Nishi replied, winking.

"Indeed we did." Seiko raised an eyebrow, giving Kyoshi a meaningful look.

"Cool." Kyoshi nodded his approval.

"I need a ride home. You picked me up, remember?" Nishi said, nodding to his brother.

"Yes, of course. I can drive you home."

"Actually, you can drive both of us there," Nishi replied, grinning.

"I see."

"What?" Nishi demanded. "Why are you giving me that look?"

"I don't know what look you mean," Sho protested.

"It's cold out here," Seiko remarked.

Nishi put his arms around him, pulling him close. "I'll keep you warm."

"Perhaps we should all go inside for a bit and have something warm to drink," Sho suggested. "I can brew up some coffee."

"Hey! I have an idea!" Kyoshi exclaimed. "Why don't we all go to my place for the Holidays? We'll have the whole place to ourselves the entire three days."

"Sounds good to me," Nishi nodded.

"Me too," Seiko agreed.

The three of them looked to Sho, who seemed a little hesitant.

"Come on, Sho," Kyoshi encouraged, giving him a poke.

Nishi joined in on the game, poking him as well. "Yeah, Sho. Why not?"

"Oh, all right," the Headmaster sighed.

"Woo hoo! This is going to be fun," Kyoshi announced.

"I'll need a change of clothes or something," Seiko remarked.

Nishi nodded. "Me too."

"Why don't we all meet back here in a couple of hours," Sho suggested. "Nish, you can take my car and drive Seiko back to Kensington Hall."

"See you in a bit, then." Nishi and Seiko climbed back into Sho's car. "Don't do anything we wouldn't do."

"That opens it up to just about anything," Sho shot back.

Nishi only grinned in response before he slammed his door shut.

"Goodness. We shouldn't be standing out here in front of the house for anyone to see," Sho exclaimed suddenly.

"Don't worry. I'm keeping a respectable distance. Let's go inside though before I freeze my ass off."

"As soon as we get inside, I'm pinning you to the bed," Sho whispered.

"Oh yeah? Pinned twice in the same night." Kyoshi smiled, following the Headmaster inside.

Chapter 14 - *Confessions and Revelations*

SHO CLOSED THE DOOR BEHIND THEM, HIS EYES GLEAMING with urgency and lust. "I want you in my bed. NOW."

Kyoshi grinned. "Ooo. You're sexy when you're like this. Maybe I should—"

The remainder of his remark was left unuttered when Headmaster Mitsuwa pushed him up against the wall, forcing his mouth open with his own. Sho felt as though he could not get enough of him; he wanted more than just to taste Kyoshi—he wanted to consume him.

The boy's tongue was hot and willing against his own, meeting him without reservation or hesitation. It was a kiss that had matured, somehow, conveying all the intimacy and history between the two lovers, full of want and need. Nothing was held back. It was a kiss that got both of their hearts pounding.

The Headmaster slipped a hand down to the youth's pants, fumbling with the zipper. He broke away, gasping for air. "Oh, Kyoshi."

Kyoshi leaned back against the wall, his legs apart, thrusting his pelvis out to show his interest. "Yeah?"

"You have no idea what you do to me. You...you've completely bewitched me."

"Perhaps I'm a witch." Kyoshi's eyes sparkled like two dark gems, his lips still parted and wet from their kiss.

"Take these off." Sho, tugged impatiently on Kyoshi's pants as he threw off his coat and began undressing.

"Does this mean I get an 'A' in your class?" Kyoshi teased, winking, and remaining exactly where he was, leaning back against the wall.

Sho pulled off his turtleneck. This small act of undressing made his hair stand on end, giving him the look of a wild man. He shot Kyoshi a disapproving look, his hands on his hips and his brow arched. "Kyoshi," he scolded.

"What?" Kyoshi laughed, shrugging. "I'm just asking. Don't you see the irony? Me acing my Ethics class because I'm sleeping with the professor?"

"We'll discuss that later," Sho answered, pointing to the bedroom. "Get undressed, and go lie on the bed."

"So I take it, that's not a definite *no*," the dark-haired youth whispered as he passed by the Headmaster on the way to the bedroom. He let his coat fall to the floor and then pulled off his shirt, turning back to give Sho another wink as he sauntered into the bedroom.

Sho followed him, shivering at the sight of Kyoshi's beautifully ripped upper body, his muscles still pumped up from the tournament. He gasped and frowned, however, when Kyoshi removed his pants and revealed the dark bruises on his ass.

"Oh, Kyoshi!" he exclaimed. "Was that from your punishment?"

Kyoshi lay down on the bed, nodding wryly. "Yes. Professor Zucyu is even worse than you. He's got a nasty arm, that one."

"That's my fault," Sho murmured. "It was because of me that you were late."

"Yes, it *is* your fault," Kyoshi agreed. "Which means you owe me. I should get to punish you, to make up for it."

"Hmmm." Sho pulled off his own pants and then joined him in bed, too distracted by the youth's nakedness to reply. He ran his hands down his body and then leaned down to suckle a nipple.

"Oooh," Kyoshi moaned, closing his eyes. "That feels good, Sho. So you agree, right? I should get to punish you?"

Sho rolled onto his back, pulling Kyoshi onto him. "Suck me," he demanded.

"You're not answering my question," Kyoshi replied, lowering to give him a kiss and then nibbling Sho's lip.

"I want my cock in your mouth," the Headmaster hissed.

"I want your answer," Kyoshi insisted.

"All right," Sho agreed, finally, pushing on his shoulders. "All right, you can punish me. Later. Please, Kyoshi. Oblige me."

Kyoshi, feeling triumphant, flashed Sho a gorgeous smile before proceeding to move down between his legs. The Headmaster spread his legs open, wiggling a bit to offer himself to the boy's willing mouth.

Kyoshi teased him at first, barely tracing his tongue down the length of his cock, and then flicking it, here and there.

"Kyoshi," Sho murmured, almost whimpering. He buried his hands in the boy's hair, thrusting his pelvis impatiently at him. Kyoshi looked so beautiful, so sexy and exciting down between his legs that it was all the Headmaster could do to remain still, especially when the boy teased him so ruthlessly.

Finally, he reached down and slipped his hand around his cock, bumping it up against Kyoshi's mouth.

"Open up," he demanded.

"This is part of your punishment, to make you squirm a bit," Kyoshi answered, flicking his tongue around the head of the Headmaster's engorged, swollen organ. He glanced up at Sho, his eyes twinkling mischievously.

"Open up!" Sho repeated, grabbing Kyoshi's hair and forcing his cock inside his mouth.

Kyoshi immediately accommodated him, opening his throat to allow the Headmaster completely inside his mouth.

"Oh, fuck!" Sho groaned, letting his head fall back on the pillow. "Oh, Kyoshi!"

Kyoshi, who couldn't remember ever hearing the Headmaster curse while they were in bed together, almost laughed, but Sho's cries were so erotic that he soon began to tremble with excitement. He gently rubbed his hands against the outside of Sho's thighs as he pleasured him, encouraging the Headmaster to cry out.

After a few minutes of this, Sho pushed him off, flipping him onto his stomach. He fumbled for a tube of lubrication on the bedside table and in the process knocked over a stack of books to the floor.

Kyoshi laughed, eyeing the mangled pile of books on the floor. "In a hurry, Headmaster? You know, if any of those are library books, you're probably in for a beating. That librarian is a total bitch. She acts like the books are *her* books or something."

"Oh? Since when do you actually read books?" Sho shot back.

"Ha. Shows how much you know. I check out books all the time."

"Hmmm."

"It's true. It's a good place to find some untouched ass, you know. The library. Or have you forgotten why I was sent to you that first time?"

Sho hadn't forgotten, nor did he care to be reminded of Kyoshi's indiscretion. "Pick up another boy in the library and I'll paddle you in front of the entire student body," he threatened.

Kyoshi smiled at this. "You're adorable when you're jealous, Sho."

Sho ignored him, rubbing the slippery gel onto his cock with shaking fingers. "You're getting a hard fucking," he warned.

He inserted a finger and then withdrew it, pushing Kyoshi's thighs open with his knees and then positioning himself for penetration. He slid his arms under the boy, grabbing the front of his shoulders, and then rubbed his cheek against Kyoshi's.

"I wish we could stay just like this forever, with you under me," Sho whispered, nuzzling the side of his face.

"That might be a bit awkward during your lectures," Kyoshi answered, closing his eyes.

"Don't be a smart-ass."

"Why not? You know you like that about me."

Despite his threat to give Kyoshi a hard fucking, Sho entered him carefully and gently, waiting until he was opened up a bit before proceeding with his more aggressive coital agenda.

"Now I'm going to tell you about the rules, Kyoshi," Sho continued, as he began slowly fucking him.

"Rules?"

"Yes. Now that we're pinned, you must abide to certain rules."

"I can't wait to hear this," Kyoshi laughed.

"Rule One. No laughing during sex." The Headmaster punctuated this rule by suddenly thrusting hard — a bit too hard. Kyoshi instinctively gasped, and then had to struggle to keep from laughing again.

"Rule Two. We ARE exclusive. That means no sex with anyone else. That means, for the record, no FLIRTING with anyone else."

"You're funny, Sho," Kyoshi replied.

"I assure you, I am perfectly serious."

"How many rules are there?"

"There are three rules. And the Third Rule is: you must never tell anyone about us."

"It might be a bit late for that," Kyoshi answered.

Sho froze for a moment. "What?"

"Well, I mean obviously Seiko knows about us."

The Headmaster relaxed and then began moving against him again. "You'll tell no one else."

"So, does this mean I get to lay down a few rules?" Kyoshi asked.

"Such as?"

"Such as: you won't give me a hard time about smoking. That's Rule One. And Rule Two is: no more little trips to your chambers for discipline. Rule Three: I get an 'A' in any class I take from you. And Rule Four is, before I submit to your No Sex With Anyone Else or Even Flirting Rule, we get to have a threesome with someone."

"Kyoshi, you know I can't agree to those rules," the Headmaster protested.

"But that's not fair. I—"

Sho silenced him by covered his mouth with his hand as he began thrusting more forcefully, finally giving him the hard fucking he'd promised. "Hush."

Kyoshi relaxed his body, shivering when the Headmaster began working him at just the right angle. Pleasure tingled all through his buttocks, the pressure building in his groin.

He loved being held down and fucked, and Sho's decision to clap a hand over his mouth added a whole new erotic element to the act. He felt as though he were being raped, and he adored this idea; it reminded him of the time when the Headmaster had taken him by force over his desk.

He wiggled a bit to encourage deeper penetration and then groaned, his lips vibrating against Sho's hand.

The Headmaster let his hand drop away, pushing himself up on his arms so he could watch himself penetrating. "Oh, Kyoshi. I'm so close!"

Kyoshi, too, was close—and then the moment swelled over him, flooding his body with such light, sweet pleasure that he whimpered, biting his lip and clutching the sheets beneath him as he raptured.

Sho was grunting like an animal, sweat dripping from his brow onto Kyoshi's back. He eased himself down and lay completely on him, his nails sinking into his shoulders. "That's it," he hissed, delighted with Kyoshi's trembling and the high-pitched, almost desperate vocalizations the youth made as he ejaculated.

He slowed his thrusting, trying to delay the moment so he could enjoy Kyoshi's orgasm before he submitted to his own need. But it was too late; he could no longer hold back, and his semen erupted from him in demanding bursts that burned release through his entire body.

"Oh God," Sho groaned, his teeth clenched hard.

The Headmaster collapsed onto Kyoshi's body, breathing hard, his head spinning. "Kyoshi, Kyoshi," he whispered weakly, his voice ragged and husky.

"Headmaster," Kyoshi whispered, his eyes still closed.

"We should stop this. I know we should stop this."

"You know we'll never stop now."

Sho sighed, withdrawing slowly and rolling onto his back, an arm flung over his eyes. "I'm a miserable Headmaster. I ought to be put in the racks for this."

"We can arrange that," Kyoshi teased softly, rolling onto his side. "In the racks, and then whipped."

"I'm serious."

"No, you're not. You just pinned me, remember? You always get this way after we've fucked. Most of the time, anyway. That was an especially good fuck, Sho."

"Yes," Sho agreed, moving his arm so he could look at Kyoshi. "Yes, it was." He touched the youth's face, marveling over his beauty. "Oh, Kyoshi. What are we going to do?"

"Well, for starters were going to get ready for our Holiday. Seiko and Nishi are waiting for us, remember?"

"Perhaps that's not such a good idea," Sho answered, frowning.

"Oh, come on. It's too late to back out now. What's the harm in it? I told you, we'll have the entire place to ourselves."

"You're sure there's no chance your uncle will return?"

"Positive. He's not even in the country."

Sho shook his head. "We really shouldn't. Seiko shouldn't see us...together, I mean."

"He's already seen us. He already knows about us. Come on, Sho. We'll have a great time."

The Headmaster was quiet for a moment, just gazing at Kyoshi. He felt a sense of helplessness, as though, for the first time in his life, he was not quite in control of himself, or of his heart. All he wanted was to be with Kyoshi. Nothing else really seemed to matter, even though he knew what he was doing with the boy was wrong.

He actually wanted to see Kyoshi's estate. He was looking forward to some time alone with him, to make up for their recent misunderstandings and separation. After their lover's spat, he knew he never wanted to be apart from Kyoshi again.

And he was glad to see that Nishi had made a connection. He wanted Nishi to be happy, too. The only thing that really bothered him was the addition of Seiko to the party. Somehow he felt it was exceedingly risky and irresponsible to allow another student to witness his indiscretion. It was one thing for Seiko Shinozaki—Valemont's star athlete—to have heard that he and Kyoshi were intimate, but quite another to actually have personal confirmation of it.

"We really shouldn't," he murmured.

"Yes, we should," Kyoshi argued. "You know you want to."

"Yes, all right," Sho sighed, continuing to stroke Kyoshi's cheek and feeling a bit overwhelmed by the boy's powerful physical beauty. He could never remember being so attracted to anyone before. And with Kyoshi, it was more than just physical attraction. He could feel his heart starting to wiggle out of his control, going where he did not want it to go. He knew he had fallen in love with Kyoshi. And he didn't feel comfortable about it.

"Good. So, are we in agreement? About my rules."

The Headmaster slowly came back to awareness, narrowing his eyes when he realized what Kyoshi was talking about. "Absolutely not."

"Then why should I have to abide by your rules?" Kyoshi demanded.

"Kyoshi, I can't promise not to punish you. If you misbehave at Valemont, I am still the Headmaster, so I *will* have to discipline you. And I can't give you an 'A' in my course, unless you earn it. And, by the way, I hope you'll have the good sense not to take any of my other courses in the future."

"What about the other rules, then?" Kyoshi pressed, not really all that surprised by Sho's answer.

"I don't like your smoking," Sho answered. "I want you to stop."

"I'm not going to stop. So you need to deal with it."

"Very well," Sho sighed, "I will *try* not to give you a hard time about it. But you may not smoke in my house."

"All right. Then at least give me Rule Four."

"Rule Four?"

"We get to have a threesome."

"No, Kyoshi."

"Oh! I have the perfect idea! Why not have a little orgy with your brother and Seiko? We'll all be at my estate for the Holidays. C'mon, Sho. It'll be hot as hell."

Sho sat up, swinging his legs over the side of the bed, and then turned to look at Kyoshi. "So, you *are* attracted to Seiko," he remarked.

"Well, of course! He's hot! You know he is!"

The Headmaster frowned at this. "And my brother?"

"Sure, he's hot, too. And I'll bet he'd be game."

"What makes you say that?" Sho asked suspiciously.

Kyoshi shrugged. "Don't know. Just a sense I get."

"Hmmm."

"So, is that a yes?"

The Headmaster shook his head. "Absolutely NOT."

"Awww, come on. You only live once."

"NO, Kyoshi!"

"But I promise you, if we do this, I'll never even *look* at anyone else."

"No, it's too awkward. You don't understand. Nish...he's my brother."

"Um, yeah, I know he's your brother. You don't have to do anything with him. You take Seiko and I'll take Nish."

Sho was silent for a moment. Kyoshi, who had never in his wildest dreams imagined that the Headmaster would seriously contemplate his demand, now felt his heart thumping hard in his chest. "Although, I want you to at least kiss Nishi once," he added boldly. "And I get to kiss Seiko."

"No." The Headmaster stood up, gathering his clothes and making for the bathroom.

"Come on." Kyoshi came up behind him, wrapping his arms around the Headmaster and forcing him to stop. "Let's do this. It would be so kinky. And then I absolutely promise to be good and obey all your rules."

Sho remained still as Kyoshi held him, contemplating the offer. He couldn't believe he was even giving the idea a moment's consideration. But after seeing Kyoshi with Jiji, he was anxious to secure some sort of real commitment from Kyoshi. He couldn't stand the thought of him dating anyone else. He knew the pin would not be enough. Would such a scenario satisfy Kyoshi? Or would it only leave him wanting more of the same?

Kyoshi, who had really only been teasing when he first posed the idea to him, was stunned that Sho might be seriously considering his proposition. He waited, excited, his head spinning.

"No," Sho said, finally. "That's my final decision."

Kyoshi said nothing, secretly feeling as though he'd made some headway, despite Sho's ultimate refusal. He decided to let the matter drop.

He kissed Sho's shoulder, hugging him tighter. "Well, let's get ready anyway. I don't know if we have more snow coming tonight, but I'd like to head out before too much longer. I hate driving in the snow."

"That's a good idea," Sho agreed. He put his hand over Kyoshi's, standing quietly with him for a moment and enjoying the comfort of their embrace. Then he turned around and held Kyoshi's chin, his thumb rubbing gently against his skin. He bent down and kissed the dark bruise and swelling that had formed on the side of his face, where Kyoshi had been punched during the tournament. "Poor boy," he whispered.

"I'm fine," Kyoshi protested. "My ass is in far worse shape than my face."

"I was so worried about you," Sho whispered. "I don't think I can ever watch you fight again."

"Well, the tournament's over for this year." Kyoshi couldn't resist smiling, his eyes shining proudly. "And I won."

"I know you want me to say I'm proud of you. But I'm just glad you weren't seriously hurt. I hated the tournament, every minute of it. Kyoshi, if you had been...if he had...." Now Sho's voice broke, his emotion constricting his throat so that he couldn't speak.

"Shhhh," Kyoshi comforted, putting a finger to his lips. "I know. It's over now. I won't be fighting again until next year."

"I wish you'd give it up," Sho pleaded, his voice lowering to a whisper.

"I can't do that. It makes me feel alive. I can't give it up, Sho. Not even for you."

"If you really cared about me, you'd...you would," the Headmaster protested.

Kyoshi laughed. "Listen to you. If you really cared about me, you wouldn't interfere with anything that made me happy."

"I do care about you," Sho argued.

"Oh yeah? I'm still waiting for you to say it."

"I just told you. I care about you."

"Tell me you love me," Kyoshi demanded.

"Kyoshi," Sho sighed.

"What? Why is it so hard for you to say?"

Sho fell silent, considering. He wasn't sure why he couldn't confess his love. He knew how he felt about Kyoshi; yet somehow he couldn't make the words come to his lips. They were there, in his heart. He knew that now. "They're not words that should be bantered freely," he protested softly.

"Bantered freely?" Kyoshi laughed. "What the hell does that mean?"

"I've never told anyone I loved them, I mean...other than family," the Headmaster explained.

"Yes, I know. You told me that."

"It's just that...it seems people say the words without really meaning them. They should be...special words....reserved for...for...." Now Sho faltered, finding himself unable to explain his thoughts.

"Reserved for when you really love someone?" Kyoshi shot back, his anger started to show.

"I didn't mean it like that," Sho protested, sighing.

"I know exactly what you meant. But guess what? I've never told anyone I loved them either. But I know I love you. And even though you won't say it, I know you love me, Sho."

The Headmaster was rendered silent by Kyoshi's declaration, his heart rejoicing in the boy's confession, though he wasn't completely sure he could believe him. After all, Kyoshi was very young. How could he really know how he felt? And hadn't he just been with Jiji, not a few hours before?

Kyoshi watched him, feeling hurt when Sho did not reply. "Well, thanks. That makes me feel just great," he said bitterly.

"Kyoshi," Sho whispered, taking his hand and looking into his eyes. "I'm touched that you'd say those words to me. And I want you to know I've never felt for anyone the way I feel for you. I just...can't say what you want me to, at least not now. I can't explain why."

Disappointed, Kyoshi looked away. Though he rarely teared up, he felt an uncomfortable wave of emotion hit him when Sho failed to profess his love. He swallowed hard, blinking and trying to push back the wave of anger and hurt that swirled up inside him, threatening to spill out and spoil his composure.

Sho's reluctance to return his sentiment pulled at something vulnerable deep inside him, a sense of loneliness, inadequacy and rejection he'd felt since his parents had died and he had been thrown into his uncle's care. He'd never felt that his uncle really loved him, even though he cared for him responsibly as a guardian should. He'd opened his heart to Sho, and he felt miserable that he'd been rejected.

Sho watched him with concern, seeing the hurt that Kyoshi tried so hard to conceal. "Oh, Kyoshi," he whispered.

"Never mind," Kyoshi snarled, wiping away an errant tear that managed to escape all his efforts to hide his deep hurt.

"But, I didn't mean—"

"I said, never mind! Fucking forget about it." Kyoshi moved past Sho, making for the bathroom and slamming the door shut behind him. Then he locked the door.

Inside the bathroom he turned on the water and tried to gather his composure. He felt a strange sensation swirling up within him, sending waves of buzzing heat through his brain. Somehow his confession had stirred up old memories, memories of a time when he knew he was loved...and when he had loved. Though he tried to repress them, the images of his mother and father appeared in his mind, unbidden, as though they were reaching out to him in his anguish.

He clutched the sink, gasping. An involuntarily sob escaped him, and he splashed cold water on his face, pushing the memories away, forcing himself to rise above his pain, as he always had, ever since that fateful night years before, when his parents had been killed in the fire.

Sho stood outside the door, worried. "Kyoshi," he called, knocking gently and then trying the doorknob. "Come on. Let me in."

"Fucking leave me alone!" Kyoshi shouted.

For a moment the Headmaster considered breaking down the door. Kyoshi's emotion had surprised him. And now there was no question he was truly upset. He put his ear to the door, listening, and then felt guilty for doing so, feeling as though he were intruding on the boy's privacy.

He moved away and sat down on the bed, shaking. Was Kyoshi really so upset because he refused to confess his love? Did Kyoshi truly love him, as he'd said?

Sho knew he loved Kyoshi, more than anything in the world. So why couldn't he tell him?

He stood up and slowly got dressed, staring at the closed door for a few moments. Then he went back out to the living room, making for the bar. He reached for the cognac and then changed his mind, splashing some brandy in a glass and then downing it in one gulp. The heat of the alcohol burned his throat and clouded his mind, but that was precisely what he wanted. He wanted out of the moment.

He poured himself another drink, took a sip and was already starting to feel warm and slightly buzzed when he became aware that the phone was ringing.

He picked it up, feeling a little disoriented. "Hello?"

There was a slight pause. "Ah. So you *are* there. I was beginning to think you'd disappeared off the face of the planet. At least, that is, until I saw you tonight at the Jufi tournament."

Sho forced back an instinctive groan. "Ukita," he answered. "I'm sorry, I'm right in the middle of something. Can I call you back?"

Ukita laughed softly. "That's a good question. Can you? I've been waiting for your call for weeks. You've been avoiding me."

"Yes," Sho admitted, deciding that it was time to be frank with the man. "Yes, I have been avoiding you. I'm sorry, but I don't think we should see each other anymore."

"Oh, I'm not really surprised to hear that. I suspected as much when you blew me off at the concert. But what really surprised me was that you'd pick a boy over me."

Sho fell silent, nearly dropping his brandy. He set the glass on the bar counter to steady himself. "I beg your pardon?"

"At first I couldn't quite believe it. But when I saw you run down onto the floor at the tournament, my suspicions were confirmed. So I decided to do a bit of spying. And I know that Kyoshi Sayuki is in your house right now, alone with you."

"How dare you," Sho hissed, looking toward the window and wondering how much Ukita had seen. The curtains were pulled shut. Surely Ukita could not have seen anything. "And...I don't know what you're talking about."

"I think you do. He's a student, Sho. He's off limits."

"My private life is of no concern to you," Sho snapped, and then caught himself. The alcohol was affecting his cognition; he was offering more than he should. He gathered himself, taking a deep breath. "That is, you're completely off-base, Ukita."

Another soft laugh. "Am I? You seem a bit flustered. I think I'm right."

"I don't have time for this ridiculous call!"

"You may want to rethink that. I'm sure the Trustees would be very interested in learning that the Headmaster of Valemont Academy is intimate with one of his students. What a scandal that would be!"

Sho felt weak at the knees. He clutched the bar counter, his heart pounding. "What do you want?" he whispered, finally.

"Ah. Now we're on the same page. You know what I want. I want...what I've always wanted. I want you in my bed."

"I told you. I'm not interested."

"You don't understand. You don't really have a choice. If you want to keep this secret from getting out, you'll submit to my demands. And this time, Sho, I'll be calling the shots. You get my meaning?"

For a moment Sho was rendered silent. "You can't be serious. That's…that's…."

"I think the word you're looking for is *blackmail*. And yes, it is. So, when shall I pick you up?"

"How dare you," Sho hissed. "How fucking dare you!"

"Such language, Sho. Kyoshi's proved a bad influence, I think. So, when shall it be? Tuesday's good for me. Let's make it Tuesday."

"Out of the question. This whole thing…is out of the question!"

"I'll let you think about it, then, about how embarrassing it will be for you when this breaks out. You'll lose your position, of course. And no Academy will ever take you, so your academic career will be over."

"This is so…despicable," Sho whispered. "I can't believe you'd stoop so low, Ukita. I'm…terribly disappointed in you."

"I'll pick you up Tuesday at 9:00," Ukita replied smoothly, completely ignoring the jab. "We'll be going to my place this time. Oh, and Sho…wear that cologne I like."

The Headmaster stood with the phone in his hand for a few minutes after Ukita hung up, stunned. He hung the phone up and then collapsed into a chair, struggling to get his thoughts around what had just happened.

It was impossible. He was being blackmailed? He couldn't believe that Ukita was capable of such deviousness. In fact, it put a whole new light on his understanding of Ukita. He'd completely dismissed the conductor from his thoughts the moment Kyoshi had come into his life.

The idea that the man would stoop to such methods to get what he wanted made him feel even more repulsed by him; only now, he could no longer discount Ukita as a harmless annoyance. His impotency, apparently, was reserved only for his organ. His threat was viciously powerful—the man knew Sho was in a corner, and he was taking advantage.

After a few moments Sho got up and filled his brandy glass again. He knew he was drinking too much, too fast. But he didn't care.

"Hey," Kyoshi said, coming up behind him and startling when Sho slammed the empty glass down on the bar.

Sho turned to him, his expression softening. "That wasn't directed at you."

"Oh. Good," Kyoshi answered, eyeing the empty glass. He watched as Sho poured himself another drink, his brow furrowed. "I heard you talking to someone."

"Yes. Ukita called," Sho replied. Just saying the name made him almost wretch, and he said it through clenched teeth. He was so angry he could hardly think straight. He downed his drink and then, in a moment of complete frustration, hurled the glass against the wall, shattering it.

"Hey. Calm down." Kyoshi put his arms around Sho from behind, actually a bit relieved that something had happened to distract Sho from their rift in the bedroom. He was embarrassed about his open display of emotion, and the last thing he wanted to do was talk about his awkwardly-received confession.

"I can't believe it! How could I be such a...poor judge of character?"

"What happened?"

"He's blackmailing me! Blackmailing *us*! He knows about us, Kyoshi."

"Blackmail? What do you mean?"

"I mean he's threatening to tell the Board of Trustees about us. He's...he's a complete rogue!"

At this, Kyoshi couldn't help but crack a smile. A rogue? "What does he want? Money? Don't worry about it. We'll pay him."

"Not money. At least, he hasn't asked for it yet. He wants sex. From me."

To Sho's surprise, Kyoshi laughed.

"I fail to see the humor," Sho protested.

"It's just that...well, the guy has balls. I find it amusing."

"It's not amusing, in the least," the Headmaster said grumpily.

Kyoshi leaned over and kissed his cheek. "Don't worry about this. We'll deal with him. We'll think of something."

"He's picking me up on Tuesday," Sho said uncertainly, though feeling a little encouraged by Kyoshi's confidence. "You really think we can do something about it?"

"Sure. My uncle has connections. We'll take him out."

"Kyoshi," Sho protested, horrified at the thought and not realizing the youth was only kidding.

"I'm teasing you," Kyoshi laughed. "Boy, you're really wound up tight, aren't you?"

"Of course I'm wound up tight! He wants to...defile me!"

Kyoshi smiled, entertained by Sho's melodramatic exclamations. "Of course he wants to defile you. *I* want to defile you."

"I don't want him to touch me! I won't be reduced to...to...being his fuck toy!"

At this Kyoshi snorted, unable to keep from laughing aloud again. "I've never heard you use that expression before. Fuck toy, I mean."

"You're not taking this seriously!" Sho wailed.

"And you're taking it far too seriously. Listen. We'll deal with him. He's nothing. Forget about it for now. Let's go now. Seiko and Nishi are waiting for us. We'll have a great time this weekend. Let's get away from here and really cut loose. We'll have plenty of time to figure out what to do about this. Okay? Look, I know people. Throw enough money at them, and they'll be satisfied. Believe me, he has a price."

Sho took a deep breath, and then met Kyoshi's gaze, nodding. "Yes, all right." Though he didn't feel it was going to be all that easy to deal with Ukita, he was comforted by Kyoshi's calm reassurance that the matter could be resolved. The alcohol was starting to take effect as well, and he allowed himself to ease into its numbness, grateful for its welcoming arms of oblivion.

Chapter 15 - *Inside Sayuki*

"Is that all you're bringing?" Nishi laughed at the enormous suitcase Seiko was loading into the back seat of the car, unable to resist teasing him about it.

Seiko grinned, shrugging. "It's the only suitcase I have."

"Hmmm. I was starting to worry about you." Although Nishi hadn't seriously worried, Seiko had taken far longer than he had expected to pack his things, and the snow was really starting to come down hard.

"I didn't know what to bring! I figured I might want to work out, so I brought extra clothes for that, but I didn't really know what all we were planning on doing, so...."

"I imagine we're going to lounge around all weekend at Kyoshi's mansion. Yes, I can see how it would be hard to plan your wardrobe around that." Nishi smiled at him, his warm brown eyes twinkling mischievously.

"Asshole," Seiko shot back, sliding into the front seat and shivering a bit from the frigid night air. "Shit! It's really cold."

Nishi resisted his first instinct, which was offer a predictable retort like, "Don't worry. I'll keep you warm." Instead he reached over and tugged on the young man's flimsy jacket. "Well, of course you're cold. That's not much of a coat."

"It's fine," Seiko protested, fumbling uncertainly with the zipper at the bottom of the expensive, leather jacket. "Don't you like it?"

"Oh, don't get me wrong. You look great in it—it's very fashionable. It's just not exactly weather appropriate." Nishi nodded to his suitcase. "Don't you have a sweater in there you can throw on?"

"We're not going to be outside much now. I'll be fine."

"You know, you don't have to worry about how you look," Nish pressed. "Not around me, that is. Why did you change your shirt?"

Seiko frowned, looking down at his shirt—a short-sleeved, cream-colored top that showed off his golden tan. "What's wrong with this one?"

"Nothing's wrong with it. You look sexy as hell. I just wondered why you changed out of the other one."

"It had semen on it."

"Oh," Nishi laughed, nodding. "Yeah, good reason." He eyed Seiko openly, marveling over the young man's incredible physical beauty. He had always admired the famous Valemont athlete from afar, but now he was able to take a closer look—and he definitely liked what he saw.

His body was lean, healthy, and perfectly proportioned, every muscle taut from rigorous conditioning. His beautiful face, with his fine features, shiny blond hair and vibrant, green eyes, would have been enough to make him look twice. But the face *with* the body made Seiko one of the most stunning young men Nishi had ever laid eyes on. And his golden tan was so radiant that he almost seemed to glow, as though he had just returned from a summer by the sea.

Nishi thought about this for a moment. "How is it you have such a nice tan, this time of year?" he asked, finally.

At this, Seiko seemed a little embarrassed, shrugging as though not wanting to answer.

"Don't tell me you go to one of those tanning booths," Nishi guessed.

"So? What if I do?"

"Is it really worth risking cancer just for a bit of color?"

"You just complimented me on my tan," Seiko argued.

"You're right," Nishi conceded, as he pulled away from Kensington Hall and slowly moved onto the snow-covered road that lead away from Valemont. "But honestly, you would look just as amazing without one."

"That's doubtful."

"Are you kidding? As physically fit as you are, you really don't need to be doing anything special to look good. Take my advice: don't worry so much about what you're wearing or bother with tanning or any of that. Just be you—just as you are. You're perfect."

Seiko listened quietly, finding Nishi's perspective rather comforting. He actually spent a good deal of time trying to enhance his physical appearance. In fact, his entire existence was built around his body. As an athlete he had come to appreciate his substantial physical gifts. But his air of confidence concealed painful feelings of self-inadequacy.

He felt inferior to his classmates when it came to academics, and he had no artistic or creative gifts. So he channeled all his feelings of self-doubt into his physique and into sports, each new trophy helping him feel a little more at ease with himself but never really truly comfortable or proud of what he had accomplished. Valemont's greatest athletic star, ironically, felt like a failure.

Seiko thrived on compliments about his physical appearance, and Nishi's obvious appreciation of his looks was flattering. He found himself powerfully drawn to the outspoken, easy-going man who had serviced him with such skillful lingual artistry earlier that evening. Nishi's suggestion that he just be himself, without worrying about his physical appearance—that he was perfect just as he was—was more effective at securing his interest than any other route of seduction the man could have attempted.

"In fact, I think you shouldn't bother with clothes at all," Nishi continued, winking at him. "I say you should just be naked whenever you're with me. So you might as well take those clothes off now."

Seiko laughed, mostly to hide a sudden surge of emotion. Panicking, he turned to the window and pretended to look out at the snow. "It's really coming down now."

"Yes, it is. I wonder how far away Kyoshi's estate is? I hope we can get there before it gets much worse."

"Are we going by your place next?"

"Yes, but I'll just dash inside. You can come inside too, if you like. I'm right here, actually," Nishi said, motioning to his house as they pulled into the drive.

"You live really close to campus."

"Yes, this used to be Sho's house, before he moved to his new one. Oh, fuck!"

Seiko frowned. "What is it?"

Nishi was staring at King, realizing then that he'd forgotten all about his dog. He couldn't very well leave the animal by himself for three days. Though King often preferred being outside, he did need to go inside sometimes to warm up, and then there was the issue of food and water. He could leave him with plenty of food, but the water would freeze. Besides, the weather would be too much, even for the cold-hardy Siberian Husky.

"What am I going to do about King?"

Seiko followed his gaze toward the large animal that was lying on the porch, looking half-asleep. "Is King your dog?"

"Yes. Shit!"

"Maybe you can bring him along. I'll call Kyoshi and find out." Seiko flipped open his phone, glad for a distraction from his thoughts. He was uncomfortable dealing with feelings, and Nishi's warm regard and unconditional acceptance had made him feel inexplicably emotional.

Kyoshi answered after the first ring. "Yeah?"

"Hey. Nishi is worried about his dog. Can he bring him along?"

"Sure. Are you two almost ready? We should head out before the weather gets any worse."

"We know. We'll be there soon. How far is it to your uncle's place?"

"About half an hour's drive," Kyoshi answered.

"All right. We'll hurry."

"Where are you now?"

"At Nishi's. We just pulled up."

"Why don't you stay there, then. We'll come by for you," Kyoshi suggested. "That way we can head over there now while Nishi is packing."

"Sure. See you in a bit."

Seiko closed his phone, giving Nishi a reassuring smile. "He says it's no problem. We can bring him with us."

Relieved, Nishi nodded. "Awesome. Now it's just a question of how we'll get him into the car."

"Kyoshi says we should just wait here. They're coming over now to pick us up."

"I guess that means no sex before they get here." Nishi sighed with exaggerated disappointment, although he hadn't seriously planned on rushing things, now that they had an entire three-day weekend ahead of them.

"I already told you that I'm not a bottom," Seiko reminded him anxiously.

"Yes, I know that's what you said." Nishi gave him a mysterious, knowing smile and then got out of the vehicle.

The night seemed strangely quiet and beautiful; there was nothing outside that was not covered in soft, sparkling snow, which gave everything an ethereal, magical quality.

Seiko fell in beside him, though held back a little as they approached the dog. "Does he bite?"

Nishi gave him an amused look. "Don't tell me you're afraid of dogs?"

"Not particularly. It's just that I'm not around them much."

"He's harmless."

"Yes, that's what all owners say until their dog chews somebody's hand off."

"You *are* afraid of dogs!"

"I am not," Seiko protested.

"He's really gentle. The only time I ever heard him growl was at Takashi — but that's because Takashi was a snake."

"You have a snake?" Seiko looked even more apprehensive at this, frowning as they neared the porch and looking around as though he expected one to spring out at him at any moment.

Nishi arched a brow. "Afraid of snakes, too, are we? If my memory serves me correctly, you claimed not to be afraid of snakes, nor anything else, for that matter."

"I'm not. Not really, that is. Only I've never actually encountered one before."

"Well, don't worry. I don't have a snake. Takashi was...my last lover."

"Oh." Seiko felt a slight sting of jealousy at the mention of a lover, though Nishi's claim that Takashi was a snake was reassuring. He found his own reaction a bit disconcerting, however. Why should he care whether or not Nishi had a lover? He wasn't going to sleep with the man. He'd made that clear. There was no way he was going to be a bottom, not for anyone.

Yet even as he told himself this, he couldn't help but wonder what it might be like to be with Nishi in bed. His obvious skill at fellatio made him curious about what other sexual artistry the man possessed. And there was no question he was enjoying Nishi's flirting and his quiet confidence; Nishi certainly acted as though he expected Seiko would eventually succumb to his advances.

King looked decidedly uninterested in either of them, continuing to lie on the porch as though completely unconcerned that he was blocking their access to the house.

The young men both carefully stepped around him.

"Is he okay?" Seiko asked, when the massive animal made no reaction to their presence.

"Yes, he's always like that."

Nishi opened the door to his house, nervously peeking in to be sure nothing embarrassing was lying around. He hadn't expected company, and so he'd left the place in shambles. "Sorry about the mess," he murmured.

"It's okay," Seiko answered, as he stepped inside. He looked around with interest, finding the man's casual, studio-like living area rather inviting, despite the clutter and disarray. The center of the room was occupied by an easel covered with a cloth, which immediately piqued his curiosity.

The house smelled of paint, but it was not unpleasant. There was another aroma, too—a citrus-like scent. Seiko turned and spied a miniature potted orange tree by the great bay window that took up most of the front wall.

"Wow, oranges?"

"Oh, yes. I love oranges. They're best straight off the tree."

"I didn't know you could grow them inside," Seiko remarked, admiring the colorful, flowering plants by the window. "You've got quite a collection here. You must like plants."

"Yes, I love gardening. That's why I hate the winter. Sit down if you like—I'll be just a minute."

Nishi rushed to his bedroom to pack, leaving Seiko to explore the room for a few minutes alone.

The place was strewn with countless unusual objects that invited further inquiry, but Seiko's interest was immediately drawn back to the giant easel in the middle of the room. The cloth over the painting only made him more curious about what it was hiding. He crept toward the easel, determined to take a peek while he had the chance.

"Don't look at the painting," Nishi called from the other room, just as he was about to lift the cloth.

"I won't," Seiko answered. He then boldly lifted the cloth anyway. He gasped, and then pulled the cloth from the painting, letting it fall to the floor.

Before him was nothing short of a masterpiece. He honestly couldn't believe his eyes—it was like a painting from a museum, or from another time, by some famous, long-dead artist. It depicted a young man sprawled out in the grass, fast asleep. He was completely naked, and he was beautiful.

"I told you not to look at it!" Nishi cried, as he entered the room with an armful of clothes.

Seiko turned to gaze at him with wonder, his eyes shining. "It's...amazing. You painted this? You honestly painted this? It's extraordinary! You really *are* an artist!"

Nishi softened at this, looking pleased with his praise. He tossed his clothes onto the sofa. "You really like it?"

Seiko looked back at the painting, feeling almost speechless. "I don't know what to say. You're so incredibly talented." The revelation that Nishi was a real artist made him view the man in a different light. He had liked Nishi well enough before. Now he felt almost inferior, as though he wasn't worthy to be standing in his presence. He knew he was no art critic, but there was no question that Nishi's painting was riveting. Anyone would think so; there were artists, and then there were masters. Nishi was a master.

"It's not quite right. It lacks depth," Nishi sighed, staring at the painting with a critical eye. "I've given up on it, I think."

"What? Are you out of your mind? It's...it's spectacular! Do you have other paintings I can see?"

"No."

"Why not?"

"Because none of them were quite right. So I destroyed them."

"What?!"

Seiko looked so horrified at this that Nishi had to laugh.

"How can you laugh?" Seiko protested. "You can't seriously destroy paintings like this! That's...that should be against the law!"

Nishi shrugged. "They're my paintings. I know I can do better. I don't want anyone to see my work until I'm ready. And I don't want my practice pieces lying around to remind me of my failures."

"Your failures!" Seiko shook his head. "You can't seriously think that about your art!"

"So, does this mean you're going to pose for me?" Nishi probed, walking toward Seiko with a meaningful smile.

Seiko swallowed, his heart immediately beating a cadence faster as the handsome man approached him. "I'll pose for you...if you promise not to destroy this painting."

"Agreed," Nishi answered. "You can have the painting, if you want it."

"You're giving it to me?"

"If you want it."

"I couldn't possibly take it. It's...a masterpiece. It should be in a museum."

Nishi had moved closer and now put his hands on Seiko's hips, caressing him suggestively. "I'm dying to see you naked," he whispered, pulling him closer. "Sprawled out before me, just like that." He nodded toward the painting, a smile tugging at the corners of his mouth.

"Who is he?" Seiko asked. "One of your lovers?"

"No. Just a depiction of ideal male beauty. But he's nothing compared to you."

"You really want to paint me?"

"I want to do more than that. I want to make you whimper. I want to make you beg. I want to kiss your entire body. And then I want to fuck you, over and over, my cock burning deep inside you. And you'll love it, Seiko...you'll spread your legs wide for me and plead with me not to stop, bucking back against me when I find that special place that makes you scream."

Special place? Seiko listened, fascinated, and at the same time feeling a bit nervous about Nishi's agenda, which the man laid out with such authority and confidence. Perhaps the planned trip to Kyoshi's estate wasn't such a good idea. What if Nishi wouldn't take no for an answer? What if he insisted on what he wanted?

"But I told you—"

Nishi silenced him with a kiss, his warm tongue thrusting deep inside him, forcing him to defend the sanctity of his mouth with his own tongue. The lingual dance that ensued made Seiko feel light-headed and weak-kneed; the man tasted like fire and honey all at once, sweet and powerful and burning, like the warmth of sudden intoxication, a slow fire moving through his body in an insistent, devastating wave.

Seiko felt completely unprepared for such a kiss. He'd never been kissed in such a manner before, in his entire life. Until that moment, he hadn't realized such pleasure was even possible, or that there was an artistry to lingual congress. Nishi was teaching him as he kissed him, patiently coaxing him to respond with slower exploration, to make every incursion deliberate — to taste him with passion and purpose.

He was trembling from head to toe, very much aware of Nishi's hands on his hips, of the slightest movement of his fingers, as though his touch burned through his jeans and into his flesh. When Nishi slid his hands around to his ass and squeezed him, pulling him up forcefully against his body, he welcomed this intimacy. His cock was so rigid and swollen it ached, and the man's hands felt good. He liked the way Nishi's hard body felt against his own and found himself suddenly wondering what he looked like naked.

Nishi slipped his hands under the back of Seiko's shirt and then down inside his jeans, one hand on each ass cheek. He began squeezing and kneading him, his fingers brushing tantalizingly close to his portal, and all the while continued to kiss him.

Seiko considered himself fairly experienced when it came to sex, but he realized as soon as Nishi began touching him that he was a mere boy in his arms. The man's confidence and skill was apparent in his every movement. Nishi was, of course, older — and now Seiko began to feel exceptionally curious about what he had to offer. He was accustomed to rather brief, somewhat desperate and sometimes even awkward sessions with his peers or boys younger than himself. He had always been satisfied and so had never found his sex life wanting in any way.

But now, the way Nishi so masterfully held him almost suspended against his body, teasing him, made him very much aware that he had never been with a real man before, or with someone who truly knew what he was doing in bed.

Nishi began circling his sphincter with one of his fingers, probing the sensitive skin with just the right amount of pressure to make Seiko long for something more. He had never experienced such an urge before, but now he wanted Nishi to penetrate him with his finger. He waited, hoping for it, and feeling a little ashamed for wanting it. He wasn't, after all, a bottom. No, of course not. Seiko Shinozaki was 100% top. And yet his entire body quivered with anticipation as the man deliberately teased him, keeping him pressed up against his body, up on his toes, working him like a puppeteer handles a marionette.

Nishi knew exactly how long to keep him waiting, carefully monitoring his every movement, the trembling of his body, the anxious whimpers that now escaped him, muffled by his kiss. He pressed the tip of his finger up against his portal and slowly but firmly inserted it, just pushing past the sphincter.

Seiko gasped, pulling away from the kiss.

"I'm going to come in my pants," he warned.

Nishi found this endearing and struggled not to laugh. "Would you like me to suck you off again?"

"God, yes."

At that moment car lights shone into the room as Kyoshi pulled into the driveway.

"Fuck!" Seiko exclaimed. "They're here. Damn it! God damn it!"

"Perhaps we can continue this later," Nishi suggested, gently kissing Seiko's throat.

"I want to come *now*."

"If you liked this, wait until I put my tongue up your ass."

"Oh God," Seiko groaned, shivering at the thought.

Nishi smiled to himself, feeling victorious as he pulled his hands from Seiko's pants. Despite his protests that he was not a bottom, Seiko was giving every indication that he was extraordinarily sensitive and responsive in the area that mattered most and would therefore learn to enjoy being taken. He felt confident he would have the boy begging to be fucked before the night was through.

"That's right," he continued, one hand behind Seiko's head as he whispered provocatively in his ear, "I'll put you face down on the bed and spread your legs wide, and then bury my face in your ass, my tongue squeezing up inside you."

"I'm seriously going to spill," Seiko pleaded. "Please stop."

"All right." Nishi moved away, turning to hide his smile.

He loved how easily Seiko was sprung and knew that he would be a delight to pleasure. The idea that he was also technically a virgin—at least in the way that it really mattered to him—was another turn-on. It would be thrilling to teach him the joys of penetration. As for himself, Nishi was looking forward to the unparalleled pleasure of an untried ass: Seiko would be so tight and resistant to his every movement that it would make even the slightest incursion nothing short of paradise.

Sho was pounding impatiently on the door. Nishi grabbed his clothes and stuffed them inside a paper grocery sack, along with some dog food, shrugging when Seiko laughed at his choice. "I don't know where my suitcase is," he explained.

Sho gave him an anxious look when he opened the door. "We need to hurry."

"Take it easy, brother," Nishi whispered, putting a reassuring hand on his shoulder.

"The weather's getting worse. Perhaps this isn't such a good idea. I'm thinking maybe we should call this off."

"What are you going on about? Of course we're going. Where's King?"

Nishi looked around and realized Kyoshi had already managed, by some miracle, to persuade King to follow him to the car, and was now instructing him to get into the back seat.

The dog obeyed, jumping into the car without hesitation.

Nishi shook his head at Sho. "How on earth did he do that?"

"I couldn't tell you."

"King doesn't respond to anyone—not even me, half the time! And I've never been able to get him into a car that easily!"

"Is that all you're bringing?" Sho motioned to Nishi's paper bag without comment, as though not the least bit surprised at his choice of luggage. "What about Seiko?"

"Mine's still in the car. I'll get it," Seiko murmured, rushing to retrieve his suitcase. He was almost glad for the cold, since it helped tame his arousal.

"Let's go," Kyoshi called as he got back inside the car. "The snow's supposed to get worse."

"The snow *is* getting worse," Sho repeated, giving his brother a worried look.

"We'll be fine," Nishi insisted.

They all piled into Kyoshi's car, Sho in the front and Nishi and Seiko in the back. King had chosen to lie on the seat behind the driver's seat and refused to move, so Nishi and Seiko sat close together, on the other side.

Once they'd all settled in, they rode in silence for a while, the furious onslaught of the snow making them all a little apprehensive. The roads were completely deserted, as though everyone else in the city had suddenly vanished.

"Traffic's a bit heavy," Kyoshi remarked, to help ease the tension.

Seiko and Nishi both chuckled at this, but the Headmaster peered outside with a gloomy sense of foreboding.

Sho was in a near panic. Ukita's call had made him revisit his own concerns over the impropriety of his relationship with Kyoshi. He had almost called off the trip, but Kyoshi had managed to convince him that it would be good to relax together for the weekend. The weather only made him even more nervous, as though nature itself were trying to tell him the trip was a bad idea.

The Headmaster felt, now, even more keenly how inappropriate and unwise it was for Seiko to witness his indiscretion. It was embarrassing, and the more he thought about it, the more uncomfortable he felt, especially now that they were all riding together in the car.

He was reliving, too, with no small amount of chagrin, his ridiculous dash out onto the arena floor at the tournament. He imagined that it must have been obvious to everyone, if it were obvious to Ukita, that he was engaged in illicit contact with Kyoshi. He almost expected to return to work after the Holidays and find a summons from Dean Gerard, demanding to know what was going on. The more he thought about this, the more he was convinced that everything was headed for a disastrous end.

And it was too late to do anything about it.

Mitsuwa no longer felt he could break things off with Kyoshi. Their lover's spat had driven this point home. Sho had hated being apart from him, even for that short amount of time. He still felt angry and extraordinarily jealous when he thought of Kyoshi with Jiji. He knew now he wanted Kyoshi all to himself.

Kyoshi noticed his brooding but said nothing about it, still feeling the sting of the Headmaster's reluctance to profess his feelings for him. He was extraordinarily puzzled over Sho's actions—which seemed to definitively suggest that the man did love him, and yet he refused to say the words. Why couldn't he say he loved him?

"Can you see all right?" Nishi asked, breaking his reverie.

"Hmmm?" Kyoshi glanced back, smiling when he saw Nishi with his arm around Seiko. Seiko looked completely relaxed, happily snuggling up with his new "friend."

Nishi motioned toward the window. "Can you see the roads? With the snow and all?"

"Oh. Sort of, but it's a bit slick. That's why I'm driving so slow." Kyoshi adjusted his mirror so he could see the couple from the front seat. "Seiko, you do realize you left your date back at that party, don't you?"

Seiko grinned. "Yeah, I know. I totally spaced and just walked out without him. My phone keeps vibrating. I think he's pissed as all hell."

"He'll get over it," Nishi remarked, delighted that Seiko had abandoned the handsome young man he'd seen him with at the tournament. He certainly had noticed when Seiko left the party without his date, though he had deliberately kept this observation to himself.

Seiko nodded. "I'm sure he will, too. He doesn't have trouble attracting interest, with that body of his."

"He didn't seem all that hot to me," Nishi said, feigning a disinterested yawn.

"Are you kidding? He was hot as hell," Kyoshi proclaimed, and almost immediately regretted the comment when Sho shot him a dark look.

Kyoshi laughed, reaching out to put his hand on the Headmaster's knee. "Come on now. Don't be jealous."

"You should keep both hands on the steering wheel," Sho answered, in a low voice.

"But I like having my hand on your knee," Kyoshi protested.

"Kyoshi," the Headmaster whispered, shooting him a meaningful look, as he motioned anxiously toward the back seat.

"What? Like they both don't already know we're going to fuck each other senseless at my place?"

Seiko and Nishi both laughed loudly at this.

"Kyoshi!" Sho hissed, mortified.

"Relax, brother. We *do* already know that," Nishi said, reaching out to pat his brother reassuringly on the shoulder.

The Headmaster sighed, and then turned to look back at Seiko. "Seiko, I can't imagine what you must think of me. I really must...apologize for my behavior. Believe me, I know how inappropriate this is. I've been sitting here thinking perhaps it would be best if we called this trip off."

"No!" the others all cried in unison, laughing when they heard each other.

"No, please don't apologize, Headmaster," Seiko answered. "I promise I won't say anything."

Sho shook his head. "You shouldn't be put in the position where that would even be an issue. You must be completely shocked."

"I was shocked at first," Seiko admitted, "but I can see you're both taking this seriously. And you seem less like the Headmaster to me now, and more like a regular guy." Although this wasn't entirely true, he was looking forward to the weekend and didn't want the trip to be called off.

Kyoshi snorted at the Headmaster being referred to as a *"regular guy,"* which earned him another sharp look from Sho.

"Yet you still call me Headmaster."

"I'm sorry," Seiko murmured, his brow furrowing. "Should I call you something else?"

"I don't suppose it makes much difference," Sho sighed, turning away.

"I still call you Headmaster," Kyoshi pointed out. "Mostly because it's kinky."

Sho only rolled his eyes at this, deciding not to even bother scolding him.

"Kyoshi, you're a man after my own heart," Nishi announced.

Seiko frowned. "What's that supposed to mean?"

"I mean he's not afraid of breaking rules in the name of kink."

"So? I'm not afraid of that either."

"Oh yeah? That's good to know."

Seiko turned to look at Nishi and realized the man was teasing him, his eyes full of warmth and invitation. The next thing he knew Nishi was kissing him again, his tongue exploring his mouth in languid circles.

"For heaven's sake, Nish," Sho scolded, after a moment.

"What?" Nishi laughed, breaking away from the kiss. He was extraordinarily aroused and absolutely loved kissing Seiko, feeling as though he could kiss him forever.

"We're in the car, too."

"So? Admit it. It turns you on."

"I assure you, it does not."

"It turns *me* on," Kyoshi announced, adjusting himself and shooting Nishi a grin.

"Why am I not surprised?" Nishi replied, giving Kyoshi a wink.

"Would you two stop flirting?" Seiko protested.

"I'll second that," Sho remarked wryly.

"Now, brother, there's no need to get jealous. You know my heart still belongs to you. Especially after our special time earlier today."

"Nish!" The Headmaster was so mortified that he turned completely around in his seat, leveling him a withering glare.

"What's this?" Kyoshi probed, turning to Sho for verification. "What's he talking about? What, did you two kiss earlier today?"

"We did more than that," Nishi whispered.

"What?!" Seiko and Kyoshi both exclaimed in unison.

"That's it! The trip is over!" the Headmaster barked. "Kyoshi, turn the car around!"

Nishi laughed. "Oh come on, brother. You know I can't resist teasing you. There's no need to throw a fit and spoil the weekend for everyone."

"So are you saying you didn't do something together, or you did?" Kyoshi pressed.

"We didn't," Nishi said quickly. "Of course we didn't."

Kyoshi looked back at him through his mirror and Nish raised his eyebrows as if to say, *Yes, we did.* The two men shared a brief smile. Kyoshi turned his attention back to the road, his mind now completely wrapped around this new idea, that Sho had already done something extraordinarily kinky with his own brother. He found this notion amazingly erotic.

He wasn't the slightest bit jealous of Nishi, who he knew could never be a serious rival for Sho's affections. Whatever the brothers had engaged in had surely been entirely sexual, a moment of sheer carnal, forbidden pleasure. He mulled over the possibilities in his mind and wondered exactly what they had done.

He hadn't been teasing when he'd said Seiko and Nishi were turning him on. Watching them kiss had aroused him, and now he began actively exploring a new fantasy — one centered around the foursome that he had suggested to Sho earlier that evening.

The fact that the Headmaster had not immediately rejected the idea had been encouraging. Now, to learn that Nishi and Sho may have already been sexually intimate put a new spin on the situation. Perhaps the foursome was not entirely out of the question. The thought that such a wickedly erotic encounter was even a remote possibility was so exciting to him that Kyoshi was having trouble concentrating on the road.

Although Nishi's retraction had momentarily pacified Sho, he was still furious with Nish and was feeling increasingly anxious about the whole weekend. He was just about to insist, once again, that the trip was cancelled. But then they arrived at the Sayuki estate.

"Ah, we made it," Kyoshi said, realizing then how tightly he had been gripping the steering wheel. "Here it is."

They pulled up to a great iron gate bearing a shield-like sign with a family crest on it. Beneath the crest, engraved in bold letters, was the word, *Sayuki*. The crest split in two as the gate slowly opened for them, its sensors recognizing the identification tracers that had been implanted in Kyoshi's vehicle. Though it was dark out, the road that led to the house was well-lit, and the house itself, situated on a slight hill in the distance, seemed to have nearly every light on, which made its magnificent, sprawling size unmistakable. It was beautiful, the windows glittering like a thousand pieces of gold.

"Holy shit," Nishi breathed. "That's your house?"

"Yes, it is," Kyoshi answered proudly. It had been a long time since he'd brought anyone to his home, and at least for that moment, he couldn't help but enjoy their reactions.

"Goodness," Sho murmured, equally stunned by the colossal majesty of the Sayuki estate. For the first time he realized the true magnitude of Kyoshi's wealth and all that he stood to inherit from his wealthy guardian.

Seiko leaned forward, peering through the windshield in disbelief. "Wow, Kyoshi! It's like a palace!"

King, as if deciding to join in on the commentary, suddenly barked.

"I thought you said no one was here," Sho said anxiously.

"That's right; I sent the servants home for the Holidays."

"But all the lights are on."

"Oh, that's just a security thing. Uncle insists on it. I know it uses a lot of energy, but actually the entire place is also powered with solar panels, so it's not as wasteful as it seems."

"It's absolutely enormous," Nishi remarked, feeling even more astonished as they approached the mansion and its true size became apparent.

"Yes, it's very big," Kyoshi agreed quietly. Privately, he found the mansion far *too* big for his tastes, and he had grown up feeling rather marginalized by the grand scale of his uncle's estate. Too much of it was empty, some parts rarely used. Kyoshi had restricted himself to certain areas of it in an attempt to make the place seem less lonely and overwhelming. The grandeur and opulence of the Sayuki estate was only surpassed, in his view, by its tremendous coldness.

"You're sure no one's here?" the Headmaster repeated.

"I'm sure."

Seiko shook his head. "This is straight out of fairy tale. It must have been something, growing up in a place like this."

Kyoshi only nodded, deciding it would make him seem rather ungrateful to explain how miserable his childhood had been in his uncle's care. He had not wanted to think about his childhood. But as they drew closer to mansion, he found himself besieged by images—a myriad dark, painful memories that descended into his consciousness, unbidden, and rather unwelcome.

Kiichi Sayuki had been the sort of man who believed children had to be regularly punished, for their own good. He been brutal when it came to physical discipline. Kyoshi's own father, by contrast, had never once raised his hand to him, preferring gentler means of parenting. So when Kyoshi came to live with his uncle, already traumatized from the unbelievable horror of losing his parents, his personal anguish was only compounded by the all-too-frequent "correction" of his uncle's paddle, belt, or cane.

Kyoshi had quickly learned what behavior was acceptable and what was not. But as a young boy he had craved, most of all, love and attention, and he had learned something else: that his uncle only paid attention to him when he needed disciplined. Eventually Kyoshi resorted to deliberately disobeying him, just for the few minutes of intimacy—however painful—that his behavior earned him with the man who was otherwise mostly absent from his life. He would dread the punishment and, at the same time, look forward to it, for only after he had been soundly thrashed would his uncle speak for any length of time to him, scolding him as he brushed away his tears. Then Kiichi would be off again on another business trip somewhere in the world, leaving his young nephew alone to plot out his next act of disobedience.

As Kiichi's patience with his wayward charge began to wear thin, his punishment had become even more brutal. Next the boy had been introduced to the bench, a device that kept him restrained while the man laid into him with such fury that Kyoshi finally abandoned his attempts to win his uncle's attention through intentional disobedience.

After that he had endured years of loneliness and neglect as his uncle essentially ignored him, leaving him for weeks at a time with only the servants for company. The man had even denied him the companionship of a pet, claiming that animals carried horrible diseases and parasites.

So Kyoshi had grown up, for the most part, alone in the massive, magnificent mansion—where he had wandered through an endless labyrinth of empty rooms that somehow mirrored the vast loneliness of his heart.

"Look at this! You have, what...*ten* garages! Ten!" Seiko shook his head as one of the garage doors slowly rose to admit Kyoshi's vehicle.

"Is that how many cars you have? Ten?" Nishi asked.

"I don't know, probably," Kyoshi answered, shrugging. "I only drive this one."

"You don't know? Wow, Kyoshi. And this is a garage? It looks like you just drove into someone's living room! You're going to give us a tour, I hope?" Seiko pressed.

"Sure, of course," Kyoshi agreed, smiling stiffly as he turned off the ignition.

"Is it all right to bring King inside your house?" Nishi asked.

"Yes, bring him inside. It's fine." Although this was a complete lie, Kyoshi knew it was unlikely his uncle would ever discover that he had allowed a dog to roam around inside the mansion. And even if he did find out—Kyoshi really didn't care.

Seiko and Nishi were both too excited to notice his change of mood, but Sho picked up on it instantly, falling in beside him as they exited the vehicle.

"Unbelievable!" Seiko murmured, as soon as they stepped inside. He and Nishi exchanged another look of disbelief, equally awed by the splendor and scale of the house. Even King seemed a bit less lethargic, looking around the room as though mildly interested.

Sho put a protective hand on Kyoshi's back. "Is something wrong?" he asked in a low voice.

Kyoshi shook his head, though thinking about his childhood had most definitely upset and unsettled him.

"A fountain!" Seiko gravitated toward the elegant fountain that formed the focal point of the room, while Nishi stood admiring the paintings that lined the walls.

The Headmaster frowned as he studied Kyoshi, feeling certain that something was troubling him. "Why don't you take us to our rooms, so we can all get settled in?" he suggested. "You can show us around after that."

"Yes, all right. Follow me." Kyoshi walked through the first great room and then through a second before reaching a corridor. He turned to Seiko and Nishi. "These are all guest rooms. Pick any room you like."

The couple peered down the long corridor, marveling at all the doors that lined the hall.

"All these are guest rooms? You must have had a lot of guests," Seiko remarked.

"Not really," Kyoshi replied, not bothering to inform him that there were, in fact, hundreds of guest rooms in the various floors of the mansion—rooms for guests that never came. Rooms that had never, even once, been used. It was a complete waste to have them cleaned regularly, in his view. But for the occasional dinner or event at the Sayuki estate, the quiet mansion rarely saw visitors.

He had only occasionally brought friends to his home, quickly learning that his wealth inspired jealousy and resentment, and that his "friends" treated him differently when they saw where he lived.

He nodded ahead to another enormous room that opened out from the corridor. "We'll meet you back here in a bit. My room is on the other side of this sitting room."

"Do you mind if I lie down and stretch my legs for a bit?" Nishi asked. "This day has been exhausting."

In truth, Nishi wasn't the least bit tired—but he had been coddling an erection for hours and was anxious to do something about it. He knew Seiko was still aroused, as well, and he wanted to take advantage of it.

"Good idea," Sho agreed. He was now convinced that something had upset Kyoshi, and he wanted to talk to him, alone.

"THIS IS MY ROOM," KYOSHI ANNOUNCED, STEPPING aside to allow the Headmaster to enter first.

The "room" was actually a collection of rooms, more like a large apartment, or a penthouse suite. It had a kitchen, a seating area, a bar, and a separate bathroom and bedroom, and though the area was spacious, it was a bit smaller than Sho might have expected, given the scale of everything else he had seen thus far. It was furnished tastefully, but with restraint — as though Kyoshi had made a deliberate effort to avoid the opulence that seemed to characterize the rest of the mansion.

King followed them inside, apparently deciding that Kyoshi's room was the place to be. He lay down directly in front of the fireplace, looking very much at home.

"Would you like a drink?" Kyoshi offered, moving toward the bar.

"Yes, actually. A spot of cognac would be rather nice."

He has his own bar, Sho thought, finding it a bit unusual that Kiichi Sayuki would allow his young nephew such free access to alcohol. He followed him to the bar, trying to collect his thoughts.

"Kyoshi...I couldn't help but notice that you suddenly appear a little out of sorts. If it's because of what Nishi said, you don't have anything to worry about. I'm not attracted to Nish, although it's true he probably feels a bit more for me than just brotherly love. What happened...what he referred to...was just a...an accident. I can explain, if you like."

Kyoshi turned to him, an odd look on his face. "You think I'm upset because of that? Surely you know me better than that. I think it's hot that Nishi has a thing for you, and even hotter if something actually happened." He smiled. "So, what exactly *did* happen?"

The Headmaster frowned. "That's not why you're upset?"

"What, now you're not going to tell me?"

"I'll tell you, but I'm more concerned about whatever it is that's bothering you."

"I don't really feel like talking about it," Kyoshi answered, turning away as he poured Sho his drink.

"Are you sure?"

Kyoshi hesitated for a moment, trying to fight back a wave of emotion that threatened to break his composure. He turned around and handed Sho the glass, shaking his head. "It's just this house...hearing you all make such a fuss about it, made me feel guilty for hating that I grew up here."

Sho took the drink, nodding his thanks. "You hate this house?"

"Not the house. I hate...the memories. The loneliness."

They both instinctively moved toward the chairs in front of the warm, crackling fire. Kyoshi sat down with an air of dejection and then stared absently into the flames.

Sho sat across from him, crossing his legs and sipping his cognac for a moment, wanting Kyoshi to open up to him and feeling as though there was something of great importance looming just beneath the surface of his words. "You were lonely here?"

"Yes." Kyoshi continued to stare into the fire, his expression unreadable.

"You're not close to your uncle, I take it?"

"Gods no," Kyoshi laughed. "He's a fucking prick."

The Headmaster studied him, deciding not to scold him for his disparaging remark about his guardian. He began to put together, in his mind, a critical truth about Kyoshi, based on a few comments he'd made about his uncle before: Kyoshi felt unloved by his guardian. And as a child—during his most formative, critical years—he had been lonely...perhaps even neglected. Despite Kyoshi's callous laughter, Sho could see the deep hurt in his eyes.

"It would be easy to feel lonely in a place as big as this," he answered carefully.

"Especially when you're left alone most of the time," Kyoshi remarked bitterly.

Sho nodded slightly, his suspicions confirmed. "So, your uncle was often away on business, then?"

"That's what he claimed. I don't even know. I only know he was never here."

Another thought then occurred to the Headmaster, one which, on reflection, made him rather angry. Kyoshi's uncle hadn't been at the tournament for his big night, hadn't been there to praise Kyoshi for his victory, or to worry when he'd been knocked out. Kiichi should have been the one who had rushed out onto the floor, risking Kyoshi's disqualification—not him. Nor had the man even called to find out what had happened, despite the fact that he must have known Kyoshi was competing in the final tournament. Sho began to harbor a distinct dislike for the great Kiichi Sayuki, for all his wealth and generous endowments, if he had neglected Kyoshi as much as he now feared might be the case.

"I can't imagine what that must have been like for you, coming here after...losing your parents, and then not getting the attention and affection you must have so desperately needed," Sho said thoughtfully.

Kyoshi swallowed hard, his eyes burning with tears. In a single sentence, the Headmaster had captured the tragedy of his entire childhood. He had nailed it. Kyoshi had never spoken of his private torment with anyone before. Now, to have Sho so succinctly validate the injury that had been done to him, almost came as a shock to his system.

He felt as though something deep inside him had just broken away from a sticking place and now burned up through his heart, carrying with it years of hurt and loneliness. He could not have stopped its trajectory even if he had tried, and in that moment he was no longer willing to even try. The darkness that had ruled his inner terrain for so long now seemed to swirl and lift, and there, for a brief moment, Kyoshi remembered the boy he had once been—a happy, carefree child whose innocence was then irrevocably ripped away.

"Fuck," he whispered, as tears began streaming down his cheeks. "Oh, fuck!" He stood up, standing for a moment as though unable to decide what to do, one hand raking anxiously through his dark hair.

"Oh, Kyoshi." Sho put his drink down and then got up. In the next minute Kyoshi was in his arms, sobbing, his face pressed against his chest.

The Headmaster held him, gently stroking his hair in a comforting fashion that made Kyoshi aware of just how long he had waited for such tenderness. He had waited for comfort from his uncle over his loss, comfort that never came. He had then waited desperately for love and affection, but he had waited, again, in vain. His guardian had never once told him he loved him, nor had he shown that he did, in any of his actions—not really. Kyoshi's cries came out in broken, ragged gasps, his entire chest heaving as Sho held him close.

"That's it," Sho encouraged, intuitively realizing that Kyoshi needed to cry, that he was releasing a terrible hurt that had been pent up inside him for far too long.

King had abandoned his place by the fire and now ventured a few feet forward to sit at Kyoshi's feet, as if somehow understanding that the young man needed comforting.

Chapter 16 - *Cutting Loose*

SHO MITSUWA HELD KYOSHI AS THE YOUNG MAN cried out years of frustration and hurt. He could hardly bear to hear Kyoshi's pain; it tore into his heart like nothing had before. At that moment Sho knew he had fallen completely in love with him, despite all the obstacles between them. It went against everything he stood for to have involved himself with a student, and yet somehow it had happened.

And now he was more than just involved. He was in love. His heart and mind screamed out his love, yet his mouth could not surrender the words he knew Kyoshi desperately needed to hear.

"There, now," he whispered, as he soothingly stroked the young man's hair. "That's right. Let it all out."

Even as he comforted Kyoshi, he was becoming increasingly agitated. His thoughts were racing so furiously he felt as though his mind were about to explode. He had done the unthinkable — he had engaged in sexual intimacy with a student. That alone was enough to cost him his career as Headmaster at Valemont Academy.

But he had done more than that. He had gotten inextricably emotionally involved with Kyoshi, so much so that he was now doing ridiculous, foolish things, such as running out onto the tournament floor to Kyoshi's side in front of thousands of spectators and then angrily crashing a private party to retrieve Kyoshi in front of his peers.

Sho knew that his actions had to have raised the suspicions of anyone who had witnessed his behavior. If Ukita had guessed what he was up to, so would others. He felt it was just a matter of time before everyone knew what was going on between them.

What was he going to do? And how was he going to deal with Ukita? Was he really going to submit to the man's blackmail? Was that what he was reduced to? But what else could he do?

Even though Sho suspected it was inevitable that his relationship with Kyoshi would eventually be made public, he wasn't ready to face that humiliation. Not yet. Even if he was just putting it off, he felt he had no other choice than to give Ukita what he wanted. But perhaps Kyoshi was right — perhaps he *could* be bought off, at least for a while.

"Shit," Kyoshi whispered, settling back on the sofa with a sigh. "I haven't cried that way in years."

"It's probably good that you did," Sho answered. "Do you feel better?"

"Yes, actually. I feel lighter, like I've been carrying around this huge weight that's just been lifted from me." Kyoshi pulled out a pack of cigarettes, tapping the end of it. He gave Sho an apologetic look. "Sorry, but I really need a smoke."

"It's your home. I really can't stop you from smoking in your own home."

"No, you can't," Kyoshi agreed with a teasing smile. "And don't forget, it's one of my rules." He lit up a cigarette and then took a slow drag, studying the Headmaster as he did so. "You should see the look on your face. You really hate it when I smoke, don't you?"

"Yes, I do," Sho admitted, finishing off his cognac in a single gulp.

"Why does it bother you so much? Is it the smell?"

"Not really. Your particular brand isn't so bad, unlike some. I hate it because you're killing yourself every time you inhale."

"I'm young. It can't be doing that much damage," Kyoshi countered.

The Headmaster shook his head. "It's a nasty habit. If you don't kick it now, it's going to be even more difficult to stop in a few years. The longer you smoke, the more damage it will cause."

"I'll stop eventually, when I'm ready."

"If I may ask, why do you smoke? What's the appeal? I don't understand it."

Kyoshi shrugged. "I enjoy it. It gives me pleasure."

"I don't understand how it could be pleasurable."

"Oh, come on. You've never even tried a cigarette before? You weren't at least curious?"

"I tried one once," Sho answered. "It was terrible."

"Maybe you have to smoke more than just one to enjoy it. I don't know how to explain it. It just...smooths out the edges, I guess."

"You wouldn't have edges to smooth out if you weren't addicted to them in the first place. Also...I don't like the way you taste after you've smoked."

Kyoshi sighed. "We agreed you're not going to constantly bitch at me about this. You really need to chill out a bit, Sho. Why don't you get yourself another drink? If it makes you happy, I'll put this out and go brush my teeth. Then you can give me a big, sloppy kiss."

The Headmaster made no answer but got up and went to the bar. Kyoshi put out his smoke and then reached down to pet King, who was still lying at his feet. "You're a good dog," he whispered.

King yawned and then put his head on his paws, closing his eyes.

Sho poured himself some bourbon, marveling over how well-stocked Kyoshi's bar was. Even as he was pouring the drink, he knew that he was probably drinking too much, too fast, especially considering that he had already started drinking earlier, at his own place. But he was still feeling anxious, and the alcohol did help him relax a bit.

In fact, he was already too intoxicated to fully appreciate that his judgment was now seriously impaired. This had the unfortunate effect of encouraging him to continue drinking beyond the point he usually stopped. He had finished one glass and was starting in on another when a sudden wave of intoxication swept through him as he was making his way back to the sofa.

"You all right?" Kyoshi asked, when Sho seemed to have a little trouble setting his glass down on the coffee table.

"I'm drinking too much. I should stop."

"I think you should cut loose tonight. Just enjoy yourself. Do whatever you want to do. Forget about all the crap that's on your mind, at least for tonight."

There was something appealing about Kyoshi's encouragement to set his worries aside, at least for the night. He relaxed back into the sofa, smiling when the young man straddled his lap. "What are you doing?"

"What does it look like I'm doing? I promised you a kiss, remember?"

Sho felt as though he had fallen asleep for a moment. He felt disoriented; the next thing he knew, Kyoshi was kissing him. But he felt removed from the experience and simultaneously felt as though he were falling deeper into the kiss.

Next he found himself wondering what a kiss was, precisely. It was more than just his mouth or the simple mechanism of his tongue movements. Somehow his entire being was pulled inside the kiss. But why was the chair moving beneath them? And who was kissing him? He pulled away, relieved to see Kyoshi smiling back at him.

"It's you," he whispered.

"Who else would it be?" Kyoshi laughed.

"I'm getting drunk. It's...really starting to hit me."

"So it appears. Let's go check on Seiko and Nishi. They're probably wondering where we are."

"All right," Sho agreed, though he felt a little unsteady as he rose to his feet. He had a moment of panic as he felt himself lose control of his body and mind, berating himself for drinking to excess. He was old enough to know the dangers of alcohol, especially on an empty stomach, yet somehow he had made a grave error of judgment in calculating when to stop.

Now he was experiencing the horror of increasing intoxication, knowing that he had set into motion a process he could not now abort. He felt helpless, as though an ocean were sweeping over him, carrying him far from land and reality to a place he had not been since his own youth.

Sho was no longer himself; the Headmaster of Valemont Academy was completely smashed.

The room seemed different than he remembered. He became acutely conscious of how strange it was for his body to move through space. He felt as though he were walking on a different planet, one where the rules of gravity were altered. In fact, he wasn't walking at all. He was simply floating, yet somehow he was able to move across the room, just with the power of his mind. It was an interesting sensation.

Kyoshi turned to him, grinning. "You have the funniest look on your face, Sho."

"I have special powers, I think," Sho replied, his speech a bit slurred. "I can walk without feet."

Kyoshi laughed. "You are drunk."

The Headmaster looked around, confused. "Where are we?"

"We're in my house, remember?"

"Oh. That's right. Your house seems...so big."

"It *is* big," Kyoshi agreed.

"What are we doing, exactly?"

"You've forgotten that already? We're meeting up with Nishi and Seiko."

Sho had to think for a moment before he realized that Nishi and Seiko had accompanied them to Kyoshi's estate. He felt puzzled, as though he had forgotten something extraordinarily important that he needed to remember.

Kyoshi was knocking on one of the guestroom doors. "Open up, you two!"

"We're busy!" Nishi answered. "Come back later!"

Kyoshi responded to this by opening the door and walking into the room. Nishi and Seiko were half-dressed, clearly engaged in an enthusiastic make-out session.

"What the fuck?!" Nishi protested. "I told you we were busy!"

"Come on, I'll take you to my favorite room. It's where I watch movies. You can fuck there. It'll be fun."

"We weren't going to fuck," Seiko clarified, hastily zipping up his pants.

"Whatever."

Nishi, annoyed to have been interrupted when he was making so much progress with Seiko, only scowled, but then shot his brother a concerned look. "Are you all right, Sho?"

"He's a bit drunk," Kyoshi explained.

"I don't know what happened," Sho murmured.

"The Headmaster is drunk?" Seiko exclaimed, eyeing Sho with surprise.

"I told him he should try to cut loose and relax a bit."

Sho startled at the word *Headmaster*, trying to figure out why it was so important. He frowned, staring first at Seiko and then at Kyoshi, and then back to Seiko again. "I'm the Headmaster," he blurted out, finally, as though just remembering his vital fact. "I'm the Headmaster of Valemont Academy!"

Seiko and Kyoshi both laughed at this, while Nishi only raised a brow. "You *are* drunk, Sho."

"Yes," Sho agreed. "I am."

"So, what's this room you're taking us to?" Seiko asked.

"Follow me. I'll show you."

Kyoshi led them through the house to a room with an immense viewing screen—nearly as big as an entire wall.

"Holy shit," Seiko exclaimed. "This is like having your own theatre!"

The seating area consisted of several large, comfortable-looking sofas and chairs, as well as a few pillow-covered bedrolls on the floor. Kyoshi flipped a switch and a panel slid aside on one wall, revealing rows of movies on mini-disk.

"We have plenty of films to choose from," Kyoshi announced. "But I think I have the perfect choice." He picked out one of the boxes, holding it up to show the cover. "Bad Boys III."

"Is it porn?" Nishi asked.

"It is, indeed," Kyoshi answered, grinning. "And these boys are mighty fine."

"Sounds good to me," Seiko said.

"Me too," Nishi agreed.

They all turned to Sho, who seemed to have trouble keeping up with the conversation.

"Sho? What about you? Does this look good?"

Sho studied the cover for a long moment. "Those boys are naked," he said finally.

"Just put it in," Nishi advised. "He'll like it."

"Help yourself to anything you want to drink," Kyoshi said, motioning to the bar.

"Can I get you something?" Nishi asked.

"No, I've had enough, and obviously Sho has, too."

"We'll have to catch up with you, then."

The group settled in and began watching the film, which depicted attractive young men engaging in various sexual acts. It wasn't long before Nishi and Seiko were all over each other.

Kyoshi wasn't sure what aroused him more—watching the movie or watching Nishi and Seiko kiss. He nuzzled up to Sho, kissing his neck and slipping his hand under his shirt. "I'm so turned on," he whispered.

"What?" Sho said, rather loudly.

"I said, I'm turned on. Aren't you?"

The Headmaster had initially felt a little disconnected from the film, his sexuality a bit deadened by alcohol. But now he was becoming aware of his arousal. "Yes," he admitted.

Next they were kissing, at first slowly and then with increasing ardor. Suddenly Sho felt as though he couldn't get enough.

"You're groaning," Kyoshi laughed, breaking away from the kiss.

"I am?"

"Yes." Kyoshi stood up, holding out his hand. "Come on. Let's lie down on the bedrolls."

The next thing Sho knew, he and Kyoshi were rolling around on the floor, kissing and groping each other. It wasn't until they were both undressed that he even became aware that Nishi and Seiko had joined them on the bedrolls. They, too, were naked.

"Look at Seiko's body," Kyoshi whispered into his ear.

Sho turned and looked. There was no question that Seiko's athletic propensities had left their mark on the young man's body. Every muscle was defined and toned, and the slightest movement created enticing hollows and ripples.

Kyoshi was massaging the Headmaster's cock as he nibbled on his earlobe. Sho found himself unable to look away from Seiko, much to Kyoshi's delight.

"You're so hard," he whispered, moving his thumb over the tip of the man's organ. "You're wet already."

"Kyoshi," Sho groaned.

Nishi broke away from Seiko, distracted by his brother's nakedness. Kyoshi caught his eye and the two shared a meaningful grin. Sho continued to stare at Seiko, who now sat up on one elbow, looking back at the Headmaster.

For a few minutes no one said anything.

"I know what," Kyoshi announced. "Let's all fuck."

To Be Continued in
In the Headmaster's Chambers, Part 2

Printed in Great Britain
by Amazon